Redemption

usa today bestselling author
jenna hartley

Editing: Lisa A. Hollett
Cover: Qamber Designs

Trust your gut.

Your inner compass
will never
lead you astray.

jenna hartley

Content Warnings

This story contains explicit sexual content, profanity, and topics that may be sensitive to some readers.

For more detailed information, visit the QR code below.

Playlist

"Ruin" by Shawn Mendes
"Losing Touch" by Virginia To Vegas
"Find" by Shallou, Kasbo, Cody Lovaas
"Star Crossed" by 3LAU
"Just For A Moment" (featuring Iselin)
by Gryffin, Iselin
"August" by Taylor Swift
"Right Now" by Nick Jonas, Robin Schulz
"Water" (featuring ZOHARA)
by KREAM, ZOHARA
"Starving" by Hailee Steinfeld, Grey, Zedd
"Watermelon Sugar" by Harry Styles
"Make Me Yours" by Borgeous, Zack Martino
"Adore You" by Harry Styles
"Never Let Me Go" by Logan and Isabel
"Be Mine" by Gamma Skies, Jaslyn Edgar
"Always" by The Him
"Holding On" by Dabin, Lowell
"Nobody Like You - Sun Soaked Mix" by Kaskade
"Unforgettable" by Aerreo, NEIMY, NSH
"Close" by 3LAU, Oly
"Love You Forever"
by Nicky Romero, Stadiumx, Sam Martin
"Perfect" by Pentatonix
"Can't Sleep Love/Sunday Morning (Mash Up)"
(featuring Skyler Hale) by Rick Hale, Skyler Hale

You can find this playlist and more at
https://www.authorjennahartley.com/playlists

CHAPTER ONE

Sloan

G raham smoothed a hand down his tie. "I know you don't want to talk about this—"

"You're right." I cut him off. "I don't."

"Sloan," Jasper said from his seat on the couch, his tone a mix of concern and exasperation. "We're trying to help. We're worried about you."

My face flushed with frustration, but I waved a hand through the air, determined not to appear ruffled. Instead, I concentrated on the feel of the plush carpet of the Huxley Grand Los Angeles Presidential Suite. It was soft beneath my feet as I padded across it.

"What's new? You've always been overprotective of me— all of you." I swung my gaze to encompass all four of them, my family.

My eldest brother, Graham. Stoic and definitely overprotective. Probably the most so, even if he wasn't always as vocal about his concerns as my other siblings. Perhaps the fact that he was so adamant this time should've been enough to scare me, but I refused to live my life in fear.

Graham's stern expression was nothing new. I simply

wasn't used to having it directed at me. Sure, there were times we argued. We were siblings. We ran a billion-dollar hotel empire together, along with Jasper. We were bound to have disagreements.

But Graham typically stayed out of my personal life, and I stayed out of his. Not that he had much of one. Apart from his dogs—a pair of Irish Wolfhounds named Queen V and Prince Albert—he was a solitary creature of habit.

My other brother, Jasper, could be just as overprotective, even if he was generally more diplomatic about it. And Knox and Nate—my cousins whom I considered my siblings—had always treated me like their kid sister.

It didn't matter that I was thirty-seven. That I was the Senior Vice President of Operations for Huxley Hotels. The four of them would only ever see me as their little sister in need of protection.

Though, this time, they might be right.

I sighed and sank down on the sofa. I didn't want to admit it, but the threatening notes frightened me. At first, I'd brushed them off as a mistake or a prank. I didn't have any enemies that I knew of. I mean, yes, my family was wealthy, which made us an easy target. But I was the only one of the five of us who'd received any threats.

And now... I sighed. Now that it had happened several times over the span of six weeks, I could no longer ignore the fact that someone was trying to send me a message. I just couldn't figure out who it was or why. And why *now*?

Their nasty vitriol floated through my mind once more.

"End your subscription to life,
you TOXIC BITCH."

I'd found that one on my desk at the office one morning. It had my picture on the front, my face covered with a large skull and crossbones. When I'd asked my executive assistant about it, Halle had been confused and upset on my behalf.

"You are poison, and you will pay."

That lovely gem had arrived at my home inside a Christmas card. Jasper and Graham had immediately flown to London and insisted on staying through the holidays.

Jasper took a seat next to me, rubbing circles on my back. As children, he'd always been the one to comfort me. I think he needed that touch, that connection, more than my other brothers. Definitely more than Graham, who had always shied away from physical affection.

"I talked to Maverick Hudson," Knox said, referring to the owner of Hudson Security, a company known for elite executive security, among other things. "He offered to send a team back to London with you."

"I *have* a security team," I gritted out.

Graham narrowed his eyes at me. "Sloan, the Huxley Grand staff is not your personal security team."

"I know that." I dug my nails into my fist until I felt the bite of them against my skin. "I would never expect them to be. But all residents are entitled to security while on the premises. Thus, I'm protected."

"Are you?" Knox asked. "These threats suggest otherwise."

"I definitely question the staff's competence in light of these threats," Nate said, and I had to agree, even if the idea of it being one of my own employees twisted my gut.

"Hudson suggested leaving those employees in place in case one of them is in on it," Knox said.

Great. Just great. That definitely did not help me feel more secure.

Even so, I grimaced. "I don't want to be surrounded by a protective bubble of bodyguards." Hell, that was how I'd felt a lot of my childhood. Suffocated by nannies and staff and four protective older brothers.

It was part of the reason I'd jumped at the chance to move to London years ago. That and the idea of putting an ocean between Jackson and me had been both appealing and necessary. But now, I just wanted to feel safe again. Unfortunately, Jackson was also the only person who'd ever made me feel that way—at least, before he'd broken my heart.

"I don't know what else to do," Graham said, and it was then I realized how exhausted he was. How concerned he was—they all were. "I've tried everything I can think of to determine the fucker's identity."

If Graham didn't have any leads, I didn't know what to think.

My brother might be the CEO of Huxley Hotels, but he was also a computer genius. He could hack in to anything, though it wasn't a skill we advertised.

"Even more reason to be concerned," Nate said, echoing my thoughts. Nate had dealt with his fair share of stalkers and crazed fans. If he was concerned...

"I've set up alerts on all the security cameras around Sloan's home and office," Graham said. "I've tried to have the paper, the ink, the writing—anything—analyzed, but it's like they're a fucking ghost."

"We could swap." Jasper turned to me. "I know that wouldn't be your preference. But I could take over in London for a while, and you could come back to New York —or LA, even."

My brothers watched me expectantly.

I hesitated but quickly vetoed the idea. "What if that's what the person making threats wants? What if my leaving emboldens them? Besides, what about Edward?"

What about Halle, my executive assistant? She was a young, single mom, and I worried for her safety. Even if she hadn't been the one receiving the notes, I didn't like the idea of putting her or her son in any danger.

I could feel my brothers' collective annoyance buzzing. Mentioning Edward had been like kicking a hive, and now the bees were angry and ready to swarm. They were not fans of my boyfriend, never had been. Graham hadn't said it outright, but I knew he didn't like Edward. Nate thought Edward was pretentious and fake. Jasper, well, he said Edward was too cold. And Knox found it strange that Edward and I spent more time apart than together.

I tried to brush off their comments as the misguided, but well-meaning, intentions of protective older brothers everywhere. But deep down, a little part of me hated that they might be right about Edward not being the right guy for me.

I sighed, knowing that what I felt for Edward wasn't much more than companionship. I'd been trying to talk myself into feeling more for him—love, even—but I couldn't. And I hated myself for trying.

"Edward is not the one being threatened," Knox growled, his legendary patience slipping. "And if he cares about you as much as he allegedly does, he should be doing anything to protect you."

I drew a deep breath. It took a lot to ruffle Knox. In that moment, it hit me how afraid for me he really was. How worried all of them were. My brothers had been searching for this creep, calling an intervention to ensure my safety.

Edward had asked me to move in with him, sure. Had suggested that I'd be safer at his London townhouse than at the Huxley Grand, but I just...I couldn't. I'd made excuses, put off answering.

I stood, going over to the floor-to-ceiling windows. I peered out at the Los Angeles skyline, marveling at how different it was from London. It might be dazzling and glamorous, but it wasn't home. And it lacked the character and the history of London.

If I couldn't bring myself to move in with Edward, what was I even doing with him?

I dug in my heels. On paper, Edward and I made sense. He was successful. Understood the demands of running a large family company. Respected my ambition.

But was that enough for me? Was what I had with Edward enough?

There was no passion. No feeling that I'd die without him, as harsh and dramatic as that sounded. I'd told myself that with passion came heartbreak. That sensible was safe. I'd certainly learned that lesson the hard way, thanks to Jackson.

I clenched my fists, knowing what I had with Edward wasn't enough. It hadn't been for a long time. I'd just been too scared or unwilling to admit it. Sometimes it was easier to stand still than to move forward.

But I hadn't been standing still, not really. I'd been moving backward. I'd been losing myself.

He'd been pressuring me to move in with him. And instead of being overjoyed, I'd been making excuses. But did he truly believe that moving in together would solve our problems? If anything, I thought it would only magnify them.

Edward and I were both busy. I was overseeing the Huxley empire with my brothers, heading up the European and Asian operations. Edward had been groomed to run his family's banking company when his dad retired and would one day be a member of the House of Lords.

Plus, there were the incessant demands of his family's social schedule. I stared at my phone screen and the picture of the two of us I'd saved for his contact ID. We were smiling, and yet...that day, I'd spent more time with a team of stylists than with him. And when we'd finally arrived at Royal Ascot

—regardless of my making every effort to fit in—his family had still looked down on me.

Despite my fortune, I lacked a title or "genteel refinement," as I'd overheard Edward's sister, Lady Amelia, say once. I tried not to let it bother me, but seriously? She was a decorated Olympic Skeet athlete, but she acted like she was God's gift to humankind.

Graham turned away and uttered a sound of frustration, but it was Knox who came over and took my hands. Knox, who was always kind and nurturing. Who always strove to keep the peace.

"Sloan," he said, compassion lighting his blue eyes. "I don't want you to live in fear or upend your life, but you have to be realistic about the situation."

Nate came to stand beside Knox. Of the four of them, he could probably relate the most to my current predicament. Nate was one of the billionaire heirs to the Huxley empire, like me. But he was a celebrity in his own right, the owner of a Hollywood film production company and an award-winning actor.

Ever since he'd become a household name, he'd had to deal with all sorts of crazed fans who crossed the line. One of his daughter's former nannies had tried to seduce him then sell his underwear on the internet. He needed a bodyguard; I didn't.

Or at least, I hadn't in the past.

My shoulders slumped. "What would you have me do?"

"Come to LA. You can live with Kendall and me, or at the Huxley Grand close to Graham." Knox gave my hands a squeeze, silently pleading with me to agree.

"For how long?" I asked.

"Until the threat is neutralized," Graham said in a menacing tone. I wondered what Graham would do to "neutralize" them if given the chance. I shuddered and Knox released me.

I considered it a moment. Part of me *was* scared. Part of me knew he was right—they all were, to some extent. But if I conceded now, they'd only push for even more security precautions.

I loved Nate, but I didn't envy him the life he lived. I didn't want to always have to tell someone where I was going. I didn't want someone to have the power to tell me no because of security concerns. I didn't want to lose my freedom.

Jasper sighed. Graham clenched his teeth. "I'd hoped it wouldn't come to this, but…the board agrees. You need a bodyguard."

My eyes widened, and I felt his words like a physical blow. "You went to the board?" I seethed, stepping forward. "This is a *private* matter."

"You are a public figure," Graham bit out.

"You need protection," Knox said. *Way to plunge the knife even deeper.* "This has gone on long enough."

I felt as if I was sixteen again and trying to go on a date, only to have my brothers scare off all the guys. I loved them, but sometimes they went too far.

I crossed my arms over my chest and stared Graham down. Just because he was older than me and ranked higher in the company didn't mean he could bully me into doing what he wanted. I knew it was coming from a place of love. I knew he had my back—he always had. But I despised his heavy-handed tactics.

"Sloan," Graham said, annoyance bleeding through his tone. "You're second in charge. You're too valuable to risk such vulnerability."

"Too valuable to whom?" I asked, hurling the words with anger. "The company?"

Graham glowered. But Jasper responded first. "Sloan," he chided. "That's not what he meant."

I knew that, but jeez, would it kill Graham to express some emotion every so often? He was always so reserved. So in control.

Edward wasn't much better. At first, I'd brushed off his lack of affection as a British thing. Or blamed it on his personality. But maybe it was just me.

Or maybe I was expecting too much. Something more. Something he wasn't capable of giving.

I sighed. It was useless—wanting something you couldn't have. Expecting someone to change.

"Sloan." Jasper placed his hands on my shoulders. *"Please. The thought of anything happening to you…"* He stared at the ceiling, and it looked as if he might cry.

My stomach sank. I hated the idea of hurting my brothers, especially Jasper. Jasper and I had always been close. Maybe it was just who we were. Maybe it was because we'd been the youngest when our parents had died in a plane crash with my aunt and uncle, and our memories of them weren't as strong.

Our grandparents had raised Knox, Graham, Nate, Jasper, and me. It had made us all close.

I gnawed on my lip. I didn't want a security detail, but I knew I needed to do something. The threats were becoming more frequent, and they'd escalated in tone. I couldn't stay in London right now. I was too rattled, even if I refused to admit it to them.

I contemplated my options then said, "I have a better idea. I could take my annual sailing trip a little earlier and for an extended amount of time." When several of my brothers opened their mouths as if to object, I held up a hand to silence them. "You wanted me to get away from London, and

I am. My absence will give you and the team from Hudson time to find and neutralize the threat."

Slowly, their expressions changed. And I could see my proposition was winning them over. Hell, I was excited about it, and I could feel my shoulders relaxing at the idea, some of my tension melting as I imagined myself back on the ocean. Back on the *Athena*.

Blissfully alone.

Away from all the drama and the threats.

I'd had to skip my sailing trip last year because of a broken arm. Time on my sailboat—alone on the open water —was long overdue.

"How long do you think you'd be gone this time?" Jasper asked.

I considered a few routes but knew that I wanted to sail from Florida down to the Caribbean, settling on… "Six to eight weeks."

The company was used to my annual sailing trip, and we had the right systems in place to accommodate my extended leave. In fact, we encouraged all our employees to take advantage of their generous vacation time, and we had an extended new-parent leave policy as well. We wanted our employees to feel valued. Appreciated. We wanted them to be able to feel free to care for their families without worrying about their jobs. To spend time on the things that lit them up so they could come back reenergized.

"An elegant solution," Graham said. "Someone from Hudson can accompany you."

I gaped at him. "You can't be serious."

"As if Graham knows how to tell a joke." Jasper balked at the idea.

"This sailing trip has always been something I do alone. And that's important to me."

"We get that," Knox said in a gentle tone. "But this time is different. Whoever is sending these threats knows your schedule. How to get close to you. I'm not trying to scare you, but they are likely watching you."

I glanced around, creeped out by the idea even though I'd had the same thought myself. Still...my sailing trip? It was the one time I got to escape the pressures, expectations, and demands of my life, and just...be.

"You don't have a bodyguard," I said to Knox. "Why do I need one?"

"I have a residential team from Hudson Security, just like Nate. And Kendall has a bodyguard, as does Jude."

I jerked my head back. "They do? Since when?"

He rubbed the back of his neck. "We should probably keep that between us for now."

"Wait." I pointed at him. "You mean to tell me that your fiancée and your adult son each have a bodyguard, and they don't know about it?"

"Ah—"

Jasper smirked. Nate sighed. "I think we're getting off track here."

"What about you?" I spun to Jasper. "You don't have a bodyguard." I turned to Graham. "Or you."

"Everybody loves me." Jasper winked, one ankle crossed at the knee.

I arched my brow. He was so damn cocky. "I have a feeling a few of your former flings would disagree."

Nate snorted. Knox coughed into his hand to cover a laugh.

"This isn't about us." Graham had clearly reached his limit. "It's about you. We're not the ones receiving threats."

"Then shouldn't it be my decision? Besides, I have self-defense training." Years of it, in fact.

"Enough!" Graham roared then turned and pinched the bridge of his nose. "Enough," he said again, more quietly.

Silence fell on the room, and I glared at him.

Knox draped his arm around my shoulder. "What he's trying to say—" he glowered at Graham "—is that we love you, and we're worried about you. And we understand that this situation is frustrating and scary."

"We've already lost so much," Nate said, taking my hand.

When I glanced at him, I could see the fear in his eyes. All of their eyes, even Graham's.

"Please." Jasper kept his voice low. "I can't…I can't lose you too."

His alarm, his vulnerability, finally made me stop and listen. The four of them might be overprotective, but I understood their fears. I understood what it was like to lose someone you loved. I sagged, unable to fight them anymore. I took a deep breath and accepted the fact that maybe it was time to hire a bodyguard.

"So…what?" I asked, trying to figure out how this would work. "They'd sail the same route?"

Nate's expression was full of pity and also…understanding. "They'd sail on the same boat as you. Your boat."

I let out a strangled cry. I couldn't imagine sharing my boat with anyone apart from the men in this room or my best friend, Greer, especially for that length of time. I straightened. "It's too small. They'll only get in the way."

"It's a thirty-five-foot sailboat," Graham said. "You have the space, even if it might be a bit cramped."

"Ha!" I pointed at him, childish as it was. "So, you admit it."

Internally, I rolled my eyes. So maybe I wasn't acting like the mature senior vice president of a hotel empire that I was, but sometimes my brothers brought out the worst in me.

"Okay," Nate interjected. "Let's pretend for a minute this was Brooklyn we were talking about."

My chest squeezed, and rage surged through my veins at the idea of anyone threatening my niece.

"Would you be okay with her going on a sailboat, *alone*, under these circumstances?"

"No," I admitted begrudgingly. "But the guest cabin is tiny." The perfect size for my twelve-year-old niece but not anyone much larger.

"They'll live," Nate said. "Or you can rent or buy a bigger boat for the trip."

"You can borrow my yacht if you'd like," Knox offered.

He didn't get it. None of them did. That was the point—I loved *my* boat. I could sail it single-handedly. I didn't need anyone else.

I'd been sailing since almost before I could walk. My grandfather had loved sailing, and it had been our thing. When I was barely eight, I'd won a sunfish sailing race. Before college, I'd considered attempting to circumnavigate the globe. Sailing was in my blood.

It was my escape. My solace.

"We can even try to find someone with sailing experience if that'll make the idea more palatable," Nate said.

"It won't," I muttered. But I could tell they weren't going to be dissuaded.

As if to hammer home the point, Graham said, "The board wanted to put you under round-the-clock protection. Police and private security. And they'd have the votes to do it, but I talked them out of it."

"Ugh." I threw my hands in the air. "Fine. *One* bodyguard. That's it."

"Excellent." Knox grinned. And from the look the four of them shared, I wondered if that had been their goal all along.

I hung my head, resigned to my fate. Hopefully my body-guard—whoever they were—wouldn't be as annoying and overbearing as my brothers.

CHAPTER TWO

Jackson

"How are things at the Crawford residence?" Vaughn asked from across his desk at the LA office of Hudson Security.

I lifted a shoulder, still trying to hide my surprise that I'd been summoned to the office. We'd already had our weekly debriefing with the team, but Vaughn had asked me to come in alone. "Good."

"Good. Wedding plans going well? How big a team do you think you'll need?"

I glanced toward the windows, making some rough estimates based on what I knew so far. "It's a pretty big guest list. Many high-profile."

The principal, Nate Crawford, was a huge celebrity. Actor and producer. His engagement to Emerson Thorne had nearly broken the internet and given me a damn heart attack.

That said, I hadn't been all that surprised. By the engagement—sure. But the fact that Nate and Emerson were attracted to each other had been obvious from the start.

She was a famous Olympic athlete. And the two of them

together had the internet salivating for details. Everyone was invested in their love story. Their wedding. Everything about them.

If it was exhausting for me at times, being on the periphery, I couldn't imagine how they handled it. But they did—with grace and generosity.

"I figured," he mused, running a hand over his chin. "It'll be a logistical nightmare. But that's why they hired us. We can handle it."

I agreed, though I wasn't looking forward to it. Too many people. Too many variables. Too many other executive protection teams fighting to be top dog. Too much fucking politics.

That was a big reason why I'd switched to a residential security team, as opposed to a movement team, over a year ago. I liked the challenge of defending my client's castle, so to speak.

I moved about the city with them to local, smaller events. And I'd even accompanied Nate and his family to Abu Dhabi. But it had only served to remind me of how many variables I had to account for. How many things could go wrong.

"I was thinking about asking Ghost to handle it," Vaughn said, referring to my colleague Nicholas. Ghost was his call sign, like Blackjack was mine.

While some of my coworkers had joked that it was because of my love of sailing or cards, I'd been given the call sign by my fellow SEALs. A blackjack was a weapon. A small but powerful lead-filled club with a flexible handle.

"Has the Crawford family asked for a change?"

Had I done something wrong? Had Graham finally decided to do something about me? I knew he remembered me. I knew he knew who I was, even if he'd never said anything.

"No." Vaughn dragged a hand over his head. "Nothing like that. I just…" He sighed, leaning back in his chair. "I could use your expertise for a different project."

I frowned. Why did I get the feeling I was being reassigned? It made no sense. I had a great rapport with the Crawford family.

"We have a client who has been receiving threats."

I arched an eyebrow as Vaughn slid me a folder across the desk. I opened it and scanned the threats. Nothing too gruesome, but I could understand the client's concern. Still…that didn't explain why Vaughn had sought my "expertise," as he'd put it. Any number of our agents were qualified to analyze threats and offer guidance. Hell, a lot of them were more qualified than me.

As a Navy SEAL, I'd been trained and tested with my skills in combat diving, land combat, parachute jumping, and Naval Special Warfare. I had other training, both from my time in the Navy and at Hudson. I could certainly analyze a threat, but some of my colleagues were better equipped and suited to do so.

"No idea where they came from?" I asked, holding up a copy of one of the notes.

Vaughn shook his head, and I waited for him to tell me where exactly I came in.

He interlaced his fingers. "The client wants to take a sailing trip and has agreed to protection."

I frowned. "What do you mean…has agreed to protection? They're not currently under protection?"

"New client. Sort of. Family referral. I sent Disco to keep an eye on things in the meantime." He shuffled some papers on his desk. "Anyway, you were the first person who came to mind, considering your experience. Are you interested?"

"How long?"

"Two months."

Wow. A two-month sailing trip sounded like heaven, even if it technically would be for work. I'd always loved being on the water, the horizon the only thing ahead of me beyond endless ocean.

"What's the proposed route?"

He handed me his tablet, and I scrolled through the plans. *Holy shit.* The more I read, the more excited I grew.

It was a dream trip. Sailing down the Thorny Path from Miami through the Bahamas and the Turks and Caicos Islands. Puerto Rico. Virgin Islands.

"What kind of craft? How many crew?" I asked, my eyes never leaving the screen.

"Thirty-five-foot sailboat. No crew."

I jerked my head back. "No crew?"

"It can be sailed by one person."

"I know, but..." Most of Hudson's clients weren't the type to sail a trip like that alone. They had yachts and crew and... My curiosity was certainly piqued. Even so... "That's a small boat for two people. I assume it would be just the two of us."

"Correct."

I nodded, considering. Wealthy. Experienced sailor. It wasn't their first rodeo if they were willing to take on that journey alone.

I leaned back in my chair. "Let me get this straight. You want to pay me to spend two months sailing the Caribbean with a client."

"Yes."

I'd had some cool assignments—some really shitty ones too. But this had to be one of the best ones I'd been offered. Even so, I was hesitant.

"It's close quarters. What if we don't get along?"

"Make sure you do."

I scoffed. We both knew that was easier said than done. Some of our clients could be a real pain in the ass. Not the

Crawfords, of course. But others. They could be demanding, condescending. Didn't listen. Didn't heed our advice or warnings.

"And after?" I asked, assuming the client and I didn't kill each other.

"New York."

"New York," I repeated, as if to confirm it.

"We've been watching you—Maverick, the leadership. You're smart. Hardworking. You play your cards right with this assignment, and the New York office is yours."

Say what? I blinked a few times, positive I'd misheard him.

After everything I'd been through—being discharged from the SEALs, working as a bouncer, finding my way to Hudson—this felt like a redemption of sorts.

"What about Wyatt?" I asked.

We'd all heard that Clay, the director of the New York office, was retiring. But surely Wyatt, his second-in-command, would take over.

"Wyatt's going to open our new office in London."

Well, shit. I sank back against my chair, resting my ankle on my knee. This would be a huge promotion—and a dream come true.

"New York," I said again.

I rubbed the back of my neck. I hadn't been to New York, apart from a few work trips with a client, in nearly a decade. My thoughts went to Sloan, as they often did. I couldn't think about New York without thinking of her.

I hadn't seen or spoken to her in years—at least, not until our paths had crossed in Abu Dhabi a few months ago. She'd visited Nate a few times in the past year, but I'd always been on vacation. Or I'd let my team handle it.

Her Abu Dhabi visit had been unexpected, and her sudden appearance had stirred unwelcome feelings.

Reminding me of a past I couldn't change and a future that would never be.

"Jackson?" Vaughn asked, tearing me away from thoughts of Sloan.

The way her skirt had wrapped around her hips—more generous than they'd been in the past. Her hair had been different too. As had the way she'd looked at me—with shock that had quickly turned into a mask of cold indifference.

"Hm?" I met his gaze.

He assessed me with a quizzical expression. "I thought you'd be more excited."

I cleared my throat and straightened, trying to mask my shock. "Yes. Yes, of course I am. I just…" I dragged a hand over my head, the short strands bristling against my palm. "Surprised, that's all. I mean…head of the New York office. That's one hell of a promotion."

It's what I'd been working toward, wanting, for years. The chance to lead not just a team but an entire office. After how everything had gone down with the SEALs, I didn't know if anyone would ever trust me to lead a unit again. Maverick's, and especially Vaughn's, faith in me was humbling and gratifying. He'd been my mentor for over a decade, and I knew he was just as invested in my success as I was.

"You'd be damn good at it."

I was still in shock but somehow had the presence of mind to say, "Thank you."

I couldn't believe it. He was offering me the chance to take on a leadership role at the highest levels of the company. The chance to honor my father and finally live up to his legacy. Not to mention the fact that I'd be closer to my sister and her family, as well as my mom. Considering my mom's recent stroke, this couldn't have come at a better time. She was going to be so happy when I told her.

"Is this your subtle way of telling me I'm getting too old

for field work?" I teased, though Vaughn had been determined to see me advance in the company.

"Blackjack, you were too old five years ago." We both knew that wasn't true, even if I was forty-four.

"What's Nate going to think?" I asked.

I'd been protecting his family for almost a year now. I felt like part of the family at times, even though I did my best to maintain a professional distance. They had always been welcoming, especially his twelve-year-old daughter, Brooklyn.

"Nate wants you to take this client. He specifically requested you."

"He did?" I asked, furrowing my brow. "Who is it?"

"One of his cousins."

Nate had a lot of cousins, though he was closest to the ones on his mom's side. They were more like siblings. Surely Vaughn wasn't referring to Graham, Jasper, or...I swallowed hard. Sloan. Right?

My heart rate ratcheted up at the thought of Sloan. Technically, she was Nate's cousin, but he'd always referred to her as his sister. Sloan did love sailing. But... *No.* Surely not.

"Nate trusts you," Vaughn continued. "That speaks volumes."

Vaughn was right. Nate's trust wasn't easily given. So, for him to request that I be reassigned to his cousin—a cousin who hopefully wasn't Sloan—meant he was entrusting them to my care. And that soothed some of the sting from the fact that I would no longer lead his residential team.

I'd be crazy to turn down an opportunity like this. The sailing trip alone... I was still trying to wrap my head around it. All of it.

I was a little rusty—at least for a trip of that duration. But I knew it would come back to me quickly. It always did.

"Here's the file." Vaughn passed it to me.

I opened the folder, and *oh fuck.* I went completely still. There she was, staring back at me as if my thoughts had conjured her.

"Sloan?" I choked on her name. "Sloan Mackenzie is the client?" My eyes flashed to his, seeking confirmation. I supposed this shouldn't have been a huge surprise, but *fuck.*

Vaughn furrowed his brow. "Why? You know her? Apart from her connection to Nate."

Images flashed through my mind. Her coy smile as she straddled me. Her head tilted back in ecstasy as I thrust into her. Lazy days spent in bed talking about everything and nothing.

"We..." I blew out a breath. "Yeah. She's my little sister's best friend."

Yes, I knew Sloan. But once upon a time, she'd known me —better than anyone ever had.

Which was why I found myself saying, "Maybe you should send someone else. Cujo or any of the other former SEALs."

Connor James, or "Cujo," was a former Navy SEAL like me, but I doubted he wanted to leave his wife for two months when she was nearing the end of her pregnancy.

Vaughn shook his head. "Nate specifically requested you."

I scratched at my jaw. "That's great, but what about Sloan?"

"What about her?" he asked, being deliberately obtuse.

He leaned forward, resting his elbows on the desk, narrowing his eyes at me. I knew he was waiting for me to elaborate.

I considered how best to phrase it. How to explain who Sloan was to me. I wasn't sure I could.

"Look, it's clear from your reaction that you guys have some...history. But how long has it been since you've seen her?" he asked.

If you didn't count Abu Dhabi… "Fourteen years." Though the moment I'd seen her in Abu Dhabi, the past hadn't felt that long ago.

Vaughn waved a hand through the air. "Water under the bridge."

I swallowed hard at the thought of seeing her, spending so much time alone with her. Maybe Vaughn was right. Fourteen years was a long time. She'd probably moved on.

She *had* moved on, if her file was anything to go by.

No children. Never married. I assumed that was because Sloan was focused on her career. But who the hell knew.

Even if I hadn't skimmed the file, I knew from Greer that Sloan was in a relationship. And wasn't that a fucking punch to the gut. Maybe I was the only one who was stuck in the past.

"Is your past going to be a problem?"

Not a fucking clue.

I didn't want to think it would be. I was a professional, but it was a fucking sailboat. With Sloan. For two months.

Vaughn leaned back, and I got the feeling he was reading between the lines. Finally, he said, "Maybe you can use your previous…acquaintance to establish trust with the principal."

I barked out a laugh. He didn't know what I'd done. I was pretty sure Sloan would never forgive me, let alone trust me.

"Come on, Blackjack." He frowned. "It can't be that bad."

It's worse.

I thought back to that night. The night I'd left, even though it had nearly killed me. And then again, at my sister's wedding and the way Sloan had looked at me. With more coldness than I'd thought she could ever possess.

But now that I knew the threats were directed at Sloan, anger surged in my veins. I would hunt the fucker down and make them pay.

"Why's she being threatened? Who are her enemies?" I

skimmed through the notes, trying to understand the assessment. "It doesn't make any sense. People have always loved Sloan."

"You're only proving my point. You're perfect for this assignment." He leaned forward. "We're still trying to figure that out. Maybe you could get her to talk."

"Pretty sure I'm the last person she'll want to talk to," I said, mostly to myself.

"I suggest you find a way to make it work if you want that promotion." He stood, and I followed suit.

I was determined not to fail. "I won't let you down." *Or Nate.*

Or Sloan. I gripped the file.

I wondered if Graham knew about this. I wondered if he was okay with it. I'd encountered him a few times over the past year, but he never acted like he recognized me, even though I was positive he knew exactly who I was.

Vaughn clapped a hand on my shoulder, guiding me to the door. "I know you won't. The Crawford and Mackenzie families give Hudson a ton of business, both as clients themselves and in referrals. They may not always like us or what we have to say, but our job is to keep them safe." He gave my shoulder a squeeze before releasing me.

"Of course." He wasn't saying anything I didn't already know.

"Good. Wrap up with the Crawfords then take a few days to prepare for your trip. The principal will arrive in New York on the twenty-sixth. You can meet at the Huxley Grand since the Crawfords and their team will be traveling there for Emerson's work engagement."

"Great," I said, swallowing past the lump in my throat. *Their team.* As in the one I'd no longer be part of. "Thank you again for the opportunity. I'll get to work on logistics."

"Call if you need anything."

I nodded, but my mind was still trying to catch up. I was leaving the Crawfords—potentially for good. Taking a two-month sailing trip with Sloan to some of the places we'd always dreamed of.

Regardless of the weather forecast, I had a feeling the voyage would be anything but smooth.

CHAPTER THREE

Sloan

"Auntie Sloan!" Brooklyn ran at me, and I dropped my bags and smiled despite my jet lag.

I'd landed in New York earlier in the day and had been ferried to the Huxley Grand by a guy named Zeke, who went by the call sign Disco—one of the members of my temporary security team. I'd slept some on the flight, but it had been fitful. I was too preoccupied with all the things I needed to wrap up at work to truly rest.

Jasper was going to keep an eye on the London office in my absence. Between him and my executive assistant, Halle, I had faith that everything would run smoothly.

I tried to blame my restlessness on work, but even I knew there was more to it. Things with Edward had been... strained lately. It was almost as if he was trying to punish me for taking too long to give him an answer about moving in together.

Then there was Jackson, and the possibility that I might run into him.

Jackson Shaw, I sighed.

My best friend's older brother. My first love. And apparently, a member of Nate's security team, something I hadn't realized until Abu Dhabi.

Up until that point, I'd tried to forget all about him. Greer mentioned Jackson every so often in passing, but I usually tried not to pay too much attention. But now that I'd seen him again, I couldn't stop thinking about him, despite not wanting to.

For months, I'd been dying to ask Nate about Jackson. About how long he'd been working for him and so many other things besides. But I didn't know how to bring it up without sparking questions I didn't want to answer.

I'd considered asking Disco about Jackson. But every time I'd come close, I'd lost my nerve. Now that I was going to meet up with Nate and his family, I was on edge. Almost as if waiting for Jackson to pop out from behind a corner.

It was silly, really. I was being ridiculous.

For all I knew, Jackson could've been temporarily assigned to Nate in Abu Dhabi, like Disco was temporarily assigned to me in London. I'd never once seen Jackson during my other visits to LA before or since our run-in in Abu Dhabi.

Yeah. I told myself. A temporary assignment—that must be it.

Even if I saw him now, I could be cordial. We'd been together...so long ago. It practically felt like another lifetime. Like a dream...

"Auntie Sloan?" Brooklyn asked, dragging me out of my thoughts.

"Sorry." I smiled. I was missing out on precious time with my niece because I was distracted by thoughts of Jackson. *Enough.* "I brought you something." I reached into my bag.

She squealed when I pulled out a tin of her favorite cookies from the Huxley Grand London.

Though there were many menu items we kept consistent

across the world, each location also had some unique local delicacies. The Huxley Grand in Paris had the best éclairs and croissants. The most amazing choux buns. The Huxley Grand in London was known for its decadent high tea. And our famed tinned cookies were provided in all the suites and sold in our gift shop. Brooklyn was obsessed with them.

"Thank you!" Brooklyn beamed then handed me a few friendship bracelets. "I made these for you."

I smiled as I peered down at the bracelets with their colorful designs and inspirational phrases. Brooklyn was a huge fan of Taylor Swift, and so was Emerson—her dad's fiancée.

I'd always been protective of Brooklyn. She was like a daughter to me. And her egg donor, Trinity, was a piece of work. But Emerson... I smiled. Emerson was everything I would've hoped for for Brooklyn—Nate, too. She was driven and kind and loving. Despite my initial hesitance because of the speed—and surprise—of their engagement, I adored her.

"These are amazing! Thank you." I slid the bracelets onto my wrist next to my watch. There was one with beads that spelled "Unstoppable." Another with "Smooth Sailing." And the third read "Captain Sloan." That was probably my favorite.

"I also brought these." I grabbed another tin from my bag. It was identical to the first, except the goodies were all gluten- and oat-free. "For Sophia and her family."

Brooklyn scanned the label and brightened. "All gluten free? For real?"

I smiled. "Yep!"

A few years ago, Jasper had issued a challenge to Huxley Grand properties across the world to make allergy-friendly versions of guest favorites. Our team had exceeded all our expectations. Even I couldn't tell the difference between the two. The texture and flavor were identical.

"She's going to love it!" She threw her arms around my neck once more. "Thank you."

"I'm glad." I smiled and turned to Nate and Emerson as they entered the room.

Emerson wore a cute matching athletic set in bright colors, her long blond hair in a bouncy ponytail.

"It's good to see you," Emerson said, giving me a hug.

"You too." I smiled. "How was your Peloton class?"

It was the second Peloton class they'd taught together, and I could see why everyone was clamoring for more. I'd streamed their first one live and had replayed it several times since because it was *that* good. I'd loved their dynamic, and so did everyone else. Emerson pushed us to work harder, and Nate made us laugh during the class.

"Great." She grinned just as Nate groaned. *Served him right.*

Nate deserved happiness, but he also needed someone like Emerson to put him in his place.

I laughed, giving him a hug. "Good workout?" I teased. He was sweaty and looked worn out, while Emerson was glowing and energized.

"You'd think I would've learned my lesson by now," he grumbled.

"So, what do you have planned for this afternoon?" I asked.

"Some shopping?" Brooklyn bounced on her toes with a hopeful gleam in her eye as she glanced between Emerson and Nate.

"Of course," Emerson said with a playful grin.

Nate shrugged, his expression full of love and affection as he watched Emerson and Brooklyn plot the stores they were going to visit. Though unlike with Nate's ex, I didn't worry that Emerson was only with Nate for the money or status. She was well-off and successful in her own right. And their love and mutual respect were clear to anyone who was in their presence. I would've been jealous if I weren't so happy for them.

After lunch, Brooklyn and Emerson went shopping. I hung back with Nate to catch up and check in with operations at the Huxley Grand New York. I was supposed to meet my bodyguard today, and I wasn't looking forward to it.

That said, having Disco shadow me in London hadn't been as awful as I'd feared. But as great as Disco had been, it was still difficult to imagine spending two months with him —or anyone—on my boat. And while I knew my brothers were right about my needing protection, I was still pissed about the way they'd gone about it.

Nate and I had returned to the suite and were just starting to discuss my sailing trip over coffee when there was a knock at the door. Disco was stationed in the hall, so anyone knocking would've been vetted by him first.

"Come in," Nate called.

The door swung open, and my eyes collided with a pair of familiar blue ones. The color of the ocean on a bright, sunny day. A full bottom lip I'd gotten drunk on many times. A jaw that had sharpened with age, the hard angles now lined with scruff.

All the air had been sucked out of the room, and my chest felt tight. My entire body was like a live wire, attuned to him. *Wary of him.*

The years had certainly been kind to Jackson Shaw. He was hotter than ever, his suit perfectly tailored to showcase his broad shoulders and narrow waist. He looked masculine and intimidating, and my body reacted to him like it always did. Leaning closer, desperate for a look, a touch. Anything he was willing to give.

Traitor.

I straightened. He was stoic. Restrained. It was a sobering reminder to rein it in.

But damn those smile lines and the gray at his temples. It was so unfair.

He stiffened, and my gut clenched with anxiety. *Surely he...they...*

"Jackson," Nate said. "I believe you know my sister, Sloan Mackenzie."

What? I stilled. What had Jackson told Nate about us?

"Yes, of course. You were my sister's roommate in college," was Jackson's response. Smooth as ever. I nodded as if in a daze.

"Sloan," Nate said with a pleased smile. "Jackson will be accompanying you on your sailing trip."

The hell he would.

"No." I stood, smoothing my hands down my skirt.

"No?" Nate furrowed his brow, glancing between the two of us.

To anyone else, nothing about Jackson's expression would indicate displeasure. But I'd always been able to read his emotions. A muscle ticked in his jaw and his nostrils flared. Dead giveaway. He was just as unhappy about this as I was.

Jackson excused himself under the pretense of taking a call.

"Sloan." Nate came over to me. "We talked about this."

"I know." I took a breath, trying to calm my racing heart. "I do. But... Are you okay with me spending two months alone on a boat with him? I mean, with a guy?" I stumbled over the words, flinging my hand toward the door Jackson had just exited.

The mere sight of Jackson set my heart fluttering, and I hated my body's reaction to him. Why? Why him? And why had these feelings still not gone away?

Nate chuckled, placing a hand on my shoulder. "Sloan, you're a grown woman, and it's *Jackson.*"

Exactly.

"He's Greer's brother. I thought you'd be happy about this."

"Happy. Right," I muttered.

Nate pressed on, undaunted. "Jackson has protected my family for the past year. I trust him with my life. With Em's and Brooklyn's lives."

"Then shouldn't you keep him with you?" I asked, grasping on to that excuse, feeble as it was, considering Nate had clearly agreed to send Jackson with me, if not in fact orchestrating it. "He knows your house, your life. I would never want to put you or your family at risk."

He smiled softly, settling his hands on my shoulders. "Then you understand how I feel about you. And Jackson will certainly be missed—not just because he's familiar with our lives. But you need him more."

Did I?

Nate had always been very intuitive. He was affectionate, sure—knowing when to give me a hug or when to give me space. But his ability to read me made it difficult to hide anything from him.

I scrutinized Nate's expression for clues. Did he know about Jackson and me? About what we'd once been to each other? Of all the history and the heartache between us?

I'd never told my family about Jackson, beyond the fact that he was Greer's brother. Never told anyone. He was my best friend's older brother, and our relationship—if you could even call it that—had only ever been a secret.

I'd loved Jackson. Given him everything. And he'd left, choosing his career over me.

I should've known. Hell, Greer had warned me.

I could remember the first time I'd met Jackson. I'd

opened the door to our apartment, and before he could even introduce himself, Greer was there. Jumping into his arms as she squealed his name.

"Jackson." I could hear the smile in her voice. Knew how much she'd been looking forward to seeing her brother.

I had to admit—I'd been curious about him. Greer and I had been friends for a year, and Jackson had been deployed for most of it. He was a Navy SEAL. While I'd seen pictures and said hi a few times while they were on Skype, I had not been prepared for his hotness.

Gorgeous blue eyes scanned me, making me squirm beneath his perusal. He smiled at me over her shoulder. She finally released him, returning to the floor before turning to me.

"Sloan. This is my brother, Jackson. Jackson, this is Sloan."

He stepped over the threshold into our apartment, sucking all the oxygen out of the room. Out of the entire space. It was the size of a shoebox, but it was the nicest place we could afford.

My family had expected that I'd live at the Huxley Grand New York, but I'd wanted an authentic college experience. My grandparents were happy to pay for tuition, but if I wanted to live somewhere else, the cost was on me.

I appreciated their offer, and I knew they were trying to persuade me to live at the hotel. But I was sick of living in a fishbowl. I didn't want to wonder if my family was using the staff to spy on me and report back. I wanted to feel free to do what I wanted.

Hell, New York was one of the most expensive places to live. But I didn't care if I had to work two jobs while attending school to afford a place of my own. A place with Greer. It was worth it.

I'd spent my childhood in hotels around the world, and it was so nice to finally have an apartment that was mine. Where I could hang art on the walls. Decorate it however I wanted. Make the space my own. A home.

Jackson held out his hand. "Nice to finally meet you in person, Sloan."

The way he rasped my name sent a quiver through me. He was handsome. He was trouble.

I hesitated a moment before placing my hand in his. "Same. I've heard a lot about you."

When our hands touched and our eyes met, I felt this...I don't know, spark of recognition. It sounded crazy, but I couldn't deny there was something there. And it wasn't just lust, though he was hot. It was... It was something deeper. A connection.

He shook his head, and I wondered if he'd felt it too. "Only good things, I'm sure." He smirked.

"All right. That's enough," Greer said, severing our contact and giving Jackson a meaningful look.

Jackson shrugged, his expression one of innocence. "What?"

Greer narrowed her eyes at him. "You know what."

"Do I?" he taunted. Or, at least, I thought he was. The devil danced in his eyes, and it was difficult to tell.

"Don't ruin this for me." She continued glaring at him, pointing at him. "I mean it."

I glanced between them, trying to understand. "Don't ruin what?"

"Jackson, here—" she threaded her arm through his "—has a way of sabotaging all my relationships."

"Not all of them." He smiled at me. That smile was wicked. Delicious. It made the most seductive promises.

And I needed to cut it out. He was my best friend's brother, for crying out loud. Any connection—real or imagined—needed to be forgotten.

Greer huffed. "Enough of them. When you're not being a cock-blocker, you're trying to get in my friends' pants."

I tried—and failed—to hold in my laughter. The two of them sounded just like my brothers and me. I loved how close they were.

"One time. That happened one time."

"With my high school best friend!" She slapped his chest. "You broke her heart and ruined our friendship."

"Maybe instead of scolding me, you should be thanking me," he said, and I wouldn't have blamed Greer for wanting to knee him in the balls at that point. "She wasn't a true friend."

Greer gnashed her teeth. "You've got some nerve..."

"Look." Jackson's expression turned more serious. "I am sorry ab—"

She held up a hand, silencing him. "Nope. I don't want to hear it." He started speaking again, and she clapped her hand over his mouth. "Jackson," she growled. "We are done talking about this."

He lifted a shoulder. "You're the one who brought it up."

Greer's expression was pinched, and she looked as if she might murder him.

He held up his hands. "Okay. Okay. I won't mention it again."

She jabbed his chest. "Not good enough."

"Right." His expression was one of chagrin. "It won't happen again."

"It better not." She glared at him. Then she came to my side and draped her arm over my shoulder. "Sloan is too important to me. We're soul sisters."

I smiled. Greer was my best friend. My rock. The closest thing I'd ever had to a sister. And I had enough older brothers to understand her frustration with Jackson. Hell, I'd even been in her shoes.

It came with the territory of being a younger sister. Some of my friends had crushed on my older brothers, especially Nate. It didn't help that he was a rising star in Hollywood. And the few guys my brothers hadn't managed to scare away had been more interested in my money than me.

Thanks to my brothers and the fortune I was set to inherit, I was still a virgin.

That wasn't fair. It wasn't entirely their fault. I had yet to find someone I felt comfortable enough with to share that kind of inti-

*macy. Just because I understood the mechanics didn't mean I was
ready for the emotions that came with it.*

Pretty soon, all that would change, though. Pretty soon,
everything would change.

I shuddered, rubbing my arms. It had been fourteen years.
I'd told myself I was over it. I'd moved on. But it was difficult
to ignore the past when we were at the site of Greer's
wedding—the last time I'd seen Jackson, apart from our
quick run-in in Abu Dhabi. This place held too many
memories.

I pushed away the thought and tried to focus on the
present. There was nothing for me in the past; I needed to
think of the future.

But when I tried to picture the future, I drew a blank.

I scrambled for some excuse, any excuse. "Edward will
hate this," I said, when I was the one who hated this. Why did
it have to be *him*?

I supposed I should've anticipated that my bodyguard
would be a man. I'd always assumed it was a male-dominated
industry, though I knew there were women in the profession. Still...in my head, I hadn't envisioned spending two
months on a sailboat with a man. With Jackson. Whom I'd
have to trust, and vice versa.

"It's not up to Edward," Nate said. "And if he cares about
you as much as he claims to, he'll be more concerned with
your safety than the man ensuring it."

I wasn't so sure about that. Time and again, Edward had
insisted that I'd be safer if I moved in with him. Now, he was
annoyed with me for leaving for two months. He didn't seem
to understand that I *needed* this trip. The fact that he didn't
get that—didn't get *me*—grated.

"Just..." Nate dragged a hand down his face. "Give
Jackson a chance, will you? I think if you got to know him,
you'd like him."

That was the problem. I already knew how much I could like him. And I couldn't put my heart through that kind of pain ever again. Losing Jackson, then my grandparents... I swallowed hard, ignoring the way the bridge of my nose stung.

I would not go there. I would not think of what could've been. What almost was...

I let out a shaky exhale.

"Sloan." Nate tilted his head, evaluating me. "Is there something you're not telling me? Some other reason you're opposed to Jackson?"

"I—" I paused, not even sure what to say. The past was in the past, and that was where it needed to stay. So I swallowed back my protests. "No."

I knew Jackson was more than qualified to sail with me. Hell, maybe I should've been happy with this turn of events. And maybe under different circumstances or a decade ago, I would've been. Jackson was a damn good sailor—instinctual. It was something we'd bonded over. Something we'd always dreamed of doing together—taking an extended trip on a boat, just the two of us.

Oh, what a cruel sense of irony the universe had.

"I know you're not happy about this intrusion," Nate said. "But Jackson has always been discreet, respectful, and professional."

I was completely at a loss for words.

"Let's just spend some time with him and talk about the trip. 'Kay?"

I swallowed hard. "Mm. Yep."

Because what else could I do at this point? I'd run out of excuses.

Had Jackson known that I was his new client? He hadn't seemed as surprised to see me as I'd been to see him. But it wouldn't be the first time I'd been wrong about him or the situation.

I straightened, telling myself this was just like any other meeting I attended. I was in charge. I was the boss. *His* boss.

God, that was weird.

This whole situation was weird. I tried to imagine spending the next two months with him on my boat and failed.

Jackson had once been the oxygen I breathed. Now, he was going to be working for me, protecting me. The prospect of my sailing trip was beginning to seem less like freedom and more like torture.

CHAPTER FOUR

Jackson

I stood in the hallway outside the presidential suite of the Huxley Grand New York while Nate and Sloan chatted inside. It made me think of my sister's wedding day. God, that day had been so fucked up. I'd barely held it together.

I paused before the door to the penthouse suite, tugging at my collar. My dress uniform felt as if it were strangling me, but I knew it was merely the idea of seeing Sloan again after so long. We'd promised not to let whatever happened between us affect our relationship with Greer, and I had to trust that Sloan would keep her word as she always had. Even though I knew today—my sister's wedding day—would be trying.

I smoothed my hands down my pants and straightened, knocking on the door. A butler, a freaking butler, answered.

And this was the world Sloan lived in. The world she'd grown up in and the world that she'd be expected to command when she was older. It was so far removed from my own, she might as well have lived on a different planet.

"Sir?" he asked.

I cleared my throat. Right. "I'm here to walk my sister down the aisle. Could you let my mom know I'm here?"

He stepped aside, inviting me in. "Of course. Would you like a drink?"

I shook my head, though the idea was tempting. "No. Thank you."

"I'll will inform Mrs. Shaw that you've arrived."

He disappeared, and I scanned the suite. There were bags and wedding stuff everywhere, but the place was huge. I couldn't even imagine what something like this would cost.

"Oh, Jackson." Mom lifted a shaky hand to her mouth. "You look so handsome."

I'd been so lost in my thoughts, I'd barely heard her enter. I shook my head as if to clear it. I was always aware of my surroundings. Always.

"Thanks, Mom." I gave her a hug. "You look beautiful." And she did. Radiant and happy despite the fact that it should've been my dad walking Greer down the aisle, not me.

"Always the charmer." She gave my cheek a pat. "Greer is so relieved you made it. We all are."

"Thanks, Mom. Where is she?"

"Through there. With the bridesmaids." She linked her arm through mine. "Marcie's daughter is free if you're—"

"I'm not." I cut her off.

"Okay. I'm sure you don't need my help with women, but, well —" She sighed. "When are you going to settle down? Give me grandchildren?"

"Mom," I sighed, trying not to lose my shit. It wasn't her fault that she didn't know about Sloan. No one did. And it wasn't like it mattered now. We were over. "I just moved to a new city. Started a new job. I'm still finding my footing."

"I know." She patted my arm. "I know. I just... I want you to be happy."

"What makes you think I'm not?" I asked, thinking of it as more of a rhetorical question.

But of course, she didn't. "I know it's been rough for you. Leaving the SEALs, changing careers. Moving cross-country."

She didn't know the half of it. But at least I'd been granted an honorable discharge in time for my sister's wedding, allowing me to wear the dress uniform everyone expected. Everyone except Sloan— the one person who knew the truth.

"You should talk to Sloan," *she suggested, and I tried not to panic. Did she suspect...something? I tried to get a read on her, knowing it would be best to keep my mouth shut despite my fears. But then Mom said,* "She's going through some similar changes herself. I bet she'd understand. I bet she'd appreciate a friend."

I wondered if Sloan had felt as lost as I had. It didn't matter that I'd moved across the country; I saw her everywhere. Even now, a year later, her face was the last thing I saw when I fell asleep. She was my home, and I couldn't escape her, no matter how hard I tried.

Before I could ask what changes Mom referred to, she ushered me toward a bedroom. "They're in there."

"Is everyone decent?" *I called, my heart rate ratcheting up at the idea of seeing Sloan.*

"Come in," *Greer called.*

I opened the door, and Greer stood in the middle of the room, a veil cascading down her back.

"Greer." *My voice cracked on her name. My baby sister looked stunning, but I couldn't help imagining Sloan standing there, waiting for me in a white dress. My heart shuddered, and I blinked away the vision.* "You look beautiful."

Greer smiled. So serene. So mature. When the hell had that happened?

"Thank you." *A tear leaked out, and she quickly wiped it away.* "I'm really glad you're here."

"Me too." *I hugged her, pressing a kiss to her forehead.* "Dad would be so proud of you."

"I wish he were here," *she whispered.*

"Me too." I gave her another squeeze. "But he's here in spirit." I patted my chest, where a few of his medals were pinned to my uniform.

I felt the weight of them, the honor. He was a hero, and I was...a failure.

"Oh, Jackson." She lifted her hand to my chest, admiring the awards. "Thank you. I love that."

I subtly scanned the room for the one person I wanted to see. All the bridesmaids were dressed in black evening gowns, but my attention was pulled, as always, to Sloan. Even when she shied away from the spotlight. Even when she was trying to avoid me, I sensed her presence.

Sloan stood off to the side, her back to me. The black dress clung to her form, making my mouth water. I wanted her. I wanted to go to her. To ask how she was.

I studied her reflection. Her expression was imperious and unreadable. This situation—unbearable.

I kept staring, begging her to meet my gaze. To look at me. Something.

But the moment she did, I regretted it. She was devastating. Her gaze was heated, burning with equal parts want and hate. Hell, I hated myself most days. Knowing what I'd done to us, to her.

Yes, I'd lied. But so had she.

And this was exactly why I'd skipped the rehearsal dinner. My absence hadn't been due to a delayed flight, as I'd told my mom. Because, as always, I was trying to protect Sloan. To do what was best for her, even when it nearly killed me.

My phone buzzed in my pocket, pulling me out of the past. *Fuck. Get your head on straight.*

> Vaughn: How'd your meeting with the client go?

> Me: That remains to be seen.

> Vaughn: Turn your history from a conflict into an asset.

He had no idea what he was asking.

I was trying, but Sloan had kicked me out almost immediately. She'd said "No" the moment she'd laid eyes on me.

Fuck if that hadn't stung.

I'd expected her to put up a fight, but I hadn't expected this. I wished there were some way to reassure her that I was a professional. That I would protect her. That our past didn't have to affect our current circumstances, even if I found it difficult to compartmentalize the two.

Was I crazy for even considering it?

I thought about how badly I wanted the promotion. How lucky I was to be offered the position. But all of that faded when I considered the threats against Sloan. My vision clouded. *How dare...*

The door opened, and I half expected to see my mom waiting there. Inviting me in so I could walk my sister down the aisle. When all I could think about—all I could see—was Sloan. Always Sloan.

"You okay?" Nate asked.

I shook my head as if to clear it. Dwelling on the past wouldn't change the present, no matter how much I might wish it would.

"Yeah." I swallowed. "Yeah. I'm good."

Nate stepped into the hall, closing the door gently behind him. "Sorry about that." He sighed. "Don't take it personally. Sloan's been resistant to the idea of protection since day one."

I wanted to laugh. She might be opposed to executive protection, but this was most definitely personal.

After our accidental run-in in Abu Dhabi, I'd avoided her. I'd been a coward. I'd swapped with one of the other members of my team so I wouldn't have to pretend I didn't know Sloan.

I shoved my feelings down deep, wanting to do what was best for her, even if it ran contrary to my goals. "Perhaps we should see who else at Hudson is available to go with her."

Two months alone on a thirty-five-foot sailboat with Sloan was asking for trouble. Despite everything that had happened, it was as if the two of us couldn't be in the same room without our connection sparking to life. Hell, the last time we'd been alone was at my sister's wedding. And I knew how well that had ended.

I knew we'd be safe—at least, as safe as a sailor on open water could be. But if I couldn't trust myself to keep my emotions in check around Sloan for twenty minutes, how could I possibly do so for two months?

Emotions were a liability in my profession. Emotions were a distraction. Emotions got you killed.

That was a big reason why we were supposed to maintain a professional distance from the principal. For the sake of both their safety and our own. And having sex with the principal was absolutely forbidden.

"No." Nate's tone was firm. He was adamant. "Maverick said you're the best person for the job. And loath as we are to see you go, I agree. I don't want anyone else. I trust you."

He was right. As much as I was dreading this, I also couldn't imagine sending anyone in my place. This was something I needed to do as much for myself as for her. She might not be part of my life anymore, but she'd always carry a piece of my heart. And I couldn't imagine a world without Sloan in it.

"How do you want to play this?" I asked, knowing we needed some sort of strategy. "Good cop, bad cop?"

He clamped a hand on my shoulder. "Only cop." He grinned. "She's all yours."

Ha. Right. Sloan hadn't been mine in a long time. Not that Nate meant it like that. Not that he'd approve of my dating his sister.

I needed to get my head on straight, but that was what happened when I was with Sloan. She became my first priority, and nothing else mattered. It was both dangerous and addictive.

He released me and backed away. "Good luck, Jackson. You're going to need it."

Fuck.

I clenched and unclenched my fists once his back was turned. Closed my eyes and tried to recenter myself. But all that came to mind was the smell of wild roses and sunshine. My legendary control was slipping, and I hadn't even crossed the threshold.

Sloan Mackenzie.

A memory drifted to me, unbidden. Sloan smiling at me over her shoulder. Dark-brown hair flowing down her back in waves. Now, her hair barely grazed her collarbone, and it was sleek and straight.

I considered my options regarding the woman in the next room. I could think of a thousand things I'd rather do, but there was only one choice—walk through that door and face the only woman I'd ever loved.

I told myself I was doing it because I wanted the promotion, but this was Sloan we were talking about. If she needed me, I'd always be there for her.

I wiped my palms on my thighs and straightened. I was a soldier going into battle, and I would show no fear.

I opened the door and entered the suite. "Ms. Mackenzie," I said, addressing her formally, as I would any client. It was agency policy. And even if it weren't, using her last name was a sign of respect. A reminder of my position as her bodyguard.

"Ms. Mackenzie?" she scoffed. "I think we're long past such formalities, don't you?"

I kept my gaze trained on the painting across the room, even as she stepped closer.

"Jackson," she snapped, but I held steady. "The least you can do is look at me."

Slowly, I inclined my head, regretting it the moment my eyes met hers. They were an unusual shade of green. Pale, mysterious, captivating. Looking into her eyes was like glimpsing into her heart. She'd never been good at hiding her emotions—or at least, she hadn't been in the past.

Looking at her now, I wasn't sure what she was thinking. The thin press of her lips indicated anger. But otherwise, I found her difficult to read. Gone was the carefree girl with smiles like sunshine. She'd gotten better at masking her emotions in the past decade. It was...disappointing, to say the least.

She almost seemed like a different woman in her perfectly tailored suit and fuck-me heels. She was as beautiful as ever, but she had a coldness to her. An edge that hadn't been there before.

I could easily imagine Sloan commanding a boardroom. But I wondered if she ever smiled. If she was happy.

"You're not coming on this trip," she hissed. "I don't need a bodyguard." But what I heard was, "I don't need you." It hurt more than it should've, especially after all this time.

"The threats you've received would indicate otherwise." She wasn't the first principal who'd rejected my intrusion into her life; she wouldn't be the last.

I fully intended to ask her about the threats when she was less hostile. Though, judging from her expression, I doubted that would ever happen.

"I'm going to be in the middle of the ocean."

"And what about when you dock?" I asked. "What about when you spend a few days on an island? I received your proposed itinerary, and I'd like to suggest several modifications."

She scoffed. "First, you want to invade my solo sailing trip. And now, you insist on making modifications?" She turned away as if offended by my gall, when I was only trying to keep her safe.

"Your plans do not account for certain…contingencies," I said, though, really, I wanted to know why she hadn't invited her boyfriend along. A sailing trip like this was the kind we'd always discussed taking—together. And yet, she was planning to go alone.

"Contingencies?" she asked, her eyes sparking with anger. "Enlighten me, then. Because my route accounted for the need to refuel, restock, and rest. And it took into account weather and wind, though obviously, those will be reevaluated throughout."

"Yes." My tone was gentle. I was already on thin ice. "And you were thorough." She had been. Extremely so. It was a solid plan, well researched and considered, at least from a sailing standpoint.

"Then what's the problem?"

"You don't seem to appreciate the threat to your safety. You can't behave like you always have. A solo traveler is already in a vulnerable position." I shuddered at the statistics for women, not bothering to relay them. Unwilling to ever let Sloan become one of those statistics.

"Add in the fact that you're wealthy," I continued, though that was putting it mildly. Sloan was a billionaire. "And you're even more of a target."

She scoffed. "This isn't my first rodeo. It's not like I go around flashing my wealth."

"Perhaps not," I said, knowing firsthand that when it came to Sloan, things weren't always what they appeared. "But there's been a rash of thefts in the Caribbean as the season ramps up. Gangs on Jet Skis wearing clown masks and boarding boats with guns. Not to mention muggings at ATMs." I didn't stop when her eyes widened. Couldn't. I needed her to understand. I needed her to stay safe. "And even if you ignored all that, someone has been sending you threats."

Sloan had always been stubborn, but I'd never considered her particularly reckless. At least, I hadn't in the past.

"Are you trying to scare me?" Anger bled into her words. But beneath it, I sensed fear. Sloan was scared, even if she refused to admit it.

I tried to keep my cool. "I'm trying to get you to be realistic. I know you're not happy about the situation, but you can't continue to ignore it." No matter how much she might want to.

She turned away, walking over to the window and peering out at the skyline. I took the opportunity to study her. The shoulders of her suit tapered to her waist, nipping in before flaring out over her hips. Curves that had always been generous seemed even more so. And the way her skirt clung to her rounded ass had my cock standing up and taking notice.

I drank her in like a dying man who'd wandered the desert in search of water.

Her skirt had a slit up the back, giving me a rather tantalizing glimpse of her thighs. I could remember the feel of her skin beneath my hands. The birthmark that stained the quad of her right leg. I'd spent hours memorizing every inch of her. Hours in her arms. In her bed. Inside her.

And now, it was almost as if we were strangers. The distance between us had never seemed so great, even when we were on opposite sides of the world. At least then, I could imagine a different outcome. Imagine us in the past as we'd once been—in love and inseparable. Or dream of a future together, even if it would never come to pass.

She sighed, playing with her necklace and bringing me back to the present as she turned to face me once more. "What do you suggest?"

This was good. She might not trust me, but she'd given me an opening.

I grabbed a set of nautical charts, unfolding them on the table before setting some makeshift paperweights on top.

"Talk about old-school," she teased.

"You love it," I retorted before catching myself. I needed to remember our roles and the circumstances. Not slip back into our easy familiarity, no matter how tempting it may seem.

She's your principal. She's with another man.

"I do," she said softly. So softly, I almost hadn't heard her.

Hell, maybe I'd imagined the words. Longing to hear something positive from her lips. Wanting to know that I'd meant as much to her as she had to me.

I turned my attention to the charts, needing to focus on the present.

Paper charts were safer and more reliable in the sense that our travel plans couldn't be hacked. That said, I'd given a copy of our itinerary to Hudson and Sloan's family. I detailed my proposed route, hoping she would see my suggestions as the improvements they were—mostly in terms of security.

"I appreciate that you didn't completely change my plans," she said, her eyes still on the charts. "And getting to see the eclipse is an added bonus. It wasn't even on my radar."

My shoulders relaxed, relief washing over me at her acceptance. "Like I said, I just made a few tweaks to make it safer. And I thought you might enjoy the eclipse. Selfishly, I wanted to see it."

She let out a long breath, causing her lips to purse and my cock to harden. *Jesus.*

She'd always had this effect on me. It was…problematic, to say the least.

Vaughn's voice rang in my head. *Turn a conflict into an asset.*

Yeah. I was pretty sure this wasn't what he'd meant.

"Did you volunteer for this assignment?" she asked.

"No." In fact, I'd tried everything I could to extricate myself from it.

"Is there really no one else?" she asked, her expression weary.

I shook my head. *There was never anyone but you.*

I might not have been a saint in our years apart, but I'd never given my heart to anyone else. How could I when Sloan had always owned it?

CHAPTER FIVE

Sloan

Brooklyn tugged on my arm. "Auntie Sloan?"

I forced a smile, turning my attention from the view and thoughts of Jackson. He'd left the suite after we'd finalized our plans, but his presence lingered. His scent—he even wore the same damn scent, the cologne I'd given him for his twenty-ninth birthday. It was indelibly linked to him in my mind. A mixture of something spicy, sensual, forbidden, and purely Jackson.

"What's up?" I asked.

She peered up at me, her eyes full of concern. "Are you okay?"

"Of course." I wrapped my arm around her shoulder. I didn't know how long I'd been standing there, thinking of the past and debating my future. "I'm sorry. I'm just... thinking about my trip."

"Are you excited?" she asked.

Was I excited?

I wasn't sure what I was. I wasn't sure the myriad of emotions I was feeling could be so easily categorized. But I didn't want to worry Brooklyn. So I said, "I'm excited to be able to take such a long sailing trip."

"I'm going to miss you." She gave me a squeeze.

I squeezed her back. "I'm going to miss you too."

She hugged me extra tight, not letting go. "Hey," I said in a calming tone. "Everything okay?"

She nodded, but her face was buried in my chest.

"Brooklyn?" I placed my hands on her shoulders, peering into her face. "What's going on?"

"I just..." She pulled back and let out a shaky exhale. "That's a long time for you to be on a boat. And what about hurricane season and bad weather and..."

"Sweetheart." I smoothed her hair away from her face, eager to assuage her fears. "It's not hurricane season yet. And I go sailing every year."

"Not like this. Not crossing an ocean."

"True," I agreed. "But I have before. Before you were born. And I'm an experienced sailor. Besides—" I ruffled her hair "—I won't be alone."

She let out a sigh of relief. "I'm so glad Jackson's going with you."

I hadn't realized how concerned she was for me. How concerned all my family was for my safety. And I found her faith in Jackson...sweet. There'd been a time when I'd had that kind of faith in Jackson. When I'd felt safe because I knew he'd never let anyone hurt me.

I was leaving the restaurant late one night after my shift had ended when someone tapped me on the shoulder. I jumped, letting out a shriek.

"Sloan?" Jackson asked. "You okay?"

I turned to face him, my heart racing. "I..." I breathed out. "Yeah. Yeah." I was still trying to catch my breath, so I flashed him a bright smile instead.

He tilted his head, his gaze assessing. "Where are you headed?"

"Home. I just got off from work. Why?"

Jackson scanned the street. "I'll walk with you," he said, and for a brief flicker of a moment, I wondered if he'd planned this. If he'd come here just to see me. He knew where I worked. He knew from our texts earlier in the day that I'd had a shift tonight. I nearly laughed at myself. The idea was ridiculous.

Still...there was something between us. Could he feel it too? This connection?

"What?" he asked, and I realized I had yet to respond.

I might be tempted to ask if he'd come here for me, but I was too scared to hear his response. Instead, I asked, "Aren't you worried Greer will see you?"

He'd put me in an incredibly awkward position.

"At the moment, I'm more concerned about you." His expression was sincere, and I tried not to read too much into that comment. Jackson was older. Hot. He probably thought of me like another little sister.

I tightened my grip on my bag, exhausted after a long shift and ready to go home. "I already have four older brothers. I don't need another one."

His expression darkened, but I turned and started walking toward my apartment.

"Sloan." He grabbed my wrist, his hold light yet commanding.

"What?" I asked, glancing at him over my shoulder.

"Just..." He looked as if he was going to say something else then stopped himself. "I'm sorry if I startled you. I read about a string of assaults on campus, and I was worried about you."

I softened at his words. I wanted to ask why, but I knew better than to push. Besides, it would be nice not to have to walk home alone at night just this once. "Okay. The company would be nice."

We fell into step beside each other. We talked about work, school, Greer. My family. I kept stealing glances at Jackson, his eyes connecting with mine every time.

We slowed as we neared my apartment, and I wanted to linger

in this moment with him. But this was reckless. What would we tell Greer if she happened to see us together? What would she think?

"I should—" I gestured toward the building. "I should head in, or Greer will worry. Thanks for walking me home."

"Anytime. Seriously. Call me if you ever need anything." When I said nothing, he pressed. "Okay?"

"Okay."

He lifted his hand as if to touch me. I wished he would. I held my breath, waiting for it. But then he dragged his hand through his hair.

"Wait." His arm brushed against me, and I wanted to sink into him. Into his strength and assuredness.

"Are you free tomorrow?"

My heart leaped at his question, but I told it to calm the hell down. "Yeah. Why?"

"Come by my place. I want to teach you some self-defense moves."

"You do?" I asked, lighting up.

"Yeah." He rubbed the back of his neck, suddenly bashful.

"I love that idea," I said, and I meant it. I loved that Jackson didn't want to coddle me but empower me.

"See you tomorrow." He smiled.

"Tomorrow." I smiled back, almost giddy. I turned and headed toward the door to my building, feeling his eyes on me the entire time.

"Will you still be able to FaceTime while you're gone?" Brooklyn asked, jolting me from the memory.

"Of course." I knew it would be difficult to keep up with our daily text messages and twice-weekly calls. But I would do anything to reassure her.

"I wish I could go with you," she mumbled in a glum tone.

She'd been saying that for years. I'd hired a sailing coach at one of the local marinas for her. And we'd been sailing together every chance we got. One day, she'd be ready. *One day*, Nate had agreed.

"How'd it go with Jackson?" Emerson asked, entering the room.

"Good." I smiled brightly, still feeling off-kilter. "Yeah. Good."

But the more I thought about it, the more surprised I was. Because I actually meant it.

"He's super nice," Brooklyn gushed. "I knew you'd like him."

"Hey, B?" Emerson ruffled Brooklyn's hair, meeting my eyes over the top of her head. "Why don't you see if the chef can rustle up a charcuterie board."

"Okay!" Brooklyn popped up and disappeared down the hall to the kitchen.

"Hey," Emerson said in a softer tone. "Are you okay?"

"I…" I glanced away, not sure what to say or if I even should. I liked Emerson. Thought she was perfect for Nate and Brooklyn. But I wasn't sure I wanted to divulge my past with Jackson to her—or anyone.

I'd kept our relationship a secret all these years. Why stop now?

"I'm fine." I only hoped my smile looked more convincing than it felt.

I was still trying to grapple with the fact that my ex was going to be my bodyguard.

It had been easier to forget about him when we were living separate lives, but now, we'd be sharing a boat. And all the feelings I'd forgotten or suppressed seemed determined to resurface.

"Mm." She smiled. "I know you say that. And I know you want it to be true, but I sense you don't quite believe it yourself."

Was I really that transparent?

"I—" I gaped at her.

She flashed me a warm smile and leaned in. "I've been in your shoes. Many times. Pretending I'm fine when I'm anything but."

"You mean since announcing your engagement to Nate?" I couldn't fathom living with the level of publicity and scrutiny they dealt with on a regular basis. It had to be exhausting.

"Yes, but even before. I guess what I'm trying to say is that it's okay not to be okay." She placed her hand on my forearm. "And I'm here if you want to talk."

"Thanks." I swallowed past the lump in my throat, overwhelmed by her generosity. I didn't have many girlfriends. And even though Emerson was younger than me, she was wise. Genuine.

"I know what it's like to have people invade your space," she continued. "To have your life turned upside down without your consent. To suddenly have a bodyguard. And if I didn't have my best friend, Kendall, and Nate, I don't know how I'd get through it."

"You'd find a way." Of that, I had no doubt.

Emerson was an Olympic gold medalist. She was an incredible athlete. She was perfect for Nate, but she was also the type of woman I'd always expected Jackson to end up with—beautiful, ambitious, athletic. She was like a ray of sunshine.

Which got me wondering, not for the first time, about Jackson's relationship status.

If he was going on a two-month sailing trip with me surely he wasn't married, right? I couldn't imagine his wife being okay with that kind of assignment. I sure as hell wouldn't be if I were in her shoes.

Greer hadn't mentioned there being anyone serious in

Jackson's life, but he didn't tell her everything. I knew that from experience.

And the idea of Jackson having a wife made me sick to my stomach. I placed a hand there to quell my growing nausea.

"Sloan?" Emerson asked. "Are you sure you're okay? You look pale."

"I am pale," I joked. "I live in London, and I'm rarely outside."

She eyed me with a healthy amount of skepticism but didn't push. Instead, she asked, "How's Edward?"

"Fine." At least, I assumed he was. We'd barely spoken all week. So, I tacked on, "Busy as ever," because that seemed more accurate.

"I'm sure it takes a toll on your relationship." I knew she was speaking from personal experience. She and Nate juggled a lot, but they always seemed to make Brooklyn and their relationship with each other the priority.

"It does."

I could hear Brooklyn talking to someone in the other room. Based on the animated tone of her voice, I assumed it was Sophia.

"I'm sure you'll be eager to return to London after your sailing trip, but I was hoping you'd attend Kendall's bridal shower."

I wasn't sure I'd be eager to return home, at least not until the threats stopped. And considering I planned to break up with Edward, I didn't think I'd have a relationship to return home to.

"I'd like to," I said. "I'll do my best," I added.

The chef delivered a charcuterie board, and I wondered if I could ask Emerson about Jackson without arousing too much suspicion. Surely it would seem natural for me to be curious about my bodyguard, right? Especially considering the fact that we'd be in such close quarters.

"What do you know about Jackson?" I asked.

Emerson considered me a moment then said, "He's a former Navy SEAL. Forty-four. Great with kids. Obsessed with safety. Discreet. Loyal."

I already knew all that, but I simply listened as if it were news to me. Her comment about Jackson being "great with kids" surprised me, despite the fact that Brooklyn had gushed about him.

"What do you know about him personally?" I asked, trying to subtly inquire about his home life. His relationship status.

She lifted a shoulder. "Not much. Like I said, he's friendly but professional. It took months before he finally agreed to switch from calling me Ms. Thorne to Emerson."

I popped a cracker into my mouth, chewing as I considered.

She tilted her head, assessing. "Why? Are you concerned about something?"

"Just…apprehensive about the situation in general." A glance at my watch told me it was getting late in London. I was running out of time to talk to Edward before my trip, and I didn't want to leave with things as unsettled as they were.

"It'll be okay." Her smile was full of warmth and under-standing. "You'll see. Having a bodyguard isn't so bad, and Jackson's the best."

I wondered if she knew about Kendall's bodyguard. I wondered if I should tell her since Kendall was her best friend. But then I decided it wasn't my place.

I stood, smoothing down my skirt. "I'd better go call Edward."

"I've got to do some stretches. I'll catch up with you later."

When I reached my room, I shut the door behind me and kicked off my shoes. I dragged a hand through my hair, padding across the carpet. I was sick of making excuses. Done with lying to myself.

I knew what needed to be done. With a deep sigh, I pressed the button to connect the call. Edward answered on the third ring.

"Sloan, darling."

"Hey." I stared at the contents of my suitcase.

We fell silent for a minute, awkward tension stretching between us. This wasn't the type of conversation I wanted to have over the phone, but he'd been too busy to meet up in the weeks leading up to my trip. And I didn't feel like I could put it off any longer.

"Do you... Do you feel like this is normal?" I asked, trying to ease into it.

"What?"

"Our relationship. It just..." I sighed, trying to choose my words carefully. "It feels like we're disconnected." Surely he could see that, right? Even my brothers could see that, and they lived on the opposite side of the world.

"I'm not the one who decided to leave for a two-month sailing trip." The words came out clipped, and I could imagine him smoothing a hand over his hair as if he could smooth away his agitation. "You know I get motion sickness."

Edward hated open water, often joking that he could get seasick in a bathtub. I'd always told myself it was okay for couples to have different interests. But sometimes it rankled that we couldn't share something that was so important to me. Something that was as much a part of me as my green eyes.

"I know," I snapped, frustration lining my tone. But he wasn't getting it. This had been simmering beneath the surface for a long time. "This isn't about the sailing trip."

"Then what is it about?"

Everything else.

Edward was perfect on paper, but I couldn't see a future with him. And I'd ignored that fact for far too long.

"Look," he said in a calmer tone. "We lead busy lives. There's a cost. But if you'd move in with me..." He trailed off, perhaps hopeful that I'd finally say yes.

"I appreciate the offer, but I'm not sure it would change anything."

"Of course it would." He was growing agitated. It wasn't the first time we'd had this conversation. "We'd get to go to bed together," he said in a suggestive tone. "Wake up together. Share meals."

It wasn't enough. And I was frustrated that he didn't understand. That he didn't even recognize there was a problem. That he thought we could solve everything by moving in together.

"You're not listening to me. You never listen to me." I straightened, feeling a sense of rightness settle into me. "We want different things."

"What are you saying?" he asked, hesitancy creeping into his tone for the first time.

I took a deep breath and let it out slowly, knowing there was no coming back from this. "I don't think we should see each other anymore."

"What? Sloan, where is this coming from?"

I didn't even know what to say to that, but I soon found myself launching into a list of reasons. When he didn't try to brush aside my concerns, he disputed each and every one until I was worn down and exhausted. This was what he did. How he handled a disagreement. But I wasn't going to be deterred.

Finally, he said, "You're being hasty."

"I'm not. I've given this a lot of thought."

"Right. Which is why you decided to spring it on me the

night before you leave for two months and become practically unreachable?"

I sighed. "I tried to talk to you about it sooner."

"When?" he asked.

"Several times." I pinched the bridge of my nose. "You were always too busy."

"Maybe you didn't try hard enough."

"You know what, Edward?" I gritted my teeth. "I'm done. Done arguing with you. Done with this relationship."

"Come on, Sloan." His tone was softer now, almost pleading. "Don't do this. Don't throw away what we have. Can't we just...can't we discuss this more later? When you're back from your trip."

I understood that he was upset and maybe felt blindsided, but postponing this conversation would merely be dragging out the inevitable.

Inevitable, I scoffed. That was the exact word Jackson had used when he'd broken up with me all those years ago. I pushed thoughts of Jackson aside.

"I'm not sure what more there is to say." I only wished we could've had this conversation in person instead of over the phone, even if it wouldn't have changed anything.

He scoffed. "Fine." Then he hung up the phone without saying goodbye.

I felt bad for hurting Edward, but I set my phone down, filled with an overwhelming sense of peace. For the first time in a while, I felt as if I was making the right decision. The decision that rang true to me.

CHAPTER SIX

Jackson

The jet engine hummed, providing sound to the otherwise silent flight. I glanced over at Sloan, her face screwed up in concentration as she stared at her laptop. The light from the screen illuminated her features—those plump lips and determined eyes. And I couldn't seem to tear my gaze away from her, despite telling myself numerous times that it was completely inappropriate.

She'd been working almost nonstop since we'd boarded our flight to Miami. Part of me wondered if it was an avoidance tactic. If Sloan had decided to ignore our past and pretend I was her executive protection agent and nothing more. Or if she really was just that busy.

Considering she was the senior vice president of operations for a global luxury hotel brand, it was likely she truly was *that* busy. Yet somehow, it still surprised me. I didn't know why. She'd always been diligent, driven, and determined. But in the past, she'd also known how to relax and have fun.

She'd been good at getting me to let go and have fun too.

I kept having to remind myself that she wasn't the same

girl I'd once known. That what little I knew of Sloan's life for the past fourteen years had come from snippets my sister had mentioned in passing or things I'd read in Sloan's file. I didn't know her anymore, not really.

Seeing her now, she was so buttoned-up. So stiff and professional.

What had happened?

And was I somehow responsible for this change?

Don't flatter yourself. It had been years since we were together. I'd changed, and so had she.

I sighed and stared out the window, the clouds drifting past. Seeing her again, being so close to her again, had everything rushing back—the good, the bad, the... unexpected.

I was standing at the entrance to the VIP section of the club near closing time when a group descended. Rich. Young. Drunk.

One of them stopped, her head tilting in confusion. "Jackson?"

It took me a minute to place her. And when I did, I could scarcely believe my eyes.

"Sloan?" I asked, barely recognizing my little sister's best friend. Damn, she looked good. Short dress. Low neckline. Glossy pink lips.

The longer I looked at her, the more differences I cataloged. And it wasn't just the makeup. It was...everything.

"What are you doing here?"

"I, uh—" I tugged on my collar. Shit. Was it tight? Panic sliced through my veins, and I glanced around. No one was supposed to know I was here, least of all my sister's best friend. "Is Greer with you?"

She shook her head. "I'm here with some friends who are in town for the weekend."

"Come on, Sloan!" a girl called to her. I'd seen her earlier, her and her friends. She was some celebrity. A model or a socialite or something. And she knew Sloan? Nothing about this was adding up with the picture I had of Sloan.

She was my sister's roommate. Young. Broke. College student. Yet here she stood, looking like...that.

And I wasn't the only one who'd noticed. She turned heads everywhere she went.

Suddenly, the floor manager was at my side. "Is there a problem?"

"No." I swallowed. "No problem, sir."

"Good. Then get back to work," he barked then quickly disappeared.

Sloan's eyes went wide. "Work?" She leaned in and whispered, "Jackson, are you undercover or something?" But all I could think of was the smell of her—wild roses and sunshine. Amid the bright lights and the loud music, it centered me.

"Please don't say anything to Greer," I begged, careful to keep my voice low. "Please."

I'd hoped to have more time before confessing to Greer. In truth, I hoped I'd never have to tell my family I'd left the Navy until after I found a more permanent job. I knew how disappointed they'd be.

Disgrace. Failure. Liar. *The words spun through my head on an endless loop.*

"I won't for now." Sloan held my gaze. "As long as you promise to explain what's going on."

"You hungry?" I asked. "My shift's almost over."

"I...uh, sure. Let me just say goodbye to my friends."

I nodded, clocking out and then meeting her at the front. We went outside to hail a cab. When Sloan shivered, I removed my jacket and placed it over her shoulders. She smiled up at me, and it was like a punch to the gut. "Thanks."

I hailed a cab, giving them directions to a twenty-four-hour diner down the street from my place. We grabbed a table and ordered some food.

"How's school?" I asked, wanting to ease into this conversation.

"How's school?" she sputtered. "Um. I think we have a few more important things to discuss. Like why you're working at a club in

New York while Greer still thinks you're deployed. Do you know how worried she's been about you?"

She didn't mince words, did she?

Before I could answer, the waitress delivered our food, and Sloan dug into her pancakes. I didn't have much of an appetite, so I pushed my food around my plate.

"I was discharged from the Navy."

"Are you okay?" She scanned my face. "Were you injured?"

I shook my head. That would've been almost preferable. At least then, I would've left with honor not in disgrace. "I got into a fight."

Sloan arched an eyebrow. "About what?"

"Doesn't matter." I shouldn't have let that asshole get in my head.

"Jackson," Sloan chided. "Clearly, it matters if it's the reason you were discharged from the Navy."

I sighed, sensing she wasn't going to drop it. I'd already told her more than I'd intended, and despite not knowing her very well, I trusted her.

Before I could stop myself, I said, "Long story short, while we were out one night, this asshole said something...derogatory to my buddy. And—" I curled my hands into fists beneath the table, remembering those hurtful, ignorant words. Remembering the way my friend had told me to let it go. To pretend it didn't matter. "—I punched him."

Sloan nodded, seemingly not surprised. "Sounds like he deserved it. You're a good friend."

It was so nice to have someone take my side. I hadn't expected that. I hadn't expected her to understand. But she had.

"The asshole filed assault charges, and the Navy was forced to discharge me." I leaned forward, lowering my voice. "I'm lucky I had such a good rapport with my chain of command. They gave me only a general discharge and the chance to earn an honorable discharge if I keep my nose clean."

She stayed close, and I realized that her eyes weren't just green.

Gold flecks danced in them. They were captivating, and I found it difficult to look away.

"Is that what you're doing at the club? 'Keeping your nose clean'?" She used air quotes.

"I'm trying to," I admitted. "And I needed a job."

"As a bouncer?" Her expression was incredulous.

"Look," I huffed, annoyed that she would look down on me for my job. Perhaps she was like those rich girls she'd been hanging out with. "You don't have to understand it, but it works for now."

"Jackson." She opened her mouth as if to speak then closed it. Opened it again. "I'm not judging you for your choices, but even I know that you don't belong there."

"Oh yeah?" I scoffed. "You know that? Because you know me?"

She rested her forearms on the table. "I know enough about you to know that being a bouncer is a respectable job, but it's not the job for you."

"What would you have me do? Huh? Do you know how hard it's been to find work? My buddy pulled some strings for me to get this job." I hadn't meant to admit that. I hadn't meant to admit any of it.

"My..." She paused. Swallowed. "I know someone who works at a luxury hotel. Maybe they're looking to hire someone in their security department."

"Thanks." I sipped my drink, annoyed with myself more than anything. "But no thanks."

"If you change your mind," she said, "the offer stands."

"I appreciate it."

"What about Greer?" she asked. "When are you going to tell her?"

"I'm not."

She choked on her drink. "What?"

"You heard me." No way in hell was I telling my family. My dad was one of the most decorated SEALs of all time, and I was a

disgrace. Worse than a disgrace, I was pathetic. I couldn't even control my temper.

The waitress brought the check, and Sloan and I both grabbed for it.

I narrowed my eyes at her, trying to claim it for myself. "What do you think you're doing?"

"I've got it." She tugged.

I growled and removed the check from her hand. "I've got it."

"Fine," she huffed. "But only if you let me buy next time." She smirked.

Sloan was different than I'd expected. More outspoken or something. Or maybe she was just tired. It was three in the morning.

"There will be no next time," I said. "After this, you're going to go home and pretend this whole conversation, this whole evening, never happened."

"So, you want me to lie to my best friend and your sister."

God, I hated hearing her say that. But yes, that was exactly what I was asking.

"I—" I dragged a hand over my head. "I want you to give me some time."

She seemed to consider it then said, "I know what it's like to want to hide something from your siblings."

I wondered what she meant by that because her tone certainly indicated something darker. My curiosity was piqued.

"And I know," she continued, "what it's like to be on the receiving end of a sibling's misguided attempt to 'protect' you." She gave me a meaningful look. "So, I will give you time, but you need to tell Greer."

"I'll consider it." That was the best I could do for now.

She stood. "Thank you for the pancakes and the honesty."

I smiled, standing as well. "Thank you for listening."

"Anytime." She patted my shoulder, and for the first time in months, it felt as if a weight had been lifted.

"We'll be starting our descent into Miami shortly," the captain announced over the intercom.

I returned my attention to my laptop, reviewing Sloan's file once more. I scrutinized the threats for new clues, combing through her contacts in search of answers. I opened the file on her boyfriend—Edward Burton, heir to Burton Banking and future Duke of Torrington.

I rubbed at my chest, seeking to soothe the ache there. Knowing Sloan had moved on and seeing proof of it were two different things.

I wasn't sure she could've chosen anyone more different from me. His family had an official website. A crest. A ducal manor. Edward was wealthy. Titled. He easily fit into her world.

I studied the articles and pictures of Edward and Sloan at various events. They looked perfect together, and though it pained me to admit it, I was glad she'd found happiness. Even if it was with someone else.

I was right to let her go.

I stood and stretched, ready to be off this damn plane. It felt too small for the two of us—fucking claustrophobic.

"Can I get you anything, Jackson?" Tabitha asked when I exited the restroom near the galley. She worked for the Hartwell Agency—a bespoke recruitment service that placed nannies, jet crew, and other household staff with wealthy clients around the world. The Crawfords always requested her when they flew. I'd interacted with her a number of times, and she was always polite and discreet. She kept to herself.

"I'm good, thanks. How have you been?"

"Good." She smiled. "Busy."

"With flying or the farm?"

"Both. But mostly the farm."

I shoved my hands into my pockets. "I don't know how you find time for it all."

She lifted a shoulder. "You make time for what matters."

"Sage advice."

"What about you?" she asked. "You're no longer protecting the Crawfords?" She gave me a meaningful look, as if to say, "What's up with that?"

"Reassigned for the time being."

"I'm sure it was difficult to say goodbye. They're such a sweet family, especially Brooklyn."

I smiled. I adored that kid. "That they are. But alas," I sighed, teasing, "I go where I'm told."

She nodded, a grim set to her expression. "As do I."

I returned to my seat, feeling Sloan's eyes on me the entire time. When I looked at her, she quickly turned her attention to her laptop, and I wondered if I'd imagined it.

I took my seat and resumed my arrangements for the trip. Today, we were flying to Miami, where the boat was docked. While Sloan met with the staff of the Huxley Grand Miami, I'd use the rest of the day to finish preparations so we could cast off in the morning—assuming the weather stayed fair. Levi, a teammate from Hudson who was already stationed in Miami, would keep an eye on Sloan while we were apart.

I reviewed the schematics of the boat, as well as the safety specs. Every so often, I'd chance a glance at Sloan. She was absorbed in her task, and I wondered if this was what I could expect for the next two months—the silent treatment.

Though when we were on the boat, she wouldn't be able to avoid me or bury herself in work. We'd have to communicate and work together.

I checked the weather again. Wind was favorable. No expected storms, though there was a front we were going to have to keep our eye on.

Sloan finally closed her laptop and peered out the

window as we began our descent. We might only be separated by the aisle of the private jet, but it felt more like an ocean. I wanted to address her, but I had to remind myself she was just like any other client. She had to be—for my sake anyway.

So instead, I focused on the view. Clear blue waters. A bright sunny day. I ached to be on the water just as much as I dreaded it.

It was still so strange to think that I'd be spending the next two months with Sloan. We'd barely spoken two words to each other the entire flight. Years ago, we would've filled the time with conversation. With touch.

Years ago, I'd been her everything. Now, I was just the bodyguard.

But seeing her again made me yearn for what we'd once shared. Yearn for easy conversation and the peace that came from being completely yourself with someone, and knowing that they loved and accepted all of you.

And yet…she'd lied to me.

She'd omitted crucial information about herself. About her family. It had made me question what else she'd lied about.

But I was a professional, and I would protect Sloan, regardless of our past. Or perhaps all the better because of it.

After we landed at the private airstrip, my counterpart from Hudson was waiting on the tarmac with a black Escalade. Levi was a younger guy, newer. Eager. He'd been here a week, preparing for our arrival.

I scanned the area from behind my sunglasses. It was warm and fucking humid, the breeze doing little to dispel the moisture that clung to my skin. My shirt was sticking to me, but I knew a shower wouldn't make a damn bit of difference.

Meanwhile, Sloan looked immaculate. Put together and composed. Not a hair out of place.

Levi opened the door to the Escalade for Sloan, and she climbed in the back seat with a thanks.

"Hey." We shook hands. "Thanks for doing the prep work and keeping an eye on the boat."

"No problem." He glanced toward the car. "You sure you don't want to swap assignments?" He gave a meaningful lift of his brow while the airport crew loaded the luggage into the back.

I clenched my teeth, annoyed by his implication. "No. I do not." She was the fucking principal. He had no business ogling her. "Now, let's get going."

He lowered his sunglasses, a sour expression on his face. "Jeez. Lighten up a little. It was a joke."

I crowded him, hardening my jaw. "I don't joke when it comes to the principal. Not about their safety or their person. You got it?"

He gulped. "Got it."

"Good. Now show me that Hudson didn't make a mistake in hiring you."

"Yes, sir." His entire demeanor changed. He climbed into the driver's seat, and I joined him in the front, grateful Sloan already had the privacy screen raised. I planned to use the time to review a few things with Levi. But more than that, I needed some fucking space.

Being with Sloan, inhaling her scent, it was fucking with my head.

And as we drove across town, I realized that maybe I'd been short with Levi. But if he couldn't handle it, he didn't deserve to be here.

Levi pulled into the VIP entrance of the Huxley Grand Miami. As soon as Sloan exited the car, the staff fawned over her. Nate and his family had always been treated with respect at the Huxley properties, but Sloan was treated like royalty. She was their queen.

Not that it surprised me. She'd always had a way with people. A kindness. A charisma that was different even from Nate's magnetism. When Sloan was with you, she made you feel as if you were the only person who mattered.

But seeing her in a professional setting was enlightening. Hell, if anything, it made me respect her even more. You could tell a lot about a person from the way they treated their employees. And Sloan treated everyone with kindness and respect, both cleaning staff and manager alike.

As difficult as it was to tear my eyes away from Sloan, I forced my attention to Levi. "You good here?"

"I've got it covered, Blackjack." He tossed me the keys to the Escalade. After our conversation on the ride over, I had more confidence in his ability to protect Sloan. At least for a short time. When assisted by hotel security.

"I'm going to do a sweep of the suite and then head to the marina. I should be back by eighteen hundred, but contact me if anything comes up. And I do mean *anything.*"

He scanned the entrances and exits, monitoring everyone who came in or left. "I already checked the suite, but staff would've delivered the luggage, so that's a good idea."

I could remember being young and cocky like him. He had some growing to do, but he had potential too.

I went up to the penthouse, conducting a thorough sweep of the suite before I was finally satisfied. Then I drove to the marina, eager to see the boat in person. I parked and went through the gate. The lack of security measures was disappointing, though not entirely surprising. At least Levi had been keeping an eye on things, providing an escort for the staff who'd stocked the boat with food and other supplies in preparation for our trip.

The marina was a hub of activity as charters returned from an adventure or prepared for a sunset cruise. I quickly found Sloan's boat, a gorgeous sailboat named *Athena*. I'd wondered at the name before, and seeing it now, I was even more curious. Athena was the Greek goddess of wisdom and war.

I didn't remember Sloan being a huge fan of Greek mythology. At least, not enough to name her boat for it. And yet, this boat was named Athena. *Interesting.*

I did an external survey of the boat, checking safety supplies and the integrity of the hull and sails. Once I was satisfied, I headed below deck. Everything had already been cleared by a local boat mechanic. Before that, it had been sailed here by a crew from the Hartwell Agency. Their crew certified that the vessel was in perfect condition, so that gave me some peace of mind.

The boat was nice. More than nice, actually. It wasn't brand-new, but it wasn't that old either. I could definitely think of worse places to spend the next two months, even if I struggled to imagine being so close to Sloan after all this time.

The main living space was high enough that I didn't have to hunch my six-foot-two frame. Most of it was clad in warm wood tones or creams, and there were multiple places to sit. The kitchen was small but well-appointed. And the storage was ample and cleverly done—allowing access from multiple points.

I double-checked that the satellite phone was where it belonged, the red lights to preserve night vision were work-ing, as was the radar system. We had a set of paper charts, personal locator beacons, first aid kit.

The main cabin, where Sloan would sleep, was cozy. The bed was covered in pale blues and fluffy whites. I had a brief vision of her lying on the bed, her hair splayed over the pillow as I peeled a swimsuit from her body.

I groaned and headed for the guest room. That was never going to happen.

The guest quarters were smaller than the main, with part of the roof sloping low over the foot of the bed. It was a good thing I wasn't claustrophobic because the size of the room was more suited to someone Brooklyn's height.

I smiled, wondering what Brooklyn and the rest of the Crawford family were up to. She'd insisted on throwing me a going-away party, and I loved her for it. After protecting them for a year and being so intimately involved in their lives, I missed them. I missed hearing about Brooklyn's day as she chatted with Emerson in the back seat on the way home from school. And it was strange not knowing what they were doing and if they were okay.

Yes, they were my clients. But over the past year, they'd become more like family. Especially since the addition of Emerson.

I knew they were in good hands. I wouldn't have recommended my replacement if she weren't up to the task. And my reluctance to say goodbye was probably an indication that it was past time to move on. I'd become too attached.

My phone rang, Vaughn's name flashing on the screen.

"Hey, Vaughn. What's up?"

"Just checking in before you head out. Everything look good?"

"Yep." I glanced around the boat once more. "Supplies are on board. Levi delivered the package from Hudson, so thanks."

"Good." He hesitated, which was unlike him. "Look, uh, I'm sure this goes without saying, but these circumstances are unique."

I frowned. Vaughn didn't typically flounder about with words.

"The principal's safety is of the utmost importance," he continued.

"I know." Where was he going with this?

"You're going to be sharing a small space for an extended period of time."

I glanced around the cabin. *No shit.*

"The Crawford and Mackenzie families are important to Hudson. And while the principal's safety is always the top priority, we want to keep our valuable clients satisfied."

Um…excuse me. *What?*

"What I'm trying to say is that you can be abrasive. Commanding."

"Wow. Thanks," I scoffed.

"It's not a bad thing, but…at least try to give the principal the illusion that she's in control."

I barked out a laugh. "Anything else?"

"Be safe out there. Check in as agreed, and we shouldn't have any problems. Right?"

"Right," I said. *If only it were that simple.*

I had a sinking feeling that of all the challenges I'd faced as a bodyguard, none would compare to this trip. To spending two months at sea with a woman I'd always desired and never been able to resist.

CHAPTER SEVEN

Sloan

My phone buzzed. I assumed it was Edward again, and I was prepared to send his call to voice mail. But instead, Greer's name flashed on the screen, along with a picture of us from her birthday trip a few years ago. We were smiling, best friends after almost two decades. My gut clenched with guilt—both familiar and unwanted.

For years, I'd suppressed my guilt over my secret relationship with Jackson. I told myself it was in the past. It didn't matter. Besides, Greer's biggest fear had been that Jackson would ruin her relationship with me. And despite how difficult it had been, I had never let what had happened with her brother come between us.

But seeing Jackson again, knowing that I'd be spending the next two months with him... It had a funny way of bringing all the guilt, all the secrets, all the lies, back to the forefront of my mind. And since Jackson and I hadn't touched on the topic of Greer earlier, I could only assume he hadn't told her about his new assignment.

Hell, he'd never been one to tell his sister the truth about us. Why should it be any different now?

I took a deep breath and hit the button to connect the call. "Greer. Hey." I placed the phone on the bed, tapping the speaker button so I could chat while I got ready for bed.

"Sloan! I'm glad I caught you before you head off on your big adventure. I had a crazy idea I wanted to run by you." She sounded strange. Almost...hyper? Or out of breath?

"Okay," I said, dragging out the word. Greer had always been more of a planner. Less...spontaneous. Crazy ideas typically weren't part of her vernacular.

"I hope you're not going to kill me, but..." I braced myself while I waited for the rest of whatever she was going to say. "I bought a plane ticket to Puerto Rico. I thought I could meet you there."

"You...what?" The last word came out as more of a shriek.

"I bought a plane ticket to Puerto Rico!"

"What about...what about Logan and the kids?" I asked, trying to wrap my head around her impromptu travel plans. "And work?"

"They'll be fine. Besides, I can use the trip for content."

I frowned. Greer owned a popular lifestyle blog that she'd transformed into a huge platform. She and her team typically planned their content months, if not years, in advance. A trip like this was completely out of character.

That said, maybe she needed a break. She ran a successful seven-figure business. She was a mom of two. A wife. It was a lot. I didn't know how she made it look so easy, even when I knew it wasn't.

"I get that, but can you really just drop everything and leave?"

"Psh." She tried to brush aside my concerns, but I wasn't buying it.

"What do you mean, psh?" I asked. Greer didn't do laid-back. She didn't go with the flow.

"I just..." Her voice cracked, and my heart ached at her

distress. "I need a break. And we haven't taken a girls' trip in years."

"I know, but...are you sure? This all seems so sudden." I asked, all worries about keeping my previous relationship with Jackson a secret fading in the face of concern for my best friend.

"Yes," she said. "Yes," she said again. More resolutely. "Besides, I'm worried about you. Two months alone at sea is a long time."

"Actually..." I hedged. "There's something I need to tell you."

"Now, *I'm* worried." She said it in a teasing tone, but I could hear her unease all the same.

"No. It's just...I won't be alone."

"Edward?" She paused. "I thought he got motion sickness."

"He does. And it's not him." I clasped and unclasped my watch, spinning it around my wrist. "We broke up." And I had yet to shed a single tear.

If anything, I felt relief. Our relationship had been built on mutual respect. Compatibility. For a long time, I'd thought that was enough. Told myself it was enough.

"For real?" She sounded almost...hopeful.

"Yes. For real."

She shrieked, and I was grateful I hadn't been holding the phone to my ear. "OMG. Who's with you, then? A new boy toy? One of your brothers?"

"No to the boy toy." To both. "And we only recently ended things."

"Are you okay?" she asked, her tone softening.

"I am." I smiled.

"I'm glad."

"About me or the breakup?"

She laughed. "Both. So, are you going to tell me who's

going on the trip with you so I can stop putting my foot in my mouth?"

"Is that even possible?" I teased.

"Har. Har. Who's going with you?"

I hesitated a moment, my heart rate always quickening at the thought of the threats. "You know those nasty notes I received?" I'd told her about the first one because I'd thought it was a joke. But then she'd insisted I keep her posted, so I had.

"Yeah."

"My brothers made me hire a bodyguard."

"Finally," she sighed. Shit. Had she been that concerned for me too? "Is he hot?"

"He's…" I swallowed hard. "Your brother." *And yes, he's hot.*

She was quiet for so long that I glanced at the screen to make sure we were still connected. We were.

"Greer?" I prompted.

"Sorry." She sounded almost…dazed. "I think it must have cut out. You said something about your brothers."

"No." I took a deep breath. "*Your* brother. Jackson. Jackson is my new bodyguard."

There was a pause, and I braced myself. "Jackson's going with you?"

"Yep."

"On the boat," she said.

"Mm-hmm." I was practically holding my breath at this point. Waiting for her reaction.

"For two months."

"Yes," I sighed. There was no way around it.

And Jackson wasn't happy about it either, judging from his exchange with Tabitha on the flight here. His terse, "I go where I'm told," echoed in my mind.

"Wow. That's…" I prepared myself for her to say "terrible," but instead, she practically yelled, "Awesome!"

"It is?" My shoulders were still coiled tight with tension.

"Yeah! I feel a lot better about the situation with him there. He's a good sailor, and I know he'd never let anything happen to you. You're like a sister to him."

I winced. *Right. Like a sister.*

"Plus," she continued. "When we're all in Puerto Rico, it'll be like old times."

Except it wouldn't be "like old times." Jackson and I wouldn't be sneaking around, stealing kisses, touching every chance we got. But we'd still be lying about our relationship.

I'd never told Greer about Jackson. How could I? I knew how much losing her high school friend had hurt her. And I'd gotten involved with Jackson anyway.

She'd known that I was seeing someone. That I was heartbroken when it had ended. And for the longest time, she'd suspected that my mystery man had been married. She'd never outright asked, but she'd hinted at it enough times.

I could never bring myself to tell her the truth, and I'd always felt like such a coward for it. But I refused to come between my best friend and her older brother. Selfishly, I couldn't fathom the thought of losing her.

Greer had been my rock. My best friend since freshman year of college. She'd been there for me when my beloved grandmother had died. And then when my grandfather had followed soon after. Their deaths had left a gaping void in my life. And then my siblings and I had been left to take on the mammoth task of running the global hotel empire.

Greer and I had been there for each other through bad dates and heartbreaks. Whether it was the best time of my life or the worst, she was always by my side. And I had her back.

Which was why my betrayal, my lies, felt like the worst possible sin.

"Sloan?" she asked, and I wondered how much of the conversation I'd missed.

"Yeah?"

"I said I'll see you in a few weeks."

I couldn't tell her no. Not that I'd want to anyway. So I tried to force myself to sound enthusiastic. "Sounds good. Love you, Greer."

"Love you too."

We ended the call, and I sank down into one of the chairs. What the hell was I going to do? The last time I'd been with Greer and Jackson had been at her wedding, and I'd sworn it would be the last. It was too painful. There were too many secrets between us. Too much potential for hurt.

My mind drifted back to that day.

I peered out the window at the Empire State Building. Still no sign of Jackson. I wasn't sure whether to be relieved or disappointed.

I hadn't seen him in nearly a year. Not since he'd broken my heart. And now, I was going to have to stand across the aisle from him and smile as we watched his sister—and my best friend—get married.

I sighed, dreading that moment. The moment when I'd have to face him. When I'd have to smile and pretend as if nothing had ever happened between us.

As if he didn't know my body intimately.

Hadn't consumed my thoughts for the past few years.

Hadn't shattered my heart completely and irrevocably.

Was he bringing a date? Was that why he was running late?

Oh god. *I held a hand to my stomach. If I had to watch him laughing with someone else. Touching someone else... I was going to be sick.*

"Sloan?" Greer called.

"Yeah. Yep?" I answered too quickly, my tone too bright.

If anyone found my behavior odd, I hoped they'd chalk it up to wedding day nerves and excitement. Not the fact that I was going to have to face the love of my life after he'd told me that the end of our relationship was "inevitable." Inevitable. Ha!

Looking back now, I could say the only thing that had been inevitable was the fact that he'd break my heart. Greer had been right.

"What can I get you?" I asked Greer. *Jackson might be running late, but I knew he would never miss his sister's wedding. He was walking her down the aisle, for Christ's sake.* "Something to eat? To drink?"

"Champagne." *She grinned, passing me a glass.* "Here."

I realized then that the rest of the bridal party were already holding their own flutes, the bubbles racing to the top. If I'd eaten breakfast this morning, I was pretty sure it, too, would be racing to escape.

"Thank you all for helping celebrate my wedding." *Greer smiled.* "I'm so grateful for each of you and the role you've played in my life."

"Aww," *one of the other bridesmaids crooned. I wanted to be present. To be there for my best friend, but it felt as if I were floating outside my body. Watching everything as it happened to me instead of being an active participant.*

Damn, Jackson.

"And thank you to Sloan." *Greer turned to me.* "For helping me have the wedding of my dreams at my dream venue." *She spread one arm wide to encompass our suite.* "The presidential suite at the Huxley Grand New York? It doesn't get any better than this."

The Huxley Grand New York was one of the most sought-after wedding venues in Manhattan. It didn't matter that it was incredibly expensive; it was booked out years in advance. But for Greer, I'd covered the majority of the cost, knowing she'd never let me pay for her wedding, even though it wouldn't make a dent in my inheritance now that I had full access to my trust.

I inclined my head. "Only the best for my bestie." I'd happily pulled some strings, doing everything in my power to ensure my best friend had the most wonderful wedding day possible. It was the least I could do.

We clinked our glasses, and I downed the champagne, feeling like the terrible friend I was. She had no idea that I loved her brother, and it needed to stay that way.

Besides, it didn't matter now. Jackson and I were over.

I was still gutted by the fact that he'd lied to me. He'd said he loved me, but he'd accepted a job on the other side of the country. He'd interviewed and searched for apartments and made plans for his future without my ever having a clue.

I tightened my grip on the champagne flute. How could I have been so oblivious? How could he have kept something so big... from me?

I guessed part of me knew I should've seen it coming. He'd lied to his family for months, allowing them to believe he was still with the SEALs. We'd both lied about our relationship—never letting on that we were together. That we were in love.

I took a gulp of champagne. Were we, though? In love?

Everything else had been a lie, so maybe that had been too. At least for him.

The bridal party finished getting ready. By the time I was in my dress, I was on my third glass of champagne. I was buzzed and determined to be happy, and I was not going to let Jackson—or anyone else—ruin this day.

"Oh my goodness." Greer's mom, Belinda, entered the suite. "Sweetheart..." She held a hand to her mouth, her gaze soft on Greer. "You look stunning."

"Mom." Greer fanned her face. "Don't make me cry."

"I have amazing news." Belinda was beaming, radiating joy as she took Greer's hands in hers. "Your brother made it in early this morning. He's getting ready and should be up soon."

Greer's shoulders relaxed, her face transforming into one of serene happiness. "Did you hear that, Sloan?" Greer turned to me. "Jackson made it. He's not going to miss my wedding."

"That's great."

She turned back to her mom. And while I was happy and relieved for my best friend, her announcement only served to ratchet up my anxiety. As Greer and her mom talked with excitement about the day ahead, I was filled with nothing but dread.

Get it together!

Belinda turned to me, while the hair stylist touched up one last curl for Greer. Belinda took my hands in her own then stepped back to look at me. "You look so beautiful, Sloan."

I was grateful that Greer had let us pick our own dresses, provided they were black. I'd opted for a halter neck dress with a low back and a high slit. Anything to feel confident and sexy.

"Thank you, Belinda." She gave me a hug.

There was a knock at the door, and the butler peeked his head in. "Mrs. Shaw? Your son is here."

"Give me just a minute, Mom," Greer called.

"Sure," she said to Greer before turning back to me. "Try not to break too many hearts out there." She winked.

I laughed, though it had a nervous edge to it. If she only knew...

Greer came over to me while the others visited. "Hey. You okay?" she asked, her voice low as she placed her hand on my shoulder.

"Are you kidding?" I smiled, but thanks to the champagne, it didn't feel as forced as before. "I'm so happy for you."

"I know, but—" She glanced around as if to confirm no one was listening. "You've been going through a lot. A really rough breakup, a move, and..."

I held up a hand to silence her. "I appreciate your concern, and I love you for it. But you don't need to worry about me. Especially not on your wedding day."

"Maybe a wedding is just what you need. Maybe you'll find a

hottie to hook up with. One of Logan's cousins is single." She waggled her eyebrows.

"Thanks, but I'm good." I couldn't imagine hooking up with another man, no matter how hot they were. Jackson had ruined me.

"Sloan," she chided.

"Greer." I mimicked her tone. "I'm fine. Promise."

"Mm-hmm." I got the distinct impression she didn't believe me.

Hell, I wouldn't either. She, of all people, knew how much of a mess I'd been after the breakup.

"Is everyone decent?" Jackson's low voice called, practically vibrating through me. Fuck. Oh fuck.

"Come in," Greer called out.

Before he could enter, I turned my back to the door and busied myself with my phone. I took a deep, fortifying breath. This was the moment I'd been dreading for months.

Act normal. Act normal. Act normal.

What the fuck even was normal in this situation?

My best friend's brother was the love of my life and the man who'd destroyed me.

I went to the mirror, keeping my eyes on my reflection as I reapplied my lip gloss. I refused to look at Jackson. It didn't matter that I could sense his presence. That my body was still attuned to him like a flower seeking the sun after all this time. That I could feel his eyes on me like a lover's caress. I knew if I looked at him, it was over. My carefully constructed façade would crumble.

Yet, when I glanced up... Yep. Sure enough. There he was, and damn, he looked good in his dress uniform, medals strapped to his chest. And he was looking right at me, our eyes locked in the reflection.

I sucked in a quiet gasp, feeling the force of his gaze like a bullet through my chest.

I quickly glanced away, my cheeks flaming with heat at the fact that he'd caught me staring. My heart was racing, and all the champagne was catching up to me and not in a good way.

I can do this. I can do this. *I turned away from the mirror, smiling and keeping my attention on Greer.*

Jackson greeted the other bridesmaids by name, giving some of them a hug. And then he came to me, and my body froze. As if I was waiting to see what he'd do first. Like he was a predator and I was his prey, and I didn't know if I'd make it out of this alive.

"Sloan," he rasped. My heart thundered in my ears, and I couldn't get a read on his tone.

I inclined my head, unable to say more than, "Jackson."

The click of a camera shutter reminded me just how many people were watching. And damn it, I was not going to ruin the day for Greer. So I smiled and tried to focus—as always—on my best friend and not her brother.

CHAPTER EIGHT

Jackson

The door to Sloan's room opened, and I pushed off the wall. Her gaze flicked to me, her expression guarded. She looked like she'd slept about as well as I had, which was to say—not well at all. She had dark circles beneath her eyes. And yet something was different from yesterday, though I couldn't put my finger on it.

She walked past me without saying a word. She didn't want me here, and I couldn't bring myself to leave. Not when she was in danger.

I rubbed a hand over my jaw. *This was going to be interesting.*

Levi drove us over to the marina so we could set out for the Bahamas. The sun was barely over the horizon, and the weather looked promising for the first day of our trip. We ran through a series of checks, preparing the boat to cast off. It was easy to fall into a rhythm, to get lost in the final preparations for the trip. And I was grateful to have a distraction.

We didn't speak much, but we didn't need to.

"Ready?" she finally asked, emerging from her cabin.

Sloan had changed into a pair of shorts and a T-shirt that

stretched deliciously over her breasts before nipping in at the waist. Her shorts ended mid-thigh, and I had to clench my fists to keep from reaching out to touch her.

She wasn't mine, and she hadn't been for a long time.

"Whenever you are. The desalinization tank is full, and the solar panels are fully charged."

"Good," she said, then added, "Thanks."

I followed her up on deck, where she fired up the engines. Her sunglasses shielded her eyes from my view, and I couldn't get a read on her. I supposed that wasn't my job, though. My job was to keep her safe.

She guided us out of the marina and toward the opening to the ocean. The wind played with her braid, tendrils of hair fluttering about her face as the boat bobbed gently through the water. She looked fucking spectacular.

I hated myself for the way I'd ended things. Regretted it almost every day since, even if I'd thought I'd been doing what was best for her. Best for everyone.

I didn't know whether to address it or leave it be.

I got the feeling she'd just as soon push me overboard as talk to me about anything that didn't pertain to sailing or safety. And I could only hope this trip would be a chance for redemption. To make up for how I'd treated her in the past.

"Why *Athena?*" I asked, finally coming up with a question I thought she might actually answer.

She kept her attention on the water, even as she spoke. "She's the Greek goddess of wisdom."

"What happened to *Escape?*"

Her jaw was set. "I decided wisdom and strength were more important."

Well, shit.

What was I supposed to say? I was trying here, and I knew things would go more smoothly if we could build some sort of rapport. Weather reports had indicated no incoming northwesterlies, but crossing the Gulf Stream could still be hazardous. It would be better if we were on the same page. If we were a team. Sure, we'd discussed the tasks each of us would perform on board, but there was still a gaping chasm between us.

"Do you remember the first time we went sailing together?" I asked, wanting to see her smile. Laugh. Something other than the sad, serious air that seemed to hover around her shoulders like a dense fog.

"Look," she sighed. "This trip is the one thing that I do for me. And now…" She glanced out at the water then back at me. "I only agreed to have a bodyguard on board to appease my family and the Huxley board. I don't want to revisit the past. This isn't the time for a trip down memory lane."

"Okay." I held up my hands. I was merely trying to make conversation. "If you don't want to talk about the past, then tell me something about the present."

She leaned her hip against the captain's chair, her gaze skeptical. "Do you do that with your other clients?"

"Not usually. But this is different."

"Because of our past."

"Well, yes. But I was referring more to our present circumstances. I'm not typically alone with a client for such an extended period of time. There are usually other staff present. Other members of my team. Family or friends, even."

I wasn't trying to make her uncomfortable. In fact, the opposite was true. We sat in silence for a while before she asked, "Do you like being a bodyguard?"

"Technically, I'm an executive protection agent. But, yes, most people refer to us as bodyguards."

"Okay," she said, dragging out the word, annoyance bleeding into her tone. "Do you like being an executive protection agent?"

I lifted a shoulder. "It definitely has its perks at times." I gestured to the view. We were nearing the edge of the breakwater, and I knew the wind would likely pick up as soon as we were past it. The waves too.

"Here." I handed her a life vest. She thanked me, and I watched as she secured it before putting on my own.

"I'm sure it's not all fun and games. Just like everyone assumes my life is full of ease and luxury. And a lot of it is," she said, her expression darkening. "But it's also a lot of hard work."

"Exactly." I nodded. "There's a lot of prep work. A lot of things that go on behind the scenes."

"Like what?" Her curiosity encouraged me to continue. There were many other things I'd rather discuss with Sloan, but at this point, I was just grateful she was talking to me. Maybe she was finally beginning to thaw.

"Like our trip, for instance. I have to check potential locations where we'll stop. Evaluate the circumstances on each island—if they are recovering from a recent hurricane or what the current political climate is. And those are the big-picture pieces. There are other considerations, such as marina safety and security. The location of the hotels and their placement. Transportation. Availability of medical facilities. I could go on and on."

"That's definitely a lot more detail than I take into account."

"That's part of the reason why I moved to a res team."

She glanced at me. "Res team?"

"Residential," I explained. "The team stays with the principal and concentrates on the security of the principal's home. As opposed to a movement team that's formed solely for the purpose of a trip."

"So what would this assignment be considered?" she

asked. "The boat is currently my home—so it's residential. But we're traveling. So, movement?"

I chuckled. "This..." *Like everything with this woman.* "...is unique."

"That's one word for it," she muttered. Or at least, that was what it sounded like. The wind had picked up now that we were past the breakwater. I didn't know what she was more upset about—someone encroaching on her trip or the fact that *I* was that someone.

We fell silent, watching as the sail unfurled. I waited until it had caught the wind, and then I tightened it around the winch. The sun beat down on me, and I tried to adjust to the idea that this would be my life for the next two months. Glancing over at Sloan, I had to admit, I didn't hate it.

THE REST OF THE DAY HAD BEEN PLEASANT, BUT SPENDING THE day in the sun had sapped the energy from me. Despite my exhaustion, I tossed and turned, plagued with thoughts of Sloan. Snippets from today and memories from the past.

"What would you name your boat if you had one?" she asked, running her hand over my chest. With Greer at Logan's, Sloan and I were spending a lazy morning in bed. She didn't have class until eleven, and I was off until Thursday.

"Hm." I was too distracted by her touch to think of much else. "Hydrotherapy."

She laughed, her body vibrating against mine. It was intoxicating—her happiness, and the idea that I'd caused it.

"Mm. How about Fantasea *but spelled s-e-a?"*

She smacked my chest playfully. "Too cheesy."

"What about you?" I trailed my fingers up and down her back. "What would you name your boat?"

"I don't know. Maybe Liquid Asset."

"Very punny," I joked.

"Okay, then," she said, a smile in her voice. "Be serious."

I didn't know why this was so important to her, but it was. So I said, "Serenity."

She pushed up on her elbow and peered down at me. Her face was all scrunched and cute. "That makes me think of a funeral home. Or that show... What was it?"

"Firefly?" I offered, pinching her side. She started giggling, batting my hands away.

"Yeah. That's the one."

I couldn't believe my sister had made her watch that. But I guessed it was a testament to their friendship. My thoughts soured. I didn't want to think about their friendship or how my relationship with Sloan might impact it.

So instead, I focused on tickling Sloan.

"Okay. You think you can do better?" I kept tickling her, making her breathless with laughter. "Huh? Tell me what you'd name your boat."

She was laughing so hard, she could barely speak. When she rolled on top of me, rocking her body against mine, I finally relented. I settled my hands on her hips.

"Escape," she said, sighing as she sank down on my cock. "Escape."

I groaned and tried to ignore my cock and the way it hardened at the memory. I tried to focus on the present instead of the past.

Today had been...nice. Surprisingly so, despite the rocky start.

Sloan and I hadn't talked much, but we hadn't needed to. There was a pleasantness, a contentedness, to taking responsibility for the various tasks that needed to be done on the boat. A sense of peace had settled over me as soon as the coast had faded from view, and it seemed to have the same effect on Sloan.

I'd always respected her work ethic, especially once I'd discovered who she was. Who her family was. They were so wealthy, she didn't have to work a day in her life. And yet, she'd worked two jobs in college to pay her rent. Even now, she put in the work that needed to be done to sail, when she could've easily hired a crew. She could've taken her private jet to a luxury hotel, but she was practically roughing it on a sailboat.

After a full day of sailing, we'd made it to our first stop in the Bahamas. We'd cleared customs and immigration relatively quickly, which was a relief. We'd docked for the night at a marina to rest up and make any final preparations before heading down to Turks and Caicos. That leg of the trip would take about a week if we were lucky.

After today, I found myself looking forward to it. Sloan still wasn't thrilled about my presence, but she'd actually smiled at me a few times. A smile of pure joy when we'd let out the sail and the wind had carried us away. A small tilt of her lips in gratitude when I'd brought her lunch.

I sighed, tucking my arm behind my head. I knew it wouldn't all be smooth sailing. There was still that cool undercurrent of disinterest. Of distrust. But at least today had been nice.

When I finally fell asleep, my dreams were filled with her. At first, they were vivid. Beautiful. A mix of the past and the present.

But then they turned into nightmares. The image of Sloan's lifeless eyes staring up at me. Accusing me. Asking why I hadn't protected her.

I jolted awake and wiped the sweat from my brow, trying to get my breath under control. I strained my ears for any sound—from Sloan, from someone who might want to harm her.

I couldn't figure out who was sending her the threats, and that only added to my irritability. When I'd asked Sloan about the threats earlier, she didn't seem to have any ideas about who might be sending them either, which made me feel even more powerless. A team at Hudson was working on it, but I wanted answers now.

I needed to keep her safe. The overpowering need to do something, anything, made it impossible to sleep. I stood, almost bumping my head on the ceiling.

I crept past the galley toward the deck. We hadn't left the red lights on since there was little need to protect our night vision while docked. The breeze felt good on my heated skin, and I checked the rigging and our position, drinking in the cooler night air. The sound of the waves lapping at the side of the boat was peaceful.

I stayed out there for I didn't know how long, thinking about life. About Sloan. About what could've been and all the mistakes I'd made.

I scrubbed a hand over my face. Sleep. I needed some sleep.

I headed back down to the cabin, and I was passing through the darkened galley when an elbow connected with my stomach.

Oof.

I glanced at Sloan's door—it was closed, and the lights were off. My body moved as if on autopilot, and I quickly restrained the assailant, the scent of wild roses wafting into my nose.

Oh shit. "Sloan?"

"Jackson?" She sounded equal parts relieved and annoyed. I released her and switched on a light.

She placed a hand over her heart, canting forward as if to

93

catch her breath. "What the hell were you doing? You scared me half to death."

"I'm sorry." I reached out as if to place a hand on her back —to comfort her—before stopping myself. "But what was I supposed to do? You attacked me."

I hated that she was scared, but I was impressed by her response. Hell, she'd been able to get a drop on me, and that was no small feat. My chest bloomed with pride—all those self-defense lessons I'd given her years ago had paid off.

"Because I thought you were boarding my boat in the middle of the night." She stood, and that was when I realized what she was wearing.

A silk tank top that flowed over her skin, her nipples pebbled beneath it. And a pair of shorts so tiny they were scarcely more than underwear. *Holy...* My mouth went dry as I greedily scanned her form, unable to stop myself.

Her hair was mussed from sleep. And with her face devoid of makeup, she looked younger. More like my Sloan and less like the billionaire SVP she'd become.

When I finally met her eyes, the look of hunger in them was undeniable. It didn't matter how many years had passed or how much heartbreak we had between us, my body still craved her touch.

God, how I wanted to touch her. Kiss her. Taste her.

What I wouldn't give to hear her rasp my name while I was buried deep inside her.

It wasn't just about the sex. Though, the sex had always been amazing. It was the way she looked at me. *Knew* me. It was in our connection.

Slowly, she dragged her eyes from my chest. "I heard a motor in the distance, and it made me think of your clown pirates."

"Clown pirates?" I frowned, still trying to get my bearings. I forced my eyes off her chest or anywhere else I shouldn't be looking.

"Yes. The ones who ride Jet Skis and board boats in clown masks."

"Oh. Right."

Right? No. Fuck. What the fuck am I doing?

I took a step back, willing my dick to calm down. She was my principal. And she was in a relationship with someone else.

I desperately needed to put some distance between us before I did something stupid. Before I said to hell with the rules and made her mine.

CHAPTER NINE

Sloan

I crossed my arms over my chest. Gratified by the way Jackson's attention darted to my breasts, his gaze lingering and heavy like a caress. The muscles of his chest rippled, along with his tattoos. God, he was glorious.

And then I saw it. The outline of his cock against his athletic shorts—thick and heavy and hard. *Oh my...*

I swallowed, my eyes darting back to his. My breath hitched when I looked into his blue eyes, which was perhaps even more dangerous. No one had ever looked at me the way Jackson did—as if I were the air he breathed and he'd die without me.

I'd forgotten what that felt like. How...all-consuming even just one look from him could be.

I took a step backward, my hip connecting with the galley counter. I gripped the edge to brace myself. It was late. This was reckless. We had a long day of sailing ahead, and we'd both need our rest for tomorrow.

I forced myself to turn away from him and head to my cabin. "Good night, Jackson."

He said nothing, but I could feel the tension in the air. It practically vibrated with desire and longing.

I closed the door to my cabin and immediately flipped the lock. I wasn't sure whether it was more to keep Jackson out or me in, though I knew he'd never enter without being invited. Somehow, even after all this time, even after the lies we'd told and the pain he'd caused, I found that I trusted him.

I willed my body to calm down. Cool down.

I wasn't aroused. I was…riding the adrenaline high from thinking there was an intruder. If I was aroused, and that was a big *if*, it was due to muscle memory, nothing more. The tightening of my nipples and heating of my core had nothing to do with Jackson.

Sure, he was handsome, objectively speaking. Rugged and strong, his muscles honed from years of service, first as a Navy SEAL and now as an executive protection agent.

But I'd just broken things off with Edward. And even if it had been a long time coming, I wasn't ready to jump into bed with someone else, let alone with an ex—tempting as it might be.

I closed my eyes and tried to steady my breathing with my back to the door. But Jackson immediately came to mind, and my fingers curled of their own accord.

His chest and arms were covered in tattoos, more than ever before. I could remember lying on his chest and asking about all of them. I'd wanted to hear the story behind each as I traced them with my fingers. My tongue. I still wanted…

No. I punched down a pillow as I climbed into bed. It didn't matter what I thought I wanted; what I *needed* was sleep. I was overtired. I hadn't slept well the past few nights, and I wasn't thinking clearly. But my body didn't listen to reason. It never had when it came to him.

I woke to the gentle rocking of the boat and the scent of

something delicious floating to me from the kitchen. A glance at my watch told me it was almost six in the morning. I logged on to my computer and checked my emails, quickly responding to the few that Halle had sent. I was finishing up an email to Jasper, and I could hear the rumble of Jackson's morning voice as he spoke with someone. A woman. I frowned.

I pulled on some clothes then headed to the bathroom to wash my face. As I dried my cheeks, I stared at my reflection in the mirror. I looked tired. And the lines at the corners of my eyes didn't help.

I wondered what Jackson thought when he saw me. Did he still find me attractive? I applied sunscreen then lip gloss, fluffing my hair. I stilled my hands and huffed, annoyed with myself for caring what he thought about me or how I looked. I yanked my hair into a braid and headed out.

I found Jackson on deck, chatting with a woman in a bikini top and cutoff shorts.

"Morning, *hayati*." He smiled, pulling me to him and pressing a kiss to my forehead.

Hayati. I hadn't heard that word in years. And only ever from Jackson.

I stilled, wondering if I'd somehow bumped my head last night. I placed a hand over my stomach as if to make the butterflies there stop. *Please* make it stop.

"Cheri, this is Sloan. Sloan, Cheri." Jackson made the introductions. "Cheri and her friends are headed down to Turks too."

The sailing community was a welcoming one, and it was always nice to connect with fellow travelers. We talked about the weather—a source of endless conversation for sailors. And the places we'd been.

"Morning," I said, my insides still fluttering from the sound of the word *hayati* on his lips.

Years ago, after much persuasion, Jackson had finally

relented and agreed to tell me the meaning. *Hayati* meant "my life," the term stemming from the Arabic word for life. *Hayati* was a common term of endearment in the Arabic world, and I'd always assumed he'd learned it on one of his missions, despite his unwillingness to confirm my theory. But as he'd once explained, using *hayati* expressed that his love for me was so strong, his life would be nothing without it.

I tried to study Jackson's expression for clues. Had he purposely called me *hayati*, or was it a slip? My brain was in knots—the weight of his arm both distracting and familiar.

Cheri shielded her eyes from the sun, and I turned my attention to her. "We leave in a few days. And we're on the *Knotty Buoy* if you need anything."

I laughed. "Thanks. Love the name. And feel free to radio us."

We said our goodbyes, and then she headed back to her boat.

"Sleep well?" Jackson asked, releasing me.

"Well enough," I murmured, still thrown by that forehead kiss.

"Winds look good. Averaging about fifteen knots from the southeast."

"Um…what was that about?" I asked, hooking my thumb over my shoulder to indicate where Cheri had gone.

"What?" Jackson's face was neutral.

"The side hug. The forehead kiss." Why was he acting like nothing out of the ordinary had occurred?

"I should've mentioned it sooner. When we go ashore or meet other sailors, it's probably best to act like we're a couple, at least when we're not staying at a Huxley Grand."

"Is it?" I didn't know what to make of that.

"From a security standpoint, yes. And it's a good cover story."

"Okay." I didn't disagree. "And what exactly would pretending to be a couple entail?"

He lifted a shoulder. "Like what we just did. It doesn't have to be complicated."

Not complicated. Right.

"When do you want to head out?" he asked, sidestepping any further objections. "I left pancakes in the microwave if you're hungry."

My eyes widened, my questions forgotten. "The banana ones?" He'd always made them for me when I'd spent the night, but I hadn't eaten them in years.

He nodded, his expression sheepish.

"Thanks." I was touched and trying not to let myself read too much into it. He'd made pancakes. So what? Jackson had volunteered to do most of the cooking after all. Still...they were Jackson's banana pancakes. "I'm going to make some coffee. Want some?"

"That would be great."

"Great," I added, then kicked myself. Why did this have to be so awkward?

I headed down to the galley, preparing the coffee before going back on deck with the pancakes and coffee. Jackson took a mug from me with a thanks. I'd considered eating below deck, but the weather was too gorgeous to stay inside, even if I wanted to hide from Jackson and all the tension that filled the air between us.

I cut into one of the pancakes, the smell of lazy mornings filtering through my mind.

"Mm." I pressed myself to Jackson's back. "What are you doing? Come back to bed."

Between my class schedule, his work schedule, and the fact that we were sneaking around, it was rare that we got to spend a morning in bed together.

"Making you breakfast." I peered over his shoulder to find him

mashing a banana with a fork. He turned his head, giving me a kiss.

"Looks more like baby food," I teased.

He smirked and turned his attention back to the bowl. "You'll see."

I gently raked my nails down his bare back, admiring his muscles and tattoos. He shivered. God...he was so hot.

"Sloan," he growled.

"What?" I asked in an innocent tone.

He glared at me. "You know what."

I slid my hands up his back then down again with my nails. "Do you want me to stop?" I wrapped my arms around him.

"You know I don't." He had a smile in his voice as he placed one of his hands over mine.

"You okay?" Jackson asked, bringing me back to the present.

While I'd been stuck in the past, he'd been preparing the boat to cast off. "Yeah." I shoved the last bite of pancake into my mouth. "Yep."

It wasn't too late to back out now. Cancel the rest of the sailing trip. Go home.

But being on the water yesterday had been so lovely. And today promised to be just as nice.

I sighed and glanced down at the friendship bracelets Brooklyn had made me. I fingered the beads, reading the text on each of them.

Smooth Sailing.

Captain Sloan.

Unstoppable.

Fuck it. This was my ship, and I was done walking on eggshells.

I glanced over at Jackson and found him watching me. "What?"

He turned his attention to the bow, where a cargo ship was far off on the horizon. "Nothing."

"It's not nothing. I…" I knew I just needed to get it over with. *Just say it.* "This is weird, right?"

"Is it?" He tilted his head, biting his lips as if to quell his amusement.

He wasn't going to make this easy on me, was he?

"Oh, come on, Jackson. You know it is. This trip. Us." I gestured between us. "We haven't seen each other in years, and now we're trapped on a boat together. Pretending to be a couple."

"Yeah." He rubbed the back of his neck. "It is a little strange."

I scoffed. "A little?"

"Okay. A lot," he admitted, and I finally felt a little better. "Though it's not the first time we've had to deal with weird and awkward situations."

"True."

"Remember that time Greer came home early from Logan's and almost caught us?"

I laughed even though it hadn't been funny. But it was sort of comical because of how ridiculous the situation had been.

The front door to my apartment opened then shut, and I jolted. "Jackson," I hissed, realizing that Greer had come home earlier than expected. "Get dressed."

Jackson had come over late after his shift at the club ended since Greer was at Logan's. He still hadn't told her about being discharged from the SEALs. And we definitely hadn't told her about us.

"Hmm." He nuzzled into my neck, his body wrapped around mine.

"Jackson." I elbowed him. "Get up. Greer's home."

"Shit." He jumped out of bed and grabbed his jeans, putting them on without his boxers.

I launched myself out of bed, throwing on the first thing I could find. "What are we going to do?"

"Sloan!" Greer called from the living room. "I'm home. Let's go to brunch and get drunk on dollar mimosas."

"I—" I called, gesturing at Jackson to hurry the hell up. "Be right there." I hopped on one foot, pulling on my running tights.

"Maybe we should just tell her," I whispered.

"I can't." He shook his head. "Not after..." He sighed. "I promised."

"You also promised her you wouldn't sleep with me," I hissed.

"You think she'd forgive us, but are you really willing to take that chance?"

I couldn't do that to Greer. She'd already been through so much. She'd lost her dad, and I knew how much Jackson meant to her. How much she meant to me.

"Fine," I sighed, knowing he was right. Besides, emerging from my room together, smelling of sex, was definitely not the way to break the news.

Jackson glanced at the window as if searching for an escape. I grabbed his arm and whispered, "You're not scaling four stories."

He eyed the drop before shrugging. "I could."

"Just..." I glanced around as if hoping the answer would come to me. It had to. "Let me go first."

"Sloan?" Greer called, her voice getting closer. "Are you okay?"

"Do you trust me?" he asked as I peered up at him.

"Always."

"Tell her you have a surprise." He gave me a quick peck.

I gestured for him to hide out of sight when I opened the door, and just as I was about to open it, he grabbed his boxers from the foot of the bed. My heart was pounding, and I had no idea what he was going to do.

I opened the door in a rush, stepping out into the living room before closing it behind me. "Hey."

"Hey!" Greer frowned. "Were you...working out?" She assessed my outfit.

"I, um—" I glanced down at my clothes. "Actually, I have a surprise for you."

She tilted her head, the corner of her mouth tipping up. "What kind of surprise?"

God, it was tempting to tell her the truth and be done with it. I hated keeping this secret from her. I hated having to hide what Jackson meant to me, even if I was terrified of how it would impact our relationship.

"Close your eyes."

She scrunched up her face. "Okay." And then did as she was told. "But it's not even my birthday."

I opened the door to my room and motioned for Jackson to come out. He crept toward the front door, and I was impressed by his stealth. Even so, my stomach felt as if it might launch itself out of my mouth at any moment.

He went over to the front door. Opened and closed it, all while remaining on the inside of the apartment.

"Open," I said, counting on the fact that Greer would be too happy to see her brother to question his sudden appearance or the reasons for it.

Her eyes fluttered open, and the moment she saw Jackson, she smiled. "Oh my god. Jackson?"

"Surprise!" I hoped I sounded excited and not nervous.

She launched herself at him, and his answering smile was brilliant. "Hey, sis."

"What are you doing here?" she asked, stepping back. "Is everything okay?"

He glanced at me over her shoulder, and I nodded, encouraging him to tell her the truth. At least about his job, if not about us.

"That was…" I shook my head. "God, that was stressful."

I still hated myself for lying to my best friend. But Jackson and I had kept our promise—we hadn't let our relationship, or lack of it, affect our relationships with Greer. Not then and not since.

"And that time on the boat…" he started to say, and then we were both laughing.

My cheeks reddened. "That was… It could've been really bad."

"I wouldn't let anything happen to you then—or now." His expression seemed too heavy for the moment we'd just shared. Like it was weighted with some unspoken meaning.

"Jackson…"

"That's why you hired me, right?"

Silly me. For a minute, I'd thought that maybe he still cared about me, but I was just another job to him.

"That's why *my family* hired you," I corrected.

"Sloan," he chided. "Don't lie to me."

I gritted my teeth, annoyed by his thinly veiled dig at our past. "I'm not lying."

"Maybe not about your reasons for finally relenting. But come on. Anyone would be scared by the threats. Hell, you attacked me last night."

I decided to let his comment about lying slide. He was just as guilty of keeping secrets as I was, but if we were going to survive this trip, avoiding any mention of the past seemed like the best policy.

"Attacked you?" I scoffed, determined to keep us rooted in the present.

He'd quickly restrained me, ending any illusions I'd had about being able to protect myself, despite self-defense training.

"And excuse you," I said, my skin prickling. "The door to

your room was closed. I was justified in thinking you were an intruder."

"If there was a real intruder—" he stepped closer "—don't you think I'd be there to protect you in a heartbeat?"

"I, uh…" I glanced out at the water. I didn't know what to think.

"Sloan," he growled.

"What?" I mumbled.

"Look at me." By now, he was standing directly in front of me, our toes practically touching.

I swallowed and looked into his eyes. *Big mistake.*

"I will protect you," he said with a solemn expression. "Always." He waited a beat and then added, "You believe me, right?"

Once upon a time, I couldn't imagine a life without him. Now, after years apart, he was asking me to trust him again. And yet, he'd always been my safe place. My protector.

Regardless of everything that had happened between us, I trusted Jackson to keep me safe. And not just because it was his job.

I nodded.

"Good. Now, I want to talk about the threats. You still didn't answer my question about them."

"I answered your questions yesterday."

He narrowed his eyes at me. That wasn't what he'd meant, and I knew it. And he knew that I knew it.

"I'm—" I stared out over the water, letting it calm me. "Yeah. I find them unsettling."

"Unsettling." He leveled me with a look.

I did *not* want to get into it. Not now. Not when we were far away from London, and I was in my happy place.

But it was more than that. I hated feeling so…helpless. So vulnerable.

And now, I had to rely on Jackson. Something I'd sworn would never happen again. Whether I wanted to admit it or not, I needed Jackson. I needed his protection.

"What do you want me to say?" I asked. "I told you everything I know. Surely between Graham's…" I trailed off, stopping myself before I mentioned his hacking. "And the team at Hudson, we'll figure out who's behind them."

"Graham's…what?" He furrowed his brow. "What does your brother have to do with it?"

"Oh, um…" *Shit.* I glanced away, searching for an answer. "You know, because he's the head of the company." And no one could ever know about his hacking skills.

"Mm." He narrowed his eyes at me, his skepticism clear.

"I just…" I sagged. "I'm exhausted. I've been on edge ever since the threats started. And now that we're out on the water, I feel like I can finally relax."

I didn't want to be scared. I wanted to feel free. And sailing helped. So did Jackson's solid presence, even if I didn't want to admit it.

"Okay," he said. "I'm sorry I brought it up."

I knew he was just doing his job, but I wanted to forget all about the threats.

I stood, clearing my plate and heading for the galley. "Thank you for the pancakes."

"Thank you for the honesty," he said, his words an echo of the past. Of a night long ago. I smiled despite myself.

When I returned to the deck, Jackson was quiet. Contemplative. We readied the boat to leave, and I fired up the motor.

The rest of the morning passed pleasantly enough, like it had the day before. Jackson and I were immersed in our individual tasks, neither of us talking unless it was necessary. Being on the water was peaceful.

I was sitting at the helm, watching a pair of birds swoop and dive into the water. Jackson placed his hand on my shoulder, startling me. "Hey. You ready for lunch?"

I turned to glance up at him. The sun glinted off his hair, and my eyes lingered on his lips. Full. Inviting.

I could practically taste the salt on his lips. Remember the feel of them gliding against my own.

I shook my head as if to clear it. The sun must be getting to me. That was the only rational explanation.

"Sounds good."

It wasn't long before he brought me a sandwich and an apple. "Nothing too fancy."

"I don't need anything fancy." I surveyed the plate. "And this looks great."

The boat was on autopilot, and we were making good time. The wind was fair, and the waves weren't so large.

"Based on your quick reactions last night," Jackson said while I crunched the apple between my teeth, "I assume you still train?"

"With someone in London. Former SAS."

Jackson had been the first to insist I train in self-defense, and he'd spent hours teaching me various techniques, making me practice until I was sweaty and exhausted. Until he felt confident the movements had become muscle memory.

Where my brothers would've tried to surround me in bubble wrap, Jackson had given me the tools to take care of myself.

"Good." He gave my shoulder a squeeze, but the feel of his touch lingered. "We should practice when we're back on dry land."

I hesitated. I could use the practice, especially with such an experienced opponent. But still, the idea of getting so physical with Jackson, of being so close to him... "I don't think that's a good idea."

"Why?" he taunted. "Because you know I'll best you?"

"Psh." I glanced away, hating the fact that he still had such an effect on me. "Don't be cocky, Jackson. I have moves you've never seen."

"Oh." He lifted his chin. "Who's being cocky now?" He took my plate to the galley and returned not long after. "Maybe when we get to Turks and Caicos. Or Puerto Rico."

I stilled at the reminder of Puerto Rico and Greer's impending visit. A visit I'd neglected to tell Jackson about.

"Actually—" I cleared my throat. "I'd like to tweak our itinerary slightly."

"What are you thinking?" he asked, pulling in the main sheet and allowing it to catch the wind once more before winching it tight.

He didn't sound annoyed. Merely curious.

"I think we should spend a few more days in Puerto Rico and shorten our time in the Dominican Republic, only stopping for fuel and food."

"Okay. Any particular reason?"

"Greer's planning to meet us in Puerto Rico?"

"She—" He choked, his eyes flashing to mine. "What? Greer? As in my sister Greer?"

"I know. I was just as surprised when she suggested it."

He furrowed his brow. "This isn't good."

"Yeah. I know."

"No. Not because of us. I'm worried about her."

"So am I," I said, hating the way my body reacted to Jackson referring to an "us." As if there was an "us." I wanted to laugh at the idea. That was past tense.

"Also..." He glanced over at me and smirked. "I know what the two of you are like when you get together."

I rolled my eyes and gave him a playful shove. "We all

make stupid decisions when we're young. I'm not the same person I was back then."

"Neither am I." His eyes were filled with an emotion that looked a lot like, well, regret.

Regret about the past? About us?

I turned away and focused on the water, checking our location. It didn't matter. That ship had sailed long ago.

CHAPTER TEN

Sloan

"That doesn't sound good." I frowned as the engine RPMs dropped, and my stomach along with it.

We were only two hours into what promised to be a long day. Yet again, we were sailing into the wind, our bow smashing into the waves. And these weren't small waves—I was staring down eight-foot seas. Waves that were considerably taller than even Jackson. Jackson and I were wearing our life jackets and personal locator beacons, and I stayed focused on making it to Clarence Town.

When the engine cut out completely a few minutes later, it wasn't surprising. But that didn't make our reality any easier to swallow.

"Shit," Jackson said, voicing my thoughts. "Didn't you just change the filter?"

"Yes, but I've had to change them more frequently lately."

Fuel supply issues were the worst. Notoriously difficult to diagnose, and there wasn't much we could do about it at the moment.

Think. Think.

I'd read a post on this issue recently, so I didn't think the problem was a particulate in our fuel. I had a theory, but it might be only part of the issue. It was at least something to go on.

"I think there's a leak somewhere in the vacuum side of the fuel supply line."

Jackson nodded. "Okay. What do you recommend? Change the filter again?"

I considered it as something crashed to the floor inside the cabin. My stomach was roiling, my breakfast threatening to make a reappearance. I didn't think changing the filter again would make much difference.

"This might sound crazy, but we could bleed the system and try to ride it out as long as possible."

He grimaced. "That means we'd both have to go below deck."

"Yep." It wasn't ideal. The last place you'd want to be in rolling conditions was below deck. But we didn't have many options.

"Okay." He sighed. "Let's do it."

We let out the jib, turned ninety degrees off our route, and set the autopilot. With the boat under full sail, we headed down below to bleed the engine. With one hand braced against the wall, I placed the other to my mouth, willing my nausea away. And Jackson looked just as miserable.

"Let's make this quick."

While Jackson cracked open the bleeder nut, I watched the mechanical fuel pump. Those few minutes we spent below deck felt like hours. I tried not to think about barfing. I tried to distract myself by watching Jackson's forearms. By imagining our next destination. But if I didn't get up on deck and soon, I was going to—

"Okay. Let's go." Jackson practically pushed me toward the stairs.

I rushed ahead of him, desperate for some fresh air. His

hand was on my back, steadying me. We burst onto the deck, and I gulped in the fresh air.

"Let's see if it worked," Jackson said.

I fired up the engine, relief washing over me at the sound of it turning over. I smiled at Jackson, and he smiled back, placing a hand on my shoulder. "Good job."

"You too." I was grateful for his help. For his faith in me.

We made it a few more hours until the engine died again. We repeated the same process as before, working as quickly as possible and trying not to throw up. One of the waves was so strong, I got knocked into the wall.

I hissed at the pain, squeezing my eyes shut, and tried to refocus myself. *I'm fine. We're going to be fine.*

Jackson eyed me with concern. "You good?"

"Let's get this over with." I gritted my teeth as I tried to ignore the pain.

By the time we pulled into Clarence Town, we'd bled the system four times. We still didn't know the source of the problem, but we knew we had an issue that needed to be resolved. We were banged up, exhausted, and I was honestly feeling a bit defeated. I sensed Jackson was too.

We were trying to scope out an anchorage when it started raining.

Jackson turned his face up to the sky. "You've got to be kidding me."

I stared at him, watching as the water ran in rivulets down his face. He was breathtaking.

I heard shouting in the distance, and I turned toward its source. "Yikes." I winced.

Jackson followed my gaze to where another sailboat had run aground. "They were just behind us. Like, right behind us. And I thought our day sucked."

"I know." I cringed, thinking of the damage to the boat. "I feel bad for them."

By the time we got the *Athena* settled in, a large megay-acht had helped the other boat off the reef. And the rain had let up.

"Look." Jackson nudged me. He pointed to the sky—and to a full rainbow.

I gasped at the sight of the vibrant colors against the ominous gray sky. "It's beautiful."

We'd made it through the storm—together. And that was perhaps the most surprising thing of all.

"I guess if you want to see a rainbow," I said, "you have to put up with some rain."

Jackson smiled back at me, and despite how rough the day had been, I found that for the first time in a long time, I was…happy.

WHEN I EMERGED FROM THE BATHROOM AN HOUR LATER, I'D showered and shaved. I'd washed my hair, and I felt like a new woman.

Jackson glanced up from his computer. His eyes dragged down my form from head to toe, lingering on my breasts, my hips, my bare legs. Heat flooded my core at his leisurely perusal.

We were supposed to go ashore to have dinner at a local restaurant. According to one of the online sailing forums, we were in for a treat. Clarence Town might have a population of less than one hundred and only a handful of buildings, but the restaurant was touted as having the best food in the Bahamas. And after the day we'd had, I was ready for a nice, relaxing meal.

I'd decided to dress up for dinner, and apparently, so had

he. Jackson was wearing a pair of linen slacks and a white button-down shirt that stretched across the muscles of his chest. The sleeves were rolled up, revealing tanned, corded forearms.

"Ready?" I asked.

He nodded, closing his laptop and stowing it away. I reached for my purse, slinging it over my shoulder. But when it grazed my side, I sucked in a breath that was more of a hiss. *Ow. Shit.*

I clutched my side. Now that I was no longer so focused on keeping my food down, I realized how much my side hurt.

Jackson frowned. "You okay?"

"I'm fine." I exhaled slowly. Or at least, I would be.

"Sloan." He raised one eyebrow, clearly skeptical.

"My side hurts from where I whacked it on the boat earlier, but it'll be fine."

"Let me see," he said, his evaluation turning more clinical. It wasn't a request.

"I'm not going to lift my dress to show you." I'd tried looking at it earlier in the mirror, but it was difficult to twist around to see when it already hurt.

He crossed his arms over his chest. "Then unzip it because we aren't going anywhere until I've checked your injuries."

"You don't get to tell me what to do." I planted my hands on my hips.

"I do—" he leaned forward "—when it comes to your safety."

I rolled my eyes. "You're making this into a much bigger deal than it is."

He barked out a laugh. "I was just thinking the same about you."

I held his gaze, and he held mine, both of us just as stubborn as ever.

"Come on. I know I'm your bodyguard, but I'm also your friend."

I arched an eyebrow. "Is that what we are? Friends?"

"It's what I'd like to be," he said, surprising me.

"Okay, *friend*." I emphasized the word because it felt ridiculous to think of Jackson as my friend, considering our past. "Let's get going. I'm hungry."

He patted his stomach. "Mm. I hear Erica's Bakery has the best rum cake in the world. And you know how everything here runs on island time," he continued. "It'd be a shame to miss out."

I narrowed my eyes to slits, even as my mouth watered. I loved rum cake, and he knew I'd been dying to visit that bakery. He was evil.

"Ugh. Fine," I huffed, unwilling to miss out on "the best rum cake in the world," according to fellow travelers. "You win. You are such an ass."

"What was that? You like my ass?" He glanced over his shoulder, lifting his hip. "Thanks. It does look good in these pants."

I laughed, unable to help myself. It did look good, but I wasn't going to admit that. Instead, I swatted at him, feeling lighter and more relaxed.

At least until he twirled his finger and said, "Turn."

He wasn't going to relent. And deep down, part of me knew he was right to insist. Out on the ocean, we were a team, and downplaying or hiding our injuries did both of us a disservice.

I swallowed hard and did as he'd asked, putting my back to him. His breath skimmed along my shoulder, and I shivered.

"Where does it hurt?"

"Here." I pointed to my side—the back of my ribs.

"I'm going to lower your zipper now." His voice was gravelly. "Okay?"

"Mm-hmm." I gulped. But I wasn't prepared for the way the zipper hissed loudly as it slid down my back. Or the way my skin pebbled with goose bumps when he gently pushed the fabric aside. I bit back the urge to cry out.

"I'm, uh, I need to lower this side of your dress to get a better look."

I slid my arm out of the strap and then held it to my chest.

He cleared his throat. "I'm going to touch you now."

I braced myself for it, but nothing could've prepared me for the feeling of his fingers as they drifted over my skin. I sucked in a sharp breath. My eyes closed of their own accord, and my pain was momentarily forgotten.

His voice was rough when he spoke again. "Does that hurt?"

"A little," I said, though mostly I was responding to his touch. It was light, but his hands were warm, sending sparks of need skittering across my skin.

"There's a little bruising, though I'm sure it will look worse tomorrow. You should ice it and take some pain medicine."

"I already did." I stared at the ceiling and tried to remain calm. "Take some medicine, that is."

"Good. Any pain when you breathe? Or difficulty breathing?"

Apart from the fact that he was standing so close? Was touching me?

All of a sudden, it was too much. He was too close.

"No." I yanked on my strap. "Like I said, I'm fine. Satisfied?"

He muttered something under his breath that sounded like, "Hardly."

"Can you please zip me up now?"

"Let me grab some arnica salve from the first aid kit." He stood and went over to one of the benches, lifting the cushion and grabbing the kit, all without meeting my eyes.

He took his position behind me, and I tried to calm my breathing as he opened the lid. When he touched my side, I jolted.

"Sorry if I was too rough." His tone was full of remorse.

"You startled me, that's all."

He rubbed the salve into my skin, his touch warm and sure and…

"Right." He cleared his throat and stood. He zipped up my dress before returning the salve to the kit and washing his hands. "Shall we?"

"We shall." Even though I was still trying to get my head on straight.

The rain had cleared, and the sunset promised to be beautiful. He grabbed the trash bag from the kitchen and carried it out. We locked up and then headed over to the restaurant after a quick stop at the bakery for rum cake. Most of the buildings on the island were colorful, and everyone was friendly.

"Good call on the fuel supply line and bleeding it out," Jackson said as we walked up to the outdoor restaurant. It was little more than a hut covered in palm leaves. Colored lights surrounded the space, and the food smelled amazing.

"Thanks," I said, both to his compliment and the fact that he'd pulled out a chair for me. "I plan to spend some time troubleshooting tomorrow, but I'm guessing we need to replace the filter system."

"Let me know how I can help." He perused the menu.

Jackson hadn't questioned or second-guessed me; he'd trusted me. Even during a stressful situation, he'd put his faith in me. It meant more than words could say.

"Thanks. I appreciate that." We'd worked well together today, and it had been surprisingly nice.

His thigh brushed against mine, but neither of us moved away. "What are you going to order? The conch salad, the fried conch, or the conch fritters?"

"Hmm." I tapped my finger to my lips. "I think the conch."

We laughed, and he leaned back, resting his arm on the back of my chair.

"Seriously, though." I grinned. "How about all of it? Let's just order one of everything and share."

"Sounds good."

Before long, my rum punch was delivered, along with Jackson's beer. I took a deep sip, barely tasting the alcohol, thanks to the fruity flavor. I kept thinking about how he wanted us to be friends. So I decided to try it out. To ignore our past and pretend as if we were just two friends out for a drink.

"Brooklyn says hi." I'd checked my email earlier and sent her a quick response to update her. "I have to tell you, she gushed about you after we were 'introduced' at the hotel," I said, using air quotes.

"Yeah?" He chuckled, but the tips of his ears pinkened. "She's a sweetheart."

"She is." I smiled, sipping my rum punch. "You like kids, huh?"

"It's hard not to like Brooklyn," he said, sidestepping my question.

"And your niece and nephew."

"They're great, but I don't get to spend as much time with them as I'd like."

"Because of work?" I asked while the fritters were delivered, along with a second glass of punch. I barely even felt the alcohol. Just a nice, pleasant buzz.

Friends. Maybe this wasn't so bad.

He nodded. "Though…"

I furrowed my brow. "Though, what?"

He shook his head. "Nothing. I just… I'm hoping to spend some more time with them after our trip."

"That will be nice," I said. "Never wanted kids of your own?"

He toyed with his glass. "That's dangerous territory."

It wouldn't be the first time we'd wandered into dangerous territory.

He cupped my cheek, threading his fingers through my hair. His gaze was so intense. So right. I could drown in his eyes. I could forget everything and everyone else when I was with him.

"I need you to promise me something." He brushed my hair away from my face.

"Anything," I breathed. I would give him anything he asked.

"Promise me that no matter what happens between us, it won't affect your relationship with Greer."

"I-I—" I swallowed hard. He was right; Greer would kill us. But I was already too far gone to try to stop. I had tried to stop. I'd tried to avoid Jackson, but I couldn't. "I promise."

The moment his lips connected with mine, I was lost. Lost to reason. Lost to anything but the feeling of his lips caressing mine. His hands on my hips.

It was everything I'd dreamed of and still so much more. It was like gliding along the water—natural and freeing. Exhilarating.

When he kissed me, it was as if the world came alive. As if I came alive.

The earth kept on spinning, the song changed, and yet, we were in our own little world. Just the two of us.

Jackson placed his hand on my arm. "Sloan?"

"Hm?" I glanced down at where his hand rested on my skin.

"Where'd you go just now?"

I blinked a few times. I needed to ground myself in the

present before the rum and memories of the past carried me away.

"Tell me about working for my brother."

"Nate?" he asked as our meal arrived. We dug in.

"Yeah. Unless you worked for one of my other brothers."

He rubbed the back of his neck. "I'm not supposed to talk about a principal with another client."

"Right. I get that." I stirred my drink. "But as your *friend* —" I winked, and it felt exaggerated "—there's just one thing I want to know."

"What's that?" he asked, brow arched in amusement.

I leaned in, never breaking eye contact. "Did you know Nate and Emerson were dating? I mean, before they got engaged."

He threw his head back and laughed. It was glorious. The sight of it did funny things to my ovaries.

I took a bite of the fried conch just to do something with my mouth beside gape at him. "Oh my god," I said around a mouthful. "You have to try this."

I held it up to his mouth, and he swallowed hard before parting his lips. He took a bite, his eyes focused on mine the entire time. *Holy...*

"How is everything?" the waiter asked.

I jerked my hand away as if I'd been scalded. "Good. Yeah. Great." I couldn't seem to stop nodding.

After the waiter had gone, Jackson leaned in, his breath teasing the shell of my ear. "I like how you're leaning in to our cover story."

I laughed, but the sound was breathy and embarrassing. If I'd turned my head just slightly, we'd be kissing. Instead, I stared ahead, ignoring his closeness and his spicy, forbidden scent that called to me, beckoning me closer. He was my bodyguard, and he was here because he was being paid to do a job. That certainly cooled some of the desire coursing through my veins.

Conversation returned to other matters, and dinner passed pleasantly enough. There were light touches, occasional flirting, but I told myself it was all part of the act.

Eventually, he flagged over the waiter and paid our tab.

I scowled at him. "Hey. I was supposed to do that."

"You can pay next time," he said. But we both knew he'd never allow that.

When I stood, I nearly toppled. I giggled. "I guess those rum punches were stronger than I realized."

"Mm-hmm." He wore a bemused expression that was so damn sexy. He offered me his arm. "Are you going to be able to walk, or do I need to throw you over my shoulder?"

"You're teasing, right?" Surely he was joking. I patted his chest, but my hand lingered there, caressing his muscle.

He leaned in. "Care to find out?"

I stepped away from him, knowing better than to push my luck. He reached for me, and I wagged my finger at him.

"Don't you dare." I laughed, despite my efforts to be stern. "Don't even think about it."

He shifted from foot to foot, looking as if he might charge at me. I tried to dart from his path but stumbled. But Jackson was there, catching me. Steadying me.

"Whoa there." He chuckled, but his expression soon turned serious. His hands remained on my hips, his eyes on my lips.

"Jackson?"

"Yeah."

"I—" I rolled my lips between my teeth. "I don't think I can be your friend," I whispered, getting a little too close to the truth.

He leaned even closer. "And why's that?"

"I—" The reflection of the moon on the water caught my eye. "Wow," I breathed.

Jackson turned to follow my gaze then wrapped his arm around my shoulder. We stood there for a minute before he ushered me down the path.

I barely remembered the walk back to the marina or climbing aboard the *Athena*. Part of me thought I'd imagined him guiding me to sit on my bed. Kneeling to the floor to remove my sandals before tucking me in.

"You're a good friend." I patted his cheek. I let out a happy sigh, my eyes closing of their own accord. "Tonight was nice."

"Sleep well," he murmured, and I felt a flutter of a kiss on my forehead. Yet another thing I'd probably imagined.

CHAPTER ELEVEN

Jackson

I glanced up from the navigation chart at the sound of Sloan's cabin door opening. Sloan and I were supposed to spend the morning troubleshooting the filter system. But if the motor continued to have issues like it had yesterday, I wanted to have some alternate routes in mind.

Sloan and I had gone sailing in the past but never in rougher conditions like we'd faced yesterday. Through it all, Sloan had been calm and confident, in command. It was sexy as fuck. Watching her ride the waves as if she were on top of the world. As if she were free.

"Morning."

She groaned. "Morning."

"Feeling a little rum-punched," I teased, trying to focus on the chart instead of Sloan's bare legs.

"Har. Har." She squinted then sank down on the chair across from me. "That stuff was stronger than I realized."

I reached over to the galley, grabbing the plate I'd prepared for her. "Here." I set it on the table in front of her. I wondered what she remembered from last night, but I didn't ask.

I'd nearly kissed her. Several times. *Fuck.*

"Thank you. And thanks for last night."

I lifted a shoulder. "It's my job."

Her expression fell briefly, and I regretted the words as soon as they left my mouth. I hadn't meant it like that. Yes, I was being paid to be here, but I wanted to take care of her. And not just because I was her bodyguard. Because I was her friend.

Right. Her friend. Even I didn't believe that.

I could never be *just* her friend. Sloan had always... I blew out a breath. I'd never imagined myself with anyone but her.

"This looks delicious." She surveyed the plate of toast, eggs, and bacon. "Thank you."

She took a few bites and groaned, dropping the fork to the plate. "Oh my god. This is so good, I could kiss you." She stilled. "I, um..."

I reached out to wipe a crumb from the corner of her mouth but then stopped myself. "I know." *You have a boyfriend.* I cleared my throat. "How's your side?"

A boyfriend who wasn't here, though I still didn't understand why. Maybe he couldn't be away for two months, but he could've joined her for part of it. I would've if we were together.

She touched her side gently. "A little better."

"I'm glad, but there's no rush. We can stay as long as you need."

She stood. "If we can get the fuel supply line sorted, I think we should push on."

"Okay," I said, trusting that she could make the best decision for herself. "But if we're heading out today, I don't want to leave much later than ten."

"Agreed."

Sloan washed up, and we headed below deck. We spent the rest of the morning removing the filter housing and replacing it with a new system. I didn't see any signs that it had been tampered with, and that was a relief. Sloan did most of the repair, while I assisted. She made it look easy even when I knew it wasn't, and I was in awe of her.

"Look at that." Sloan smiled, dusting off her hands. "It's nine thirty."

"Look at that." I smirked, wishing I could fix our relationship as easily as we had the filter system.

That said, for the first time since we'd left Miami, I felt hopeful. For the first time, we were united.

It wasn't long before we were casting off. Our voyage to Pittstown Point was mostly uneventful. I still had concerns about the fuel supply line, but the only way to test our current "solution," if you could call it that, was to run the motor for long periods of time. So that's what we'd done.

Sloan planned to have the boat evaluated once we reached Turks and Caicos. My guess was that there had been a leak in the filter housing or coalescer, but we wanted a mechanic to look at it for both our peace of mind.

I wasn't naïve enough to consider it—or our relationship —fixed, but we'd encountered no issues since. And that was certainly an improvement. Our tentative friendship was also an improvement.

"We should reach Plana Cays today," I said after she'd emerged from the bathroom the following morning. Her hair was freshly braided, and the smell of sunshine and wild roses clung to her.

We'd spent the night at an anchorage that had been peaceful and isolated. Our only company had been the sharks that had shown up after dinner, swimming slow circles around the *Athena* for a few hours.

"I'm glad we decided to press on yesterday." She joined me at the table, tucking her leg beneath her. It had the effect of revealing more of her tanned, toned thigh, and I had to bite the inside of my cheek and glance away.

I'd already spoken with the staff at the Huxley Grand Turks and Caicos via satellite phone and confirmed our plans with the head security officer. Even though I'd hoped it was unnecessary, I'd requested round-the-clock surveillance on the *Athena* while it was docked. When it came to Sloan's safety, I wasn't taking any chances.

There'd been no new threats since she'd left London, but that didn't mean we could let down our guard. Not until the culprit was caught. And I was determined to give Sloan the peace of mind she seemed to have reclaimed on the water.

"This was a nice spot," Sloan said, surveying the anchorage.

"Very peaceful."

Last night had been clear, the sky full of stars. It was the first night since starting our trip that I'd slept deeply, secure in the knowledge of her safety. She looked better rested too, and, for that, I was grateful.

Sloan sighed wistfully and stood, wincing slightly as she did so. "It is, but I suppose all good things must come to an end."

I'd always hated that expression. Probably because I didn't want it to be true.

I closed my laptop and stowed it away. I was concerned about Sloan's side, but she'd assured me she was fine. And the arnica and ice seemed to have done their job. Her skin was still bruised, but her pain had lessened.

"Ready when you are." I followed her up to the deck.

I raised the anchor, and then we motored out. The first few hours were spent beating directly into the wind, much like the past few days. We were once again reduced to tacking—zigzagging across the water.

"If this continues," I said to Sloan. "We won't even need GPS. All we'll have to do is navigate directly into the wind each day, and we'll reach our destination."

She laughed, though she didn't seem at all daunted by the challenging conditions. If anything, she seemed to relish them.

"Not ideal," she finally admitted. "But better than our trip to Clarence Town."

"True."

Around lunch time, we raised the sails and turned south. That made a huge difference—it was as if the *Athena* had let out a sigh of contentment. I patted her side as she proceeded to slice through the water.

Sloan smiled and tilted her head back to soak in the sun. "That's more like it. *Athena's* happy, and the sunshine will top off our battery bank."

I nodded, scanning the horizon. No cargo ships. No other sailors. It was as if we had this part of the world all to ourselves.

It was both peaceful and strange to sail for hours on end without seeing any signs of human life. It almost felt as if we were the last two people on earth.

"It's desolate out here," Sloan said, echoing my thoughts. "Beautiful, but even more remote than I'd expected."

"What type of route do you typically sail for your annual trip?"

"It varies. I'm usually gone for three, four weeks, tops, so I stick to trips that allow for more island-hopping. I've done the Greek Islands, the Grenadines, the South Pacific."

"Always alone?" The fact that her boyfriend wasn't here still niggled, but I didn't want to ask about him. I didn't want to think about him.

She nodded. "Until this year anyway."

"Damn." I rubbed a hand over my mouth. "I didn't realize…"

"How experienced I am?" she joked, waggling her eyebrows in a suggestive way.

I laughed, but her comment had me thinking of the first time we'd slept together. About her lack of experience at the time, at least when it came to sex.

"Are you sure?" I asked, hovering above her, my cock hard and seeking her core.

This woman was going to be the death of me.

As much as I'd tried to deny it, I wanted her. I wanted her, and it was wrong. But I couldn't help myself.

The more I got to know Sloan, the more she'd burrowed beneath my skin, the easier it was to forget that she was my sister's best friend who was off-limits.

Sloan nodded, her pupils blown wide with desire. "I want this, Jackson. I want you."

She locked her hands behind my neck, pulling me down for a kiss. She wrapped her legs around my waist, tugging me closer.

I writhed against her, my cock sliding through her wet heat. "God, hayati. You feel so good."

"Yes," she moaned. "Yes, Jackson." She dug her heels into my back, edging me closer.

I slid inside her, hissing at the tight grip of her pussy. Fuck me, she felt good. So good.

She winced a little but then seemed to relax, taking me in fully.

"You okay?" I asked, brushing her hair away from her face.

"You're just…really big."

"You sure know how to stroke a guy's ego. Here." I rolled us so she was on top. "You control our pace. You control how deep I am. Take as little or as much of me as you want."

She placed her palms on my chest. "I want all of you."

"You have me," I groaned, watching in awe as she slid all the way down.

"You know," Sloan said, jolting me from my memory. "At first, I wasn't happy about giving up my solitude on this trip." Her expression was contemplative, and then she dipped her head. "But I'm glad you're here."

I tried to gauge her expression behind her sunglasses. "I'm glad I'm here too," I said, surprised by her admission.

I wasn't sure she'd feel that way if she knew I'd been taking a mental walk down memory lane. But I appreciated her saying it.

"I mean, it's nice to know I have something to feed the sharks if they decide to circle again," she joked.

"Ha-ha." I laughed, though it was without humor. "I'm too tough to be tasty."

She gripped my bicep, her touch like a brand. "I beg to differ." She seemed to realize what she'd said belatedly, her eyes going wide.

I shuddered. "Was this your plan all along? Agree to bring me on board only to cast me out as shark bait?"

"You're only just now realizing that?" Her answering smile was wicked and fucking sexy.

This was the Sloan I knew and loved. The woman I'd fallen in love with all those years ago. I could remember another time she'd smiled at me like that.

"Put this on," Sloan said, handing me a sleep mask. It was navy and silky, but it was the middle of the day.

"Why?" I asked, immediately suspicious.

Greer was out of town for the week—staying with Logan and his family for spring break. I hated that I was lying to my sister, and I knew Sloan hated it. I didn't blame her—she was in an impossible situation.

At least we were no longer lying about my job. I'd told my family that I was leaving the Navy, though I hadn't shared the circumstances that had led to it. I was still so ashamed that I'd been discharged. I couldn't bear the thought of disappointing my mom.

I was still looking for another job, but for now, the club paid well, even if the hours sucked. Still, it allowed me to spend time with Sloan, especially on days like today, when the club was closed. I was surprised Sloan didn't have plans. She'd quit working at the restaurant and started a paid internship at a luxury hotel. Between that and a full class load, she was busy.

"Please." She batted her eyes.

I narrowed my eyes at her. We were standing in the kitchen of her apartment, and I didn't get the feeling she was trying to blindfold me for sex. Not that I would've been opposed, but my heart was fully at her mercy. I didn't know how much more I could take.

I stepped closer, taking the sleep mask and then turning her so her back was to me. "Maybe you should wear the sleep mask," I rasped in her ear.

She shivered, and I cascaded my hands down her arms. But then she straightened and seemed to shake herself out of it. She turned to face me, and I was so distracted by the feel of her lips on mine that I barely noticed her slipping the sleep mask from my hand.

"Nope." She smiled against my lips before leaning back. "I need you to wear it. I have a surprise for you."

"What kind of surprise?" I waggled my eyebrows.

She rolled her eyes. "Yes, there will be sex involved, but we have to get to our destination first."

"Which would be..."

She shook her head. "You can put it on now or when we get in the car."

I narrowed my eyes. "I don't like surprises."

I meant it. Surprises as a SEAL were deadly. And my training was so ingrained in me that the idea of covering my eyes and leaving the apartment went against the very fiber of my being.

She looped her arms around my neck. "I know. But you like me, right?"

"Mm-hmm." I nuzzled her neck.

I more than liked Sloan. I loved her, but I couldn't tell her that. Not when we were still keeping our relationship a secret from my sister and I had no idea what the future held.

I hated that we had to sneak around, but the idea of hurting my sister nearly killed me.

And I knew what would happen if we told her. When Greer had found out about my relationship with her former best friend, she hadn't talked to me for weeks. And they hadn't been nearly as close as Sloan and Greer were. Telling Greer would only end in heartbreak for everyone.

"And you trust me," Sloan said.

"Yes." I peeled her shirt aside, kissing every inch of available skin I could reach.

She moaned. But then she pushed me away. "Stop trying to distract me."

"But it's so much fun." I smirked.

"Jackson," she huffed.

"All right. All right." I slid the sleep mask over my eyes. "Happy now?"

It was dark, and I didn't like giving up my sense of sight. But I had to trust Sloan, and I did. Besides, my curiosity was definitely piqued about whatever she had planned.

With my vision darkened, my other senses were heightened. I heard a loud zipper. The jangle of her keys as she locked the door behind us. Felt the warmth of her skin as she slid her hand in mine.

I'd had to step up into our ride, which meant it wasn't your typical taxi. And the seats were a soft, buttery leather. Where was she taking me, and how could she afford this?

After nearly an hour car ride that had left me grumpy and still clueless as to our destination, we stopped. Sloan thanked the driver before helping me out of the car. The noise of the city seemed magnified, and was that...a ship's horn?

I itched to remove my blindfold. I hated not being able to scan my surroundings, to make sure Sloan was safe. But I was trying to be patient—for her. Because whatever this surprise was, she'd clearly gone to great lengths—and perhaps considerable expense—to make it happen. For me.

"Here we are," she said, finally sliding the sleep mask from my face. "Surprise!"

I squinted against the bright morning sun. A row of sailboats bobbed in front of us, glass skyscrapers rising dramatically behind them.

"We're having lunch by the water?" I asked.

"Nope." She grinned. "We're going sailing."

"In one of these?" I encompassed the boats with a sweeping gesture, my excitement growing. I loved sailing, and Sloan and I had been talking about going together. But it had always seemed like something that was out of reach. We either couldn't find the time or the price of renting a sailboat for a weekend was astronomical.

"Come on." She tugged my hand, leading me past the row of sailboats used for tourist charters and over to a locked gate.

I surveyed the area, only a few people out. The boats were very expensive. What was she...

She unlocked the gate and pushed it open. I stood there a moment, gaping at her. I followed, trying to put together the pieces of a puzzle that weren't fitting.

Sloan stopped before a gorgeous sailboat that had to cost six figures. Easily. If not more.

"Come on." She smirked. "You can check out the cabin while I get us ready to cast off."

I grabbed her arm, holding her loosely. "Cast off? Sloan, whose boat is this?"

I didn't know what answer I was expecting—or even hoping for—but it certainly wasn't the one she gave. "It belongs to my grandfather."

She didn't meet my eyes when she said it. And all I could think was, who are you?

Our GPS signaled, indicating our destination was near. I glanced away from Sloan to scan the horizon, squinting at something in the distance as a strip of land came into view. A sliver of golden sand bisecting blue skies and bluer waters. It was…

"Paradise," Sloan sighed, taking the word right out of my mouth. "It's so beautiful." Her tone was full of awe.

"Pristine," I said, amazed at the miles of white, sandy beach. The water was crystal clear, and there were no people or boats in sight.

"How are there not more people here? Enjoying this unspoiled beauty?"

I lifted a shoulder. "I don't know, but I'm certainly not going to complain." I was in one of the most beautiful places on earth with the most beautiful woman I'd ever seen.

Because I was being paid to be here.

I straightened. Right. This was my job. Not a vacation. She was my client. We were friends—or, at least, we were trying to be. And I didn't want to lose the progress we'd made.

"Let's head over there to anchor," Sloan said.

"Aye-aye, Captain."

She grinned, cutting the engine so we slowly drifted toward the island. "Captain, huh?"

Once we were in a more sheltered area, we worked together to lower the anchor. She'd been more playful today, less serious. Less withdrawn. It was nice.

"I figured you preferred it to Ms. Mackenzie," I teased. I'd stopped calling her that days ago.

"Oh, definitely. But you know you can call me Sloan."

"Nope. I like Captain. It suits you."

She smiled, and the sight went straight to my chest. *Fuck.*

For so long, I'd been convinced she'd never look at me that way again. As if...

She tilted her head. "What?"

"I should check the anchor," I said.

Before I could respond, she headed over to the stern. She stripped out of her clothes, and I stood there, gaping at her. She wore a bright coral bikini that left little to the imagination.

Holy...fuck. I'd had principals who were celebrities. Models, even. But no one had ever affected me like Sloan.

"What are you doing?" I asked, watching as she grabbed a snorkel and a pair of fins and dove into the water.

"Sloan!" I rushed to the edge and peered over. She was treading water, smiling up at me.

"The water's perfect." She used her goggles to peer beneath the surface, even though I could see clearly to the bottom from the boat. "Jackson!" She surfaced. "You have to see this—it's amazing. Fish and coral and—" She gasped. "A manta ray."

"Someone should stay on the boat," I grumbled. "Keep an eye on things."

She spun around in the water. "There's no one here. We have this entire deserted island paradise to ourselves. When will this ever happen again?"

Likely never.

I was still in disbelief that this was my current reality.

Still, I was supposed to be protecting Sloan. Not allowing myself to be distracted by the coral reef and her bare skin. Not when it made me want to cross lines I shouldn't.

When I continued to hesitate, Sloan said, "As your captain, I order you to join me." Then she hastily added, "If you want to, that is," with a smile.

Of course I *wanted* to. When it came to Sloan, it had never been a question of want.

I glanced around once more, satisfied we were completely alone. Safe from outside threats apart from those posed by mother nature. I stripped out of my shirt, gratified when Sloan couldn't take her eyes off me. I could feel her gaze lingering on my skin, and the fact that I'd stolen her attention from the reef felt like a prize of its own.

I grabbed some goggles and checked our position and the forecast once more before jumping in. Sloan squealed— splashing water at me as soon as I'd surfaced.

"You scared away all the fish with your cannonball," she teased, and I slicked water away from my face.

"Hopefully all the sharks too," I joked, though we both knew they could show up at any time. If we were lucky, we'd only see the more harmless kinds—lemon, nurse—if any.

I peered beneath the water with my goggles, amazed by the colors and vibrancy of the reef and all its beautiful creatures. Sunlight filtered through the surface, spearing the water with its rays. A school of dark black fish with brilliant cobalt fins and tails darted by.

"Look over here!" Sloan called, and I swam closer, smiling at her excitement. It was almost more fun to watch her than the show beneath the water.

She grabbed my hand and pointed in the distance where a sea turtle swam among the reef. I smiled, unable to focus on anything beyond the fact that she was touching me. Holding my hand. We swam for a while, pointing out various things to each other and reveling in our discoveries.

I tried to capture the moment in my mind, the feeling of being with Sloan. I didn't want this to end. Not just today, or even the trip, but my time with her.

Sloan had made it very clear she didn't want to revisit the past, but being with her called so many memories to mind. So many good memories, even ones I'd long forgotten or suppressed.

And now, we were creating new memories together. Exploring new places. Revealing new facets to each other.

When I was younger, for a long time, I'd thought being discharged from the SEALs was the biggest mistake of my life. But seeing her now, I knew what had happened with Sloan was my biggest regret. I should've never let her go.

CHAPTER TWELVE

Sloan

Jackson and I had spent the afternoon snorkeling the reef. The pads of my fingers were wrinkled, and my body was exhausted.

I climbed up the sugar sloop, feeling Jackson's eyes on me the entire time as he followed. For a second, I thought I felt the brush of his hands on me, but then I told myself I was imagining it. Maybe I just wanted it. Wanted him to touch me. *Want me.*

Wanted to know if it would be the same as it had always been—electric. Shattering my world and then putting me back together in the way that only he could.

"That's it, Sloan. That's it," he urged, his own movements becoming more frantic.

My pleasure had been building and building, and I didn't know how much more I could take. I'd never felt so full. So complete. I couldn't imagine sharing this moment with anyone else.

Jackson cupped my cheek, pressing his lips to mine. Claiming me. With his cock buried deep inside me, it was the most intimate and intense thing I'd ever experienced.

"I've got you, Sloan," he whispered, urging me on. "I've got you."

Stars exploded in my vision, my mind emptying completely. I didn't have to think; I only had to feel. And everything felt... wonderful.

Jackson's movements turned frenzied, until he was panting out my name. Unleashing his own release. He was there with me. We were falling together. Always together.

We fell back on the bed in a tangle of limbs, and I could feel his heart racing beneath his skin. It matched the cadence of my own.

"Fuck, baby. That was incredible."

"Is that unusual—incredible sex?" I joked, but I was curious. Because that had definitely exceeded all my hopes and expectations.

Jackson stilled. "Wait." When I lifted my head, I could see the panic in his eyes. Feel it coming off him in waves. "Wait. Are you... were you a virgin?"

I rolled my lips between my teeth.

"Oh my god." He sat up and shrank back. "You're a virgin? You were a virgin? I took your virginity?"

"First of all," I said. "You didn't take anything. I gave myself to you. And secondly—" I placed my hand on his chest, annoyed by this conversation "—virginity is a social construct. It's outdated and heteronormative."

"You're right, but still..." He dragged a hand down his face. "It was your first time. I wish you'd told me. I would've been—"

"More careful?" I asked. "Gentler?"

"Yes."

I cupped his cheek. "I didn't want you to be gentle. And I would've told you if I was uncomfortable."

Finally, eventually, he seemed to relax. "Are you okay?"

He scanned my body as if searching for any signs of injury. It was ridiculous, really. But it made me feel special that he cared.

"I'm great." I smiled, my body still buzzing after my orgasm. I was happy and light and in love.

I hauled myself on deck and grabbed a towel, wrapping it around my waist.

"That was fun." I sank down on one of the benches. My limbs were exhausted from an afternoon of swimming along the reef, but I hadn't felt this happy, this light, in such a long time.

Jackson nodded, but my mouth went dry at the sight of him and all that glorious bare skin. Water sluiced down the hard planes of his chest, making his tattoos glisten even more in the sun. Looking at his torso was like playing a "spot the differences" game. Except with the most gorgeous living, breathing canvas.

I'd been on this boat with this man for nearly a week now, and it was impossible not to want him. It wasn't just about his looks, though he was hotter than ever. Jackson was thorough and kind and commanding and respectful.

He made me pancakes, checked in with me about the threats and how I was feeling. Cared for my injuries.

He hadn't taken over the boat, as I'd feared. He was supportive; he'd allowed me to lean on him. He'd make suggestions, but he always deferred to my opinion.

He was the same man I remembered—and yet somehow more. More mature. More patient. More nurturing.

We weren't the same people we used to be, but maybe we were...better.

"You're staring," he rasped. But when I met his eyes, they were hooded, greedily drinking me in.

"So are you," I said, challenging him.

"Yeah. Well..." He toweled off his head. "Can you blame me? You're gorgeous."

Based on his earlier insistence to remain professional, I didn't know what to think. But standing there, staring at him, I couldn't deny it. I wanted Jackson, and neither time nor distance had dulled my body's reaction to this man.

I swayed a little on my feet, but I knew it had more to do with the man standing before me than the gentle waves rocking the boat. Jackson placed his hands on my waist as if to steady me. He'd once been my rock. My protector.

I wanted to feel that way again. Safe. Secure. Loved.

Being with him on the *Athena*, I felt that again. Not only because it was my happy place, but because Jackson made me feel safe. Taken care of.

"Hey." He peered down at me. "You okay?"

"I—uh…" Suddenly, I'd lost the ability to form words in his presence. Without realizing what I was doing, I'd placed my hands on his bare chest. Our faces were inches apart.

I licked my lips, remembering the taste of him. The feel of his body pressing into mine deliciously. The…lies. The thought came to me unbidden and unwanted.

"Were you ever going to tell me?" I asked, devastated that Jackson had accepted a job across the country and was moving to LA. I'd only found out because Greer had congratulated him in front of me.

Talk about heartbreaking. The man I loved was moving, and he hadn't even mentioned the fact that he was interviewing, let alone had accepted a job. Was he just going to leave? Without telling me? My body felt as if it might rip in two.

Jackson stalked toward me, crowding me. His expression was like a thunderhead. "I'm not the only one who's been keeping secrets."

I crossed my arms over my chest, my heart rate racing. "What's that supposed to mean?"

"I don't know, Sloan. Maybe the fact that you're a hotel heiress."

I scoffed. Right. Of course. "So that changes things, does it?"

"Yes. No." He dragged a hand through his hair, pacing the kitchen floor. "It only reaffirms what I already knew."

"And what's that, Jackson?"

"All this time, we've been kidding ourselves. My sister. Your family. Your…future." He shook his head.

Wait. What? I could feel the panic rising. No. He couldn't do this to me. To us.

"You're my future." I placed my hand over his heart. And he was mine.

And yet, he hadn't asked if I'd go with him to LA.

He took my hand in his, and then he shook his head, his expression downcast. "This was the only potential outcome. Face it, Sloan. It's inevitable." He gave my hand a squeeze before releasing me. And when he took a step back, it felt as if he'd erected a wall between us.

Inevitable.

I lowered my hands and took a step back, trying to calm myself. To clear my head. While I had faith that I could weather any storm with *Athena*, I couldn't survive another round with Jackson.

"Sorry. I, uh, I think I must have gotten too much sun."

He dropped his hands as well. "It is warm out." But his gaze was focused on my lips when he said it.

The tension between us pulled taut. He looked as if he was going to kiss me or break me. I knew both were equally likely when it came to him. I could practically feel the desire and restraint rolling off him.

I'd never had someone look at me the way Jackson did. As if he'd die if he didn't touch me. As if it took everything in his power to hold himself back.

I knew what I wanted. What I'd always wanted—*him.*

I licked my lips, and his eyes darted there, his nostrils flaring. Desire blazed inside me, and my chest rose and fell in great, shaky breaths.

I wasn't sure who moved first, or if it even mattered, but I blinked and we were touching. He was kissing me. Holding me. Igniting every nerve ending that had lain dormant for the past decade. Reviving me.

I gasped into his mouth, unable to get close enough. "Jackson."

I wanted to be swept up in that frenzy. That rush that only Jackson could evoke in me. Right now, I didn't care if it killed me. Not when his touch was the only thing that made me feel truly alive.

"Fuck," he rasped. "Fuck, you feel so good."

His erection dug into my stomach, and his hands were everywhere. On my hips, sliding up my ribs to cup my breasts, in my hair. I was just as out of control, touching every inch of bare skin I could reach.

"We shouldn't," he said between kisses, his words an echo of the past. Though—then and now—he didn't seem inclined to stop. I didn't want him to stop.

"Don't stop," I begged.

He kissed me again, making me dizzy. Delirious.

"But I'm..." He leaned his forehead against mine. "And you're..." He tightened his grip on my hips and groaned. Heat flooded my core, making my nipples pebble with desire. "We can't."

He tasted like mint and salt. Like all my best memories and the source of my greatest heartbreak.

And somehow that, coupled with his words, cleared my head enough to realize that this was a bad idea. A mistake. I placed my hands on his chest, gently pushing him away.

"You're right," I said, my lips swollen from his kisses. "We can't."

I swallowed. I couldn't do this again. I couldn't go down this path—knowing heartbreak was the only thing waiting for me at the end.

He peered down at me with concern but didn't try to come closer.

I straightened my swimsuit top and covered my chest with my arms as if to shield myself from him. I supposed a handful of nights at sea with Jackson, sailing the beautiful Caribbean, was enough to make anyone lose their senses.

Jackson shook his head, his vision clearing as if from a trance. "I'm sorry. That was completely unprofessional."

Unprofessional, *right*. I bit my lip and glanced away. There was always some excuse, some reason, why we couldn't be together. In the past, it had been his uncertain future. His sister. Just when I'd thought we could finally move past one of them, something else would pop up like a twisted game of Whac-A-Mole.

He turned his back to me and grasped the railing, peering over the side of the boat. I took a moment to study his back —the tattoos that came to life every time his muscles rippled. Some were familiar and others were new. All beautiful and captivating.

"I'm going to shower," I said, needing to be somewhere, anywhere, else. Unfortunately, on the boat in the middle of the ocean, there were only so many places to go.

I headed below deck with a heavy sigh. This wasn't me. I wasn't some horny teenager who forgot all reason, but that was how Jackson made me feel. Insatiable. Uncontrollable.

I blamed it on the sea air. The vacation mentality.

That was all this was. All any vacation was. A chance to escape the ordinary. To ignore responsibilities and expectations and reality for a little while. I might fantasize about Jackson, but that was all it could ever be. At the end of the trip, Jackson and I would return to our separate lives, and nothing would change.

I STARED AT THE CEILING. I COULDN'T IMAGINE A MORE peaceful setting—floating in the calm waters off the coast of a secluded paradise. It was a cloudless night with no rain in the forecast. Even so, it felt as if a storm was approaching. My body was tense. And I felt...restless. On edge.

I sighed and rolled to my side. We had another full day of sailing tomorrow to reach Mayaguana. I needed my rest, but I couldn't stop thinking about what had happened earlier. About Jackson.

He'd been...well, even better than I'd remembered. His kiss. His touch. They had the power to consume me. They nearly had once.

And while I knew it was a good thing we'd stopped, that didn't mean my body was happy about it. No. It was achy and frustrated and woefully unsatisfied.

I kicked the covers aside and padded to the galley for some water. The space was bathed in red light, and I was halfway across the main cabin when I heard a groan. I paused. Maybe it was the groan of the ship, but it sounded more like the groan of a man.

The sound of another low groan had me rushing to Jackson's door, my gut clenching with concern. What if he'd eaten something that didn't agree with him? What if he was hurt?

We were in the middle of the ocean. If something bad had happened, I needed to act fast.

In my panic, I twisted the handle to his quarters without knocking. The boat rocked, carrying the door open with it. Red light spilled into his bunk from the main cabin, his breaths suddenly even louder in the small space. His torso was bare. He'd kicked off the sheets, and there was just enough light to see the outline of his hand gripping his cock as he pumped himself furiously.

Oh my god. Oh my...

I was too stunned to move. Too entranced to do anything but stare.

When I met his eyes, they were hooded as he scanned my form. Daring me to watch him. Or at least, that was how it felt.

I swallowed hard, easily falling under his spell once more. I hadn't set foot into his room. Hadn't removed any of my clothes, and I was already on edge just from the sight of him. God, he really was glorious. And the longer I stood there, the more my eyes adjusted, allowing me the most erotic and tantalizing glimpses of this beautiful man.

I felt as if I couldn't breathe. As if my whole body was wound tight, my being wrapped up in him. Everything tingled and ached and wanted. Wanted him.

Before I realized what I was doing, my hand had drifted down, sliding beneath the silk of my pajama bottoms. I just… I needed a release. Something. This past week had been torture, and seeing Jackson now, touching himself, pleasuring himself, had finally pushed me over the edge.

Our eyes locked. I rubbed my clit, imagining it was his hands. His tongue. It still wasn't enough, but it was as far as I dared go.

"Fuck," he grunted. "Yes, *hayati*."

I knew he was close. Hell, I was nearly there too, the pleasure building and building to an almost impossible crescendo.

Jackson's muscles tightened, his abs clenching as he increased his pace until he was hissing through his teeth, ropes of come spilling on his skin. I loved seeing him lose control, and my own orgasm barreled through me. Making my vision darken and my legs shake.

"Oh god," I whispered. I hunched forward, still feeling the aftershocks. Wondering what the hell I'd just done.

So much for staying away. For being professional. For being...friends.

I let out a shaky exhale, and when I lifted my gaze to him, we both stared at each other as if to ask, "What just happened?"

Shit. This was bad. Really bad.

But it had felt so, so good.

I closed his door and crept back to my room before I could make an even bigger mess of things. I had no idea where Jackson and I went from here, but I had a feeling there was no going back from this.

CHAPTER THIRTEEN

Jackson

I jolted upright, nearly hitting my head on the ceiling of my berth. "Fuck," I said. "Fuck," I repeated, more softly this time.

The sun was shining through the porthole in my cabin, turning the sky a beautiful pink. It was time to get moving. Today, we'd head to Mayaguana, our last night on the boat before spending the week at the Huxley Grand Turks and Caicos.

After everything that had happened yesterday, putting some space between Sloan and me didn't seem like a bad thing. I didn't know how much more temptation I could resist. I mean...first, that kiss. God, that kiss. My memories hadn't lived up to the shattering reality of it.

But the look of hurt in her eyes that had followed had nearly gutted me. I hated seeing her so upset, especially when I was the cause of it.

I dragged a hand down my face. I was trying to do the right thing here. I always tried to do the right thing by her, even if it didn't always seem that way. But there was only so much a man could take.

My cock was almost always hard around her. So, in an attempt to relieve some pressure, I'd taken matters into my own hand. I'd tried to be quiet, but then she'd…she'd opened the door. *She'd* watched. Touched herself. Made herself come.

Fuck me, that had been hot.

But also… I buried my face in my hands. *What the hell was I thinking? What was she thinking?*

Sloan was my principal. My boss didn't care that we had a past. And when he'd told me to use it to my advantage, he sure as hell didn't mean jacking off in front of the client. Daring her to watch me even though she was already in a relationship with someone else.

I squeezed my eyes shut, feeling completely adrift.

She's with someone else.

The idea of Sloan with anyone else made me sick to my stomach.

Yes, we'd crossed a line. Several lines. But I didn't share. And even if I'd been willing to overlook the fact that she was in a relationship, I knew it would eat Sloan up inside.

I knew what it was like to sneak around. To lie.

We'd lied to my sister for years. Hell, we were *still* lying to her. It had been a point of contention for us. It had caused us both a lot of pain, especially Sloan.

And while I respected Sloan for keeping her promise to me—to not let what had happened between us affect her relationship with Greer—I hated myself for it. If I could go back, that was part of a long list of regrets when it came to Sloan.

I wouldn't ask that of Sloan again. Which was why this had to stop. *I* had to stop doing this—thinking we could be something more.

I sighed, rubbing a hand over my chest. The problem was, I didn't know if I could. Sloan had always been my anchor, grounding me when life was difficult.

When I'd been at my lowest after leaving the SEALs, she'd been there for me. She'd been supportive, listening without judgment. With her, I could be vulnerable in a way I'd never been before.

After my dad's death, it had felt as if the weight of the world rested on my shoulders. The responsibility to take care of my mom and Greer. To become the kind of man he would've respected—a hero, like him.

And then I'd gotten kicked out of the SEALs, and everything had come crashing down. But Sloan had been there for me. She'd loved me. Healed me.

But that was in the past. I needed to focus on the present. She was Hudson's client, for fuck's sake. And I'd worked too long and too hard to give up that promotion. It was within my grasp. All I had to do was keep my eye on the prize and my cock in my pants.

I dressed and headed out to check our position and the weather.

"Morning." Sloan peeked her head in from the deck. "Breakfast and coffee are in the microwave. Everything else looks good. I'm ready to leave whenever you are."

I scrutinized her expression, but she was as calm and beautiful as ever.

*Okay...*Was she just going to pretend last night never happened? Hell, maybe it was for the best if we simply acted like nothing had changed.

I was tempted to ask, but I reminded myself that she was the client. And after last night, I'd resolved to treat her as such. No more flirting. No more...touching. Kissing.

Fuck.

No. Not fuck. Definitely no fucking.

It was my job to keep her safe and, when possible, happy. So I swallowed back my questions, realizing that perhaps ignoring the problem in this situation was best.

I said, "Sounds good," and got ready to head out.

We motored into the wind, and as the island faded from view, I gave it one last lingering glance. On the island, it had felt as if anything were possible. As if something between Sloan and me could be possible.

If I were honest, I still wanted it to be possible. But I knew that was a fantasy, nothing more. I'd ignored protocol, discarded my principles like my swim trunks, and that couldn't happen again.

I checked and double-checked the weather, using the satellite phone to email security at the Huxley Grand Turks and Caicos. Everything was ready for our arrival tomorrow, and that should've given me some manner of calm, but it didn't.

When it was my turn to take the wheel, Sloan went below deck. I wondered if she was avoiding me. We'd barely spoken all day, and I had no idea what she was thinking. It felt as if all the progress we'd made the past few days had come undone.

I hated the idea of her pushing me away. Though it wouldn't be the first time, and I couldn't say I blamed her.

THE DOOR TO MY APARTMENT OPENED AND THEN SLAMMED SHUT. I found Sloan pacing in the living room.

"What happened?" I asked, immediately on edge. "What's wrong?"

"I can't keep doing this." She continued pacing. "I can't keep lying to her. To everyone."

"I know." I went over to her, relieved, even as my stomach churned with guilt. "I understand, and I'm—"

"No." She raised a hand as if to silence me. "You don't. When I leave to come to your place, I have to lie. When I'm texting with you, I have to lie. When Greer asks who put that dreamy look on my face—"

"I get it." I smoothed my hands up and down her arms. "You have to lie."

Her shoulders slumped. "I hate lying to her. I'm a terrible friend."

"And I'm a terrible brother," I said. "But we can't control who we fall in love with."

She gasped, and I realized it was the first time I'd said the word aloud. I'd thought it a thousand times. It was always on the tip of my tongue.

She glanced up, meeting my gaze. "You...you love me?"

"Yeah, hayati." I cupped her cheek, wishing I'd told her sooner. "I do."

She wrapped her arms around my neck and squealed. I held her close, my heart pounding as the realization sank in. I loved her. I am so fucked.

It was a good thing she wasn't fluent in Arabic or she would've figured that out months ago.

"I love you too." She peppered my face with kisses. "God, I love you so much, Jackson."

I didn't deserve Sloan or her love. I dropped my head to my chest. How could I ever give her the kind of life she deserved, when I'd been discharged from the Navy and we were hiding our relationship from friends and family?

"Hey." She angled her head so she was meeting my gaze. "What's that about?"

"You deserve more than this. More than I can give you." More than lies and secrets and...

"Jackson." She gripped my shirt, her gaze intense. "I don't want anything but you. But I can't keep living like this."

"What are you saying?" I asked.

"I want to tell Greer about us."

I jerked my head back. "What? We can't. You know we can't."

It wasn't the first time we'd discussed this, but I thought we were on the same page.

"We can," she insisted. "We love each other. Surely that will show her how serious we are, right?"

"Maybe," I hedged, still doubtful. "But if we tell her that we love each other, then she's going to realize how long we've been keeping this from her."

"What do you think?" Sloan asked as we neared our destination. The wind had shifted, and we were flying through the water, making good time. "Should we stop for the night or press on?"

"How do you feel?" I asked, deferring to her.

She lifted a shoulder, never meeting my gaze. "I'm good to keep going if you are."

"Maybe a few more hours. Just to put us closer to Turks and Caicos." And a villa where we'd have more space and less temptation.

"Agreed." Her tone was cold, distant.

We eventually anchored in about eighteen feet of water, and it was the first time we'd stopped all day. I could see straight to the bottom of the clear blue water, and everything looked good. That said, I didn't think I could handle another moment on the boat, avoiding the topic of last night. My skin felt hot. Itchy. Like it was too small to contain me.

I gestured toward the water. "I'm going to swim down to check the anchor."

"Why?" Sloan asked. "It looks good to me."

"Yeah." I scrubbed a hand over my head. "Peace of mind and all that." Though I knew it wasn't the anchor's position that was weighing on me.

She considered me a moment. "Okay. Thanks."

Sloan was in her cabin when I returned, the door closed. I

could hear her talking to someone on the phone, and I assumed she was working. Or hell, maybe she was talking to Edward. I groaned.

A plate of dinner waited for me on the counter. Was this what the rest of the trip would be like? Impersonal interactions. Silent days of sailing. Meals alone.

I sighed and showered quickly, carrying my dinner to my quarters when I was done. I did some reading and then tried to sleep, but the boat kept rocking and rolling. Finally, around midnight, I went on deck to check our position but stopped short when I spied Sloan on the sugar sloop. She turned and looked at me over her shoulder. Her skin was bare, apart from a narrow spaghetti strap.

"Sorry. I'll, uh—" I moved to return below deck, but the look of absolute wonder on her face stopped me in my tracks.

"Jackson," she whispered, her tone almost reverent. "Come here. You have to see this."

"See what?" I furrowed my brow and went to join her. The boat no longer rocked and rolled as much as earlier, and I was grateful.

"Look." She swirled her hand through the water, and it came alive, twinkling as if filled with tiny green stars.

The sight was beautiful, but I was more in awe of her than the bioluminescent bay, cool as it was. Her legs were curled up to her chest, her chin resting on her knees. Her feet were bare, and my eyes cataloged every birthmark, every freckle.

"Incredible, isn't it?" she asked.

I sank down beside her, mesmerized by the gentle way she moved her hand through the water. For the first time all day, a sense of peace and contentment settled over me. I loved sailing with Sloan, experiencing new things. But these quiet moments with her were what I longed for.

"Do you ever wish you could go back in time?" she

mused, her attention still on the water and the almost magical creatures who lived there.

All the fucking time.

But then I wondered if she was referring to last night. Treading carefully, I said, "Sometimes, sure. I would imagine most people have memories they'd like to relive."

"Mm." She gave a thoughtful hum. "If you could relive or redo any moment from your life, what would you pick?"

Relive?

Every moment with her. Good and bad, happy or sad, I would gladly take them all. But I didn't say that—couldn't. It wouldn't be appropriate for oh-so-many reasons.

"That's a big question," I finally said.

She laughed, lying back to look at the stars. Even surrounded by endless beauty, I couldn't look anywhere but at her.

"Why?" I asked. "What about you? Anything you'd redo? Any regrets?"

"Doesn't everyone?" She was clearly evading my question. Fair. I'd done the same thing only moments before.

I was afraid that all her regrets centered around her memories with me. That if she had the chance to go back, she'd not only change last night but everything between us that had come before it.

I'd caused her pain, and more than anything, I didn't want her to hurt anymore. If that meant erasing our past, I would've done it. All so she would've never experienced hurt.

But I was here to do a job, and getting involved with Sloan would put more than my future at risk. If my focus was compromised, her safety was too. I needed to put the past to rest once and for all.

"I'm sorry," I said, unwilling to let the words go unsaid any longer.

She kept her eyes on the sky, but she stiffened. "For what?"

"For contributing to your list of regrets." I placed my hand over hers, needing to comfort her even though it was far too late for that. "For disappointing you. For causing you pain."

She sighed, turning her hand so our fingers were interlocked. "I'm sorry too."

We were quiet a moment, drifting along. She yawned, and it was then I realized how tired she was.

"It's late." I stood, even though I didn't want the moment to end. "We should get some sleep. Tomorrow's going to be a long day."

We were hoping to set out early, and the Caicos Passage might be rough. We hadn't had any more issues with the fuel system or the motor, but the passage was a big undertaking.

I offered her my hand. She accepted it, and I pulled her up, slowly releasing her despite my reluctance to do so. The wind tossed her hair about, and I brushed some of the strands away from her face without thinking.

I dropped my hands and looked away. *Shit.* "Sorry. I…" I inhaled deeply and turned to go below deck. My willpower was clearly nonexistent when it came to Sloan.

"Jackson, wait." She grabbed my arm.

I stilled, my existence reduced to that one point of contact. Her hand on my skin. My name on her lips.

I couldn't keep doing this. It was going to break me— being so close to Sloan again after all this time. I didn't want to add to her list of regrets when it came to me.

I wanted to believe I was the best person to protect her, but I was so twisted up about Sloan, I was afraid of making a mistake. I was distracted. And distractions could be deadly in this line of work.

I rubbed my free hand over my face even as my heart felt

like it was being ripped to shreds. She'd only just come back into my life, and I was going to have to give her up again.

My chest tightened at the idea of leaving her. *Losing her* for good. To hell with the promotion, the cost was too high—both to her safety and to my heart.

"I—" I swallowed hard and turned to face her. "Sloan…" Her eyes sparkled in the darkness like a beacon guiding me home. She was my home. My heart. My everything.

CHAPTER FOURTEEN

Sloan

Jackson sighed, peering down at the deck. He squeezed the back of his neck. "When we get to Turks and Caicos, I'm going to ask Hudson to send a replacement."

I couldn't breathe. It was as if he'd punched the air from my lungs.

"What?" I gasped. "No." I shook my head. "You can't…" *You can't leave me. Not again.*

"I have to." He didn't even have the decency to look at me.

"Why? Because of what happened last night?" I asked, anger and fear surging through my veins.

"Yes, and because it's eating me up inside—knowing you're with someone else. Wanting you for myself." He placed his fist to his chest, pounding the space over his heart. "It's tearing me apart."

I gaped at him in disbelief.

"I don't want to leave, but you're still my principal. Hudson's client. It's my job to protect you, and I can't do that if… I just can't. I'm sorry."

"Can't or won't?" I demanded.

"Sloan," he growled. "Don't ask this of me. Don't ask me to betray all my principles."

"I thought we were friends." I crossed my arms over my chest, remembering how he'd suggested friendship only a few days ago.

He scoffed. "Oh, come on, Sloan. We could never be *just* friends."

I flung out my hands. "Then why'd you say it if you didn't mean it?"

"It wasn't—" He turned away, grabbing the railing and making his muscles pop. "It wasn't that I didn't mean it. I *do* want to be your friend. But I also want things a friend shouldn't."

"Like sex."

He turned to face me. "Yes, but not just sex. I don't want this to be like it was before. But that's—" He let out a frustrated groan. "That's just not possible."

Just not possible.

It felt too close to "inevitable." Which was exactly what he'd said when he'd ended things fourteen years ago.

Perhaps I should've told him that Edward and I had broken up, but I wanted to see what Jackson would say first. Were his objections confined to Edward, or was there something more?

"Why?" I asked.

"Why do you think?" Jackson asked. "Because of Edward, and my job, my sister, and..."

"Excuses," I spat the word, anger zinging through me like a bolt of lightning. And all the old pain came rushing back in. "Always with the excuses. If you really wanted to be with me, you'd find a way. You would've found a way back then. And you would find a way now. If you'd loved me, you wouldn't have let anything stand in our way.

"If you loved me." I took a deep breath, as if that would

help me find the air I needed. The strength. "Our breakup wouldn't have been inevitable, but *unthinkable.*" I hurled the words at him.

By the time I was done, my heart felt ragged, and yet nothing had changed. Not really. I'd wanted to believe it had, that *we* had. But deep down, we were still the same people.

Jackson was one of the bravest men I knew. If there was a situation that needed to be handled or a safety concern, he was your guy. But when it came to vulnerability and taking emotional risks, he couldn't be relied on. He couldn't be trusted.

"It's fine," I said, some of my anger shifting to hurt, exhaustion. "Honestly, I probably should've expected this." But that didn't take away the sting of my disappointment.

I turned and headed for the stairs. How could a night that had been so magical turn into…this?

"What is that supposed to mean?" he asked, his tone low, lethal.

I faced him, unable to let it go. If this was it, I wanted to speak my mind once and for all. "Don't you remember what you told me when you ended things? That our breakup was inevitable."

"I was trying to spare us both from more pain."

"That's bullshit, Jackson. And you know it."

"It wasn't bullshit. Surely you realize that we're from two different worlds." He gestured to the boat. The ocean. Whatever.

"What I see—" I leaned forward, venom in my words "—is that *this* is what you do. When things get tough, you bail." I lifted a shoulder. "I guess I should be grateful you had the decency to tell me you were leaving this time instead of letting me hear it from someone else."

Before I could even blink, he was standing in front of me,

our toes touching. "That's not fair. That's not fair, and you know it."

"Is it fair to interview for a job across the country without telling the woman who loves you? Is it fair to accept that job and plan to move, all without ever telling her—"

"I was going to tell you," he huffed.

"When?" I straightened, unwilling to back down. "*When* were you going to tell me, Jackson? When your apartment was packed? When you'd boarded the plane to move to LA?"

He threw his hands in the air. "What do you want from me, Sloan? You want me to apologize?" He stepped closer. "I did. And I will say it again and again and again, until you believe me. I'm sorry. Okay?" His expression was full of remorse, his voice softer when he said, "I'm sorry. What I did was wrong, but you also can't place all the blame on me."

I scoffed. He wasn't wrong. I had kept things from him, but... "I can't believe you're still hung up about my family."

"I'm not—" He shook his head. "I'm not 'hung up' about your family." His breath hitched. "I'm upset that you felt like you needed to keep that part of yourself from me. Especially after I trusted you."

"You are unbelievable. Do you even hear yourself?" I gnashed my teeth. "Yes. I omitted some things about my family. And maybe it was wrong to do so, but I had my reasons."

His expression was pained. "Did you honestly think I'd try to take advantage of your money?"

"No. Though, that had happened in the past." But with Jackson, it had never been a concern.

"With guys you dated?"

I nodded. "And even with people I thought were my friends."

He clenched his fists, but I knew his anger wasn't directed

at me. "I'm sorry. That's—" He blew out a breath. "Really shitty."

"Yeah. It was." I crossed my arms over my chest.

"So what, then?" he asked. "You thought I'd look at you differently?"

I hated to admit it, but… "Yeah. Kind of. I know how much you value hard work. I've seen the sacrifices you and your family have made. And I guess I was scared that—" I lifted a shoulder and peered out over the water. I took a deep breath. "I was scared you'd see me as some spoiled little rich girl."

"Sloan." He took my hand in his. "You could never be some spoiled little rich girl."

I appreciated his saying that, but the fact remained that it had changed things. "Maybe not, but when you found out I was a hotel heiress, it still affected how you saw me." When he opened his mouth to say something, I preempted him. "Don't try to deny it, Jackson."

He considered it a moment then said, "You're right. But you're also wrong."

I furrowed my brow. He was talking in riddles, and my emotions were already frayed. "What does that mean?"

He sighed, sinking down on one of the benches. "It means that it only confirmed what I already knew." He rubbed the back of his neck and glanced away briefly before meeting my eyes. "I'm not good enough for you."

"What?" I jerked my head back, his words piercing me. Gone was the anger, replaced by concern. Regret. "How could you think that? Did I—" I went over to him. "Did I ever make you feel that way?" I asked, feeling as if I might shatter.

"No, *hayati*." He held my hand. "I realize now that I had a chip on my shoulder. That I was putting these expectations on myself about what my mom needed me to be, what Greer needed me to be. What I thought you needed me to be."

His comment stopped me in his tracks, both with his vulnerability and the fact that he'd felt that way. It calmed my anger, making me realize that perhaps I'd misunderstood the situation. Misunderstood him.

I placed my hand over his heart, his skin warm beneath my palm. "I only ever needed you to be yourself."

"I know." He smiled at me, though it was tinged with a sadness that echoed in my heart. "I do. It's just... When I was offered the job at Hudson, I couldn't believe it—my luck was finally changing. I was still hoping the Navy would grant me an honorable discharge. And the job with Hudson felt like a way to redeem myself for getting expelled from the SEALs. A way to make my dad proud and honor his legacy. A way to build a better future for myself and my family."

I noticed that he hadn't mentioned a future for us. Because he saw our demise as "inevitable." I was trying to keep an open mind, but that word still haunted me.

I was determined to finally get all the answers to all my questions, even if it hurt.

"How did you find out about the job?" I'd always assumed he'd heard about Hudson from a friend or discovered them online.

He rubbed the back of his neck. "It's funny, really. One night I was working at the club, and a guy introduced himself and handed me his card. He was working his way up at the LA office, and he wanted to recruit me. I went to interview, and I was offered the job.

"The pay, the opportunity, everything was amazing. Except the fact that it was in LA, and you were in New York."

So, he *had* considered how this would impact our relationship. Maybe not. Either way, I needed to know. Not trusting myself to speak, I nodded, encouraging him to continue.

"You were about to graduate, and I knew you didn't want

to move back to LA. You'd made that..." He scoffed. "Very clear."

He was right. I hadn't wanted to move to LA. I still didn't want to move to LA. New York and now London felt more "me." And I craved the freedom that came with some space from my family. "But maybe if I'd known..."

"Sloan." He shook his head. "That's exactly what I was afraid of. And I didn't want you to change your plans for the future because of me."

I stood, unable to remain so close to him. I wasn't sure if I could handle the truth, but I needed it all the same. "Why?" I whispered, wondering why he'd been so intent on pushing me away when he'd always been my future.

"Because I knew from the things you'd told me about your family that you loved them, but you also felt like they'd held you back at times."

"I..." I swallowed. He'd gathered that from what I'd told him? I...I didn't know what to say.

"And I knew if I asked you to go with me, and you'd said yes, that eventually, you'd come to resent me."

In that moment, he sounded just like my brothers. Jackson had decided what he thought was best for me. He'd built up this entire narrative, and he'd convinced himself it was true, all without ever consulting me.

"You still should've given me the choice," I said.

"What's done is done." He stood. "And it doesn't really matter anymore. You've moved on." I could hear the pain in his voice. The longing. I felt it too.

Being so close to him but not being able to be with him. Wanting him but being scared to take that next step. It was ripping me apart like the wind shredding a sail. I could either continue to fight our past or I could accept it. I could let it go.

"It's over between Edward and me," I admitted, wanting to release Jackson of any guilt he'd felt on that score.

"Since when?" Jackson's gaze jerked to mine. "Because your file says…"

"I know what the file says, but it's wrong."

"It's…" He furrowed his brow. "Wrong. Why are you telling me this?" He groaned. "I can't…" He heaved in a breath. "As long as I'm your bodyguard, I can't be with you."

"Because it's against the rules?" I asked.

"Because it compromises my ability to keep you safe."

"But I only ever feel safe with you."

His shoulders relaxed. "You have no idea how much it means to me to hear you say that. I'd give my life to protect you."

I swallowed hard. "I know."

His statement wasn't something I took lightly—Jackson's willingness to lay down his life to protect me. I could've brushed his comment off as something he'd do for any client, but I sensed it wasn't because I was his client but because I was me.

Jackson had always made me feel safe. Made me feel like I could be who I was, not who everyone expected me to be.

I didn't want him to ask for a replacement. I didn't want him to leave, but I understood. I didn't want him to risk his job for me. His life for me. And he didn't want to jeopardize my safety.

But right now, I didn't want to think about that. We were all alone. There was no one else here. No one threatening me. No one watching to make sure he was following the rules. It was just the two of us.

The two of us on this great big ocean. Yes, he'd hurt me once. But he'd also made me feel. He'd made me understand what it was to claim something for myself. To express *my* wants and *my* needs.

I wanted to feel that way again so badly. I wanted to feel that sense of empowerment and strength. I wanted to feel… alive, even if only for one night.

I peered up at him, placing my hand on his chest. It was shaking. *I* was shaking. With want, with fear…I wasn't quite sure. "If you're going to leave anyway, why can't we have tonight?"

"Sloan," he groaned when I dragged my nails over his chest, his hands balled in tight fists at his sides. "Please."

"Please, what?" My voice was a whisper on the wind.

"I don't…" A muscle in his neck twitched. He bowed his head. "I…"

I smiled, gratified that I'd reduced this man to incoherent sentences. That he felt just as out of control as I did. I wanted to unravel him completely.

"There's no one else here. It's just the two of us."

"And what about tomorrow?"

I lifted a shoulder. I just wanted one night. One night of pleasure. One night to finally get closure. One night to say goodbye to the past and move on. "Tomorrow, we go back to being—" I gestured between us "—whatever we are."

He stepped closer. "And what's that?"

"I don't know." I finally met his eyes. "Friends?"

"Friends," he scoffed. "Right."

"Fine. Principal and executive protective agent. Captain and skipper," I teased.

"Sloan," he groaned. "I'm trying to do the right thing."

"I'm sick of doing the right thing," I blurted.

For the past fourteen years, I'd "done the right thing." I'd done everything that was expected of me and more. Taking over European and Asian operations. Focusing on my family's hotel empire. Dating Edward. I was done doing what was "right"; I wanted to do what was right for me.

"Besides," I asked, "who's going to know?"

He narrowed his eyes. "*I'd* know."

I scoffed, turning away and crossing my arms over my chest. Here I was, offering myself up to him, and he was going to cling to his honor? Part of me respected him like hell for it, even if it was inconvenient and annoying.

That said, Jackson was right. He might be an independent contractor, but it wouldn't reflect well on me to sleep with someone in my employ. Not to mention the fact that the idea of sleeping with him while I was paying him for executive protection services felt ick.

And then I had an idea. If he was going to be a stickler for the rules despite the fact that he was leaving anyway, I'd make this easy for him. For both of us.

"Jackson." I turned to him, unable to hold back my smile. "You're fired."

He gaped at me. "I—what?"

"You're fired," I said again, trying not to laugh. He hadn't caught on yet. "You're no longer my bodyguard, which means..."

"Which means we wouldn't be breaking the rules."

I bit back my smile. "Exactly."

He chuckled, shaking his head. "If only it were that simple."

"It could be. As long as you don't think you'll regret it," I said, thinking about his job. About how we'd spin this with Hudson.

He frowned. "Is that what you think?"

I lifted my shoulder, rolling my lip between my teeth.

"Sloan." He slid his hand through my hair, cupping my cheeks. "I could never regret loving you. You are my solace. My *da zra qarara*. When I'm with you, my heart is at ease."

My body relaxed at his words, even as my mind replayed them again, trying to search for answers. He nuzzled my nose with his, prolonging the torture. It felt as if everything in my life had led up to this moment. To him.

"Jackson," I pleaded. I didn't know if I wanted him to release me or never let go.

He swallowed hard, his Adam's apple bobbing. He looked ready to pounce, but then he sobered. "You sure this is what you want?"

It wasn't about what I wanted, but about what I could give. One night. A chance for closure, once and for all.

"Yes."

He closed his eyes. "Say it again."

I furrowed my brow. "What?"

He slowly opened his eyes once more. "My name. Say it again." He kissed the spot behind my ear.

"Jackson," I said on a sigh.

His eyes were locked on mine, scanning them as if seeking permission. Whatever he saw must have satisfied him, for in the next moment, he brushed his lips against mine. Gentle. Reverent. Tentative.

Even so, it was a claiming. This man dominated me like he always had.

I whimpered at the feel of his hands on me. It was like coming home. It was…everything.

I tugged at his shorts. I didn't care that we were out in the open. That anyone could've seen us if they'd happened to sail by, which I doubted. We were well and truly alone.

He wore a glazed expression. "God, look at you." He cupped me, bending forward to nip at my breasts through the thin material of my silk tank. I gasped at his touch, at the way he made me feel. In his arms, I came alive.

"You are so fucking incredible," he rasped, the words sending butterflies skittering through me.

Jackson looked at me as if I was the answer to all his

prayers. The object of all his desires. He made me feel wanted, seen, cherished.

My body was on fire from his touch. All rational thought gone.

"What do you want?" he asked.

"I want…" I swallowed hard. There were so many things I wanted. "You."

It was the first time I'd claimed something for myself in years, and it felt good.

He dragged his thumb down my lips. "God, Sloan," he groaned.

I parted my lips, and he pushed his finger inside my mouth. Filling me. Reminding me of just how good he could make me feel.

I sucked, swirling my tongue around his thumb. Licking the salt from his finger like I wanted to lick the come from his cock. My legs quivered, desire pooling in my core.

He lifted me so my legs were wrapped around his waist. Oh god…his cock. It was hard and insistent, and I wanted him inside me now.

"Fuck, I missed you." He buried his face in my neck, and a sense of rightness washed over me.

His familiar smell. The comfort of being in his arms. The words he said were exactly what I'd needed to hear.

Closure. I reminded myself. But it was difficult to remember my end goal when he set me down on the bench, his gaze tender as he kneeled before me. His eyes scanning me as if to memorize every freckle, every birthmark, every *everything*.

He kissed me, savoring me as if I were the most decadent treat. There was no rush. Nothing was hurried about his movements. He was just as lost to this moment as I was.

"Let me taste you," he said, kissing his way up my legs. He

peeled off my silk sleep shorts. Then he wrapped his hands around my thighs, hauling me toward him.

I swallowed hard and pushed away my fears. It had been a long time since I'd had a man go down on me. And none of them had ever compared to Jackson. He was always so... intense. And the filthy words he said, the way...

He pressed a kiss to my inner thigh, his lips soft. My skin was incredibly sensitive to his touch, and I nearly jolted off the bench.

"Nervous?" he asked, peering up at me from between my thighs.

I felt like a virgin again. With the hottest guy I'd ever seen nestled between my legs. About to cross a line we shouldn't.

"Stay here." Jackson linked his fingers with mine. "With me."

I forced myself to focus on the present even as it blended with the past. Honestly, when he nuzzled my clit, he made it difficult to think about anything else. I gripped the edge of the seat, the boat rocking gently as he licked and sucked and teased me, his eyes never leaving mine.

When my legs started to shake, my pleasure churning inside me like the powerful waves in the Gulf Stream, he rasped, "That's it, *hayati*."

He smoothed his hand over my thigh, before reaching around and pulling me even closer to his mouth. Positioning me exactly how he wanted. I felt as if my skin couldn't contain me. As if my body was coming apart in the best possible way.

"Oh god. Oh yes," I panted.

Pleasure. So much pleasure.

It was as if my body had lain dormant for years. Suddenly —thanks to Jackson—everything was brighter, clearer.

God, I'd missed this. Missed feeling like this.

On a boat beneath the stars with Jackson's mouth on me, my toes curled. I was flying. I was...free.

CHAPTER FIFTEEN

Sloan

I fell back against the bench, trying to catch my breath. My heart was racing, and Jackson kissed me with a satisfied grin.

"That's my girl."

In that moment, I was twenty-two all over again. And I would've given him anything and everything, if only he'd asked. But he'd never given me the choice.

This was my chance. I was seizing what I wanted and rewriting our ending.

He tugged off my shirt, tossing it below deck along with my shorts. "Fuck," he rasped. "Fuck, you're gorgeous when you come."

I wanted to see him come. I wanted to make him feel as wild and out of control as I felt.

I grabbed the hem of his shirt, and he yanked it over his head in one fluid motion. He smirked then pushed down his shorts, and his cock bobbed. Thick. Hard. Wanting.

My breath caught in my throat. *He* was stunning. So much ink. So much raw power.

He sat on the bench across from mine. "You just going to

sit there and watch, baby girl?" he taunted, pumping his cock. "Or are you going to ride my cock?"

I shuddered at the erotic sight. At his filthy words. "Why can't I do both?"

He smirked. "You can. We will. Tonight is ours, and I fully intend to make the most of it."

I stood and stepped closer. He looked at me like a predator watched its prey. Hungry. Deadly. Ready to pounce.

I placed my hands on his shoulders, preparing to straddle him.

"Shit." He squeezed his eyes shut. "I didn't bring any condoms."

"Good thing I came prepared." I ducked into the galley to get one of the intimacy kits that came standard in all the Huxley hotel rooms. I'd snagged it at the last minute from the Huxley Grand Miami.

The kits had been Jasper's idea. He was always so focused on the guest experience, and he was damn good at it. The kit contained a few condoms and some lube, and I'd never been more grateful for it.

"Mm." Jackson grabbed me by the waist, the heat of his hands branding my skin. He hauled me onto his lap for a searing kiss. "I knew I lo—iked you for a reason."

"Oh, is that the only reason?" I teased, glossing over the fact that he'd almost said "love." He didn't love me. He didn't *know* me. Not after all these years apart.

"You're also beautiful." He kissed the skin behind my ear. "Smart." He punctuated each statement with a kiss. "Sexy. Considerate. Fiercely independent. Stubborn—"

I removed the condom from the package. "Okay. I think I get the point."

He chuckled, but the sound came out strangled when I sheathed his hard cock.

"You're also resilient." Another kiss. "And resourceful."

"You sure have a lot to say," I teased.

"Fourteen years' worth of things to say, yes," he said. I glanced away, his expression too intense. I couldn't...

"Hey." His tone was gentle as he cupped my cheek, bringing my gaze back to him. "If you changed your mind, and you don't want this—" The words turned strangled as I lined him up with my core.

I kissed him—hard. "I want this."

I just didn't want to forget what *this* was. One night of wild sex. Nothing more. It couldn't be.

He lived in LA, and my life was in London. And when we arrived at Turks and Caicos, he'd ask for a replacement. He'd no longer be my bodyguard. But I didn't want to think about that right now—any of it.

He hissed as I sank down on him. I reveled in the sensation of fullness. Completeness.

"Fuck." He grunted. "You feel so good."

He threaded his fingers through my hair until he was cupping my nape. Our noses touching. Eyes locked.

He kissed me, his gentle touch at odds with his punishing thrusts.

"Fuck," he rasped, cupping my breasts. "These tits." He pushed them together, teasing one then the other with his mouth. Biting them.

It sent jolts of pleasure straight to my already overheated core. Not to be outdone, I raked my nails down his chest in the way that had always driven him wild. It was like performing the steps to a dance you already knew by heart. It was beautiful and breathtaking, even as we tried to push each other's limits.

In this instance, reality was even better than my memories.

He reached down, rubbing my clit with his thumb, his

eyes intent on mine. "You feel…" He shuddered. "God, Sloan. Nothing compares to this. With you."

"Jackson." I gasped his name when he pinched my clit, making me see stars. Even after all this time, he still knew my body best. "Oh fuck. Oh…"

"Yes." His thrusts were harder. Less coordinated. "That's it. Come for me again, *hayati*."

Oh god, yes. I shivered from his words. From the way he touched me with both reverence and barely restrained passion.

He pulled me closer. As close as possible. Our foreheads were touching. Our bodies were connected in the most intimate and primal of ways, and suddenly everything felt like too much.

My chest was tight, and I needed space. I needed… I stood and turned, putting my back to him. If he noticed, he didn't say anything.

He placed his hands on my hips, guiding me as I sank back down on him. I loved the feel of his large, callused hands roaming over my skin. I loved the strength of his body and the feeling of safety I got from being in his arms.

"That's it," he rasped against the shell of my ear as I began to move once more. "Take charge."

He palmed my breast with one hand while using the other to tease my clit.

"Tell me what you need. What you desire." His voice was low in my ear, and it felt as if everything was within my grasp.

I was a billionaire. I could buy whatever I wanted. And yet, the thing I'd wanted most—*him*—had always been out of reach.

He pinched my nipple, and I had to bite back my cry of ecstasy. His dark chuckle had my orgasm rising to the surface once more. My pleasure built with every powerful stroke.

This was what I needed. Not sweet nothings or expensive gifts. Not lavish dinners or someone who was perfect on paper. I needed someone raw and real. I needed Jackson.

I needed him to set a relentless pace until he pushed me over the edge into oblivion. Until I forgot about the past or the future. Until my entire existence boiled down to where our bodies connected and nothing else.

"I've got you." He slid a hand down my throat, collaring me. I was completely at his mercy and under his control.

He guided me so our bodies were pressed together. Until the weight of his hand rested over my heart. And for that moment, I allowed myself to relax in his hold, to trust that Jackson would keep me safe.

"That's it," he said, coaxing my orgasm from my willing body. "Shout my name to the stars while I fill you with my come."

I spasmed around his cock right before he increased his pace, losing control of his movements as he unleashed himself.

I leaned my head back against his shoulder, trying to catch my breath as I stared at the stars as if for guidance. Jackson's chest was warm against my back. He held me, nuzzling my neck as he whispered words of praise. Tears formed on my lashes. *So much for keeping my emotions out of it.*

Now that some of my earlier desire had cooled, the enormity of what I'd just done came crashing over me. I shivered.

"Come on." Jackson gave me a squeeze. "Let's go to bed."

He followed me down the stairs to my cabin, his hands on my hips as we made our way to my bed. I lay beside him, and he pulled me into his arms. It felt so natural, yet strange all at the same time. A few weeks ago, the idea of spending a night with Jackson would have been inconceivable. And yet...here we were.

"What's this one for?" I asked, tracing a line of text along Jackson's ribs. It had the words *"Acta non verba"* in a hand-written font.

"My dad used to say that phrase a lot. It means actions, not words."

I hummed. "You are definitely a man of action."

He arched his hips as if to emphasize my statement, and I laughed. "Jackson." I slapped his chest playfully. "That's not what I meant."

"Mm." He rolled so that he was leaning over me, his cock already hard against my thigh. "You sure?"

"Is this his handwriting?" I traced my fingernail along the line of his ribs, and he let out a shaky breath. I smirked, and he fell back on the bed.

"Yeah. When we were helping my mom move last year, I found some of his old letters."

"How is your mom?" I asked. I'd tried to check on her more regularly since the stroke.

"She's good. Yeah." He seemed distant, but maybe he was just lost in thought.

"Hey," I said, caressing his jaw. I couldn't seem to stop touching him. "You okay?"

"Yeah. Yeah. I'm good." He tucked one arm behind his head, keeping the other wrapped around me. "I just worry about her, you know?"

"I get it. I worry about her too, and she's not even my mom."

"You say that, but I know she thinks of you as her honorary daughter."

I smiled. "She's always made me feel like part of the family."

"You are part of the family. Greer thinks of you as a sister.

And you've probably spent more time with my family than I have."

"You could do something about that, you know," I said, half teasing, half serious. I knew Belinda would love to spend more time with Jackson. Greer as well.

"I've just been so busy, especially since I was assigned to the Crawford residence."

"The Crawford residence," I chortled. "It sounds so formal."

"Hey." He tweaked my nipple, and I hissed as my core flooded with heat. "The safety of our clients is serious business."

"I know, and I appreciate your dedication. I'm sure it isn't easy to protect someone like Nate."

Jackson nodded. "Protecting a celebrity definitely has its challenges."

"I'm sure every client presents a challenge of some sort."

"Yeah. I recently had this assignment where the client was super demanding. And then she had the gall to fire me. *Me.*"

I laughed, though I worried about the consequences for Jackson, even if I'd been joking about "firing" him. "You know why I fired you."

He took my hand in his, bringing it to his mouth for a kiss. "I do. And I don't regret it."

"I hope it won't get you into too much trouble at work," I said. I would've asked him to stay till the end of the trip, but I didn't think he had that kind of vacation time. And even if he did, could he afford to take so much time off? Would he even want to?

It was probably for the best. One night was safer. One night wouldn't muddle the situation or my heart.

"We'll find a way to spin the situation so it won't reflect adversely on you," I said.

"Thanks," he said, his expression darkening. "But what's done is done."

"Maybe you should get that as your next tattoo," I teased, noticing it wasn't the first time he'd said it. And both times, he'd sounded so...resigned. Downtrodden. I hated to think that I was responsible for it.

I hated to think that our choices might impact his career. I knew how much it had cost him to be discharged from the SEALs. I didn't want anything to happen to his position at Hudson because of me.

I propped my head up with my hand. "You said you were hoping to spend more time with your family after our trip. What will you do next? After this assignment, where are you supposed to go?"

He seemed to hesitate, then said, "I'm not sure yet. And you? Will you go back to London?"

I sighed, not wanting to imagine being anywhere but here. With him. "That depends."

"On..." he prompted after I said nothing more. He traced my hip, smoothing his hand over my skin.

"On whether Hudson is able to find and apprehend the source of the threats."

"We will find them," he said in a menacing tone that made me confident they would.

"I hope so," I said. "Otherwise, I'm afraid to see what my brothers will try to do."

Jackson frowned, brushing my hair over my shoulder. "What does that mean?"

"They can be very protective," I said. "I love that they care about me, but sometimes it feels suffocating."

"Is that why you chose to live in London even though everyone else is in LA?"

I chewed on my bottom lip. "That's certainly part of it."

"And the other part?"

179

I sighed. "The other part was that I needed a change. When I decided to move there, my grandparents had just died, and we'd…"

He tilted his head back in understanding. "Ah. Yeah." He cleared his throat, tucking my hair behind my ear. "I am sorry, Sloan. For the way everything went down. For the things I said."

I captured his hand and drew his palm to my mouth for a kiss, appreciating his apology more than he could ever know. Even so, I didn't want to dwell on it. Not now, when I was still naked in his arms and feeling so vulnerable.

"Do you spend all your time in London?" he asked.

"I travel around to various locations, especially in Europe and Asia. But I consider London my home." I didn't want to talk about myself or my life in London. I wanted to hear about him. What he'd been up to the past fourteen years. What had inspired his tattoos. "This is new." I circled the sextant tattooed on his chest.

The design was simple yet so well rendered it almost looked 3-D. It was one of my favorite new additions to his ink, but maybe that was because it was nautical. And it was part of a larger piece of artwork with a horizon and…

He covered me. "I'll show you something else that's new." He rocked into me, turning my laughter into a moan of pleasure.

CHAPTER SIXTEEN

Jackson

I woke to the scent of sea salt and wild roses. I smiled into Sloan's neck. Heaven. That's what this was.

When my alarm went off, I tried to silence it, only to realize it was Sloan's and I was still in her cabin. In her bed. It felt like I was in a dream. As if we existed in this sacred space between the past and something I'd only ever imagined. I didn't want to let it go. I didn't want to let her go. Not now and not ever.

She'd said it was one night, but last night had only solidified what I already knew. I loved Sloan, and this trip was a gift. A chance to reconnect and heal after all these years apart. I was determined to use it as a springboard to a second chance.

Even now, in the cold morning light, I knew that, given the chance again, I'd choose Sloan over the promotion any day. Years ago, I'd prioritized my career, but it was what I'd needed at the time. I'd needed to prove myself. To redeem myself. Now, I knew the only thing I needed was her.

The love I felt for her overpowered everything, and I realized that trying to fight it had been as futile as trying to outrun a hurricane. I'd have to figure out what this meant for my place at Hudson, for my career. But I tried to have faith that it would all work out.

We'd also have to decide how to navigate the situation with my sister. Sloan's family could be another potential obstacle. But I was getting ahead of myself. First, I had to make Sloan see that we belonged together.

Sloan turned off the alarm and moved as if to get up. I groaned and pulled her closer. "Don't go."

Sloan laughed, oblivious to the more serious turn my thoughts had taken. "C'mon, sleepyhead. We want to get an early start if we're going to make it to Turks and Caicos tonight."

Fuck Turks and Caicos.

"Or..." I flipped her onto her back, not ready to give this up. To give her up. "We could just stay here."

"Jackson." She smiled up at me, cupping my cheek. Gone was the sadness from last night, the heaviness of whatever emotions she'd been feeling. "We can't stay here. We're running low on food that isn't canned beans."

"You'd be surprised how creative I can get." I waggled my brows.

She patted my cheek. "Oh, I know. But it's time to get a move on. The staff at Turks and Caicos are expecting us, and I don't want to have to navigate the channel at night. Do you?"

I groaned, flopping over onto my back and dropping my arm over my forehead. "You're right."

Sloan slipped out from beneath me. I grabbed her and hauled her back onto the mattress. "Surely—" I kissed her collarbone "—we have time—" I pushed her down and kissed the side of her breast "—for me to make you come—" a peck on her stomach "—first."

I traced a finger over her breasts, teasing her nipples

without actually touching them. She sighed, arching her back, encouraging me to continue even as she said, "It was only supposed to be one night."

"Yeah," I said in a teasing tone. "It was, but then you fell asleep on me."

And I realized that I'm still in love with you.

She laughed. "After two rounds, can you blame me?"

"No." I nuzzled her. "But I had plans for you. I think we could accommodate a slightly later departure time. Don't you, Captain?" I teased, smoothing my hand up and down her thigh.

Her eyes darkened. "I suppose it could be arranged, Skipper," she said with mock seriousness.

I scoffed, bracing myself above her. "Skipper? I'm definitely a first mate."

"Mm," she hummed, her eyes hooded as I slipped my hand between her legs. She was already slick with desire. "We'll see."

I knew she was teasing, but it only made me more determined to prove how indispensable I was. Not just on the boat, but in her life. I'd made the mistake of letting Sloan go once, and I vowed not to let it happen again.

THE SUN DIPPED LOWER IN THE SKY, AND I EYED ITS POSITION nervously as we waited at the entrance to the channel markers. The approach to Providenciales, Turks and Caicos, bristled with coral reefs that would shred the hull. The channel was marked—supposedly. It was rather poorly done, with scattered green and red markers that looked like the worst obstacle course ever.

I'd spent the day thinking about my decisions and my future, and I didn't regret any of it. Yes, I'd worked hard for that promotion. And yes, it was disappointing to give it up after all my efforts. But I wasn't as disappointed as I would've expected. If anything, I knew I'd gained so much more than I'd lost.

Did I hate that my decisions would have a negative impact on a friend? Of course. But I wasn't naïve enough to think that I was irreplaceable. They would find someone else to take over the New York office. And I would find another job.

This wasn't like when I'd been discharged from the SEALs. This was my choice, and I had connections, opportunities. I'd built a solid reputation in the private security industry. I had a network that I could lean on to find another job in this field or another.

Sloan scanned the water. "I sure hope our pilot arrives soon."

We'd called ahead for the free piloting service, but it was getting late with still no sign of our pilot. Sloan was tired. Hell, I was tired. Neither of us had gotten enough sleep, and then we'd had a late start across the Caicos Passage, thanks to me.

But we'd made it. And I couldn't wait to fall into bed with her. A real bed, with a real bathroom—both built for someone my size. Where I wouldn't have to crouch to wash myself with a wand better sized for a kitchen sink.

I hugged Sloan to my side, full of love and pride for this amazing woman. I kissed the top of her head, unable to resist touching her. Despite what she'd said, one night wasn't enough. One lifetime wouldn't be enough. But if that was all we had, then I was going to make the most of it.

She stepped out of my hold as a boat neared. "Hopefully that's the pilot." She waved, and he came alongside us.

"And Jackson?" she said before he was in earshot.

"Yeah?"

"You know that when hotel staff is present, we have to maintain a professional distance, right? Until things are settled with Hudson, giving people the wrong impression wouldn't be good for either of us."

"Of course," I said, trying not to take it personally.

She was right. I knew she was right. But it stung.

The pilot informed us he'd been delayed because of engine trouble. He instructed us to follow him without deviating.

Sloan steered the *Athena* with calm precision, focused intensely on the task at hand. He certainly knew the channel better than we did. Even if he was weaving in and out of the channel markers, departing from the designated path.

Sloan and I shared a concerned look, but she pressed on. Committed to getting us safely to our destination. I was in awe of her—the way she handled every situation with confidence and ease. She wasn't afraid to take charge, even when others might hesitate.

I trusted her to keep us safe. I trusted her with my life, and that wasn't something I gave freely.

Sure, I'd trusted my fellow SEALs. I'd found that kind of family and trust with some of my coworkers at Hudson. It was part of the reason why I'd be sad to leave the company. But to have found that kind of respect and trust in a partner, in the woman I loved...well, I knew it was even more rare.

I hauled our luggage on deck, where a driver from the Huxley Grand was already waiting. Sloan locked up, and we were soon on our way. I itched to cover Sloan's hand with mine, but I restrained myself. As far as everyone else was concerned, she was still my principal, and I was supposed to be protecting her. And I would—with my life.

But I needed to sort out the situation with Hudson. I

needed to find a way to convince Sloan to give me another chance.

Her gaze was on the scenery as we trundled down the bumpy roads. My hand was on the bench seat between us, reaching out like a vine seeking the sun. I grazed her pinkie, but she soon pulled away, typing something on her phone.

I clenched my teeth and glanced out the window. I hated this already.

Our driver was quiet, speaking only when Sloan asked him questions about the island. About the local cuisine. He grew more and more animated when she asked him about his granddaughter.

As we pulled up to the Huxley Grand, I sensed a shift in her. A straightening of her shoulders as she withdrew even more and became the billionaire SVP she was.

On the *Athena*, out in the middle of the ocean, it was easy to forget. To me, she'd always been just Sloan. Smart. Beautiful. Kind.

But I had to remember she was even more than that. She held herself personally responsible for the success of her family's hotel company. For the lives of all her employees. And damn if that didn't make me admire her even more.

It was how I'd felt when I was a SEAL and now at Hudson. Sure, maybe the stakes weren't life or death at Huxley, but that didn't mean they weren't still important.

The Huxley Grand Turks and Caicos was different from some of the other properties I'd visited. Smaller but just as opulent as you'd expect from the luxury hotel brand. The manager greeted us, and we were whisked away by a golf cart to our private villa. It was getting dark, but what I could see of the view was gorgeous.

We pulled up to our villa, and I went in to inspect it while Sloan spoke with the manager. I slowed when I reached the living room. It was occupied.

"Is that the champagne?" the man asked in a posh English accent, and I frowned.

I recognized Edward from Sloan's file. What the fuck was *he* doing here?

"You need to leave." I crossed my arms over my chest, planting my heels.

He remained seated, a bored expression on his face. "So… not the champagne, then."

"You are not authorized to be here." I was furious that security hadn't thought to inform me of our unexpected—and unwanted—visitor.

He finally stood, smoothing his hands down his expensive designer slacks. "How dare you speak to me with such impertinence. I could have you sacked."

Fucking wanker.

"Jackson," Sloan called. "Is everything o— Oh!" Sloan stopped short, quickly schooling her shocked expression into something more neutral. "Edward, what are you doing here?"

"Darling," he crooned, and it fucking grated on my nerves.

He took a step forward, and I shifted, putting myself between him and Sloan. If he wanted her, he'd have to go through me.

"Get out of my way," he sneered.

My entire body was tense, my muscles coiled tight and itching for a fight. I didn't know what had happened with Edward and Sloan, but she'd told me it was over between them. There was no reason why he should be here.

I glared at him, hoping my intent was clear—touch her and die.

"Jackson," Sloan said softly, placing her hand on my shoulder as she stepped around me. "It's okay."

I shook my head, my expression solemn. He was a security risk.

187

"Edward would never hurt me."

"Exactly," Edward said, swooping in to place his arm around her. I glared at his hand on her as if my gaze alone would burn his skin. "This is all just a big misunderstanding."

Sloan silently pleaded with me—to let it go? To stay quiet about what we'd done? The fuck if I knew.

Was this what she'd meant when she'd said it was over between them? Over but not actually finished? Because clearly, Edward was under the impression they were still together. And the security staff had allowed him on the premises without consulting me first.

"Can I speak to you in private?" I asked Sloan.

"Just—" Sloan smiled brightly at Edward "—give me a second."

We went over to the kitchen, where I kept my eyes on Edward and my voice low. "What's he doing here?"

"I don't know." Sloan dragged a hand down her face. "If you'd given me a chance to talk to him, maybe I could've found out."

"It's too risky."

I had a bad feeling about the situation. About *him.*

"Jackson." Sloan rolled her eyes. "You truly believe *he's*—" she gestured toward Edward "—a security threat?"

"You don't?" I pinched the bridge of my nose. "You've been receiving threats. You said it was over with Edward, but he's here now. Unless—" A darker thought occurred to me. "Unless it isn't over between the two of you."

My stomach bottomed out at the idea. But Sloan wouldn't do that, right?

"We broke up before I left for Miami."

That was a relief, even if I was still alarmed by Edward's presence.

"When?" I asked, needing to know how recently.

"In the days before we left."

Well, shit.

"Who broke up with whom?" I told myself it was for the security assessment, but I found myself wishing I'd asked sooner for my own personal sanity.

I prayed that Sloan had broken up with Edward and not vice versa. I hoped I wasn't a fucking rebound. My stomach curdled at the idea.

"I broke up with him."

My brain was a tangled web as I tried to keep the security assessment separate from my feelings for Sloan. My gut told me to get rid of him, but I wondered if it was actually my heart that was speaking.

I was relieved that she'd been the one to end the relationship, but it stung that she'd broken up with him only a few days before jumping into bed with me. *And this is yet another reason why it's a bad idea to sleep with the principal.*

I pushed all those thoughts aside. Regardless of my reasons, I wanted him gone. *Now.*

"He needs to go."

"Jackson," she sighed. "Be reasonable."

"I am being reasonable. We don't know his motives. We don't know why he's here. Hell, for all we know, he could be behind the threats."

Sloan leveled me with a flat look. "He's not."

"Until we find the culprit, we can't rule anyone out."

"By that logic, you could be the culprit," she hissed. "Maybe you sent me the threatening notes so I'd have to hire you as a bodyguard. Maybe you set this all up."

"Now you're just being ridiculous."

She leaned forward. "And so are you."

She didn't understand. She hadn't spent the last fourteen years working in private security. Seeing the types of wackos our clients dealt with. I wasn't taking any risks.

I leaned in. "Sloan," I said, my voice laced with a threat. "Get rid of him, or I will."

Perhaps I was being unreasonable and heavy-handed, but I wanted him gone.

"I will handle it," she said through gritted teeth. "But Edward came all this way for a reason. I'm not just going to throw him out without letting him say whatever he came to say."

God, I hated how feral this woman made me. Deep down, I knew I couldn't stop this conversation from happening. But I didn't like it.

I leaned in. "I'm not leaving you alone with him."

She scoffed. "Possessive much?" Though she couldn't hide the desire in her eyes.

My blood boiled with lust and frustration. Hell yes, I was possessive. But this wasn't about what I wanted. It was about Sloan. "Whether you realize it or not, your safety is my priority. And you have no idea why he's here. He could be seeking reconciliation or revenge."

"Fine," she huffed. "But stay here."

I hadn't waited this long, only to lose her once more. This was my shot. It wasn't a second chance; it was my last chance with Sloan—and I sure as shit wasn't going to let Edward or anyone else screw it up.

CHAPTER SEVENTEEN

Sloan

I took a breath and turned to face Edward. He'd made himself comfortable in my absence, helping himself to a drink and the view.

I'd ended a long-term relationship over the phone, and I could understand why Edward might want closure. But I was still surprised he'd traveled all this way to try to get it. At least, I hoped that was the only reason he was here.

"Is everything okay?" Concern tinged his features, and it seemed genuine.

I nodded. "It's fine."

"Do you want a drink?" he asked, and I tried not to balk at the fact that he'd invaded my space and was acting like he owned the place. *Typical.* "I ordered champagne, but it hasn't arrived yet."

I wanted a shower. I didn't want champagne, and I definitely didn't want to have an uncomfortable conversation with my ex in front of Jackson.

"What are you doing here?" I cringed when the words came out harsher than I'd intended.

His attention darted to the kitchen, where Jackson sat, likely watching us. God, talk about awkward.

I was still on edge from my conversation with Jackson. Overheated, annoyed, and turned on by his display of possessiveness.

Edward set down his drink and took my hands in his. "I missed you, and I didn't like how we left things the other night," he told me in a calm tone.

God, that felt like a lifetime ago. So much had changed for me in such a short span of time. I thought I'd made myself clear, but Edward was acting as if we'd had a disagreement, not broken up.

He leaned in as if to kiss me and then pulled back, his lip curled upward. Whether it was in a smile or out of distaste, I could never be sure. "Have you eaten yet? Why don't you take a shower while I pour us both a fresh drink, and then we can talk over a nice meal."

I wanted to laugh at the differences between Edward and Jackson. Jackson had just spent a week with me on a boat, both of us smelling of salt and sweat. And he couldn't keep his hands off me. He would've never let my appearance or anything else keep him away from me.

"Sloan?" Edward said.

I snapped my attention to him. "What was that?"

"I said you look tired."

I slid a hand through my hair, but it caught. It was tangled from the wind. My body was caked in salt water and sunscreen. I desperately wanted a long soak in a hot bath. A quiet, peaceful evening alone to collect my thoughts after the whirlwind of the past twenty-four hours.

"I *am* tired," I admitted. Jackson had been ravenous last night, and I felt well and truly fucked.

"What's with the guard dog?" Edward gestured toward the kitchen.

Guard dog? How demeaning. My blood boiled.

"I told you my family insisted that I hire a bodyguard. And don't call him a guard dog. He has a name." I tried not to think of Jackson in there, possibly listening to what was going on in here. This entire situation felt like a ticking time bomb ready to explode.

"Wait..." Edward paused. *"That* guy?" He peered toward the kitchen and frowned. "I thought he was Huxley Grand security."

"No. He's my executive protection agent."

"He's—" Edward spluttered. "The one you've been sailing with? *Alone?"*

I nearly laughed. "Yes. That's Jackson."

"Bollocks." He downed the rest of his drink then poured another. I was supposed to be getting rid of Edward, not encouraging him to stay. Not that I had. But he didn't seem to be taking the hint.

"What are you doing here?" I asked again, more than ready to get to the point so I could move on with my evening.

Edward stepped closer. "This past week—without you— made me realize just how important you are to me."

Our time apart had made me realize the opposite.

"I know I haven't always made our relationship a priority. But that's going to change—starting now."

"Edward, I—" I held out my hand as if to stop him or whatever he was going to say.

Edward knelt to the floor, and all the words I was going to say flew from my brain. I rolled my lips between my teeth, resisting the urge to see what Jackson was doing. If he was watching. Listening.

"I promise to spend every day showing you how much you mean to me." Edward opened a small antique box with a unique latch to reveal an enormous diamond ring that had to be worth a fortune.

I blinked a few times, wishing I could freeze time.

"I-I—" I didn't even know what to say. This was so completely unexpected. First, the impromptu visit and, now, the proposal. "I…can't," I finally said.

He frowned. "I don't understand."

I gently tugged on his hand, wishing he would stand the hell up. Wishing I could erase the past twenty minutes of my life. "I'm sorry, but I can't marry you."

"But we're so well suited. Who else would understand the commitments and duties we have—to our families, our companies. I need you, Sloan."

Not *I love you*, but *I need you*. It wasn't the same. It wasn't enough.

"That's just it." I wondered how we could be so very far apart in our opinion of what was best for our future. A week on my boat, with the wind in my hair and Jackson at my side, had clarified some things for me. "I don't want to marry someone because we're well suited. If I'm going to marry," I said, "it will be for love."

Out of everything Edward had said or promised this evening, he'd never once uttered that word—love. And rarely ever in the past.

"You're tired," he said with an indulgent smile that felt almost patronizing. "And I sprung this on you. You should rest. We can revisit this conversation in the morning."

"In the morning?" I frowned.

"Yes." He stepped closer. "I took off the week to be here with you."

Warning bells signaled in my head. Maybe it was Jackson's concern or my exhaustion, but I found myself asking, "How did you know I'd be here? How did you know I was staying for a week?"

He furrowed his brow. "I thought you'd be happy to see me."

"I—" I couldn't find it in me to lie. "I'm certainly surprised."

"If you must know, I asked your assistant Holly for your itinerary. She thought it was incredibly romantic that I was coming to surprise you."

He sounded miffed. Like he'd expected me to fall at his feet for his grand gesture. Yet it felt hollow. Like he was going through the motions. I didn't understand why.

Maybe I was misreading the situation. My mind and my heart were chaotic after everything that had happened with Jackson and now Edward.

"It's Halle," I said, wishing I'd told more people about the breakup, especially those closest to me. Maybe then, this whole situation could've been avoided.

"Same difference," he said, waving a hand through the air.

"Edward—"

He placed his finger on my lips as if to silence me. "Just... give me a chance. Give *us* a chance."

When I looked at Edward, I felt nothing. No sadness or regret. Nothing, really. Sure, we were compatible. But I wanted love. Devotion. Passion.

Everything you have with Jackson.

I sighed. My answer wasn't going to change, but I was too exhausted to argue at this point. And then it dawned on me —Edward had probably been so confident I'd accept his proposal. He likely didn't have a Plan B. Which meant, he was expecting to stay here.

Fuck.

No fucking way. "I'll call reception and have them find you a room for the night."

I turned my back to him and picked up the villa phone without waiting for a response from Edward. The front desk answered immediately. "Ms. Mackenzie. How may I be of assistance?"

"I have a guest who will be needing another room."

"Of course. When will they be arriving?"

"They're already here. We'll need the room for tonight. As soon as possible. Whatever you have available." I didn't care how much it cost—no way in hell was I sharing this villa with Jackson and Edward.

I could hear the sound of a keyboard in the background and then, "I'm sorry, ma'am. We are at full occupancy. It's peak season, and with the eclipse, the island has been booked for months since we have 99 percent totality."

I squeezed my eyes shut. *Right. The eclipse.*

"Even the ones you typically hold back?"

There was a brief silence, and then she said, "Unfortunately, yes. The governor decided to come to the island at the last minute, and he was offered the last of the rooms for himself and his staff."

I sighed. I was thrilled the hotel had one hundred percent occupancy, but the timing couldn't have been worse. "Can you check around with the other local hotels?"

"I can," she hedged. "But to be honest, I don't expect much luck. Give me a little bit. I'll do my best."

"Thank you. That's all I ask."

Edward came up behind me, wrapping his arms around my waist. I yelped and moved out of his hold.

"Sloan?" Jackson appeared in the doorway. My heart faltered at the sight of him—handsome, imposing, and protective. I might not appreciate his bossy attitude, but I was grateful for his presence.

He glanced between Edward and me. "Everything okay?"

I nodded. "I'm working on accommodations for Edward. Why don't you order some room service?"

"You want anything?" he asked, his eyes roaming me. "Maybe the conch?"

I couldn't help it. I burst out laughing, dispelling some of the tension that had gathered in my body. "No." I held up my hand, thinking of that night in Clarence Town. "No more conch." *Or rum punch.*

Edward's gaze whipped to me. "You like conch?"

He sounded like such a snob. How had I never noticed it before?

"She loves it," Jackson said, smirking. He was right, but it felt as if he was trying to prove a point. Trying to goad Edward. I glared at Jackson, silently commanding him to back down.

It had been a long day, and I wasn't relishing the prospect of having Jackson and Edward in the same space for any amount of time. I only hoped my staff would find a solution before this situation could spiral even more out of control.

AFTER AN AWKWARD DINNER ON THE PATIO, EDWARD EXCUSED himself to make a phone call. I'd taken a shower and was leaving my room when Jackson pulled me aside.

"Hey," he said, his expression and tone soft. "You okay?"

"I—" I blew out a breath. "I don't know what I am." I wrapped my arms around myself, scared to meet his gaze when I asked, "How much of our conversation did you hear?"

"Enough." His expression was hard and unreadable.

Shit. I didn't even know what to say to that. "Look, Jackson…" I placed my hand on his arm, hoping my touch would calm him. When, really, I needed his touch to ground me.

The fact that I was already falling back into that pattern of thinking scared me. I quickly released him.

He shook his head, and his deadly calm demeanor was unnerving. "I don't trust him, Sloan. I want him gone."

"I'm just as eager for him to leave as you are," I said, on edge from the situation. "My staff are doing everything they can."

Jackson cast a quick glance to where Edward was pacing the patio. Then he ushered me into the bedroom, locking the door behind us.

"What are you doing?" I hissed, knowing that Edward could return inside at any time. This was reckless.

He smirked. "Having a security meeting."

"In my bedroom?"

He lifted a shoulder. "You don't owe Edward anything, least of all an explanation. And before you go back in there —" Jackson's lips were centimeters from mine, and he bracketed my head with his arms "—let me remind you of a few things."

"What's that?" My heart was pounding with adrenaline and anticipation.

His nostrils flared. Maybe it was wrong, but Jackson had always made me feel so…desperate for him. It was nice to see that anguish reflected back at me.

He claimed my mouth, kissing me like a man possessed. I was consumed by him. He was the oxygen I breathed, and I couldn't get enough.

I wanted him closer. *Needed* him closer.

He slid one hand up my ribs to cup my breast, while he delved beneath my sundress with the other. "It was my cock buried deep inside you."

He pressed his thumb against my clit, and I gasped.

"My name." He plunged a finger inside me, and my body clenched down as if to hold him in place. "That you screamed. My come." He worked me, his touch rough as his forehead kissed mine. His eyes intent on mine, watching me. Checking in with me. "On your ass this morning."

I drew in a sharp breath, both from the way he was touching me and his words. From the fact that we might get caught.

"I was your first," Jackson said, jerking me even closer. "And I *will* be your last. Your everything. Because that's what you are to me."

I gasped. *His...what?*

Oh shit. He hit that spot that made me lose all reason, and I couldn't think of anything else.

"That's it, *hayati*," he said in my ear, his voice low, commanding. "Come for me, beautiful. Only me."

My knees felt weak, and my body took over as my pleasure overrode everything else. Until all I could feel, all I could see, was Jackson.

He was still there, holding me, as I floated back down to earth. As the impact of his words sank in.

I will be your last.

Your everything.

Because that's what you are to me.

He smoothed my hair away from my face, cupping my cheeks. "I love you, Sloan." His voice was clogged with emotion, and he regarded me with a watery smile. "I never stopped."

I swallowed hard, trying to wrap my head around what he was saying. Was this a dream? Was this real life?

He took my hand in his and placed them both over his heart. "I know I fucked up in the past, but I'm ready to fight for us."

I... Wow. I hadn't been prepared for that. I hadn't been prepared for any of this. As always, Jackson had blindsided me.

I'd longed to hear those words from him, but... I needed more time. The sex was great—that had never been the issue —but it couldn't magically fix my broken trust. Jackson wanted a future together, but I was still haunted by our past.

We'd lied to each other once. And while we'd both grown and changed since then, I worried we were moving too fast. At least, that was what my head argued. My heart said this was long overdue. Was how it was always meant to be.

"Jackson, I—"

Perhaps sensing my hesitation or fearing my rejection, Jackson said, "You don't have to say anything now." He smiled. "I just...needed you to know." He gave my hand a squeeze before releasing me.

I straightened my dress and smoothed a hand over my hair. I was pretty sure it wouldn't matter what I did; I was a mess. Physically. Emotionally.

Edward's proposal had had little effect on me. But Jackson's declaration... It had taken my breath away.

CHAPTER EIGHTEEN

Jackson

I studied Edward as he sat on the patio, facing away from the villa. What was he up to?

Sloan was still trying to find alternate accommodations for him, so I'd been keeping an eye on him from the kitchen. I couldn't believe he'd proposed. The seconds I'd spent waiting for Sloan's response had felt like hours. And then she'd turned him down, despite the fact that he had everything—money, connections, hell, even a title. She'd still said no. *Thank fuck.*

Why? Because she didn't love him? Had she ever loved him?

I paced back and forth across the kitchen floor like a caged tiger. I hated feeling like this, so out of control.

Did she love me? Did her reaction to seeing Edward mean I had a chance?

Fuck. My head was all over the place. But I had no idea how she felt about what I'd said. I'd poured my heart out to her. Granted, it wasn't the best possible timing, but Hurricane Edward had made landfall and everything had spiraled. Including me.

Oblivious to my inner turmoil, Edward continued to make himself at home. Even now, he'd kicked off his shoes and was headed over to one of the lounge chairs with a drink in hand. I clenched my fists, my blood boiling. I was on the verge of throwing him out when Sloan joined me in the kitchen. Just the sight of her had my pulse slowing to a more normal rate.

"What's wrong?" I asked. I could tell from the hard set of her jaw that she had bad news.

"Thanks to the eclipse, everything is booked. Edward is going to have to stay here for the night until we can get him on a flight home."

I shoved my hands into my pockets, resenting his intrusion even more. "And that's our problem, how?"

"Jackson." She toyed with her necklace. "I can't do this with you. Not right now."

I frowned. "What's that supposed to mean?"

"It means that it's late. I'm tired. And right now, I need you to be my protector."

"That's exactly what I'm trying to do," I said, clenching my fists. "Protect you."

"Tell me something. Do you truly believe Edward is a threat to my safety? Or are you feeling threatened?"

Her comment rankled, partly because it was true. Professionally, my opposition to Edward was motivated by safety. But personally, I was struggling. I was going to have to continue to pretend Sloan meant nothing to me while we were sleeping in the same house as her ex.

She pinched the bridge of her nose. "I'm sorry. I shouldn't have said that. But I've tried everything. The staff called every hotel on the island. I tried arranging for a jet crew or a helicopter or a—"

"Boat," I suggested.

She shook her head. "He's incredibly prone to motion sickness. Will not set foot on a boat."

I chuckled darkly. "I'm surprised that wasn't a deal-breaker for you."

Sloan had always loved sailing. It was in her blood. She needed it like I needed her.

She lifted a shoulder. "It probably should've been."

I stepped closer. "We could sleep on the *Athena* tonight." I didn't love the idea, especially since it meant a bumpy ride back down to the marina. But I'd do it, if that was what Sloan wanted.

She might have "fired" me, but until I contacted Hudson, she was my principal. She was under my protection. But also... there was no way in hell I was leaving her alone with that prick.

She sagged. "I was really looking forward to sleeping in a bigger space tonight. Besides, why should we have to vacate the villa for him?"

Why did we have to accommodate him at all?

"It's just for one night." It sounded like she was trying to talk herself into it.

Fuck. We were really going to do this, weren't we? I dragged a hand down my face. The thought of spending even one minute with that pretentious...

But then I saw the exhaustion in Sloan's eyes, the desperation, and I put aside my own wishes to do what was best for her. What was one night when she was my forever?

"You're right." I rubbed her arms. "It's only one night."

Her shoulders relaxed. "Thank you."

Edward returned inside, and she stepped out of my touch. I took a breath and shoved down my feelings toward her ex. The mere sight of him set me on edge, but I was going to be polite for Sloan's sake.

"Unfortunately, the island is booked solid," Sloan said.

"So, Edward, you're welcome to the couch." She gestured to the sofa.

Edward scoffed. "You're joking, right? He's your employee." He pointed at me. "He should sleep on the couch."

"*Jackson*," Sloan said pointedly, "has spent the last week crammed into a small berth because he was protecting me."

I wasn't going to point out the fact that I'd spent last night in her bed, though it was tempting. I merely crossed my arms over my chest and stared at the wall.

"I could protect you." Edward's tone was sincere, and I coughed to cover a laugh. "If you'd let me."

"Edward." Sloan jumped in before I could interject. Or better yet, punch him in the face. "This isn't up for negotiation. Jackson was expecting a bed, and he will have a bed."

His eyes flashed with anger. "And I was expecting to sleep with you."

God, he was petulant, wasn't he? Used to getting everything he wanted. I knew his type. He probably turned on the charm, fooling everyone into believing he was this kind, patient man, when he was actually a huge dick.

I thought back to the photos in her file. The ones of them as a couple. She'd looked happy, but the smile hadn't reached her eyes. And her body language had always been a little closed off from him—just as it was now.

"Unless you'd rather sleep on the *beach*," Sloan said in a tone that left no room for argument, "I suggest you find a way to enjoy the couch."

Edward's face was tight, and he looked as if he wasn't going to let it go. My hands were itching for a reason to grab him and haul his ass out. But I was trying to stand back and let Sloan handle this.

He smoothed a hand down his shirt. "Of course, darling. We can spend time together tomorrow."

The fuck they would. Not if I had anything to say about it.

But I didn't. Couldn't. Because right now, I was just the bodyguard. So I tapped into years of training for both the SEALs and with Hudson and maintained a neutral, bored expression.

Sloan ignored his comment and went to her room, leaving me to lock up for the night. I did one more sweep of the perimeter, ignoring Edward's huffs of disbelief and feigned discomfort. I secretly rejoiced in the fact that Sloan had spoken up for me, had chosen me, even if it was something as trivial as a bedroom. Not that I was happy about spending the night alone, but at least I hadn't been relegated to the couch.

I showered then considered going to Sloan, but ultimately decided better of it. It had been a long day, and Sloan had dealt with a lot, both on and off the water. I wanted her to see me as her protector, her refuge. So for now, I'd bide my time. I'd be patient.

I lay awake for a long time. I was sick of this shit. Tired of losing sleep because I was apart from Sloan.

I was finally drifting off when there was a loud crash. I jolted upright and was at the bedroom door in moments.

"Oh fuck," a man grumbled. *Edward.* "Jesus, Sloan."

I bolted across the hall, through the open door to Sloan's room, my heart racing. "Sloan?" I called, flipping on a light. "Are you okay?"

Edward was balled up on the floor by the foot of the bed. Sloan was against the far wall, arms wrapped around herself.

"Sloan?" I approached slowly, hands out, always with one eye on Edward. "What happened? Did he hurt you?"

She shook her head. "He…" She swallowed hard. "He startled me."

"That's all?" I asked, not breaking her gaze. Desperate to

reassure her that I was here and I would never let any harm come to her. Not that she needed my help. She'd handled the situation all on her own.

"Should it truly be surprising to find your fiancé in your bed?" Edward asked.

My lip curled.

"You're *not* my fiancé," Sloan said. "And I thought I'd made it clear that you were not welcome in my bed, based on the fact that I asked you to sleep on the couch."

"I wonder why that is?" Edward sneered.

He stood, and I turned so my back was to Sloan. Shielding her.

"Because you welcomed me at first," Edward said, and my blood boiled. "But then she said, 'Jackson.'" He tried to imitate Sloan with a wispy, high-pitched voice as he turned to look at me. "Now, why would she say the name of her bodyguard? Why would she call out for you in bed?"

Sloan placed her palms on my back. A warning? A plea? The fuck if I knew. I just wanted this fucker gone once and for all.

Edward scowled. "I flew across the world to show you how serious I was about us. To propose."

Sloan sighed. "I can appreciate that you came all this way, but you didn't even bother to propose until *after* I'd ended things. And when you did ask me to marry you, you never once said you loved me, nor did it seem to factor into your reasons for wanting to spend your life with me."

He scoffed. "Would it have even mattered?" He turned his gaze on me, his fists clenched, color rising on his cheeks. "I asked you to move in with me, and instead, you broke it off to fuck someone else." He flicked his hand in my direction. "To fuck him." He spat the words with such disdain.

Sloan straightened. "I ended our relationship because I couldn't imagine a future with *you*." Sloan hurled the words at him with the force of a hurricane. "And I only let you stay here for the night because there was literally nowhere else on the island that could accommodate you. Clearly, that was a mistake."

"Can I throw him out now?" I kept my voice low but not low enough that Edward wouldn't hear.

Edward glared at me then took a breath, seeming to compose himself. "Darling, I'm sorry. I shouldn't have" —he looked close to tears. It was a masterful performance, truly— "said that."

"You're right." Sloan blazed with anger. God, she was practically vibrating with it. "You shouldn't have."

"You say you don't envision a future together, but just imagine all that we could accomplish. And I do care about you," he said. "Can't that be enough?"

"It's not enough. At least, not for me," she added quietly.

The question was, would *I* be enough for her?

I pushed away that tired narrative. It was part of the reason I'd ended things years ago. Because I was afraid I wouldn't be enough.

When my dad was alive, he'd always pushed me to run faster, think smarter, be stronger because he knew I wanted to follow in his footsteps to become a SEAL. He wanted me to succeed. Not because that was what he'd wanted for me, but because he knew I'd wanted it.

After his death, my mom and sister had looked to me for strength and reassurance. I was always trying to live up to the standard set by my dad. I was always trying to be enough for my sister and my mom.

And when I'd started training for the SEALs, it had only gotten worse. The comparisons had been more frequent. I'd lost count of how many times I'd heard about my dad's service record. About how he was a hero.

He was a hero, but no one was perfect. And even though I

knew all that, it was impossible not to let it affect me until I became driven by the fear of failure instead of the promise of success. Until I *had* failed. I'd been discharged from the SEALs, and I'd thought it was the worst moment of my life.

I was a disgrace. A disappointment.

And then I'd met Sloan. And the thought of disappointing her had terrified me. The constant fear that I wasn't enough and never would be.

I knew part of me would always fear letting her down in some way. But I was willing to try. I was willing to silence that voice of fear and focus on what I could give her—the things you couldn't put a price on. And I could definitely give her my protection, my support, my loyalty, and my love.

Edward's cheeks reddened. "You're making a huge mistake."

She lifted a shoulder. "Even if I am, it's my choice to make."

He glared at me then turned his attention back to Sloan. "Think of all I can offer you—"

"I have everything money can buy." Sloan cut him off. "What I want is *love*. Loyalty. Devotion. I want passion. I want a love that is all-consuming."

"What you want...is a fantasy. You speak of love. Of passion. But those things can and will fade. I can offer you something more durable. Something you can rely on."

"Stop." She held up a hand. "Just stop. No matter what you say, my answer is still no. And my answer will be the same whether it's tonight, tomorrow, or in a week. Please—" She shook her head. "Just go."

Fucking finally.

I edged closer, forcing him to move toward the door. "You've overstayed your welcome."

He got all huffy, and I grabbed his shoulder, guiding him

toward the door. He tried to shake out of my hold. "Release me, you brute."

I remained silent—for Sloan's sake. But Edward wasn't done.

"You think this is over, but it's not," he said to me. Even with him rising to his full height, I had about five inches and fifty pounds of muscle on him.

I tightened my grip on his shoulder. "Sloan said it's over, so it is."

"They'll never accept you," he hissed once we were out of earshot. "Her family. The board." He sneered. "Look at you. You're the help. By definition, you're beneath her."

"Okay, Downton Abbey." I squeezed his shoulder to the point of pain.

"Unhand me," he hissed through his teeth.

"Time to go. Pack up your shit."

"Go where?" he asked. "It's the middle of the night."

"Should've thought of that before you tried to sneak into Sloan's room uninvited." While he grumbled, I texted Huxley Grand security and arranged for an escort off the property.

"I've been sharing Sloan's bed for the past year." He shoved his clothes and things into his bag.

"That's irrelevant now." I was barely holding my anger in check as I waited for him to finish packing. He was lucky I was even giving him the courtesy. I was tempted to throw his shit on the beach outside, but I didn't want it to mar Sloan's view in the morning. "It's over."

He zipped up his designer rollaboard and stood, glancing toward Sloan's room then back to me. "She'll regret this."

"Is that a threat?" I was beyond done with this dickhead.

I'd encountered all sorts of personalities in my work as a bouncer and now as a bodyguard. I'd seen everything from entitled assholes to drunk socialites, but this guy and his attitude were definitely among the worst.

"An observation," he said in a cool tone.

I herded him toward the door and followed him outside so Sloan wouldn't overhear. Once the door was shut, I grabbed his shirt and hauled him up against the wall. His eyes widened and then flooded with fear.

"Let's get one thing straight." I spat the words. "I know countless ways to kill a man without leaving a trace. If you come near Sloan again, if you so much as utter her name with anything other than politeness and respect, I will end you."

He gulped.

"Is that understood?"

He gasped for air, and I released my hold ever so slightly.

"Yes," he choked out. "Yes."

I let go of him, and he nearly fell to the ground. A moment later, a set of small headlights swung our way.

"There's your ride."

I waved at the driver then turned and walked inside, locking the door behind me. Shutting Edward out—of the house, of Sloan's life.

I'd already shot off a quick email to the team at Hudson. I wanted them to dig deeper into Edward and his family, especially now that Sloan and he were broken up.

I had questions for Sloan, but those could wait. The immediate threat had been neutralized, and right now, Sloan was my biggest concern. She always had been, but I hadn't done the best job of showing her that in the past. I'd chosen my job. My duty. My fears. Even Sloan's relationship with Greer.

I took a breath and relaxed my shoulders. The past was in the past. I was focused on our future.

I peeked my head in Sloan's room, but she wasn't there. My heart rate ratcheted up, and I marched into the bathroom. Empty. *Fuck.* I strode down the hall and discovered her sitting on my bed.

"Hey." I took a seat next to her, wrapping my arm around her. "You okay?"

"I'm…" She shook her head before leaning it against my shoulder. "I don't want to sleep in there tonight."

"You don't have to. Come on." I guided her to lie down then crawled in bed behind her. I wrapped my arms around her, and I could feel her muscles loosen.

"What's going to happen now?" she asked.

"We sleep. You're safe."

She burrowed deeper into my arms, silencing some of my concerns—at least for now. "I always feel safe with you."

I knew Edward was no longer a threat—to Sloan's safety or her heart. But I still had no idea where we stood. For now, I'd settle for being her protector.

CHAPTER NINETEEN

Sloan

I opened my eyes to the sight of Jackson's shirtless form. He was lying on his side facing me, his breathing deep and even, his eyelashes inky against his tanned skin. He was so handsome, he seemed almost unreal. I wanted to reach out and touch him, but I needed to get my head on straight first.

It wasn't just about his physique—though his body was incredible. It was... Being with Jackson was like coming home. And I hadn't realized how lost I'd felt.

Admitting that to myself was scary. But the idea of trusting him again was even more terrifying.

I closed my eyes and replayed the past few days, from reconnecting with Jackson to Edward's surprise to Jackson's declaration to Edward's departure. It had been...a lot.

I didn't regret turning Edward down. There was no way I could marry him. I think, deep down, I'd always known that. But his comments about wanting something that was "a fantasy" had struck their mark, even if I hadn't deemed them worthy of a response.

Love. Passion. Those things can and will fade. And when they do, you'll realize just how wrong you were.

Maybe those hadn't been Edward's exact words, but that was what I'd heard.

I didn't want to think this…thing between Jackson and me was lust, but sex had never been an issue for us. Trust had. Honesty.

Would this time be different?

I'd said this was only for one night. I'd wanted closure, and yet here I was, considering more. More…sex? A relationship?

So much had changed, including us. We were better equipped to withstand challenges, but would our passion cool with time? I didn't want to think so. Besides, the mere idea seemed laughable. Jackson and I were just as attracted to each other now—fourteen years later—as we had been then.

I inhaled and let it out slowly, trying to push away the negative thoughts and consider what I wanted. What I believed.

Jackson made me feel safe. He'd kept me safe throughout the trip, even if he worried his feelings for me compromised his focus. I understood his concern, but if anything, the fact that he loved me made me believe he was even more motivated to protect me.

Sure, I'd accused him of acting out of jealousy last night, but Jackson was right to remain vigilant. And of the three of us, Jackson was the one who'd kept his cool.

I wanted him to stay. On the boat. In my life.

I wanted more time with him. More time to explore what this was. What we could be, despite my fears.

"I can hear you thinking from over here." Jackson's morning voice was deeper, husky.

I couldn't help it. I laughed and opened my eyes. "Morning."

I still couldn't believe he was back in my life. In my bed. It had been a shock to see him there yesterday morning, and the results still hadn't worn off today. I didn't know how long it would take me to get used to the idea of waking up next to him every day, but it made me smile.

"How are you feeling?" Jackson asked.

I stretched. "Okay. You?"

"Okay," he said, though he seemed unsure.

"I'm sorry for putting you in an awkward situation last night."

He scrubbed a hand over his face, tucking his arm behind his head. "It wasn't your fault your ex showed up."

"No." I slipped my hand beneath my cheek. "But I shouldn't have accused you of acting out of jealousy."

He chuckled. "You weren't wrong. I was jealous."

I linked my hand with his. "Surely you see that it's over between Edward and me, right?"

Jackson gave my hand a squeeze then released it. "For you, yes. Though I'm concerned."

"About what he'll do?"

He lifted a shoulder. "I'll tell Hudson, and they'll keep an eye on things."

"Then what's concerning you?"

He dragged a hand over his head, his eyes focused on the ceiling. "I laid it all on the line last night. And I know the timing wasn't ideal, but I just have to ask…is this a rebound for you?"

"What?" I propped myself up on my elbow. "Jackson. No." I placed my hand on his chest, hoping he'd hear the sincerity in my tone. "This isn't a rebound."

"Then what is it?"

I gnawed on my lip, not wanting to ruin whatever this was. I ultimately settled on, "A…reconnection."

He groaned. "That sounds even more vague."

"I didn't mean for it to sound vague. I guess I'm just still

214

trying to process everything. I know that's probably not what you want to hear. But it's the truth."

"I get it," he said. "I do. And I'm not trying to pressure you, but I want you to know that I meant what I said last night." He took my hand in his. "I want more. I'm willing to fight for more."

Jackson wasn't the same man as before. He was willing to *fight* for me. It was…it was a lot to take in. I had a lot to consider.

He'd been assigned to protect me temporarily. But he lived in Los Angeles and often traveled for work. I lived in London. Would he move? Expect me to?

I dragged a hand through my hair, watching a palm tree swaying through the windows. "What would that even look like?"

"Whatever we want it to," he said.

Could it truly be that simple?

I shook my head. Why was I even considering this?

I'd spent a week with the man. One glorious week. I tried to tell myself that this was a fling, a consequence of being in such close quarters. But even I knew it was more than that. I couldn't imagine many people spending every waking moment together, navigating all sorts of challenges on the *Athena*. We were a good team.

But that didn't mean our relationship would hold up in the real world. We were living on island time. This was a vacation. Of course it was easy.

Or as easy as sailing the Thorny Path in a thirty-five-foot sailboat could be.

"Sloan." He took my hand in his and held it over his sextant tattoo. Over his heart. "Do you want to know why I got this tattoo?"

"Because you like sailing?"

His eyes searched mine as if waiting for me to realize something. Some piece of the puzzle I was missing.

"Look closer." He tapped his chest, and I leaned in.

Right on the horizon, worked in so subtly I'd missed it before, were the letters SEM in tiny print. My initials. I didn't think that was a coincidence, but I wanted to hear the words from his mouth.

"It was around the time of Greer's wedding, and I'd never felt so…lost. I got it because it reminded me of you. You've always had this…" He smiled. "Incredible urge to explore. To push yourself. When you put your mind to something—" he tucked my hair behind my ear, cupping my cheek "—you're unstoppable."

I smiled, both at his praise and because his words reminded me of the friendship bracelet Brooklyn had given me with "unstoppable" on it. But Jackson wasn't done.

"As you know, the sextant is a symbol of orientation. A valuable navigation tool that will help guide you home. And I always hoped it would bring me home—to you."

That was why my initials were inked on the horizon, tattooed over his heart.

"Jackson," I whispered, a tear trailing down my face.

He'd done this. He'd branded his skin with a visible reminder of me that he'd carried with him for years. The words "I love you" sat on my tongue, begging to be spoken. But…they wouldn't come out.

It wasn't that I didn't love him. I was scared.

"You don't have to say anything." He dried my tears with his thumbs. "I know you're not ready. But I also need you to know that I'm not going anywhere."

"Thank you." Hearing him say that meant a lot to me. There was no pressure. No expectations. Just love.

I melted at his words and the sincerity and tenderness in

his eyes. I leaned in and kissed him, craving his touch as much as the connection.

"What about Hudson?" I asked.

"I was thinking…"

"Uh-oh. That's dangerous," I teased, a smile playing at my lips. He narrowed his eyes at me. "Okay." I smiled, a full one this time. "What were you thinking?"

"Won't Greer think it's strange when you show up in Puerto Rico with someone else?"

I scrunched up my face. "Good point. I hadn't considered that."

But I had been thinking about how it would look if Jackson asked for a reassignment. How it might reflect poorly on him. I didn't want my decisions to negatively impact Jackson's career.

"What if…" He sighed. "What if I stayed on until Puerto Rico?"

"And then what?"

"And then—" he lifted my hand to his mouth, kissing each of my fingers "—we'll reevaluate."

"We can't sleep together if you're going to stay on as my bodyguard." I brought his hand to my cheek, sinking into his touch.

"I know," he said. "It won't be easy. But it'll be nice to have the time to get to know each other again without sex confusing matters."

I arched my brow. Part of me had expected him to fight me on that.

He chuckled, still touching me. Always touching me. "Why? You don't think I can do it?"

I let out a puff of air. "I don't know if *I* can."

He laughed then stood.

"Hey." I grabbed for him, not ready to stop cuddling. "Where are you going?"

"Breakfast then boat repairs." He pulled on a shirt. "Staying in bed is only going to tempt me."

I flopped back on the bed with a groan. I knew he was right, but that didn't mean I was happy about it.

"Come on." He yanked on my leg. "I'll make you breakfast."

"You know you don't have to cook for me, right? We can have the private chef come over, or we can order room service."

I stood, and he pulled me into a hug. My body melted into his hold, his touch conveying so much more than even his words. *I love you. I'm here for you. I've got you.*

"I like cooking for you." I smiled at his words. He released me and headed for the door. "I'll give you some privacy to get changed."

I could hear Jackson moving around in the kitchen as I got ready for the day. I didn't know what the future held for Jackson and me, but that was okay. All I had to do right now was focus on taking things one day at a time.

When I joined Jackson in the kitchen, he was cutting up vegetables. "Whatcha making?" I leaned against the counter.

"Omelets." He placed his hand on my lower back as he reached around me for a spatula. "Sound good?"

"Sounds great." I felt a zing race up my spine just from that simple touch. "What can I do?"

"You want to cut up some fruit while I do the eggs?"

"Sure." I went over to the fridge. There was something relaxing about being in the kitchen together. We fell into an easy rhythm, sharing tasks and making conversation.

"What did you want to do today?" he asked.

"I'd like to go to town at some point. I was hoping to get a souvenir for Brooklyn."

He grabbed some eggs from the fridge. "We could do that

after we talk to the mechanic. I also need to check in with Huxley security and update Hudson."

"Sounds like a busy day."

He lifted a shoulder. "All in a day's work."

"Is that what I am to you?" I teased. "Work?"

He grasped my chin, bringing me closer as if to kiss me. "No." He released me and stepped back. "Sorry."

"Don't be sorry," I said. "I like it when you touch me."

"Sloan," he groaned. "You're going to be the death of me."

I smirked. It wasn't the first time he'd told me that. And I didn't think it would be the last.

"So, besides going into town," Jackson said, clearly trying to steer us to safer ground, "is there anything you want or need to do?"

"I need to check in with my family. I promised Brooklyn I'd call, and I know Graham is waiting for an answer from me on a few things."

"You probably don't want to hear this," Jackson said, chopping the bell peppers. "But Huxley needs better security protocols. This isn't the first time they've failed a high-profile guest—an owner, no less."

"I'll mention it to Graham and Jasper, so we can discuss it with the board after I return. If you have any specific recommendations, I'd love to hear them."

"Oh, I have plenty of suggestions," he said. "But the board probably won't like them."

"Tell me about them. Please?"

Jackson sautéed the peppers while I washed the fruit. It was so nice to have an abundance of fresh produce. During our longer stretches on the boat, food choices could get limited.

"First, I'd conduct a security assessment of the organization as a whole, as well as specific Huxley Grand properties —mostly those in larger cities or with higher traffic. Based on my stays with Nate, I already have a number of suggestions for facility and asset security, as well as human security. Many of them are simple tweaks that will ensure the safety of all guests. But I also have more targeted recommendations for the VIP or high-profile guests."

I nodded, impressed. "The comfort and safety of our guests and employees are paramount."

"Yet it seems like an afterthought. First, the incident with Brooklyn's birthday, and now this?" He set down the spatula and dragged a hand over his head. "You're one of the owners, for fuck's sake. What happened is unacceptable."

"Brooklyn's birthday was…" I gnashed my teeth. The thought that paparazzi had been able to sneak in and take a picture was infuriating. "Wrong."

"Should've never happened," Jackson said.

"I completely agree. But as to last night, security can't keep someone out if I forget to tell them." That was on me.

"No, but this isn't the first time I've been disappointed by the lack of protocols and proper training."

I loved how passionate Jackson was. How knowledgeable. It was sexy. I leaned over to kiss him then stopped myself. Right. No sex. No…kissing. "If you didn't already have a job, I'd hire you."

Though the idea of hiring him had merit.

Jackson said nothing, his attention on the omelets. His silence felt somehow intentional. But I didn't understand why.

When the food was ready, we carried it out to the patio. The waves crashed, and a gecko scurried across the stone. I stared out at the horizon, watching a boat in the distance. As much as I loved sailing and looked forward to being on the water, I was grateful to be back on land. Even if it didn't feel like I was on very solid footing at the moment.

After breakfast, Jackson went inside to call his boss, so I decided to call Brooklyn. She answered on the second ring.

"Brooklyn, hey." I smiled at her face on the screen.

"Auntie Sloan!" She squinted. "Jeez. It's so sunny there."

"It's a beautiful day." I panned the camera around, showing her my view.

"You're in Turks and Caicos, right?"

"That's right." I turned the camera back to me. I'd been sending my family emails and updates of my sailing adventures. Brooklyn always replied almost immediately, and I loved that she was so interested in sailing.

"Are you going to be able to get your boat fixed?" she asked.

"Hopefully." I dragged a hand through my hair. "Jackson and I are going down to talk to the mechanic in a little bit."

"Where is he? Can I talk to him?"

"Jackson?" I glanced toward the house. "He's inside. He's on the phone right now, or I'd let you say hi."

She leaned in, cupping her mouth as if to impart a secret. "I didn't realize he had so many tattoos."

I laughed, though it sounded nervous to my ears. "I, uh… Yeah. He does. What makes you say that?"

"One of the pictures you sent from the snorkeling had Jackson in it."

"Oh." *Oops.*

"The snorkeling has been amazing," I said, eager to take the spotlight off Jackson.

"I loved the picture of the coral. And the manta ray. And the sea turtle," she gushed. "So cute!"

"Not the one of the shark?"

Her eyes went wide. "No way. Weren't you scared?"

"Nurse sharks are pretty docile, fortunately."

"That's what Emmy said when I showed her the pictures, but still!" Her eyes were wide.

"Is that Sloan?" Nate called in the background.

"Hey, Nate!"

He came into view, chewing an apple. He seemed to scrutinize me. "How's it going?"

"Good," I said quickly. Perhaps too quickly. "Yeah."

He arched an eyebrow, questioning. I gave a subtle shake of my head, silently asking him to drop it. Nate turned to Brooklyn with a smile. "B, can you give Auntie Sloan and me a minute?"

"Sure! I'm going to grab my guitar so I can play a song for you." She ran off, and I braced myself for whatever Nate was going to say.

"Tell me the truth. Are things not going well with Jackson?"

Quite the opposite, in fact, not that I was going to admit that to my brother. Jackson had told me he loved me. That he was ready to fight for us. And I wanted to believe him.

I cleared my throat. "It's going fine."

I changed topics, and we talked for a little bit, about the new show his studio was producing and what was going on with Knox, Jasper, and Graham.

Finally, I said, "Can I ask you something?"

"You can ask…" Nate grinned, implying that he might not choose to answer.

I rolled my eyes.

His expression softened, his teasing tone gone. "What's going on, Sloan?"

"How did you…" I chewed on my lip. "After everything with Trinity, how did you get past that to be able to trust someone and let them in?"

He rubbed the back of his neck. "I'll tell you what I told Brooklyn. Trusting someone is a leap of faith. There are no guarantees."

"But how did you *know* you could trust Emerson? How

did you know she was the one?" I wanted something more concrete. Needing something more solid after everything I'd been through.

"It was less about me and more about Emerson. She showed me time and time again that she was here for me. For Brooklyn. Whether it was tackling a paparazzo at Brooklyn's birthday party or supporting me, Emerson is always here for us."

"What about..." I tried to think of how to phrase my question so it wouldn't be offensive. "Well, are you ever worried she's with you for the wrong reasons?"

He furrowed his brow. "Sloan, what's going on? Is this about my relationship or yours?"

"I was just curious. That's all."

He frowned. "Because of Edward?"

"Um..." I rolled my lips between my teeth then said, "Edward and I broke up."

His shoulders relaxed. "Thank fuck."

"You really did *not* like him, did you?"

"Since you're no longer with him, I can finally say that he was smarmy."

"Smarmy?" I shook my head. "What are you—eighty?"

"When you live and work in Hollywood, you get used to spotting who's fake. And he always seemed..." He paused as if considering his word choice. "I could never quite tell if he was being genuine."

"Why didn't you say anything?"

"Would you have listened?"

I rolled my eyes. "Fair."

"He was fine, but he wasn't the man for you."

"And who do you imagine is?" I asked, both annoyed that Nate knew me so well and genuinely curious.

He rubbed a hand over his face. "I don't know. But off the top of my head...someone who's adventurous. Who likes sailing. Someone who won't be intimidated by you or your wealth. Someone loving and supportive but also strong. Confident in themselves."

It was almost as if he was describing Jackson. But how would Nate actually feel if I told him about Jackson? Would he be supportive? I wanted to think so, but I was scared to ask.

"Wait." Nate furrowed his brow. "So, if this isn't about Edward, then who..." His voice trailed off, and then he lifted his chin in understanding. "I see."

"No," I blurted. "You don't see anything."

"Mm. Is Jackson the reason you ended things with Edward?"

"No." My voice came out strangled, the word sounding more like a question.

"Oh shit." His eyes widened. "He is, isn't he? I totally called it."

"I—" I swallowed hard. "What? What are you talking about?"

"I could tell there was something between the two of you in Abu Dhabi."

"How?" I'd done my best to hide my reaction to Jackson, but I should've known Nate would see right through me. He always had.

I glanced back at the villa, confirming that Jackson was still inside. I considered denying it, but I knew Nate. And he knew me.

I glared at him. "Promise you won't say anything to the others."

"I won't..." He leaned back, crossing his leg at the knee. "But only if you answer my questions."

"Not fair!"

He chuckled, and I wanted to reach through the phone and strangle him. "When did it start?"

I sighed. "It's a long story." Even if it was a relief to talk to someone about it.

"I've got time."

"I sincerely doubt that," I said, knowing that Nate was always short on time. Between his family and his production studio, his time was a rare commodity. That said, he'd always made time for me.

"Come on, Sloan. Tell me."

I hesitated a moment, debating. If I didn't talk to someone about this, I was going to explode. I'd been keeping this secret for years, and the past had finally caught up with me. I wanted—no, I needed—a second opinion. And I trusted Nate to be honest.

Before I knew it, I'd told him everything. How Jackson and I had met. How he'd broken my heart. How he wanted a second chance. Through it all, Nate listened patiently, only occasionally interrupting to ask a question.

"I had no idea, Sloan. I wish you'd told me sooner. I'm sorry you were in so much pain and dealing with all of that on your own."

I lifted a shoulder. At the time, Nate's career had been taking off. He'd left the family business to become an actor, and his life was insane.

"I had Gran," I said. "I told her about Jackson and me before she died."

"I'm glad, but you know I'm always here for you, right?"

I nodded. "I do."

"And I think you're smart to take it slow," he said. "To focus on getting to know each other again, as you are now. You've changed a lot in the past fourteen years. I'm sure he has too."

"Thanks, Nate." I chewed on my lip. "So, you don't think I'm crazy?"

"Love makes us all a little crazy."

That it does.

"And who am I to judge?" Nate grinned. "After all, I fell in love with my daughter's nanny."

"True." I nodded. "But seriously, how do you think everyone else would react?"

"Knox can't say anything, considering his situation. Jasper would probably be happy for you. And Graham, well, who knows."

"What about Greer?" I asked. "I've kept this secret from her all these years, and I'm terrified of losing her."

It almost seemed worse to tell her now, though the idea of telling Greer had never been easy. She'd always made it very clear to Jackson that her friends were off-limits.

Nate turned more contemplative. "You two have been friends for a long time. I'd like to think she'd support you. Hell—" He dragged a hand through his hair. "If Jude can get over the fact that his dad is marrying his ex-girlfriend, then you can only hope Greer will be as forgiving about her brother."

I took a deep breath, considering everything he'd said.

"Trust yourself," Nate said. "You've always had a strong inner compass. I know you'll make the best decision for you."

"Thanks, Nate."

"Anytime. Now, I better get going. I know Brooklyn wants to play her song for you, but Em's going to kill me if I make us late to dinner at her parents'," he said. "I'll send you a video of her song. Chat more soon?"

"Absolutely. Go." I waved him away.

"Love you."

"Love you too, Nate. Even if you are a pain in the ass."

"Takes one to know one," he joked.

I rolled my eyes and disconnected the call, feeling like more of an equal to Nate than ever. I took a few minutes to center myself, enjoying the view and the sound of the ocean.

I called Jasper to check in briefly, wanting to run an idea by him before putting it to Graham. He was enthusiastic about it and encouraged me to tell Graham.

Finally, knowing I couldn't put off talking to Graham any longer, I took a deep breath and hit the button to contact him.

"Sloan."

"Teddy Grahams." I stood and walked along the patio, needing to stretch my legs. To move.

He sighed but ignored my nickname. "Someone's in a good mood."

"It's always good to get away from the office. You should try it sometime."

"Unlikely," he muttered. "Though I'm glad you're enjoying yourself."

"Thank you," I said, touched by his sincerity.

"And I realize now that I may have been harsh the last time you were in LA. I'm sorry."

Wow. Okay. "Thanks for saying that. It means a lot."

He cleared his throat, and I knew that talking about feelings made him uncomfortable. So it wasn't surprising when he changed the subject. "What do you know about Edward's financial situation?"

I furrowed my brow. "Huh?"

"I finished my review of Halle Lovejoy. And I'm doing a financial deep dive on Edward."

I groaned. My assistant, seriously? He hadn't seen her face when I'd showed her one of the threats.

She'd been terrified for me. Outraged. Halle was one of the best people I knew. I trusted her implicitly. There was no way she was involved.

"Graham. We've talked about this. You can't go investigating someone just because you don't trust them."

"I was right not to trust Edward, and you shouldn't either.

His family's company is not as successful as they portray. They've sunk a lot of money into the ducal estate as well."

"So…?" I asked. "I can understand why he might not want to go around broadcasting that fact. Wait." I paused. "*Why* are you investigating him?"

"I've been thinking. Edward's close to you. Has access to your place—opportunity. This money situation gives him a motive."

God, he sounded like Jackson. Maybe the two of them were more alike than I cared to admit.

"Okay, Sherlock. Let's not get carried away. It wasn't Edward. He wouldn't have asked me to marry him if he were behind the threats."

"He proposed?" Graham sounded genuinely surprised. Hell, I was surprised myself. I hadn't planned to tell him that. "Did you accept?"

"*If* I marry…" I said, trying not to smirk at his horrified tone. Graham so rarely showed emotion, it was nice to know that something had riled him up. "It will be for love."

"Sloan," he growled. "That's not an answer."

I considered dragging it out, torturing him a little longer. But ultimately, I said, "I don't love Edward. So, no. I'm not marrying him."

"So glad to see that you've finally come to your senses."

"Yes, yes. You all made it very clear how you felt about him."

"Maybe we were harsh—" Graham admitted reluctantly.

"Not maybe." I cut him off. "Definitely."

"But he wasn't the right guy for you."

"And if he were?" I asked. "What if I met the right guy for me? Would you be supportive then?"

"This conversation seems a bit premature."

Considering how I felt about Jackson, I wasn't sure that it was, actually. But I didn't mention that. For now, I wanted to get to know Jackson again on my terms. Without my brothers butting in.

"Unless…" He trailed off, and for a minute, I wondered if he suspected something between Jackson and me.

"Look," I sighed. We were getting off track. "I called because I wanted to run something by you."

I told Graham about the improvements Jackson had suggested, as well as my idea, and he seemed amenable. I was following my inner compass as Nate had suggested, and I trusted that I was headed in the right direction.

CHAPTER TWENTY

Jackson

I monitored Sloan's movements from inside the villa as I went about my tasks. I was trying to give her some privacy, but I couldn't keep my eyes off her. She was pacing the deck, her expressions animated and intense as she spoke to someone on FaceTime. I wondered who it was. She'd mentioned needing to check in with her brother. Was she talking to Nate? Jasper? Graham?

I worried about Sloan's family's response to our relationship. Sure, Nate liked me—as his bodyguard. Would he be okay with me dating Sloan? Would Graham? Or would he try to intervene like he had in the past?

I finished climbing the stairs but stopped when I spied a man standing outside Sloan's apartment. I studied the man as he leaned against the wall and typed something on his phone. He reeked of money, from the bespoke suit to the impatience lining his face. He looked woefully out of place, almost comically so.

He couldn't be much older than me, but despite any similarity in age, we were worlds apart. This guy looked like he'd stepped out of a boardroom or worked on Wall Street. While I'd been kicked out of the Navy and was trying to make ends meet as a bouncer.

My phone rang, and I glanced down to see my boss's name from the club on the screen. He probably wanted to see if I could pick up a shift tonight, but I had plans with Sloan.

I silenced my phone, and when I looked up, Mr. Money was studying me.

"Can I help you?" I asked, thinking he must be lost. His suit had to cost more than a month of rent for this shithole.

"No." The man went back to his phone.

I hated that Sloan was living here mostly alone. It wasn't safe, and I'd been trying to figure out how to convince her to move in with me. If only it wouldn't mean telling Greer about our relationship.

Sometimes it almost felt as if that ship had sailed—telling my sister about us. At first, there had been nothing to tell because Sloan and I had both been so busy lying to ourselves, pretending there was nothing between us. And then, after we'd started sneaking around, Sloan and I had wanted to see where things would go without the pressure of telling Greer.

Not to mention the fact that I was looking for more permanent jobs. Something with more long-term potential. With options for promotion and advancement.

If I wanted a future with Sloan—and I did—I needed to prove that I was worthy of her. That I could provide for her. That was something my dad had always hammered into me—the need to provide for your family. To take care of the people you loved.

Was this taking care of Sloan? Sneaking around? Making her hide our relationship? I sighed. I knew it wasn't.

At the sound of footsteps on the stairs, I turned. Sloan emerged from the stairwell, then paused.

"Graham?" she asked, looking past me. Graham? She knew that guy? He was here for her? *"What are you doing here?"*

I glanced between them. How did she know him? Was he an ex?

"Nice to see you too. Aren't you going to invite me in?"

Sloan's skin paled. "Is everything okay?"

"I can't come visit my sister and check in?"

Sister? He was her brother?

She'd told me little about her family, and the longer I looked at him, the more I saw the resemblance. It was in the eyes. The way they carried themselves—with this quiet confidence.

"You?" She scoffed. "Um, no. Knox or Jasper, yes. But not you. Is Pops okay? Gran?"

He glanced around. "Is there somewhere we can talk that's a little more—" His gaze flicked to me. He peered down his fucking nose at me. "Private?"

"Oh, right." Sloan sprang into action, unlocking the door. "Come in."

Sloan shot me an apologetic look over her shoulder.

I moved to follow, and Graham tried to shut the door on me. I stuck out my foot, blocking it. Graham sneered.

"Oh, sorry," Sloan said, pushing the door open. "Graham, this is Jackson. Jackson, this is my brother Graham." Her tone was breathy, nervous even.

Something wasn't adding up. First, her grandfather's six-figure sailboat, and now, her brother wearing a bespoke suit. I felt as if I was missing something. Something important.

"And Jackson is..." Graham's question hung in the tense silence.

I waited to see how Sloan wanted to play this.

"He's, um..." Sloan shifted on her feet. "Greer's brother." It was disappointing but not surprising.

I held out my hand. Graham made a show of looking around, then finally, begrudgingly, he accepted my proffered hand, his distaste—for the apartment, for me—evident.

My phone buzzed with an incoming call, snapping me out of my stupor. I shook my head and stood to grab it from the counter. Graham hadn't been welcoming in the past. And while I now knew some of it came down to his personality, I also couldn't imagine him accepting my relationship with Sloan.

I was getting ahead of myself, but Sloan's family was important to her. If we were going to have a future together, I wanted their support. Just as I wanted Greer's blessing.

I leaned back in my chair and dragged a hand over my head. I felt...unsettled. I loved Sloan, and I'd do everything in my power to earn her trust. To prove that I was worthy of her.

Vaughn's name flashed on the screen, and my gut clenched with concern. I knew this conversation was necessary and unavoidable, but that didn't make it any easier.

I connected the call. "Vaughn."

"Blackjack. Give me a sit rep."

"We made it to Providenciales without too much excitement."

"Good." I could hear him typing on his keyboard in the background.

I gave Vaughn a quick recap of what had happened with Edward, keeping his accusations about Sloan and me out of it. I'd since spoken with the head of security for the Huxley Grand Turks and Caicos. He'd apologized profusely for the situation with Edward and promised it wouldn't happen again.

I understood why the mistake had occurred—everyone had still believed Sloan was with Edward. And he'd been on a short list of approved guests. I'd promptly made sure he was removed. I'd also confirmed that Edward had left the island.

After I finished updating Vaughn, we discussed our frustrations with the Huxley Grand security staff and event site staff generally. Most employees were well-meaning but under-trained. It was frustrating but not necessarily surprising.

"What's next?" Vaughn asked.

"We're going to stay here until the repairs are completed and then head to Puerto Rico."

"Smooth sailing. That's what I like to hear." His voice was full of pride, and I hated the idea of disappointing him. "Keep it up, and the New York office is yours."

I pinched the bridge of my nose.

"Actually..." I glanced outside to make sure Sloan was still occupied. "There's something I want to talk to you about."

"Mm." He seemed distracted.

I smoothed my hand down my thigh, preparing myself to say the words that would throw my life into a tailspin. "I'd like to tender my resignation effective as of the end of this trip."

"Not accepted. Next."

I chuckled, eager to keep things light as I delivered the bad news. "Vaughn, I'm serious. I'm resigning from Hudson, and I won't be accepting payment for this assignment."

I had more than enough money in the bank. I'd always lived frugally and saved and invested heavily. I'd be okay until I landed on my feet again.

"What?" he blurted. "Why the hell would you do that?" And then he went silent before he said, "Aw. Shit. You slept with her, didn't you? Please tell me I'm wrong. I'm wrong, right?"

When I didn't respond, he asked, "Why?" And I knew he wasn't asking why I'd slept with Sloan but rather why I was doing this.

I could remember Sloan asking me that same thing years ago.

"Why are you doing this?" Sloan begged, tears streaking down her face.

I said nothing. What could I say? I loved her, but this couldn't continue. For all our sakes.

So, when Hudson had offered me the job in Los Angeles, I'd taken it. I'd accepted, even knowing it would break Sloan's heart. Break my own.

She gripped my shirt, clinging to me. And then she pushed me away. "I don't understand. Why didn't you talk to me? Why didn't you tell me what was going on?"

Because you would've wanted to go with me.

"Because I don't want you to make decisions about your future based on me."

She reeled back as if I'd slapped her. "You...what?"

"Come on, Sloan. You're about to graduate. You've got your whole life ahead of you. You—"

"How dare you," she seethed. "How dare you presume to make decisions for me and my future without consulting me." She turned away. "You're no better than my family."

"Jackson?" Vaughn asked. "You still there?"

I was taking a gamble—quitting my job in the hopes that Sloan would realize she meant more to me than anything. Words were one thing. Actions were another. As my dad would always say, *"Acta non verba."*

Despite the fact that I was quitting my job—a job I loved and excelled at—I thought my dad would be proud of my decision. He'd been devoted to my mom. And he'd always put family first. I knew he'd understand my choice, even if not everyone else would.

"Yeah," I said. "I'm still here."

"You've always followed the rules. Why would you do this? You're on the precipice of everything you've worked for. Everything *we've* worked for."

I knew I was letting him down, and I hated that. I'd not only broken the rules, I'd upset his plans. And disappointed someone who'd mentored me and given me a second chance.

Finally, I said, "Because I love her."

"Love her or the lifestyle she can offer you?"

I would never expect Sloan to pay my way. I would never take advantage of her. And for him to even say that...

"Take that back." I bit out the words.

The line went quiet, then he finally said, "You're right. That's not you, but I find it hard to believe that you'd throw away your promotion, your career, for a woman."

"Vaughn." I clenched my teeth, not wanting to get into it. "She's my past, my present, and my future. Nothing matters more than Sloan."

"Well, shit." I could imagine him leaning back in his chair and staring at the LA skyline. He let out a deep sigh, and I didn't know what to expect. Clearly, he was disappointed, but there was nothing I could do about that. What was done was done.

I rolled my eyes, thinking of Sloan's suggested tattoo.

"I appreciate you being honest with me," Vaughn said in a detached tone. "But I also have to consider what's best for Hudson."

"I know." Sweat dripped down my back, but I strived to sound professional after he'd insulted me and my relationship with Sloan. I knew he was upset and lashing out, but that didn't excuse his behavior. "I understand." I wouldn't have expected anything less. I hated that I'd betrayed the company—and the man—that had given me so much.

"Technically, I should fire you and send a replacement."

I held my breath, hoping he wouldn't do that. But he sounded mad enough that he might.

Finally, he said, "But I'm guessing she doesn't want a replacement."

"Correct."

"Nor do I want to have to explain to her family why we'd be sending one." He sighed. "I really *hate* the position you've put me in."

"I know." I felt shitty about it.

If he left me in place, he was breaking the rules too. But if he pulled me, it would lead to unwanted questions within the company. Among Sloan's brothers. Potentially with other clients as well.

"Are you sure you're the best person to keep her safe?" His tone stressed the importance of answering truthfully.

I'd given it a lot of thought, and I wouldn't have suggested this if I didn't think I was capable of protecting Sloan.

"I would never let anything happen to her. If you want me to sign something terminating my professional relationship to limit your and Hudson's liability, I will. But I'm not leaving her."

"Who else knows about this?" he asked.

"The ex suspects there's something between us, but I don't think he'll be a problem."

"We'll keep an eye on the situation." Vaughn's tone was curt and to the point. He was pissed.

"Thank you," I said. "And I'm sorry, Vaughn. Truly."

"Too late for apologies," Vaughn scoffed. "I mean... goddamn it, Jackson. You are one of the best. And..." He sighed. "I trust that you'll refrain from *violating* the code of ethics again until your assignment ends." It wasn't a question.

"Yes, sir. I've already discussed it with the principal."

"Good. Because I'd hate to have to terminate you for cause."

I didn't want that either, but Vaughn would be completely justified in firing me for sleeping with the client. Yet he hadn't.

"Does she know you plan to resign?"

"No. I wanted to talk to you about it first."

"Good," he said. "Since you're determined to finish this assignment, I'd like to wait to formally announce your resignation until after it ends."

"Understood." I was more than happy to comply. I'd spent years building and ensuring Hudson's reputation. I didn't want to do anything to jeopardize it more than I already had.

"The fewer people who know, the better," he said. "Including the principal."

"I'm not sure I'm comfortable with that." I didn't want to keep any secrets from Sloan.

"It doesn't matter. You signed an NDA, agreeing not to disclose components of Hudson's operation that would compromise our business."

He was right, but that didn't mean I had to like it.

"Look..." He sighed. "Regardless of the NDA, I'm asking you to give me some time to figure out how to spin this situation. We hadn't formally announced your promotion, but everyone expected that you were going to take over the New York office. That would be enough to create instability at Hudson. But when people realize you're together..." He trailed off, then finally said, "The last thing I'd want is for her family—or anyone else—to question Hudson's professionalism. Our ability to protect our clients."

"I know," I said. "I don't want that either."

"Then we're in agreement. Your resignation stays between us for now."

"Yes, sir." What else could I do but agree? Especially not after the bind I'd put him in.

We ended the call, and I dropped my face into my hands. That hadn't gone as I'd expected. I felt both better and worse.

The door opened, and I straightened.

"Hey," Sloan said. "Everything okay?"

"Yeah." I stood and shoved my phone into my pocket. "You ready to head out?"

"Let me just grab my purse, and then we can go."

We locked up. There was a car waiting, the keys inside. I'd arranged it with the staff earlier, and I was grateful they'd handled everything without question. I checked the perimeter and the trunk.

When I was finally satisfied, I held open the passenger door for Sloan, and she slid inside. I rounded the car and climbed in, turning the keys in the ignition. I pulled out of the resort and headed for the marina. I adjusted my hands on the steering wheel, still upset after my conversation with Vaughn.

"Graham told me something interesting." She adjusted the air vents.

"What's that?" I asked, my gut twisting with dread.

"Edward's company isn't doing as well as it seems. And the family has sunk a lot of money into the ducal manor."

I wondered why Vaughn hadn't mentioned that to me, unless...

Graham had somehow discovered the information himself. There was no reason to hire a PI when Hudson had the tools and the expertise to get the information. And if our team hadn't uncovered it, then... My mind searched for other possibilities, but it kept landing on one.

One that seemed improbable at first, given the fact that Graham was a billionaire CEO of a luxury hotel brand. But the more I thought about it, the more he fit the profile of a hacker. Graham was highly intelligent, curious, individualistic, and nonconformist.

My eyes widened as the pieces of the puzzle finally clicked into place, but I kept my revelation to myself for now. Maybe I was wrong. I mean, Graham wouldn't want to do anything that could jeopardize his position or hurt Sloan. But still...my gut told me I was right.

"Not surprising—about the ducal manor," I said. "Those gorgeous old estates are giant money pits."

"I guess you wouldn't want to live somewhere like that, then."

"You know me. I'm a man of simple tastes. Hell, I'd be happy living full time on a sailboat." And if I didn't find another job in the next six months, I might actually have to consider the prospect.

"Why? Wouldn't you?" I flicked my eyes to her then back to the road.

She considered it a moment. "Maybe." She puffed out a breath of air. "But after spending so much of my childhood moving from hotel to hotel, it's nice to feel settled. Don't get me wrong. I love being out on the water, but I think I enjoy it more because it feels like such a treat. Does that make any sense?"

I lifted my hand as if to place it over hers and then stopped myself. This whole *not violating protocol thing* was going to be difficult. "It makes perfect sense. Does London feel like home?"

She smiled. "It does. It's a great mix of modern and traditional. I love the accents and the history and the people. What about you? Does LA feel like home?"

I shook my head. Nowhere felt like home. At least, not until this trip. With her. She was my home.

"Even after all these years?"

"You have to remember, I spent a lot of that time on movement teams. I traveled the world with clients. It's only in the past few years that I transitioned to a residential team and actually spent some time in LA."

I pulled up to the marina, effectively ending the conversation. We spoke to the mechanic, and Sloan was totally in her element. She was just as at home in a mechanic's shop as a boardroom. She was confident and intelligent and fucking incredible.

After everything was settled, we drove into town for some shopping and lunch. She checked her phone and laughed.

"What's up?"

"Jasper's been working on ideas for our annual retreat,

and he wants to pitch a new idea to Graham. But Graham's going to hate it."

"What do you think of it?"

She shook her head, a rueful smile on her face. "I think it's out of the box and maybe a little off-brand but also sounds super cool."

"What is it?" I asked, curious.

"He wants us to go to this luxury glamping village in Marrakesh."

"Is that a Huxley Grand property?"

"No. But Jasper wants it to be. He's definitely the dreamer of the three of us. A creative thinker. He's great with details, but his passion lies in the guest experience. And he's good at it too, even if Graham doesn't always recognize or appreciate that," she added in a darker tone.

"And what is Graham?"

"The critic." That didn't surprise me.

"And you?" I switched on my signal and then turned into a parking lot.

"The realist." I wasn't sure that had always been the case, but it was true now. I'd seen it in action on the boat. She was definitely good at making a plan and implementing it. She could also adapt and think on her feet.

I put the car in park and turned to her. "Perhaps, but I also think you're the glue."

We climbed out of the car. I monitored the area from behind my sunglasses. Nothing suspicious, but I was on high alert. There had been an influx of guests, thanks to the upcoming eclipse.

"Does that bother you?" I asked, returning to something she'd mentioned earlier. "Graham's lack of recognition for Jasper's ideas."

"Sometimes, yeah." She dragged a hand through her hair. "Jasper likes to tease, and it can grate on Graham. And

Graham's…stiffness can chafe Jasper. They just have very different personalities. At times, it's great because it means that we see things the others don't. But it can also lead to a lot of discord."

"It sounds like you get stuck in the middle a lot."

"Not as often as you'd think. But when I do, it gets old real quick."

"If you didn't run the family hotel business, what would you want to do?" I asked.

"I'm not sure I ever gave it much thought. I knew from a pretty early age what was expected of me. I just didn't antici-pate having to step up so young."

I placed my hand on her lower back as we crossed the street. "I'm sorry about your grandparents. I know how close you were to them, especially your gran."

They were the only parents she'd ever known. Her parents had died in a plane crash when she was so young, she barely had any memories of them. I didn't know which was worse—never knowing your parent and always wondering what you'd missed out on, like Sloan. Or having a close rela-tionship and years of memories that only made the loss feel more profound, like me losing my dad. It didn't really matter. Any loss was painful.

Sloan slipped her hand in mine, and I held it there. I rubbed my thumb over the back of her hand, wanting to reassure her that I wasn't going anywhere. We might not be allowed to have sex, but surely holding hands was okay. Especially if it helped with our cover story.

Right. Even I didn't buy that.

"Ooh, this one looks cute." She indicated to a store with a bunch of conch shells and stuffed animals in the window. "Maybe I'll find something for Brooklyn here."

I held open the door, and the seashells over the door

chimed. The salesperson greeted us and then left us to our own devices.

Sloan tried on some wild sunglasses.

"Nice." I chuckled.

She put a ridiculous hat on my head. I rolled my eyes and set it back on the rack. She smiled. It made me happy to see her so carefree.

I scanned the store for threats while she looked for Brooklyn's name on the personalized keychains. Perused the glass case of jewelry. Other customers shifted around the space, and I kept an eye on them while Sloan shopped.

"What do you think of this for Brooklyn?" I finally asked, holding up a stuffed sea turtle. "I know she has a million stuffed animals, but this just seemed like her."

Sloan smiled brightly. "She'll love it." She pushed up on her toes and kissed my cheek.

Her hair brushed my jaw, the smell of it filling my senses. I clenched my fists so I wouldn't grab her and pull her in for a searing kiss.

"Sloan," I cautioned under my breath.

"Sorry, but…" She cupped her hand to my ear. "I couldn't resist. Besides, aren't we supposed to be a couple when we go ashore?"

She settled back to the floor, looking rather pleased with herself. I didn't bother mentioning that I'd had the same thought earlier. Instead, I narrowed my eyes at her. "You're incorrigible."

"Me?" She held a hand to her chest, her eyes wide with mock outrage.

"Yes. You." I smirked.

"Can you blame me, though? You got a tattoo for me."

"Mm." I wrapped my arm around her shoulder. "You like that, huh?"

"I'm honestly still so blown away by it."

"Sloan." I gripped her chin, forcing her gaze to mine. "I would cover my entire body in tattoos dedicated to you if it meant you'd give me another chance."

She blushed, and she looked so beautiful, I was tempted to kiss her. But I didn't. Not yet.

"Even your—" She gave my crotch a pointed look.

"Even that," I said, not wanting to imagine how painful it would be. But if that would convince her of my love, I'd do it.

"Let's not go too far," she said. "I like *that*, and your face, as they are." She patted my cheek, and I laughed.

"Good to know you like something about me," I teased as she headed for the counter to check out.

She turned and smiled at me over her shoulder. "There are many things I love about you, Jackson."

Her words made me stop in my tracks. It wasn't a declaration of love, but it was definitely a step in the right direction. And for the first time, I felt hopeful. Hopeful that Sloan would give me a second chance.

CHAPTER TWENTY-ONE

Sloan

Sweat dripped down my forehead, and I wiped it away. The sun was beating down on me, but I wasn't going to give up. Jackson and I had been practicing my self-defense maneuvers every day since the morning after we'd arrived in Turks and Caicos. It had been three days now, and every day showed me just how out of practice I was.

And just how horny I was. The past three nights, Jackson and I had slept in the same bed, but our clothes had remained on. He'd been opposed to sharing a bed at first, but I'd promised to follow the rules, frustrating as they might be.

The no-sex rule was both great and terrible. Great because it had given us time to reconnect as Jackson had suggested. To deepen our emotional bond. But also terrible for obvious reasons.

For instance, how was I supposed to resist this man when he was shirtless and his skin glistened from the sun and exertion?

Though he wasn't exerting himself nearly as much as I was. Jackson looked hot, while I was a sweating, panting mess. My face was probably red, my hair sticking to my skin. And he still looked amazing.

So unfair.

"Sloan," he chided. "Stop looking at me like that."

"Like what?"

He narrowed his eyes at me. "You know what?"

"I'm sorry. I was just…admiring the view."

"Admiring the view is what landed you on your back last time."

"I didn't hear you complaining," I said.

His eyes darkened, likely replaying the moment when he'd pinned me to the mat, straddling me. I'd stared up at him, panting, his crotch only inches from my face. At that point, I hadn't even cared that he'd beaten me—again.

"Come on." He turned for the patio. "Let's take a water break and cool off."

"Fine," I huffed, shoulders slumped as I shuffled over. I gulped down some water. "I thought I was doing well until I started training with you again."

"You *are* doing well." He placed a hand on my shoulder. "I know you're frustrated, but I want you to be challenged. I want you to grow. I want you to be able to protect yourself no matter what size or how skilled your opponent is."

"I know." I grabbed a towel and dried my forehead. "I do. And I want that too, but…I feel like I'm never going to be able to beat you."

"You defended yourself on the boat the night you thought I was an intruder."

"True," I said. "But it was dark, and you weren't expecting it."

"No, but it goes to show that you have good instincts. And the more we train, the more it becomes muscle memory. I trained for years in the Navy and then at Hudson. It shouldn't be easy for you—or anyone—to take me down. Otherwise, I wouldn't be very good at my job."

"I thought you never wanted it to get to that point," I said, thinking of a conversation we'd had the other day while walking on the beach.

I'd learned a lot about the strategy that went into Jackson's job. The goal was always to prevent any issues before someone could even get remotely close to the client—or, rather, principal. To minimize potential problems through planning. To de-escalate situations if they arose.

He'd asked about my job and my role in the family business. He'd made me think—asking me questions like, what I would've done if I hadn't become the SVP for Huxley Hotels. Or what I was passionate about. It had been so long since anyone had been interested to hear my answer without expecting me to say the right thing.

The truth was, I loved my family and my job. Maybe it wasn't what I would've chosen if given the chance, but I didn't regret it. I knew how privileged I was. And I loved making an impact on employees' lives. I loved getting to travel the world and see amazing places. I loved creating an experience for our guests, giving them the luxury service they could depend on no matter what Huxley Grand location they visited.

Besides, even if I'd wanted to step down—which I didn't —I couldn't. I took my responsibility seriously. My role was about more than just me; it was about carrying on my family's legacy.

My grandparents had built something incredible. I knew how important the brand had been to them. How important it was to Graham and even Jasper. Sure, they could hire someone to replace me if I stepped down, but this was a family business. And we were a team.

Since our parents' deaths, it had always felt like us against the world. That was a big reason why Jackson and I had always understood each other so well. Loss, grief, responsibility brought on by death shaped people. And Jackson understood and respected the sense of duty I felt toward my family and the Huxley brand.

Part of me wondered if I'd told him about it when we were younger—told him who my family was and what would be expected of me one day—how he would've reacted. But I'd never given him the chance. So, while there were times in the past when I'd wanted to blame him for the breakdown of our relationship, I could acknowledge that my decisions had played a role as well.

But this was a fresh start. A chance to get to know each other. We'd had so many conversations lately. It had been nice. Our exchanges were deep and meaningful, genuine. It was so…refreshing.

We'd discussed a wide range of topics, from music to the big questions of life, and I'd enjoyed getting to know Jackson again—as the man he was now. He wasn't all that different from before, just more…confident. More secure in himself in a way he hadn't been when we were younger.

I loved that we could talk about anything and everything. I loved that he made me smile, made me laugh. I loved that he encouraged me, empowered me. I loved him.

I stilled. *I love him?*

A sense of peace settled over me at the acknowledgment. *I love him.* I smiled, realizing it was true. It was just as true now as it had been fourteen years ago.

"Sloan?"

I turned to him, wondering if my thoughts were written across my face. "What was that?"

He wore a bemused smile. "I asked if you were done for the day."

I smoothed back my hair. "Let's practice a little more before we shower and go into town and check on the boat."

"Sure." He gulped down some water. His Adam's apple bobbed with every swallow, and I'd never been more entranced by someone's throat.

I turned and headed for the area where we'd been practicing. I took a deep breath and tried to center myself. Tried to ignore how unbelievably attractive Jackson was and the fact that I was falling for him. Had already fallen for him, if I was being completely honest with myself.

I sighed. This was... This wasn't supposed to happen. But there'd never been any other choice. Not when it came to him.

I'd never been able to resist Jackson. And he'd been showing me that I could trust him in so many ways. The man had gotten a tattoo for me. I was literally inked on his skin.

"Ready?" Jackson asked.

"Yes," I said. And even though I knew he was referring to our sparring, it felt like I was agreeing to so much more.

"TOMORROW'S THE ECLIPSE," JACKSON SAID OVER DINNER A FEW nights later. We were sitting on the covered patio enjoying the sunset and a meal prepared by one of the resort's private chefs.

I took a sip of my wine. "Hopefully the weather will hold out."

There was a thirty percent chance of rain, and visibility was on everyone's mind. Everywhere we went on the island, it was all anyone talked about. The eclipse. The best place to view it. The concern for visibility during the totality.

I hoped it would all work out, but if not, I was still enjoying myself. Part of me couldn't believe we were over halfway through our trip. I wondered what would happen when it ended and we went home. What would that even look like?

The board was still deliberating about the proposed chief of security position. I was hopeful, but I wasn't going to tell Jackson until they'd agreed. If they didn't, well, I was going to have to think of another plan to make sure Jackson and I would have job options in the same city. But with Graham and Jasper on my side, I felt confident we could push it through.

Graham had done some more digging, even though I'd told him not to. It was too risky while Hudson was sniffing around, but he'd assured me no one would ever know. I hoped his confidence wouldn't bite him in the butt someday.

And for the first time since I'd been gone, another threatening note had appeared—this time at my office. I was glad I wasn't in London, though Jackson assured me that Hudson was close to wrapping up their investigation. We were scheduled to have a debrief with their team and the Huxley board soon.

"You're awfully serious." Jackson placed his hand over mine. "You okay?"

I shrugged off my thoughts and forced myself to focus on the present. I didn't want to ruin the rest of this trip—and my time with Jackson—by worrying about the future.

I'd loved our time on Turks and Caicos. We spent our days exploring the island, swimming in the pool, and practicing self-defense. Life here, with Jackson, was romantic and easy and fun. We still hadn't discussed the future, but I tried to be content with what we were and the promise of what might be. Because any time I let myself imagine the future, *this* was what I wanted.

I took a sip of wine. "What do you think will happen at the debrief?"

The flavors of tangerine, mango, and honeysuckle exploded on my tongue. The wine was both flavorful and refreshing.

Jackson set down his silverware and scanned the horizon. "Hudson has narrowed down their list to a few suspects. We're close."

"Can I see it?"

"Are you sure that's a good idea?"

"What if I know something that could help solve it? What if I could clear someone who was innocent?"

"At this point," he said, "you have to assume that any one of the suspects is guilty."

"What happened to innocent until proven guilty?" I joked.

"While we're investigating, it's best to remain suspicious of everyone until the culprit is found."

I stared off at the horizon, startling when Jackson placed his hand on mine. "Hey. We will find whoever is responsible."

"I..." I swallowed hard. "You're right. I'm not sure I want to see who's on the list. And I don't want to talk about this anymore. I think I'm going to go for a swim. Want to join me?"

"Sure," he said. "I need to make a call, and then I'll meet you out here in a little bit."

"Okay." I headed inside, thanking the chef for the meal and refilling my glass of wine.

Jackson was in the spare room, so I chatted with the chef before heading back to our room to change. I combed through my suitcase before settling on my most daring swimsuit, one I hadn't worn yet. Had never worn since it was on the more risqué side.

At first glance, it looked like a classy one-piece white swimsuit. It wasn't until after I'd received the suit that I'd realized it was a thong and there was no lining. It was quite sheer, and it would be even more so when wet.

It wasn't particularly practical, especially for sailing or snorkeling. Or anything except perhaps seduction. But it would definitely torture Jackson, and that was the point.

It must have been on the bed when I'd been packing, and maybe my housekeeper had thrown it in the suitcase. Who knew. I hadn't intended to wear it, but this seemed like the perfect occasion.

I threw on a cover-up just in case the chef was still cleaning up, but I was fairly sure he'd already left. Fortunately, my suspicions were confirmed when I went to refill my wineglass. I grabbed the bottle and Jackson's glass and carried them out to the pool.

I turned on the jets for the hot tub and climbed in. The house was mostly dark apart from a light in the kitchen, and the patio glowed softly from the lights that lined the walkway and edges.

It wasn't long before Jackson joined me, stripping out of his shirt before slipping beneath the water. It was warmer than I'd realized, and the sight of a shirtless Jackson made me even hotter. I took a sip of my wine, hoping it would cool me down, but I was beginning to perspire. My sexy seduction was turning into a sweaty one.

Jackson rested his arms on the back of the tub, his eyes gleaming with amusement. "Hot?" I nodded. "I was surprised you chose the hot tub."

"It sounded nice for my sore muscles."

He regarded me with a bemused smile over the top of his wineglass. The waves crashed in the distance, and I pushed my hair away from my face, clipping it up.

I stood and sat on the edge of the hot tub, my legs still dangling in the water. Jackson made a choked sound, and when I glanced up, he looked like a cartoon character whose eyes were bulging out of their head—comically so.

"You okay?" I asked in a sweet tone.

"What—" He wheezed. Coughed. "What the fuck are you wearing?"

I glanced down at my suit, and yep, it was completely sheer. The material clung to my nipples like I was in a wet-T-shirt contest. "A swimsuit," I said, being deliberately obtuse.

"It's—" He started to say, and I stood and turned to grab a towel to dab at my face. "Oh, holy fuck. You're trying to kill me."

I smiled to myself, pleased that my plan was working.

"Damn, *hayati*. Your ass looks fine as fuck."

With my back still to Jackson, I smiled and took my sweet-ass time bending forward to get the towel. When I turned to face Jackson, he was gripping the edge of the hot tub so hard I thought he might crack the tile.

I was desperate for him to touch me. My nipples were hard points against the material, and I knew he could see them. He swallowed hard, his breath quickening.

He smoothed his hand up his chest and over his throat. "Spread your legs," he commanded. "I want to see you."

I bit my lip, considering. "Not unless you show me something."

He stood, his cock bulging against his swimsuit. He pushed his suit over his hips and sat on the edge of the hot tub. "Does that work?"

"Definitely," I said as he took his cock in hand, reminded of that night on the boat not so long ago. His muscles flexed with the movement, the entire thing so freaking sexy.

If I'd thought I was hot before, I was molten lava now. I knew we were skirting the rules, but I didn't care. I needed him more than I needed my next breath. And if this was the only way I could have Jackson right now, then I'd take whatever I could get.

I took my time, spreading my legs, the water sliding down my skin. His jaw dropped even lower. "Touch yourself," he rasped. "Slowly."

I did as he'd asked, circling my clit in lazy movements. I could feel his eyes on me the entire time, his blue irises dark with desire. He started pumping his cock, and I wasn't even sure if he realized he was doing it.

He stood and inched closer to me, splashing water as he did so. "I really—" he took few more tentative steps "—*really* want to kiss you."

"I really want you to kiss me." But I waited on my perch, letting him look his fill. Basking in his attention.

"I…" He swallowed, his eyes scanning me. "You…" He inhaled a shaky breath and let it out slowly.

"It's okay. You can touch me," I panted, silently begging him to do just that.

"If I do, I won't be able to stop."

"Would that be so terrible?" I wasn't above begging. I needed this man.

And at this point, I wasn't sure what difference it would make. Yes, he was technically still my bodyguard, but there was little reason to be concerned for my safety in a gated resort. And I knew Jackson would never willingly put me in danger.

"No. And yes."

I stood, and he placed his hands on my hips, smoothing them over my ass. He groaned. "I *love* this swimsuit."

"And I—" I gave him a quick peck "—love—" another kiss, slower this time "—you." The words came out unbidden, but they were true. It was so easy. So simple. So…right.

I didn't know what the future held, but I wanted Jackson to be a part of mine.

He blinked a few times, and I smiled back at him. He cupped my face, his eyes full of adoration. I leaned in to kiss him, and his lips curved against mine. This kiss was a home-coming and a revelation. A second chance and a new beginning.

CHAPTER TWENTY-TWO

Jackson

S loan and I had kissed countless times, and yet this one felt different. It wasn't the stolen kisses of our youth or the bittersweet ones. Nor was it quite like our recent kisses—passionate and full of longing and regret. This kiss was a fresh start.

Hearing her say those words—that she loved me—was a precious gift. I pulled Sloan even closer, loving the feel of her in my arms. She loved me. Trusted me. I vowed not to fuck this up.

I tugged her onto my lap, my cock slipping against the slick, wet material of her swimsuit. She felt so good. Too good. It would be so easy to pull the material aside and slide into her. She wanted it, and so did I.

But I was also determined to do things right this time. No more sneaking around. No more secrets from family and friends. Until everything was settled with my sister and Hudson, this was the way it had to be.

I was lucky Vaughn hadn't fired me on the spot when I'd told him I'd slept with the principal. I'd gotten the feeling he was tempted to, but I was thankful he'd only threatened it.

He was trusting me, counting on me, and I'd promised him it wouldn't happen again. He wasn't just my boss; he was my friend and mentor. And he'd done so much for me that I felt like I owed him this.

But Sloan was the woman I loved, and she loved me. I still couldn't believe it. Even after everything, she loved me.

I was ready to say fuck it, fuck the rules. But Sloan stilled her movements. I rested my forehead against hers, her breath coasting over my lips, my restraint being tested like never before.

"I'm sorry," she whispered. "Sorry." She moved to leave. "I lost control. I shouldn't have—" She shook her head. "I'm going to shower and change for bed."

Wait. What?

Was this part of her plan to torture me? Because fuck, that swimsuit had made me nearly lose my goddamn mind. Even now, I was still obsessed with it. With her. She was so fucking... I bit my knuckles to stifle a groan.

Sloan stepped out of the hot tub and headed for the outdoor shower. "I'm going to go rinse off."

I followed her with my eyes, unable to look away. She turned on the water and stepped beneath the spray, and it was over. The water cascaded down her skin, the white material clinging to her body. It was the hottest thing I'd ever seen.

Without thinking, I bolted from the hot tub and went to her.

"Jackson, wh—"

I removed the detachable showerhead from the hook and turned down the temperature. "Is this okay?" I sprayed water on her stomach to let her get used to the temperature.

She nodded, her expression full of tentative hope. "What are you...?"

I glanced around for something for her to rest her foot

on. There was a stool nearby with towels on it. I grabbed it and tossed the towels aside. "Foot," I grunted. "Here."

She did as I asked, and then I shifted the spray to her clit. She let out a sound of pleasure, her legs shaking. "Yes," she hissed, and I kept adjusting my angle to maximize her pleasure. "Yes, Jackson."

I was definitely skirting the rules, but I wasn't breaking them. I wasn't touching her. At least, not directly.

With my free hand, I palmed my cock, stroking myself to the sight of her. To the sounds she made. Fuck, she was something.

And she loved me.

"Do you have any idea how sexy you are?" I asked, watching her thrust her hips. She wanted more, and I did too. The idea of sinking into Sloan as she said "I love you" nearly sent me over the edge. But I wouldn't come, not until she did first.

"Play with your tits," I said, knowing how much she liked nipple play. God, I couldn't wait to touch her again. To put my mouth on her.

Soon, I vowed.

She complied, running her hands over her breasts. Pinching her nipples. Arching her back and moaning my name as she convulsed.

I sped up my pace, gripping my cock tighter until I painted her stomach with ropes of come, feeling both satisfied and yet not. It wasn't the same, but it would have to be enough for now.

Sloan placed her hands on her thighs, bending forward to catch her breath. She lifted her head, and we shared a secret smile.

"Come on." I rinsed her down, then myself, then the tiles before switching off the water. "Let's go to bed."

I wrapped her in a towel, and she went inside. I checked the perimeter as I did every night and locked up before heading down the hall to the bedroom. I checked my phone for any missed calls. Vaughn had left a voice mail that the man behind Sloan's threats had been caught. But when I'd tried to call him back after dinner to find out more, he'd been unavailable.

Sloan was already in bed, a book in hand, when I arrived. I wanted to tell her the news but not until I had more information. I knew the topic upset her, understandably so. And I didn't want to send her into a tailspin when she was winding down for bed.

I put on some athletic shorts and brushed my teeth before joining her in bed. "What are you reading?"

"It's a steamy romance. Nate's next movie, in fact."

"Ah. Right." I'd seen some of that author's novels floating around Nate's house. But I didn't remember Sloan reading much romance in college. "What do you like about reading romance?"

"This might sound cheesy, but I like that there's always a happily ever after."

"That doesn't sound cheesy." I took her hand in mine. "Sometimes when life feels crazy or beyond our control, it's nice to return to something that feels safe, maybe even predictable in a way."

"Exactly," she agreed, shutting the book and placing it on her nightstand.

"So just how steamy are we talking?"

"There's definitely a plot," she hedged, her cheeks pinkening. "And the sex scenes further the plot."

"Are they hot?"

"Yeah." She gave me a heated look. "They're hot."

"One of the guys I worked with at Hudson is big into romance." Not that I'd be working with Connor or any of the

Hudson team much longer. But I didn't tell Sloan that—I couldn't. At least, not yet.

"Seriously?"

"Yeah." I nodded, thinking of Connor or "Cujo." "His wife works for a big publishing house, and they fell in love over books."

"So he read romance to impress her?"

I chuckled. "Something like that. But then he fell in love with the stories too."

Sloan turned and faced me, tucking her hands beneath her cheek. "I'm surprised you never married."

I lifted a shoulder. "It was hard to fathom spending my life with someone when my heart has always belonged to you."

She smiled. "I love you, Jackson."

"Love you too," I said, still in a state of disbelief. When she'd said it earlier, I could've chalked it up to something in the heat of the moment. But now that things had cooled down, and she'd looked at me directly as she said those words, I knew she meant them with her whole heart.

She laughed.

"What?" I asked.

"You seem surprised."

I caressed her shoulder. "I'm grateful. I wasn't sure I'd ever hear that again from you."

She leaned in, cupping my cheek. Her gaze was sincere and full of love. "I love you." She said the words slowly, enunciating each syllable.

I kissed her. "I love you too."

"Can we...cuddle?" She wore a sheepish expression.

"Of course," I said. "You know you never have to ask."

"I know, but I pushed your limits earlier, and I didn't want to make things more difficult for you."

I chuckled, pulling her into me, holding her close. "I'll live."

We fell asleep like that with her in my arms.

When I woke the next morning, she rolled over to face me. Damn, she looked fucking radiant. Hair mussed, green eyes sparkling. Her lips were full and pouty, her cheeks flushed from sleep.

This woman loved me. *Me.*

I reached out gently, smoothing her hair away from her face. "Morning."

"Morning." She smiled. "Breakfast then drills?"

"Sounds good," I agreed.

She met me out on the training area a little while later. We ran through some drills, and I could see improvement in both her strength and the quickness of her responses. I knew she got frustrated that she couldn't take me down, but I was proud of her tenacity and determination.

With the repairs finished on the *Athena*, we were supposed to head out tomorrow on the next leg of our trip. The weather looked favorable, and with our visit with Greer coming up, I had something I'd been meaning to discuss. I'd put it off as long as I could, but I didn't want to wait much longer.

"I think we should tell Greer about us while we're all together in Puerto Rico."

"I don't know." Sloan kicked my legs out from beneath me, and I used a move that brought her to the padded mat. I rolled us so she was on top. I brushed her hair away from her face, and she leaned forward so our lips were nearly touching.

"Jackson," she moaned, my cock hard against her. Apart from our interlude in the outdoor shower last night, this was the closest we'd come to having sex. The daily temptation, especially when we sparred, was going to kill me. And the memory of her in that white swimsuit…

I rolled us again so that I was pinning her to the ground; her hips arched up as mine pressed down. We writhed against each other, and I couldn't seem to stop.

Sloan loved me, and I loved her. And in this moment, that was all that mattered. Fuck the consequences; she was my everything.

I told myself it was fine as long as we stayed fully clothed. Okay, semi-clothed, considering my shirtless state and the fact that Sloan was wearing a sports bra. Sloan raked her hands down my back, nipping at my chest.

I groaned. "Are you trying to distract me?"

"Should I stop?" she asked, but her hips kept moving in time with mine.

Instead of answering, I kissed her hard and deep, my tongue mimicking what I wanted to do with my cock.

"Yes," she moaned. "Right there. Don't stop." She panted. "Don't stop."

She rocked against me, and it felt as if my last tether of control was close to snapping. "Sloan."

Unable to resist, I rolled us again. My brain was no longer in control of my body. My movements were primal and rough, and I knew from her expression that she was loving it. That she was right there with me.

I used my hold on her hips to guide her over my cock, bringing me closer and closer to release. The friction was driving me wild, and Sloan looked just as out of control.

I linked our hands, and she squeezed mine. I could feel her heat and desire through the fabric, and I didn't think I could hold on much longer. My pleasure was coiled so tight, I was going to fucking explode.

"Oh god. Oh, Jackson." Her mouth opened as her pleasure crested, and she let out a string of unintelligible words.

She was glorious. The most beautiful thing I'd ever seen. And not a moment later, lightning shot down my spine. My muscles clenched, and then I felt that rush of satisfaction and relief that came with release.

I stared up at the sky, completely spent. And so fucking happy.

She fell against my chest, laughing. Panting. "Oh my god. I can't believe—"

I chuckled, the ground warm beneath my skin. "That we're acting like horny teenagers."

"Yes," she sighed. "That's exactly what I feel like."

"I'm not complaining," I said.

"Maybe there's something to your no-sex rule after all."

I swept her hair away from her face. "Not sure I've been the best at following the rules, considering..." I gestured at my crotch and the mess I'd made of it.

"There was no penetration," she said, adopting a serious tone. "Oral or vaginal."

"I love it when you talk dirty to me," I teased.

She laughed, pushing off my chest to stand. "Come on," she said. "Let's get cleaned up so we can watch the eclipse."

I pulled her in for a hug, and she buried her face in my chest. "I can't believe we just did that."

I chuckled and kissed the top of her head before releasing her. Sloan showered in our bathroom while I used the other. We were skirting too close to the rules, and I needed to stop putting myself in situations where I'd be tempted. The idea was laughable. When Sloan was around, I was always tempted.

I joined her on the patio a little later. I put on my solar eclipse glasses and peered up at the sky. The moon started its trek over the sun.

I sank down on the lounge chair next to hers. "So... Greer?" I asked, returning to our earlier conversation.

Sloan shook her head. "I don't know…"

"I know you're nervous," I said. "And so am I. But we're all adults, and I hope she can be happy for us."

"And if she's not?" Sloan asked, voicing my biggest fear aloud.

My gut twisted. "I'd rather not consider that outcome."

An outcome where my sister wasn't talking to me and Sloan had lost her best friend. An outcome where Greer felt like we'd betrayed her or she was all alone.

"Neither do I. But we have to at least consider the possibility. I mean, how's she going to feel that we kept this from her for years? *Years*, Jackson. We lied to her all that time."

I said nothing. I didn't know what to say.

Sloan's expression was forlorn, and something inside me cracked. "I can't lose her. She's always been there for me. I can't imagine my life without her in it."

"I know," I said. "But if we want a future together, that means we're going to have to tell her at some point."

She let out a heavy sigh.

"Tell me what's going through that pretty head of yours." I tucked her hair behind her ear. "Hm?"

"I just… I don't think now is the right time. Something is going on with Greer, and she needs our support."

"I don't disagree, but there will always be a reason not to tell her. We will always worry about her reaction." It felt as if I'd been waiting my whole life to be with Sloan. Not in secret, but in a truly meaningful way. "I don't want to hurt my sister, but I'm done hiding my feelings for you."

I thought Sloan would say no. I prepared myself for it, but then she said, "And what if she asks about our plans for after the trip?"

"What would you want to tell her?" I sensed we were using Greer as a guise for a conversation Sloan had been wanting to have. I was fucking thrilled—it meant she wanted a future with me.

But it was frustrating that I couldn't tell her about my resignation. Not yet anyway. I hoped Vaughn would figure out how he wanted to handle it soon, because I hated keeping secrets from Sloan.

We kept putting on our glasses to check the progress of the moon and then taking them off. It was pretty wild.

"I think we need to be prepared to tell her something. Are we going to do the long-distance thing? Should I plan to stay in Los Angeles for a while? I can't relocate permanently without the board's approval."

"I want to be wherever you are," I said, and I meant it. "I don't want to do long-distance."

"Agreed. My life is busy as it is, and long-distance takes its toll on a relationship. Does that mean you'd consider moving to London?"

"Yes." Now that I no longer worked for Hudson, I could look for jobs anywhere.

There were private security companies based in London, and working at Hudson Security for the past fourteen years came with a cache of sorts. That said, any future employer might ask why I was leaving Hudson, and I was going to have to figure out how to handle that.

Just then, it got darker. It was strange, as if someone had applied a filter over the sun that made everything appear like it was twilight even though it was the middle of the day. The temperature dropped, and when I looked up in the sky, the moon had almost completely covered the sun.

"Oh my god." Sloan's voice was full of wonder.

I reached out and grabbed her hand, staring up at the sky and this amazing astronomical sight. As the moon continued on its path, the sun was completely covered, leaving only a bright ring around it. It was...incredible, truly.

I glanced over at Sloan and smiled. She was completely in awe of the eclipse, and I was enthralled by her.

"Good call on staying for this." She gave my hand a squeeze.

We watched the rest in silence until, finally, the moment had passed and the sun was being revealed again.

"Okay," Sloan said. "We'll tell Greer when we're in Puerto Rico. But only after we see how she's doing."

Okay. Wow. Part of me couldn't believe she'd relented, even if she'd pushed to tell Greer about us in the past.

"Of course. It's not like we're going to spring it on her as soon as she lands." Though, the idea was tempting, if only to be done with it. Rip off the Band-Aid, so to speak.

"And I think we should tell her together."

"I agree," I said. "Then we can answer any questions she might have."

"Oh…" Sloan dragged a hand through her hair, and I sensed her nervousness from that one gesture. "I'm sure she'll have questions."

I didn't care how many questions Greer had; I'd answer every one of them as long as she kept talking to us.

CHAPTER TWENTY-THREE

Sloan

"You ready for this?" Jackson asked the following morning.

"As ready as I'm going to be."

He gave my thigh a squeeze. "It's over now. Okay?"

I rolled my lips between my teeth and nodded. Jackson had told me that the culprit had been apprehended but that he was waiting on details. We both were. I was relieved they'd caught the person behind the threats, but I dreaded finding out their identity and the reasons behind the notes.

"He can't hurt you anymore. I won't let anyone hurt you."

I'd needed that reassurance, more than I'd realized. Jackson always knew what I needed to hear.

I took a breath and pressed the button to connect the video conference. The LA boardroom came into view, the table surrounded by members of the board, a team from Hudson, and my brothers. Graham was sitting at the head of the table, flanked by Nate and Knox. Jasper joined us on the screen from London.

"Hey, Knox. Nate." I smiled at them, trying to project a

calmness I didn't feel. Knox and Nate rarely attended board meetings. "This is a nice surprise."

"Hey, Sloan." Knox smiled. "We asked to be kept in the loop." Instead of being annoyed like I might have been in the past, I was grateful. It was nice to know my family cared.

Sure, they could sometimes take things too far. But maybe I could keep more of an open mind regarding their suggestions in the future.

I greeted the board members and introduced Jackson before Hudson made their own introductions. When Jackson's boss, Vaughn, stated his name, I tried to maintain a neutral expression. I didn't want to do anything to call attention to my relationship with Jackson.

When we finally settled into the reason for the call, it was Vaughn who addressed everyone. "I'm happy to report that Hudson caught and apprehended the culprit." A rumble of interest went through the room. "It was an employee named Sheldon Lansberger."

I furrowed my brow. "One of the butlers?" I couldn't believe he was behind the notes. Sheldon had been at the Huxley Grand London for years. I hadn't known him well, but he'd always been polite. Professional. "You're sure?"

"Our team caught him on camera then handed him over to the authorities."

I chewed on my lip. "Do you... Did he say why?"

Jackson took my hand in his out of view of the camera. His touch was reassuring, and it grounded me.

Even though I'd been scared to ask, I wanted to know. I needed to understand why Sheldon had felt compelled to send me such nasty, terrifying notes. Maybe then I'd finally be able to put the matter to rest.

I doubted it, but I wanted to try.

"Sheldon's aunt used to work in housekeeping," Vaughn said. "When the Huxley brand changed the cleaning schedule after the pandemic, Sheldon claims it promoted an unsafe working environment. He believes it pushed housekeeping to complete too many tasks and too many rooms in too short of a time. And that led to a fall that broke her hip."

"That's terrible," I said. "Is she okay?"

"She is. Or rather, she was. She's since died, but she stopped working after the fall."

I furrowed my brow. "Because of her injury?"

"Because of the time it took to heal, and the fact that she was no longer able to perform the tasks required for the role."

"But surely we would've found an alternate position that would've accommodated her needs. The Huxley Hotels are a family. We don't just—" I waved a hand through the air "— kick someone out, especially if they've been a loyal employee."

Graham nodded. "I looked it up. She was offered another position, but she turned it down. During her treatment from the fall, the doctors discovered that she had Stage 4 cancer. She died a few months later."

"Oh my gosh. That's terrible." My heart ached for this family and the suffering they'd endured. "But what does that have to do with Huxley and Sheldon's threats?"

It was Vaughn who responded. "Sheldon believes the cleaning products used by Huxley employees were responsible for his aunt's cancer and subsequent death."

Suddenly, the threats made a lot more sense. *Toxic Bitch. Poison.* The skull and crossbones even looked like the ones you might find on a cleaning label.

"Is there any truth to that claim?" I asked, hoping like hell there wasn't. Not just for the sake of limiting the brand's liability, but for the well-being of our employees.

Graham shook his head. "Absolutely none. We use the

best nontoxic cleaning products available, and we train our employees to use them safely."

"He's right," one of the board members chimed in. "I've read studies and spoken to a number of top health officials."

That was a relief, but still... "So why did Sheldon threaten me? What did he want?"

"He was clearly angry and grieving," Jasper said with a meaningful look. We all knew what that felt like, and we could definitely relate. But still, my siblings and I had never sent anyone death threats regarding our parents' deaths or our grandparents'.

"He claims she spent hours in pain on the floor of the hotel bathroom waiting for help when she broke her hip," Vaughn said.

"What did the accident report say?" I asked. We always performed an internal investigation in cases like these—whether an employee or a guest was injured, not that it occurred frequently. But despite all our best efforts, accidents did happen.

It was Graham who answered. "She was lying there for an hour."

"Why so long?" I asked. Housekeeping staff weren't allowed to carry their personal devices, but they were issued radios each shift. "Did she use her radio to call for help?"

"It was hooked to her cart in the hall."

I frowned. That went against protocol, and it was clearly something we should remind all housekeeping employees to keep on their person. "Did no one hear her call for help?"

Assuming she'd followed other protocol, her cleaning cart should've been parked in front of the room, blocking the door. But the door would've been open.

"Apparently not," Graham said. "She was working a room at the end of a hall during the middle of the day when most people would be out."

Everyone on the screen wore somber expressions that I knew matched my own.

"And he somehow thought I was responsible?" I asked.

Of course I was responsible for the care of my employees and their safety. And we'd definitely revisit training and protocol. But there wasn't much I could do about an accident.

"He wasn't thinking rationally," Vaughn said. "He wanted someone to blame."

I could understand that. But still, it felt personal. Like an attack on me specifically. Because it was.

I sighed, feeling heavy from all these revelations. I felt bad for Sheldon and his loss. And I felt bad for his aunt and what she'd endured. "What will happen to him now?"

"The team from Hudson handed him over to the authorities. He'll be sent to trial, and you might be asked to testify."

Great. Just when I'd thought this nightmare was finally over. Still, it was a huge relief to know he'd been caught.

"And you think that's the end of it, right?" I asked.

"Correct," Vaughn said. "But we will continue to investigate. Regardless, I'd still recommend a bodyguard."

The rest of the call went fairly quickly, and Graham dismissed the board and the team from Hudson. Everyone filed out of the room, leaving Jackson and me alone with Graham, Knox, Nate, and Jasper.

"Should I—?" Jackson moved as if to leave.

"No. Stay." I placed my hand on his arm. "Please?"

A look passed between us. "Of course."

When I returned my attention to the screen, Nate was watching us with a bemused smile. And Graham's lips were set in a firm line, though there was nothing new about that. It was his typical RBF, or "resting brooding face," as Jasper liked to joke.

"How do you feel?" Knox asked, breaking the silence.

"Conflicted," I said. "Relieved that it's over, but also…sad."

"Sad about the situation that led to the threats?" Nate asked, always reading me so well.

Jackson placed his hand on my back, rubbing circles in a calming motion. Jasper arched his brow at that, as did Graham. I ignored their curious looks, hoping they'd assume Jackson was my friend who was comforting me.

"It's just a sad story," I said. "And it's unnerving, to think that a trusted employee could turn like that."

"His actions have nothing to do with you, Sloan," Jackson said. "You know what grief is like. How it can…skew the way you think." I nodded, feeling my family's eyes on us. Watching us intently. "He needed someone to blame, and you were a convenient target. That's all."

I could understand that, but Sheldon was so angry. I'd been devastated when my grandparents had died, but I'd leaned on my brothers. On Greer. I wondered who was there for Sheldon. Maybe no one.

"Can you give us a minute, Jackson?" Graham said to him.

I kept my attention on the screen. "Jackson's staying."

"Are you—" Jackson started to ask, but I squeezed his hand. He fell silent.

Graham and I had a wordless staring contest in which he told me to get rid of Jackson and I told him that Jackson wasn't going anywhere. Normally, Graham would've dug in his heels. And eventually, I might have let it go, backed down. But perhaps Graham sensed that I wasn't going to budge.

"Fine." He pinched the bridge of his nose then glared at Jackson. "He has an NDA, and I have other ways of silencing someone."

"Graham," I hissed, annoyed by his threats. I took a deep breath and opened my mouth to speak.

"Sloan," Graham cut me off. "I know you hate it when we

step in—or rather, when we overstep. But I'm your big brother, and I love you. It's my job to protect you."

I gaped at him. I couldn't remember the last time he'd said those words. Sure, they were there, always beneath the surface, but it was nice to hear them all the same. And maybe I'd been a little too harsh, a little too stubborn.

"I was going to say thank you." I smiled, appreciating both his acknowledgment of the fact that they had a tendency to overstep and shocked that he'd told me he loved me. "And I love you too."

Even Graham seemed surprised, though it barely registered on his face before it was gone.

"I'd still like to have HR review our sick leave policies as well as our housekeeping procedures." It was easier to focus on a path forward, on something to do.

"Agreed," Graham said.

"And Jasper," I said, "when I get back, I want to sit down with you to brainstorm some ideas on how to improve the employee experience."

"Of course," he said. "I'll let Halle know."

"Thanks."

We ended the call, and I stood and stretched. I turned to Jackson, wrapping my arms around his neck.

"You okay?" he asked.

I considered it a moment. "Surprisingly, yes."

The situation with Sheldon was disappointing, but it reminded me how fortunate I was to have so many people in my life who loved me. I had my family and Greer. My health. I had Jackson. Those were the things that mattered.

CHAPTER TWENTY-FOUR

Sloan

I fidgeted with my bracelets, but it did nothing to calm my nerves while Jackson and I waited at the airport for Greer to arrive. I would've sent the private jet for her, but she'd booked the tickets before telling me of her plans. She waved as she rode down the escalator to where we were waiting, her eyes hidden behind her sunglasses.

"Oh my god. Look at you." Greer pushed her glasses back on her head and gave me a hug. She pulled back, grinning at my flowy and colorful caftan. "You look so tan and relaxed and happy."

"I am. Hudson caught the person behind the threats."

"They did?" When I nodded, she sagged with relief. "Finally. Oh, I'm so glad. I knew my brother would keep you safe. I'm so sorry you had to deal with that."

She gave me another hug then turned to Jackson and smiled. "Hey, Jackson." She hugged him, and then he took her bag. "So who was it?"

I gave her a quick rundown.

"I'm so glad it's over. And this is so great." She hooked an arm around each of our waists. "All of us together."

I smiled brightly at Jackson, and he gave a subtle shake of his head. We'd agreed to tell Greer during her visit, and I was already dreading the conversation.

"What do you want to do first?" I asked. "Settle in? Go to the beach? Tour the old fort?"

"I hear they have good rum here." She waggled her brows.

Jackson and I shared a look. "Isn't it a little early for alcohol?" I asked.

"Not if it's part of a rum distillery tour. Come on." She linked our arms. "We're on island time now."

A muscle twitched in Jackson's forehead. "We can't just—"

"Oh, it's fine." Greer pulled me along with her. "We'll be safe. You'll be with us."

I glanced at Jackson over my shoulder as Greer dragged me through the airport. Greer had always liked to party and have fun, but this seemed out of character, even for her. She seemed...desperate for a distraction or something. Not simply eager to have a good time.

"It's your call, Sloan," Jackson said, deferring to me.

"You don't want to go back to the hotel and freshen up first?" I asked Greer. "Maybe visit the spa or hang out by the pool?"

"If we go to the spa, what will he do?" She hooked her thumb at Jackson.

I lifted a shoulder. "I don't know. That's new territory for me. Jackson?"

His mouth was set in a line, and I knew he was scanning the airport for any threats. Even if it hadn't been part of his job, it was a skill that was deeply ingrained in him after so many years. And I wondered if he ever relaxed. Truly relaxed. Apart from our time on the *Athena* with no one else in sight, I doubted it.

He pulled Greer's suitcase behind him. "I'll wait outside the treatment room."

Greer laughed as we headed out to the parking garage. "He really is all up in your business, huh?"

I laughed, though there was a nervous edge to it. "You have no idea."

"It must be annoying," she said while he loaded her bag into the trunk.

"Honestly, it's been nice having Jackson around."

"Good. I know this is a dream trip for him, and I'm glad you got to experience it together."

I smiled. "Me too."

She leaned in and lowered her voice. "Do you know if my brother's dating anyone?"

I swallowed hard, glancing away. Was this a trick question? Did Greer know?

"Why do you ask?" I tried to evade the question. Jackson and I had planned to tell Greer about us while we were all together, but this wasn't how I'd imagined the conversation going.

"Because he never brings anyone home to meet us. So I'm wondering if he told you about anyone or if he's just as much of a player as he ever was."

"You ready?" Jackson called.

"Yep," I chirped, grateful for the interruption.

While Jackson drove us back to the hotel, I texted the staff about spa treatments and responded to a quick email from Halle. Despite Greer's cheerful demeanor, I could feel the stress radiating off her in waves. I hoped the spa would be more relaxing and restorative than a rum tasting.

I would've asked Jackson if he wanted me to schedule him a massage, but I knew he would never agree. We'd enjoyed a couple's massage in Turks and Caicos, but he'd only relented because we'd been together.

When we reached the hotel, Jackson pulled into the VIP

entrance. One of the bellhops took Greer's bag to our suite, and Jackson accompanied us to the spa.

"This is gorgeous," Greer said as soon as we stepped through the large doors. I followed her gaze to a huge bowl that had orchids cascading down in rows. "Mm." She closed her eyes with a smile. "It smells so good. I love that scent."

"You can thank Jasper for that. And—" I headed over to one of the shelves where various beauty and self-care products were on display "—you can even take the smell home with you." I picked up one of the candles and handed it to her.

Greer removed the lid and inhaled deeply, closing her eyes with another smile. She already seemed more relaxed, and for that, I was grateful.

"That's divine. What is it?" She scanned the candle for information.

"It's our own custom scent." I leaned in and whispered, "It's oud wood, bourbon, and vanilla. We pump it through the public spaces in the hotel."

For all the times Graham razzed Jasper, he had good ideas. The intimacy kits provided in every room. The allergy-friendly menus. And the signature scent that created a sensory moment and an olfactory trigger of good memories.

He was good at creating an experience. At making people feel welcome and at ease despite the opulent surroundings, just like Gran had always been. He was also passionate about sustainability. We all were, but Jasper especially.

"Damn. That's clever."

"Right?" I turned to the front desk employee. I scanned her name tag. "Alondra, can you please add several of the candles to my tab?"

"Sloan, no," Greer said. "You know I'm paying for my

portion of the spa, right?" She stepped up to the counter and opened her purse.

"Greer." I placed my hand on hers. "I've got it."

"You sure?" she asked.

"Of course."

She smiled. "Thank you."

"Please add them to my bill, Alondra," I said, to avoid any confusion. "And anything else my guest would like."

Greer narrowed her eyes at me and opened her mouth as if to protest. I mouthed, "I've got it."

"Of course, Ms. Mackenzie." Alondra typed something on the computer.

"I love your name," I said, leaning on the counter. "So beautiful."

She smiled, her shoulders relaxing a little. "Thank you, ma'am. It means lark, but my mom heard it on a Spanish show and fell in love."

"That's lovely. There's actually an Alondra Valley in California. It's quite beautiful, and the Huxley Grand AV is nestled in among the mountains and the vineyards."

Greer sighed. "I love that location. My husband and I had our honeymoon there." And then her expression darkened, and she clamped her mouth shut.

Hm. If her reaction was anything to go by, her stressed-out state had something to do with Logan.

"I just love name meanings," Alondra said. "They're so interesting. For instance, your first name, Ms. Mackenzie, means 'warrior.'"

"Thank you," I said. "I think my gran told me that at some point."

"She was a lovely woman," Alondra said. "Very business-savvy but also just kind." I smiled, hoping that someday I could live up to my grandmother's legacy. Even now, years after her death, people still talked of her and Pops with love and reverence.

"She was," I agreed.

Alondra glanced at her computer. "Let me take you through."

When Jackson moved to follow us, Alondra frowned. "I'm sorry, sir. The spa is for patrons only."

I leaned in, lowering my voice. "He's my executive protection agent." When she furrowed her brow, I added, "My bodyguard. So he's going to have to come with us."

"Oh." Alondra's eyes widened. "Of course. I apologize for the misunderstanding."

"Not a problem." I smiled, hoping to reassure her that it was no big deal.

"Please, follow me."

Jackson waited outside the changing area. Gentle nature music played softly through hidden speakers, and the dim lighting added to the relaxed atmosphere.

"How was your trip?" I asked Greer as we changed into our robes.

"Good. Not nearly as exciting as sailing here, I'm sure." She smiled at one of the employees, accepting a cup of our signature herbal tea with gratitude.

I sipped my tea, the flavors coating my throat in warmth. "It's been quite the adventure." In every sense of the word.

"Jackson's not going to want to go to New York after this."

"Perhaps not," I said, smiling. "But I know he's looking forward to visiting you and your mom."

"Visit?" She laughed. "Jackson's not coming to visit. He's moving to New York."

My hand stilled, my tea hovering midair. "What?"

What was Greer talking about? Jackson didn't know where he was headed after this assignment.

"Yeah." Greer set her tea on a nearby table. "I don't know all the details, but Mom said something about him moving to New York for a promotion. Hudson asked Jackson to run the office there."

"Oh. That's…" I swallowed, feeling as if the words were made of glass. "That's great."

My stomach dropped. How could he possibly pass up an opportunity like that?

She tilted her head, considering. "I'm not surprised he didn't mention it. You know how Jackson is. As my mom always says, he's a tough nut to crack."

I tried not to panic, but I wondered why he'd never said anything. Why he'd said he'd be willing to move to London, despite the promotion in New York.

After everything Jackson had said, after everything we'd been through, surely… The room spun.

"Hey." Greer placed her hand on my arm. "You okay?"

Fortunately, I was saved from responding because it was time for our first treatment. An employee led us to the massage room. Jackson followed, but I didn't dare look at him. I was afraid my emotions would be written all over my face, and I wanted to discuss this later when we were alone.

He'd told me he loved me. He'd said I was his everything. But we'd been living in a bubble, and it felt as if it had just popped.

"What's new with you?" I asked Greer after we'd disrobed and were lying on the tables side by side. I didn't want to overthink the situation with Jackson, and I'd been worried about Greer. I knew she'd be more likely to confide in me if her brother wasn't around.

She blew out a breath. "I needed a break."

"Do you want to talk about it?" I asked, sensing there was more to the story.

"Maybe later. I just want to relax and enjoy this massage. But thanks for asking."

"Of course," I said as our massage therapists entered the room.

The massage felt amazing, but as much as I wanted to relax, I couldn't. I couldn't stop thinking about what Greer had said about Jackson and his promotion. About New York and the future.

I thought about this trip and all the ways he'd been there for me. I'd never felt so taken care of or cherished. I'd never felt more at ease than when I was with him. He made me feel desired and wanted, yes. But he also made me feel seen.

He showed me in so many ways—big and small—that he loved me. And I loved him. I'd always loved him.

Jackson was my everything, and I was done being scared. I was done holding back. I'd lost Jackson once before, and I'd do everything in my power to prevent it from happening again.

I FINISHED APPLYING MY LIP GLOSS AND HEADED FOR THE living room. I felt refreshed after spending the day with Greer at the spa. And while I hadn't gotten the chance to talk to Jackson, I had a plan. I took a deep breath and straightened.

When I entered the living room, Jackson was sitting on the couch. His head snapped up, his eyes lingering on my lips. The low neckline of my dress. The high slit that revealed my thigh.

He prowled over to me. "Damn, *hayati*." He rubbed his

chin, circling me. "You look good." He sounded both pained and pleased by the idea.

I smiled and met his gaze, admiring the fit of his linen button-down and pants. I smoothed my palms over his chest. "So do you."

He slid his hands up my thighs, grabbing my ass and hauling me closer. He growled and kissed my neck, and I forgot about everything but him. His hard length pressed against me. His scent surrounding me.

The door to Greer's room opened, and I dropped my hands and stepped back, my skirt falling back into place. Jackson inhaled slowly and turned away, adjusting himself. I smoothed my hands over my hips, hoping everything was covered.

"That dress looks gorgeous on you," I said to Greer, hoping she didn't notice how breathless I was. How guilty I looked.

"Thanks." She looped her arm through mine. She still hadn't told me what was going on, but she definitely didn't seem as frazzled as she had when she'd first arrived.

Even so, I knew her well enough to know that something was wrong. And her comments earlier about Logan had me concerned. They'd been together forever.

The three of us made our way down to one of the on-site restaurants, where we were seated overlooking the beach. Jackson was scanning the exits, studying everyone around us as always.

"This is amazing," Greer said, marveling at the alcove that surrounded us. It was as if we had our own little orchid grotto lit by lanterns. "I forgot how nice it is to travel with you."

I bumped her shoulder with mine. "We should do it more often."

"We should."

Though I didn't know how enthusiastic she'd be about the idea after she found out about Jackson and me. Maybe I'd blown the situation out of proportion, but this conversation had been years in the making.

My mind couldn't settle. Between the mystery situation with Greer and Logan, my secret relationship with Jackson, and Jackson's promotion, I had a lot on my mind. I needed to find out what was going on with Greer. And I knew I wouldn't be able to relax until I talked to Jackson about New York.

"I feel like I've barely seen you all day," Greer said to Jackson. "How have you been?"

He slid his hand onto my thigh beneath the table. "Good. Really good. What about you? How are the kids? How's Logan?"

"The kids are good. Work is busy."

"And Logan?" Jackson asked, pushing Greer despite the fact that she clearly didn't want to talk about her husband.

Greer waved a hand through the air. "I'm here to have fun and forget about Logan."

"Greer," Jackson chided. "What's going on?"

She shook her head, holding back tears even as she forced a smile. "It's not something I want to discuss right now, let alone with my brother. Can you please just drop it?"

He sighed, and I knew he was torn between respecting her wishes and dragging the truth out of her. I placed my hand over his beneath the table and gave it a reassuring squeeze.

"Please?" Greer pleaded. Jackson relented—for now, at least.

Conversation turned to other matters as our meal arrived. Then more drinks—at least for Greer and me. Jackson had relaxed some, but I could still see him scanning for threats.

"Doesn't it get exhausting?" I asked while Greer was in the bathroom. She'd texted to say she'd gotten a call from the kids and would be back in a little bit.

He placed a finger beneath my chin, tipping my gaze to his. "Protecting you is an honor and my privilege."

He looked as if he might kiss me, and god, how I wanted him to. Despite a few almost missteps, we'd made it through a week of forced celibacy, and I was more than ready for it to be over.

"You really do love your job," I mused.

"I love *you*."

I smiled. "I love you too."

I didn't want to ruin the moment, but the question of New York and Jackson's promotion had been weighing on me all day.

"Tell me about New York," I said.

"Hmm." He smoothed his hand over his chin. "It's on the East Coast. It's where Greer was married—"

"Jackson." I narrowed my eyes at him.

"What?" He lifted a shoulder. "You asked me to tell you about New York, and I am."

"Yes," I huffed, trying to ignore the little voice of doubt that had started screaming in my head. The one that said he was going to leave me again. "But I was hoping you'd tell me about your promotion." He stilled. "Greer mentioned it earlier in passing." I toyed with my napkin. "She, um, didn't realize…"

He tilted his head back, and he seemed to be warring with himself. Because he was worried how I'd react? Because he hadn't expected me to find out?

"What is it?" I asked, trying to remain calm despite my rising panic. I couldn't… My palms were clammy.

"There is no promotion."

My stomach plummeted at his words. I'd told myself that he'd changed, but it felt like déjà vu.

I was determined to give him the benefit of the doubt. But instead, I found myself blurting, "You lied to your family?"

He scoffed. "I can't believe you jumped straight to that."

"Can you blame me? It wouldn't be the first time you've lied to them. To me." God, that hurt to admit. This whole conversation hurt.

He pinched the bridge of his nose. "You still don't trust me, do you? Even after everything we've been through."

"I *do* trust you." I placed my hand on his, because it felt as if the conversation was spiraling out of control. "I'm just trying to understand. Greer's under the impression that you're moving to New York and going to lead the Hudson office there. Yet you've never mentioned it to me, and now you're telling me there is no promotion."

He shook his head. "If you trusted me, you wouldn't immediately jump to the conclusion that I lied."

"I—" I took a breath. "I'm sorry. I'm trying, Jackson. But can you blame me, after all the things you kept from me in the past?"

He dragged a hand down his face. "What did you honestly think would happen with my job after I slept with a client?"

I searched his eyes for answers, processing his words. "Wait. You lost the promotion because of me?"

"I gave it up for *us*. And I didn't lie about it to my family. At the time, I'd planned to take it."

"Jackson." I stared at the table, trying to ignore the tightness in my chest. "I'm sorry."

I was sorry for doubting him. For putting him in that position. For jeopardizing his future.

"So am I." Part of me expected him to say that we were done. That this was never going to work. Instead, he said, "I know I hurt you in the past, and I will keep doing whatever it takes to show you that you can trust me. So, in the interest of full transparency, I also resigned from Hudson."

I reared back. "What? When?"

He'd taken a leap of faith for me—for us. And I'd jumped to conclusions. I'd let my fear of the past overwhelm my hope for the future.

"Our first morning in Turks and Caicos. But I asked that it wouldn't take effect until after this assignment ended. And my boss demanded my discretion in return, which he had every right to do. I signed an NDA with Hudson."

I dropped my head to my chest. "I'm sorry this is such a mess."

He blew out a breath. "You have to understand... Vaughn's more than just my supervisor, he's my mentor, and I put him in an awkward position. I'm sorry I didn't tell you sooner, but I felt like I owed it to him."

"I can understand that." I could. I admired Jackson for his loyalty. "But why would you do that? Why give up a promotion and a job at a company you love?"

He took my hand in his. "Because you're more important to me than anything. I made the wrong choice once, and I vowed not to make that mistake again."

"Jackson." I melted from his words. "I would've never asked you to give up your job for me."

"I know you wouldn't." He cupped my cheek. "But you didn't have to. I *chose* to."

I closed my eyes and leaned into his touch, reveling in this moment. The significance of Jackson choosing our relationship over his job wasn't lost on me. He'd jeopardized his future to place his trust in us, and his admission was both healing and profound. I vowed that his sacrifices wouldn't be made in vain.

CHAPTER TWENTY-FIVE

Jackson

Sloan placed her hand over mine then lowered them both to her lap. Something shifted in her expression, and she seemed almost…nervous.

"Sloan? What's wrong?"

When she glanced up at me, she was smiling. "*Acta non verba.*"

I nodded, repeating, "*Acta non verba.*" Exactly.

"I also might have done something…" She gnawed on her lip. "I wasn't planning to spring it on you quite like this, but I talked to my brother, and we want to hire you to oversee all security operations at the Huxley Grand brand."

"Graham?" I asked, surprised that he'd agree.

I mean, holy shit. They wanted to hire me? To oversee all security operations of Huxley Grand worldwide? It was enough to make my head spin.

"Yeah." Sloan tilted her head. "Why?"

I rubbed the back of my neck, trying not to get too excited about what she was offering me. "I don't get the impression that Graham is my biggest fan."

She frowned. "What do you mean?"

"I met him once when we were together. Remember? At your apartment."

"Oh my god. I almost forgot about that." She laughed. "I can't believe I forgot. I almost introduced you as my boyfriend and blew the whole secret."

I debated telling her this, but I felt like she should know. "Graham is actually the one who told me the truth about your family—and your future role in the hotel empire."

She jerked her head back. "He…what?" It came out as more of a shriek, and I debated telling her the rest. I didn't want to drive a wedge between Sloan and her brother.

"I think he suspected something between us. He made it clear that I had no place in your future."

Sloan reached for her phone, likely to give her brother a piece of her mind. I placed my hand over hers, stopping her. "He was just looking out for you. I would've done the same for Greer."

"You're not pissed about this? Because I am."

"I understand where he was coming from. And at the time, his comments definitely played into my insecurities. But that's on me, not him."

She bared her teeth. "I could…"

"Sloan," I said, bringing her hand to my mouth for a kiss. "It's not worth it. And if he agreed to hiring me, that has to mean something, right?"

"With Graham, it's hard to tell. But yeah, I'd say that's a good sign." She shook her head as if to clear it. "Has he ever said anything to you about it? About us."

I shook my head. "No. But I'm positive he remembers."

Sloan nodded. "I understand if that complicates things for you. But I hope you'll consider accepting the position. We want you to be our COS."

"Chief of Sexy Times?" I joked, needing a minute to wrap my head around the enormity of this offer. I'd never expected to find another job so soon, let alone one at such a high level.

She rolled her eyes but smiled anyway. "Chief of Security. You have the experience. You know our vulnerabilities. And you'd be perfect for the role."

"I'm honored, truly," I said. "And surprised."

"Because of Graham?"

"Yeah, and because it's just…" I lifted a shoulder. "I never imagined myself in a role like that. That would be a huge advance for my career."

"A well-deserved one," she said. "I would've told you sooner, but I was waiting for the board's approval."

I was stunned. She'd done this for me. For us. Because she believed in me and our future.

This job, the opportunity to be the chief of security for such a large organization, was a dream come true. It would be a lot of responsibility, sure. But it was also an exciting challenge that would allow me to make meaningful change.

I leaned in, both honored and turned on by what she'd done. "What if I want to be the Chief of Sucking Your Clit?"

She swatted at me. "That's too many letters."

I captured her hand and held it to my chest. "Chief of Sloan's Heart."

"Still too many letters." She grinned. "But, yes. You're the chief of my heart, and I want us to be together, whether that's in London or New York or even Los Angeles. I got the board to agree that the position could be based in any of those locations, and I would push to relocate if that's what you want."

I jerked my head back, in awe of this woman and what she'd done. I was filled with so much happiness at that moment, I thought I might burst. To hear Sloan say those words. To know that she'd put this in place for us to be together.

"I know this is a lot—fast," she said. "So I understand if you need some time to think about it—the job and where you'd want to live."

"Are you kidding?" I cupped her cheek. "Yes. My answer is yes."

"We can start off living in the same city or—"

"The same city?" I barked out a laugh, cutting her off before she could say something even more ridiculous. "Sloan, *hayati*, I want to move in together. I love that you did this for us, and I absolutely want to be together. Wherever that is."

"Don't you want to know what your salary will be?" she teased.

"I'm sure it will be more than enough." I nuzzled her. "All that matters is that we'll be together."

"We'll be together." Her voice was filled with wonder. "Together." She grinned, and then she kissed me. It felt like a promise. Like a fresh start.

"What about your family? Our relationship?" I asked.

"We'll have to disclose it to my family and the board, but I think they'll approve."

"Of us or my new role?" I was anxious to hear her answer.

"Both." She smiled. "I know one person who will be particularly happy about the news."

I dragged a hand over my head, smiling at the thought. "Brooklyn." She nodded. "How did I get so lucky?" I pulled her close.

"Mm. How did *we* get so lucky?"

I kissed Sloan's neck, on the verge of breaking my promise to Vaughn.

But even as distracted as I was by Sloan, I kept an eye on our surroundings. Our table was in a secluded alcove that faced the ocean, but we were still in a public place. Thanks to the walls of the alcove, we were hidden from security cameras, but the waitstaff could come by at any time.

"Since you quit your job, does that mean we can have sex now?" she joked.

I chuckled. "No. I promised my boss there wouldn't be any more *infractions*—" I gave her a meaningful look full of heat "—until after the trip had concluded.*"

She groaned, covering her face with her hands. "I can't believe you told your boss we slept together."

"It's not like I told him that you like it when I bite your nipples," I rasped against the shell of her ear, my already hard cock pressing against my zipper. "Or how you like it when I pinch your clit."

"Jackson." She shuddered.

I smoothed my hand up her thigh. "I bet if I slid my hand between your legs, you'd be wet for me. Wouldn't you?"

"I-I—" She gulped. "Oh god."

"Tell me, Sloan." I traced the edge of her underwear, fully intending to stop. "You used to get off on the thrill of being caught. Do you still?"

Her chest rose and fell, and I knew she was barely holding on. Hell, I was right there with her. When I glanced down, her nipples were hard points against her dress.

Fuck me.

Unable to resist, I glided over the wet silk of her underwear, letting out a growl of satisfaction. Her body trembled beneath my touch, both of us aching for more.

"Fuck, baby. You're so wet for me." I continued teasing her clit, and I thought I might explode.

"Please, Jackson."

"Is that what you want?" I asked, slipping my hand beneath her underwear, sliding a finger into her. Sliding home.

"Yes," she gasped, gripping my thigh. "Yes," she said again, this time more insistent.

She was already close. So close. Keyed up from a week of

torture and now this…knowing we were in public and could get caught.

"Come for me," I rasped against her neck before trailing kisses over her skin. "Come on my fingers like you want to come on my cock."

Sloan gasped and buried her face in my neck, stifling her sounds of pleasure. Her pussy clenched around my finger, and she bit me, sending sparks skittering down my spine. She was so sexy I almost came in my pants. And the sight of her coming apart was nearly my undoing.

When she sagged, I held her to me. I kissed her forehead, then withdrew my fingers. "You're so beautiful."

I brought my hand to my mouth, licking each of my fingers as she watched with a heated expression.

"Jackson…" She warned. "Don't start something unless you're prepared to finish it."

"Oh, I'm more than prepared." I placed her hand on my cock, letting her feel just how hard I was for her.

She squeezed my shaft, and I groaned into her hair. "Sloan."

Her phone buzzed, and she pulled away to check it. "It's Greer." She frowned down at the screen. "She's going to stay in the room. I think I should go check on her."

Talking about my sister effectively killed my desire. Not to mention the fact that Sloan was concerned about Greer, and so was I.

I sighed. "As soon as the waiter comes back, we can go."

"Yes," Sloan said, tapping out a reply to Greer. She handed me a bottle of hand sanitizer from her purse. Always prepared.

"Thanks," I said, handing it back to her after I'd cleaned my hands.

She signed for the check and thanked the waiter. I placed my hand on the small of her back, standing just behind her to hide my crotch as we crossed the lobby. She smirked at me over her shoulder.

We were alone in the elevator, and Sloan reapplied her lipstick and kept smoothing her hand over her hair. I was so damn tempted to crowd her against the wall and kiss her senseless, but I wouldn't. Not when our every move was being monitored by a security camera.

Since Sloan was one of the owners of the hotel, it was likely that her movements were followed closely by her staff. They wanted to anticipate her every move; they wanted to make her stay as wonderful as possible. Fortunately, the cameras didn't have audio.

"You look perfect." I maintained a neutral expression for anyone who might be watching the CCTV.

"Perfectly fucked," she muttered. "Wait until Greer sees me."

"Sloan." I waited until her eyes met mine in the reflection of the elevator doors. Yes, her lips were still swollen from my kisses. And her cheeks were red. But she'd also been drinking. "She probably won't even notice. But if she does, just tell her you ordered another drink after she left."

"Right." She swallowed. "Good idea." And then she dropped her head. "Ugh. I don't want to do this anymore. I don't want to lie to Greer."

"So, let's tell her," I said. "It's not going to get any easier, and we can't put it off much longer. Not if we're going to live together."

"That sounds crazy, right?" But even as she said it, she was smiling.

"What sounds crazy," I said, "is wasting any more time."

I couldn't wait to start our new life together. To live together. To have no more secrets. To one day make her my wife.

The elevator dinged, and the doors slid open. Sloan

unlocked the door to our suite, and I held it open for her. She brushed against me as she walked past, the scent of wild roses and sunshine lingering in the air.

Such a tease.

"You're sure?" she asked, and I sensed her nerves.

"One hundred percent." I hoped my confidence would reassure her that we were doing the right thing.

"We're back," Sloan called.

"Hey," Greer said, returning to the living room. "Sorry for ditching you."

"Is everything okay?" Sloan asked.

"The kids wanted to tell me about their day, that's all."

"Oh. Good." Sloan twisted her bracelets, a nervous habit. "But they're good?"

"They're great." Greer's smile was full of love.

"Great. Um—" Sloan cleared her throat. "Jackson and I have something we need to tell you."

"Okay," Greer said, taking a seat. "What's going on? You're making me nervous."

Sloan shifted on her feet. "I, um—" She turned to me, her expression pinched. "I don't know if I can do this."

"Do what?" Greer glanced between us, confusion marring her features.

I knew this was it—the point of no return. There'd be no going back after this. I took a deep breath. "Sloan and I are together."

Greer blinked a few times. "Together? As in…"

I stepped closer to Sloan, sliding my arm around her waist. She felt so right in my arms. In my life.

"Oh." Greer dragged out the word. "Oh! You're… Wow. Okay."

Sloan tensed, and I braced myself for something more.

"Okay?" I asked after a minute. "That's it?"

"I'm…still processing. Jeez." She rolled her eyes.

Sloan took a seat next to Greer. Sloan's voice shook when she spoke. "You know that my relationship with you is so, *so* important to me. You have been there for me through everything."

"And you've always been there for me," Greer said with a watery smile, patting Sloan's hand.

"I hope..." Sloan wiped away a tear. "I know you were opposed to the idea of Jackson and me in the past, but I hope —" her breath hitched "—you can be happy for us. Because we're so happy together."

Greer said nothing, silently considering. She hadn't lashed out, which was good. But I didn't know what to think of her reaction.

She turned to me, narrowing her eyes. "You better not break her heart."

I didn't blink. Didn't flinch. Didn't look away. "I love Sloan, and I'm not going anywhere."

"Love?" Greer blinked a few times. "*Love?* You love her?" I nodded, and she turned to Sloan, who smiled and nodded as well.

"We love each other," Sloan said.

Greer's eyes looked as if they might bug out of her head. "This is a lot to take in," she said, clearly shocked by the news. "But I guess I should've realized it was serious if you decided to tell me."

Sloan caught my eye, casting me an anxious glance.

"But—" Greer frowned. "You just got out of a relationship with Edward," she said to Sloan. "I want to be happy for you, but aren't you moving a little fast?"

"Ah. Um..." Sloan glanced to her lap.

"Jackson?" Greer looked to me for answers.

"Sloan and I..." I drew in a deep breath, hoping this wouldn't ruin everything. "Sloan and I fell in love years ago, but the timing wasn't right."

"Years ago." Greer furrowed her brow. "Just exactly how long ago are we talking?"

"College," Sloan whispered.

"College?" Greer reared back. "You were…" She waved her arms before her. "Wait. What?" She stood and started pacing. Her questions came out rapid-fire. "When did it start? For how long? Were you together at my wedding?"

I finally explained the truth behind my discharge from the SEALs. A tear trickled down Greer's cheek, and I hated that she was hurting—because of me.

"Jackson." She shook her head. "I wish I'd known. I wish you'd told me."

"I just…" I blew out a breath. "At the time, I was so ashamed. I'm your big brother." *Your hero.*

"Leaving the SEALs wouldn't change that," she said. She gave me a hug, and I felt a wave of love and acceptance wash over me. "So after you were discharged you came to New York?"

I nodded. "I accepted a job as a bouncer. Sloan came to the club where I was working one night, and she made me tell her what was going on. After that, we started texting, but we were just friends at that point."

"At first, it was nothing. Jackson watched out for me. He offered to teach me self-defense."

Greer listened, and I couldn't get a read on her.

"Over time," I said, "we spent more time together. We fell in love."

"How much time?" Greer sank back onto the couch with a pinched expression. She rubbed her brow as if to ward off a headache. "How long were you sneaking around behind my back?"

Sloan winced. "I'm sorry we didn't tell you. We were going to, but then…everything fell apart."

"Wait." Greer straightened and turned to Sloan. "Was *he*

your mystery man? Is Jackson the one who broke your heart?"

Sloan rolled her lips between her teeth and nodded. Greer gasped, covering her mouth with her hand. "And you had to…" She shook her head. "That's why you were such a wreck on my wedding day. I thought it was nerves."

"I hadn't seen Jackson in nearly a year at that point, and I didn't know how on earth I was going to face him."

"I wish you'd told me," Greer said with a sympathetic expression. "And you—" She turned to me with narrowed eyes.

Sloan swiped away a tear. "I know how important your relationship with Jackson is, and I never wanted to come between the two of you. I'm sorry, Greer."

"And I know how important Sloan is to you," I said. "And I refused to jeopardize your friendship. I'm sorry."

Greer's expression was contemplative, and Sloan gripped my hand. I knew she was concerned. Hell, I was worried how my sister would react.

Finally, Greer sighed. "So am I. I was young, and it was selfish of me to try to forbid you from seeing each other. At the time, I was still hurt about losing my high school friend, but I didn't think anything would come of my comment. I wish you'd talked to me sooner, but I guess I can understand why you didn't."

"You were justified for making that comment," I said. "I was young and selfish too, but I've matured. We all have."

"I still have so many questions," Greer said on a laugh.

"Like what?" Sloan asked, seeming to relax.

"Does Mom know? Or *did* she know?"

I shook my head. "No. I never told her."

"I can't believe you guys were able to keep it a secret for so long. How did I never catch you?"

"There were certainly a few close calls."

"*Way* too close," I said, thinking of a few of them.

"I feel like everything I ever knew is wrong," Greer said, but she was smiling. "I'm happy for you. Both of you."

Sloan smiled at me, clearly relieved. And then she leaned her head on Greer's shoulder. "Thanks for being so awesome."

I finally relaxed, knowing that we had my sister's support. Everything was finally falling into place. My relationship with Sloan. Our future. It was more than I could've hoped for.

CHAPTER TWENTY-SIX

Sloan

When I padded out to the living room the following morning, the door to Jackson's room was open. I peeked my head inside, but I wasn't surprised to find it unoccupied. I knew he'd planned to go the gym and make some calls, so he'd asked some of the Huxley Grand security team to stand guard in the hall outside. The curtains fluttered, beckoning me to where Greer was sitting in a fluffy white robe. She sipped her coffee and peered out at the ocean.

I hadn't had a chance to talk to Greer alone since Jackson and I had told her about our relationship, and I'd wanted to give her some time to digest the news. I hoped she was still as supportive as she'd been last night. Though, I knew it might take her some time to adjust to the idea of us as a couple.

"Hey." I peeked my head out onto the balcony. "Can I join you?"

"Sure." She smiled.

"Did you sleep okay?"

"Best sleep I've had in months. The beds here are magical."

I laughed. "I'm glad to hear it. Jasper personally tested them out before we purchased them."

"I might have to ask him for the info."

"Just go on the Huxley Grand website," I said. "There's a whole store where we sell sheets, towels, the mattress. Pretty much anything you like can be purchased."

"That's new, right?"

"We had so many requests for information on the pillows, the mattresses, the candles, whatever, that we decided to start selling them. Graham was opposed at first because he worried it would dilute the luxury aspect of the brand. But I thought everyone should be able to take home a little of that luxury to their ordinary life. And Jasper argued that it would remind people of their positive experience and make them want to come back." I was rambling, but I was nervous.

"I could definitely use a little luxury in my ordinary life." Greer wore a forlorn expression.

I crossed my legs. "What's going on with you and Logan?"

She stared out at the water and said nothing. But I knew Greer well enough to know that she'd feel better if she talked.

"Come on." I nudged her foot with mine. "Talk to me."

She took a deep breath, and my heart rate accelerated. "Logan and I are getting a divorce."

"What?" I jerked my head back. When she turned to look at me, her expression was full of sadness, and my heart ached for my best friend. "Oh, Greer." I went over and wrapped my arms around her.

Divorce? She and Logan had always been so happy together. At least, that had been my impression. Sure, they had their ups and downs. What couple didn't? But on the whole, they loved each other. They had built a life, a family, together.

Greer started crying, and I hugged her close. "It's okay. I'm here. You can tell me about it when you're ready."

She sniffled, so I went to grab a box of tissues from the living room. I set them on the table then returned to my seat, holding her hand in mine.

"I can't do this anymore," Greer said. "I can't do *everything.*"

"It's difficult to feel like you're the one putting in all the work," I said. "A relationship takes two people."

"I know you get it. Edward was..." She swallowed. "Yeah. I'm glad you found happiness, even if it is with my brother," she teased.

"Thank you for saying that. I was so nervous to tell you."

"Sloan," she sighed. "You're my best friend, and I love you unconditionally. You'd have to do something truly heinous for me not to be able to move past it."

Which was why the fact that she was getting divorced was so surprising.

"Thank you," I said. "And ditto. So..." I paused, trying to find the best way to ask her what I really wanted to know. I sensed that she didn't want to talk about Logan, and I wasn't going to push—for now. Instead, I kept the conversation focused on Jackson and me, assuming she'd appreciate a distraction from her own drama. "You're okay with this? Truly?"

"If you're happy, I'm happy." She smiled. "And I can tell that you're really happy."

I finally felt myself relax. "Jackson is... He's everything to me."

She sipped her coffee then set her mug back on the table. "I'm curious. How did you move past all the hurt? Move past...the past?"

"It wasn't easy. Being trapped on a sailboat definitely helped." I laughed, and she joined in. "But it was more than that. It was Jackson's willingness to show up time and again. His actions, not his words."

"*Acta non verba*," Greer said with a wistful expression.

"Exactly."

Her expression changed, shifting to something more downcast. "That's my problem. I keep hoping and waiting for Logan to step up, but I'm done. I'm done trying to be the perfect mom and have the perfect home. I'm done trying to be the perfect wife to a husband who won't even stuff my stocking."

I started laughing. I couldn't help it. "Is that a euphemism?"

Greer joined me. "Oh my god. I didn't even..." She caught her breath. "But yes, that too."

We were quiet a moment. Then she ran a hand through her hair. "All joking aside, he just doesn't seem to care about anything anymore. At least, not anything that pertains to me." She slumped. "It's a really shitty feeling. Nearly fifteen years of marriage. Eighteen years together and now..." She shrugged, and I knew she was fighting back tears. Hell, I was.

"Now?" I prompted.

"I told him I wanted a divorce, and he said nothing. *Nothing!*" Her admission pained me. "Whatever." She scoffed.

She seemed so downtrodden, so discouraged, that I had to say something.

"It may not seem like it now," I said. "And it may take some time. But I'm confident you'll find happiness again." With or without Logan—though, I didn't say that.

She bit her lip as if to stem her tears. "I hope you're right."

I hugged her, holding her tight. "I know I am."

If Jackson and I could find our way back together after all these years, anything was possible.

A FEW DAYS LATER, JACKSON AND I HAD DROPPED GREER AT the airport and were headed back to the hotel. We'd had a really nice visit, and I'd loved spending time both just with Greer and with Jackson and Greer. It was such a relief that she knew about us. That she supported our relationship and seemed genuinely happy for us despite what was going on in her marriage. Part of me almost wished I'd told her sooner, but I was just glad it had all worked out in the end.

"One sibling down." I blew out a breath. "Four to go."

"Sloan," Jackson chided. "We told Greer, and it went great. Trust your family to be just as supportive."

Maybe he was right. Nate had been supportive when I'd spoken to him about it a few weeks ago. But still...

"Mm," I mused. "You don't know them. And they don't know you. I suppose Nate does, sort of. But I'm not sure that counts."

"Then let them get to know me. You're probably not going to like this idea, but we could cut our trip a little short to spend some time in LA with them."

I jerked my head back. "You'd give up sailing alone in paradise with me to spend time getting to know my family?"

"I'd love to say that's my only motivation, but it would mean my assignment would be over and..."

"We could finally have sex," I said, connecting the dots, growing excited at the prospect. "I like the way you think."

"Yeah?" He looked over at me and grinned.

"Yeah." So much passed between us in that brief unspoken moment before he returned his attention to the road.

"I'm happy to continue our trip, or cut it short and spend time with your family. But only if that's what you want," he said. "I want to be part of your life. I know how protective they are of you, and I want them to trust me. To realize how happy we are together."

I smiled, beyond happy. "I suppose if we went to LA, you could meet the board in person, and we could disclose our relationship," I said, cataloging the merits of the idea beyond just sex. Though, sex with Jackson in and of itself was more than enough motivation.

"Exactly." He smirked, inching his hand higher up my thigh.

He teased the edge of my panties and groaned. "God, Sloan. These past few weeks have been torture."

"I know," I gasped, wishing he'd touch me. "I thought I'd never want this trip to end, but strangely, I find myself eager to return home."

He chuckled. "So am I, *hayati*. So am I."

He slid his hand toward my knee, a safer distance from where I needed him. My body was still wound tight with tension, but I tried to focus on something else. "And if we went back to LA, we could spend time with Brooklyn."

Brooklyn made me think of Jackson's niece and nephew. About divorce and about Greer. I sighed and stared out the window. "Do you think Greer will be okay?"

"I hate seeing her so unhappy. I just don't get what's going on with Logan."

"Me either." He gave my thigh a quick squeeze before returning his hand to the steering wheel.

After we returned to the Huxley Grand, Jackson went for a workout. Hotel security was stationed outside in the hall. I ordered some room service for lunch then directed my attention to my inbox until there was a knock at the door.

"Room service."

I was in the middle of washing my hands, so I called out, "Come in."

The door opened, and a cart was rolled in, the gentle clanking of dishes accompanying it. When I entered the dining room, the woman turned. I tilted my head, studying her. She looked familiar, but I couldn't place her. At least, not until she started talking.

She pulled out a chair for me. "Sit down. Don't scream. Don't call for help. Or I will shoot." The words rang out in a posh English accent.

"Amelia." I didn't bother to hide my annoyance. "To what do I owe this pleasure?" I scanned the room for my phone, inching toward the coffee table where it was resting.

"Don't even think about it." She removed a gun from beneath one of the silver domes. "And it's Lady Amelia."

I sat down, considering my options. She had a gun with a silencer. And I knew she was a good shot. Hell, she had a silver medal to prove it.

"Hands on the table. I want to see them at all times."

I did as she asked. "What now, Amelia?" I intentionally didn't use her title just to piss her off.

She shoved my shoulder. "You will address me as *Lady* Amelia."

I said nothing, adrenaline pumping through me. I wondered what she wanted. How long she'd been planning this. If Edward was in on it.

And where the hell was security?

"What can I do for you, Lady Amelia?" I sneered. I needed to keep her talking until I could devise a plan.

"I want you to transfer fifty million dollars into this bank account." She slid a piece of paper in front of me. It contained the number of an offshore account.

I scoffed. "And why would I do that?"

She moved to stand before me. "Because if you don't wire the money within the next twenty-four hours, I will release these…" She dropped a handful of photos on the table, and a few cascaded to the floor.

My eyes widened at an image of Jackson sitting on the edge of the hot tub in Turks and Caicos, naked. Another of my front, the sheer material of the swimsuit leaving nothing to the imagination. Another of us touching. Kissing.

"What the hell?" Someone had been watching us? Photographing us? I clenched my fists. "You have no right…"

She threw down another—a blurry photograph of us in the outdoor shower, though it was clear what we were doing.

"Shall I keep going?" She tossed a few more on the table.

Photographs of him shirtless and straddling me. Others of us dry humping. I covered my mouth with my hand. *Jesus.*

I wanted to cover them all. Remove them from her view. These were our private moments.

"Mm." She scanned the photos, and my blood boiled. "He's hot. I get why you'd want to fuck your bodyguard."

I gnashed my teeth. There was so much wrong with that statement, but I figured she was trying to bait me. I needed to rely on my logic, not emotions, if I was going to survive this. "Did Edward put you up to this?"

She cackled. "Put *me* up to this. That's cute." She shook her head and paced, waving the gun in the air. I needed to find a way to disarm her. Maybe if I kept her talking, she'd get distracted.

"No," she continued. "He was definitely in on it, but this was my idea."

I tried not to show that her words stung. In on it, how? What did that mean?

Instead, I asked, "Because of your family's money troubles?"

Amelia's eyes flashed with shock that barely registered, before it was replaced by the mask of cold indifference I'd grown to expect from her.

"My father is an incompetent fool. I should be the one running the family business." She jabbed her chest, her fire returning. "Me. Not him. Not when he's running it into the ground."

"So, why aren't you?"

"Because my family is old-fashioned. And my father has always seen Edward as his successor and heir."

"That's bullshit," I said, and I meant it. My grandparents had always made me feel just as capable of taking on the role of managing the family business as any of my brothers.

"Right?" She sank down into the chair across from me with a sigh. "Which is why I'm going to save us from ruin. Then Father will realize that I'm the one who should be at the helm. And Edward will finally be free to pursue his passion."

I felt sick to my stomach. Her plan was flawed, but I wasn't going to point that out to her. At least now I knew what she wanted the money for.

"And how will you explain such a large infusion of cash?"

"My father knows I'm good at networking. I will simply say it came from a Chinese investor."

"Clearly, you've thought it all out."

"I have." I wanted to slap the smug look off her face. "And now it's time to hand over the money."

"Ah." I leaned back in my chair, feigning a nonchalance I didn't feel. "But you see, any transaction over five million requires the approval of a majority of the Huxley board."

She flinched at that. She hadn't expected it. "You're lying."

I shook my head, trying to project a calm demeanor even though I was sweating bullets. I had no idea when Jackson was going to return, and I didn't want him—or anyone else—to walk in and startle Amelia. I got the feeling she was in the mood to shoot first and ask questions later.

Her breathing quickened. "You're a billionaire. Surely you have private accounts."

"Everything is held in trust. If you'd like me to make a call…"

She trained the gun on me once more with a menacing expression. "I know what you're trying to do, and I'm not going to fall for it. Give me the money, or I'll release the photos."

I swallowed hard, trying not to let her see my fear. Those photos could never get out. There would be no more hiding the fact that Jackson had broken the rules. He'd lose everything.

And what would my family think? What would Brooklyn think? My stomach churned with unease.

"And if I pay you," I said, deciding to let her think I was playing her game. No way in hell was I letting her walk out of here with the money or the photos. "You'd give me all the photos and erase all digital copies on any device where they're stored."

She rolled her eyes. "Once the money is in my account, yes."

"I want your assurance that you won't come back to me for more money later."

"Yes, but as you said, you can't access that sum."

"I—" I tapped a finger to my lips, testing her resolve to keep my hands on the table. She said nothing. "Not from the Huxley corporation. But there might be another way."

She leaned forward, a gleam in her eye. "What is it?"

I stood, pressing my advantage further. Amelia was so intent on the money, she didn't care that I was standing. Even better, she wasn't stopping me.

I inched closer, preparing to disarm her, when the electronic lock on the door beeped. *Shit!*

Everything seemed to happen in slow motion. I was so

focused on the door and warning Jackson that Amelia was able to pull me toward her, pressing the gun to my temple.

The door to the suite opened. Jackson stood there, wiping sweat from his forehead. The door closed behind him.

"Sloan, I—" He stopped short. Glanced at Amelia, the gun, my face. His eyes connected with mine, silently asking if I was okay.

I pressed my lips together and gave the briefest of nods. If only I'd listened to him when he'd tried to warn me about Edward in Turks and Caicos.

"Sit down. Hands on the table," Amelia hissed.

"Let's just calm down," Jackson said, stepping closer to me, trying to put himself between us. "Put away the gun. And talk rationally."

"No," Amelia spat. "I'm done waiting. Sit or I'll shoot her."

Jackson sat, his expression eerily calm.

"What's your plan, Sloan?" Amelia asked, her eyes wild. "How are you going to get me my money?"

"I—" I needed a plan and quick. *Think fast, Sloan.* "I need to talk to my brother."

"No. Absolutely not."

"He's the CEO. If he and I agree to transfer the money, we can get you the sum you asked for." I was lying, but she didn't know that. I tried to remain calm.

She shifted. "Fine. Do it. Do it!" she practically yelled.

She turned the gun on Jackson, and my heart rate ratcheted up. *No!* That wasn't supposed to happen.

I went over to the table where my phone was resting. I picked it up with shaking hands, then met Jackson's eyes, hoping he would realize that I was about to cause a distraction.

"Hurry up!" Amelia commanded, swinging her gun back to me.

Jackson held my gaze. I wanted to defend him, protect

him, but I knew I needed to put my faith in him. This was what he was trained to do.

I turned and dropped the phone. When I crouched to the floor, I heard the sounds of a struggle. The gun went off and Amelia screamed, or maybe that was me.

I popped back up, terrified that he'd been shot. I moved closer, ready to help him. But Jackson had already wrestled her to the floor. Her cheek was pressed to the carpet, and he tossed the gun aside.

"You okay?" he asked me.

I nodded, searching him for any sign of injury. My heart felt as if it would pound out of my chest. "I am. Are you?"

"Yes," he said through gritted teeth, hauling Amelia to a standing position.

"Let. Me. Go." Amelia struggled against his hold. It was laughable, really. There was no way she would be able to escape. Jackson would never allow it.

"Not a fucking chance. You're lucky I don't shoot you right now and make it look like an accident."

Her eyes widened, perhaps sensing that wasn't an idle threat.

He glared at her. "Apparently your brother didn't take my message to heart."

I realized he must have seen Amelia in my Hudson Security dossier and recognized her. *Impressive.*

"What message?" Amelia's voice trembled with fear.

He leaned forward, getting in her face. "No one threatens the woman I love and gets away with it."

Oh shit. Why was that so hot?

"Is he here?" Jackson glanced around, tightening his hold to the point that she winced. "Is your piece-of-shit brother here?"

Amelia shook her head. "No." She looked close to tears,

her bravado gone. "No. We knew it would be too suspicious if he showed up again."

"Again?" I frowned, and then understanding dawned on me. "The proposal."

"Yes." She rolled her eyes. "The proposal. If you'd agreed to marry him, all of this unpleasantness could've been avoided."

I blinked a few times, positive I'd misheard her. She was clearly delusional on so many levels. It made me even more grateful that I'd ended things with Edward when I had.

I supposed I shouldn't have been surprised to learn that he'd never loved me. But if anything, it made sense. It was still disappointing to think that he'd only wanted me for my money, but it didn't hurt as badly as it should've. Because I'd never loved him.

"There are some zip ties in my bag," Jackson said to me. "Do you think you can grab them?"

I nodded. I went to his bag and pulled them out, watching as he restrained Amelia. He picked up the gun and removed the clip before collecting all the photos from the table and depositing them in his bag.

We stepped into the kitchen, keeping an eye on Amelia the entire time. "What are you going to do now?" I asked, keeping my voice low.

He pulled out his phone. "I'm going to call Vaughn. He'll send in a team to handle this."

"Shouldn't we call the police?"

"Not if we want everyone to see those photos." He gave me a pointed look. Neither of us wanted that. He was right. It was best to handle this matter quickly and quietly.

"What will happen to her?" I asked.

"What do you want to happen?"

My muscles still quivered, whether from adrenaline or rage, I wasn't sure. "I want answers."

He gestured toward the dining table. "Ask her."

While Jackson spoke to Vaughn in hushed tones, I went over to Amelia. "Was Edward behind the threats?"

"No," she scoffed. "But when he told me about them, I saw an opportunity."

"What kind of opportunity?"

"I told him to use the threats to motivate you to move in with him. To marry him."

I thought back on my interactions with Edward. He'd been pressuring me to move in with him, arguing that I'd be safer. All the while, he'd been trying to manipulate me into doing what he and his sister had wanted. Just so they could get their hands on my money.

Unbelievable.

Then to propose... I understood the desire to save his company. His family's legacy. But...had he ever cared about me?

I didn't realize I'd said the last part aloud until Amelia said, "Aw." She pouted. "You actually thought he cared about you?" She shook her head, but she didn't look at all remorseful. "I hate to break it to you, but we targeted you. He was playing you the whole time."

I'd had enough. Whether it was true or not, it didn't matter. Edward was no longer part of my life. I turned my back on her, keeping an eye on her reflection in the window.

Jackson went to the door and opened it, and a group of three men and a woman streamed in. Damn, that was fast.

"Blackjack."

"Thanks for coming so quickly. There's the trash that needs to be disposed of." He gestured toward Amelia.

Her eyes went wide. "What does that mean? What are you going to do to me?" One of the guys latched on to her arm and pulled her to a standing position. "Where are you taking me?"

"Come on." They tugged her toward the door.

As they were leaving, one of the Huxley Grand security officers ran inside. "Is everything okay?"

I crossed my arms over my chest. "It is now."

Yet again, my own security team had disappointed me. The problem was bigger than I'd realized, and it made me even more grateful that we'd hired Jackson as our chief of security.

"I'm so sorry, Ms. Mackenzie," he said, wide-eyed. "We know that you like to get to know your employees. We just assumed..."

"You assumed incorrectly." The adrenaline was fading, and I couldn't maintain this façade much longer.

"I'm sorry," he said again. "I didn't recognize her, but she was wearing the uniform. I did question her, but she said she was new."

"We will discuss this later," Jackson bit out, his eyes never leaving mine.

"Yes, sir. Of course." The security guard backed out of the room.

As soon as the door closed, I sagged. It was as if everything hit me at once. The blackmail. The gun. My fear for Jackson.

He caught me before I could fall to the floor. He scooped me up and carried me to the bed.

"Are you hurt?" He scanned my face, my body, with fear in his eyes. "What's wrong?"

"I'm..." I closed my eyes, but I saw an image of the bullet hitting Jackson. I opened them to block out the picture, but I started crying instead, unable to shake it. "I was terrified she was going to shoot you."

"Me?" He placed my hand over my heart. "Sloan, baby. You did so well. You were so brave. And you gave me the perfect opening. I'm okay." He kissed me. "We're both okay."

I nodded even as tears streamed down my cheeks. "I know." I was so choked up, I could barely speak. "I know."

He pulled me to him, holding me close. Letting me hear the reassuring cadence of his heartbeat. He was alive. We were okay.

"I'm so sorry. I should've had another bodyguard come from Hudson, but your threat level had been downgraded after Sheldon was caught."

"It's not your fault, Jackson," I said to his chest, soaking his shirt with my tears. "I wish I'd listened to you and my brothers. You were right about Edward. About everything."

He sighed, brushing a hand over my hair. "I don't want to be right. I just want you to be safe. And once I'm chief of security, I can assure you that shit like this will never happen again."

He held me tight, giving me the time and space I needed.

After a while, I'd calmed down and the tears had stopped. "What will happen to her?"

"The team might scare her a little. Give her a taste of her own medicine. But then they'll turn her in to the authorities. Her dickhead brother too. And we'll make sure all copies— digital or physical—of the photos are destroyed."

"I'm—" I opened my mouth. Closed it. Opened it once more. "I don't even know what to say."

Deep down, I'd always known I didn't belong with Edward. I only wished I'd trusted my gut sooner, that I hadn't been so stubborn.

"You don't have to say anything." He brushed my hair aside. "It's over now. I promise. The only thing that would devastate me is the thought of losing you."

Surprisingly, I believed him. Because I trusted in my ability to protect myself. And I trusted that Jackson would never let anything happen to me.

CHAPTER TWENTY-SEVEN

Jackson

Sloan smiled at me over her shoulder, my hand in hers as she tugged me down the hall toward the bedroom of our suite. We'd arrived in LA earlier in the day, and it was official—my assignment was over. I was no longer Sloan's executive protection agent, and I was no longer employed by Hudson Security.

I still needed to turn in my badge, but soon, everyone at Hudson would know that I'd resigned. It was bittersweet—leaving the company that had given me purpose again after being discharged from the SEALs. But I knew this transition was a good thing, especially since it meant I got to work with Sloan.

And after witnessing yet another failure of the Huxley Grand security protocols, I was eager to get started on overhauling their systems. I certainly had my work cut out for me, but I was excited to have the power to make positive change.

Vaughn had already sent a team to the Huxley Grand LA where we were staying, and they would keep an eye on Sloan when I couldn't. We'd met her new executive protective agent, and Vaughn had promised us that Shea was the best. She'd better be, though I'd never let anything happen to Sloan.

Shea, aka Beef, had come from the New York office. I hadn't worked with her before, but everyone at Hudson spoke highly of her. Vaughn and I were on better terms. And while I knew he was still disappointed about my resignation from Hudson and the circumstances surrounding it, he'd congratulated me on my new job and wished me all the best.

Fortunately, Sheldon, Edward, and Amelia had been arrested. Sloan seemed a lot more at ease, though I could tell it still bothered her. It was understandable—she'd been betrayed and threatened. Blackmailed. Held at gunpoint.

I sighed. She didn't deserve it—any of it. But I also knew how resilient Sloan was. She had already bounced back some, and I knew it wasn't just a front.

If anything, the altercation with Amelia had made Sloan more confident. Both in her skills to protect herself as well as my ability to handle any threat.

"So…" Sloan draped her arms around my neck. "I have a few hours before I have to leave for Kendall's bridal shower."

"Mm-hmm." I placed my hands on her hips. "Did you have something in mind? Maybe a trip to the spa?" I teased.

"Maybe," she said, considering. "That does sound relaxing."

"I can think of something even more relaxing." I slanted my lips over hers.

"Mm." She smiled against my mouth. "So can I."

She tugged me into the bedroom, and I tore at her clothes, buttons flying to the floor. She yanked on my pants, and I kicked them off, nearly tripping on the way to the bed.

Our kisses were sloppy and heated as we fumbled to undress. I'd take my time later, but right now, we were both too desperate.

"God, I missed you. Missed this," Sloan said.

"Fuck. Yes." I yanked off her skirt, bringing her underwear with it in my haste. I couldn't wait to be inside her.

"You're gorgeous," I said. She was naked and stunning, and just as I crawled on top of her, I heard a knock at the door.

"Are you expecting anyone?" I kissed her neck.

She furrowed her brow. "No. Are you?"

I shrugged and went back to kissing her. We writhed against each other, her body slick and welcoming. Mine hard and eager.

"Need you," she moaned. "I need you—now."

Whoever was at the door knocked again, this time calling, "Come on. Open up, Sloan."

Sloan squeezed her eyes shut. "Jasper has impeccable timing. I thought he was going to stay in London until I returned."

"Can we just ignore him?" I joked. Sort of.

"Have you met my brother?" She laughed, pushing off the bed. "Hell, we're lucky he didn't simply barge right in."

I frowned. "But he doesn't have a key."

"I wouldn't count on it. He probably sweet-talked some poor staff member into giving him one."

"Argh." I groaned, going to the closet and tossing her a robe. "Here."

I pulled on my pants and undershirt, willing my cock to calm down. "I'll tell him to come back later."

"Good luck with that." Sloan smirked and covered herself with a robe.

I took one last lingering glance at her then went to the door. I peered through the peephole, and sure enough, Jasper was standing there, looking at his phone.

I swung open the door. "Jasper, hey. Sloan's in the shower."

Jasper leaned forward and frowned. "I don't hear any water running."

Damn. Busted.

"She, um, must have just finished."

Jasper gave me a once-over, lingering on my rumpled shirt. He arched an eyebrow, and I realized the innuendo only too late. I cringed. So much for making a good impression.

"I'll just wait in the living room until she's ready. Graham, Knox, and Nate should be here soon, so you might want to —" He pointed at me and made a circle with his finger.

Graham, Knox, and Nate were coming too? *Shit.*

"Help yourself to a drink," I said, feeling awkward as hell. "I'll be right back."

He arched one eyebrow, and I ducked back into the bedroom, closing the door behind me. Sloan had already pulled on a casual dress and fixed her hair. The sheets were rumpled, her lips were still swollen from my kisses, and I ached to climb back in bed with her.

"No luck getting rid of Jasper, huh?" She sounded equal parts exasperated and smug.

"He insisted on waiting. He said that Graham, Knox, and Nate should be here soon."

Sloan tilted her head back to the ceiling. "Why? Why do they all have to come now?"

"I don't know." I stepped closer, placing my hands on her hips. "But I hope it doesn't take long, because I have plans for us."

"Mm." She grinned. "Tell me more."

I gripped her chin, kissing her deeply and passionately. I slid my other hand up her ribs until I was cupping her breast, rolling her nipple between my fingers.

"How 'bout I show you?" I whispered.

"Yes," she moaned. "More."

"Sloan?" Jasper called.

"Coming," she chirped. She pulled her shoulders back. "If I'm not back in five, come out with some excuse."

"Okay. Deal." I smacked her ass. She winked at me over her shoulder.

I went over to my suitcase and pulled out a fresh shirt and pair of pants. I changed, and the door to the suite opened then closed again. I could hear more male voices join the conversation.

I waited a few more minutes, checked my appearance in the mirror, then went out to the living room. Nate greeted me with a warm handshake and a smile, as did Knox. Jasper gave a polite wave, and Graham stood.

"Ah. And here's our new chief of security now," he said, coming over to me. "Jackson." He shook my hand, his gaze assessing.

"Mr. Mackenzie."

"Oh, please—" Sloan waved a hand through the air. "You don't need to be so formal, Jackson. You can call him Graham."

"I heard there was an incident in Puerto Rico." Knox smoothed a hand over his beard.

"Graham," Sloan gritted out. "You promised not to mention that."

Sweat dripped down my back. I knew why she'd told him. She'd wanted to make sure all the photos of us were destroyed. I'd agreed. He was skilled and discreet. But that didn't mean I liked it.

Hell, if our roles had been reversed, if it were Greer we were talking about, I would've wanted to kill me.

"What kind of incident?" Jasper asked, frowning.

Sloan glared at Graham. "It's been taken care of."

Knox regarded us with concern, but Jasper wasn't ready to let it go. "As a co-owner, I'm entitled to know."

319

Sloan sighed and threw her hands in the air. "Fine. Edward's sister, Amelia, tried to blackmail me into giving her fifty million dollars."

"She what?" Jasper's voice boomed, along with similar expressions of outrage coming from Nate and Knox.

Nate frowned. "What kind of leverage could she possibly have on you?"

"Not just on me." Sloan linked her hand with mine, and I tried not to let my nerves show. "On us. Jackson and I are together." She explained what had happened, in PG terms.

"Unbelievable," Nate said. "Wow. Just when you think people can't get any worse."

Jasper nodded. "I'm sorry that happened to you, Sloan. That's bullshit."

"I'm glad Jackson was there to protect you," Knox said.

Graham said nothing. And while I knew he was a man of few words, his silence was putting me on edge.

Nate was the first to offer his congratulations, and Knox shook my hand, offering his as well. I appreciated their support. Two down, two to go.

Jasper spoke next. "This is actually perfect timing."

"It is?" I asked.

"Yeah. The four of us were going to hang out tonight." He turned to me. "You can join us."

"I don't think that's a good idea," Sloan interjected.

"Why not?" Jasper asked, a mischievous lilt to his smile.

"Yeah?" Knox furrowed his brow. "Why not? We want to get to know your new boyfriend. You should be happy."

Sloan narrowed her eyes at them, and I got the sense that this evening was going to be a test of some sort. *Shit.*

"Come on," Knox said, heading for the door. "We can go to my house since the bridal shower is at Nate's."

"You agreed to have the shower at your house?" I asked Nate. "Is the team—"

He cut me off, placing his hand on my arm. "The team has it covered. Besides, you no longer work for Hudson, or me, remember?" He said it with a teasing grin.

"I—" I chuckled. "Yeah."

"You work for me now," Graham said.

"*With us.*" Sloan emphasized each word. "Jackson works with us as the CSO."

"Technically, he's still our employee." Graham wore an imperious expression. "Your relationship is a conflict of interest."

"Which is why we'd planned to disclose it to the board," Sloan said.

"Great. Sounds like it's settled, then," Knox said.

Nate clapped his hand on my shoulder and ushered me toward the door. "We'll leave you to get ready for the party," he said to Sloan.

"Wait. Stop." Sloan grabbed his arm. "Jackson and I had plans."

"Yeah, I—" I rubbed the back of my neck. "We had plans."

"You're not her bodyguard. You're no longer contractually obligated to spend every moment with her," Jasper teased.

"Besides, Sloan's going to be at the party," Knox said. "And she'll have Shea with her."

Sloan huffed, but we both knew it was a losing battle.

"Are you good?" I asked Sloan, my eyes locked on her. Because if she wasn't, I would fight tooth and nail to stay with her. "Shea's in the hall if you need anything. But if you'd rather I stay…"

"Beef has it covered," Nate said. "What's up with that call sign anyway?"

I lifted a shoulder. Shea was five foot four, which made her call sign all the more amusing. I'd heard it was because she'd had a grudge against her commanding officer when she'd been in the Air Force. But someone else from Hudson had told me it was because "beef" was her nickname for cactuses. Apparently, she was an avid collector of them. Whatever. I didn't care so long as she did a good job.

"*Hayati?*" I wanted confirmation from her.

Sloan had barely nodded when Jasper called, "See you later!" as he herded me out into the hall.

"*Hayati?*" Nate asked. "What does that mean?"

"Don't ask questions you don't want the answers to," Knox muttered, and I tried not to laugh.

I patted my pockets. "Wait. I don't have my phone." I tried to turn back for the room.

"You'll live." Graham marched down the hall. Then it sounded like he muttered, "Let's get this over with."

"Come on, big guy." Jasper draped his arm over my shoulder.

"What about Sloan and keeping her safe?" I asked, knowing nothing was more important to them.

"Like we said, Shea's got it covered," Nate said to the Hudson Security employee posted in the hallway. "Right, Shea?"

"Right, sir." She gave me a nod of understanding.

Another guy from Hudson—Nicholas—pushed off the wall, shadowing us as we proceeded to the elevator. With no more excuses, I followed Sloan's brothers to the VIP exit, where a black Escalade was waiting.

I started to open the door for Nate as I had always done when I'd worked for him, and he chuckled. "I'm sure this will take some getting used to." Nicholas, aka Ghost, opened the door for us instead, and Nate gestured for me to climb in. I did after a moment's hesitation.

This was all so strange.

It was one thing to be with Sloan while we were sailing or even when we went ashore. I was learning that being in a relationship with her was an entirely different thing when it came to her family. To real life.

I didn't know whether to talk to Ghost or her brothers. I wasn't sure where I fit in. It was as if I was straddling two worlds—my old one and the new. The bodyguard and now the billionaire's boyfriend.

CHAPTER TWENTY-EIGHT

Jackson

W hen we made it to Knox's, I was already somewhat familiar with the place from the times I'd visited with Nate. I knew the staff, and it was nice to see them again, even if it was still strange to be here as a guest.

"Is Jude coming?" Nate asked, referring to Knox's son.

Knox shook his head. "Figured he didn't need to be part of this."

Part of what? I wanted to ask but didn't. I had a feeling I knew.

Knox's chef prepared some appetizers, while Knox poured us each a drink. "Jackson, do you know how to play poker?"

"Of course."

"Good." He clapped a hand on my shoulder, and the five of us sat at the table. It felt as if each of them was sizing me up, and I knew from working for Nate that they played together regularly.

"What's the buy-in?" I asked Knox.

"It doesn't work like that. We don't bet money."

That was a relief because when it came to money, these

guys were way out of my league. Surprisingly, though, I didn't feel intimidated.

"At the beginning of each round," Jasper said. "We take turns naming the prize."

I nodded slowly, wondering exactly what that looked like. But I didn't have to wait long to find out. "I'll go first," Jasper said. "A weekend at Nate's cabin in Bear Creek."

"Ooh. Trying to impress someone with a romantic getaway?" Knox teased.

"If you're going to use my cabin as your sex shack..." Nate glared at Jasper.

"He named the prize," Graham said. "And it's something that's within your power to give."

"Fine," Nate sighed. "God, I hope you lose," he added to Jasper.

"So, if I win the round, I get a weekend there?" I asked, trying to understand if there were any more stipulations.

"You're in the game, aren't you?" Nate asked.

"I... Yeah. I guess I am." This was so strange. I felt as if I'd stepped into an alternate universe. Play proceeded, and Knox ended up winning the hand, much to Jasper's lament. I wasn't playing particularly aggressively. I was mostly using the opportunity to study my opponents and to get to know Sloan's family to find out how they felt about us.

"Nate?" Knox asked. "What do you want?"

He glanced around the circle, taking his time to evaluate each of us before landing on Graham. "Winner gets to borrow the Monet for a year."

Shit. Graham owned an original Monet?

I hoped he had adequate security and insurance for that. What would that even look like? My mind started to play out the various options as Graham and Nate argued over the duration of the loan.

"A month," Graham shot back, not even looking up.

"Six months," Nate said.

"Four."

"Six." Nate held firm.

Graham leaned back in his chair and sighed. "Five. But winner pays for transport and insurance."

"Of course," Nate said.

I watched the four of them, using the game to study them and their strategy. They each took a different approach, but they were all just as competitive, even if some were more obvious about their desire to win.

Nate won the round, and he seemed immensely pleased with himself. "Graham. You're up. Name your price."

Graham turned to me. "Winner gets to ask Jackson three questions of their choosing, and he has to answer."

My gut clenched with dread. Graham was out for blood. And no matter who won, I knew the questions would be probing. I'd been waiting for something like this, but still... Suddenly the game had lost a lot of its appeal.

"Jackson?" Nate asked.

I merely grunted to indicate my assent, while I tried to prepare myself for whatever they might ask.

Knox shuffled the cards, and everyone seemed a lot more focused and intent all of a sudden, despite their earlier casual demeanor. Or maybe it was just me, anxious about who would win and what they'd want to know. Still, I did my best to maintain a calm façade.

Graham ultimately won the hand, and the others groaned as they pushed their cards away.

I knew I was fucked the moment my eyes met Graham's. "What makes you think you're worthy of our sister?"

Once upon a time, when I was younger, his words would've made me flinch. Even now, I still recoiled at them internally. But I wouldn't let Graham or anyone stand in the way of Sloan's and my happiness.

"Shit, Graham." Jasper shifted in his chair. "You couldn't use just a little finesse?"

Graham was silent, his eyes still focused on me like a large panther stalking its prey. They were similar to Sloan's, though a shade darker and much more intense. He watched me expectantly, waiting for my answer.

"I'm not," I said, clearing my throat. "Worthy of her."

Jasper leaned in, whispering *sotto voce*, "You weren't supposed to agree with him."

I glanced at each of them. "I fucked up with Sloan once before. I thought I wasn't enough, but I realized that was my own insecurity talking. Ultimately, Sloan's the only person who can decide what she needs."

"Damn," Nate said. "Good answer."

"Thanks," I said, a little relieved now that we'd gotten one question out of the way.

"When you say you fucked up with her once..." Jasper asked.

"They were...involved," Graham said, seeming to choose his words carefully, "when Sloan was in college."

"Wait..." Jasper turned to me. "Are you the guy who broke her heart? The reason she was so messed up for so long?"

"I believe *I'm* the one who's supposed to be asking the questions here," Graham said in a lofty tone. For a minute, I thought I could get by without answering Jasper's question, but then Graham added, "But yes, Jackson is *that* guy."

Four faces full of menace were now focused on me. *Shit.*

"What are your intentions toward Sloan?" Graham asked.

"She is my everything, and I intend to show her that every day for the rest of my life."

"Marriage?" Knox asked.

"If that's what she wants," I said, instead of pointing out the fact that I'd already answered Graham's question and completed all that was technically required of me by the rules.

Graham nodded but said nothing more.

Knox's expression softened, but Jasper said, "Wait. What? Am I the only one who's not okay with this? He screwed up. He broke her heart. Are we seriously going to let this go so easily?"

"Oh, for fuck's sake," Nate muttered. "Jackson's a good guy," he said, as if I weren't sitting right there. Listening. "And Sloan seems happy."

"How can you know? You've seen them together for like two seconds," Jasper said.

"I spoke with her at length about it, and I checked in during her trip. So, yes, I believe I can confidently say that she's happy with him."

Jasper gawked at him. "You did? Why didn't you say anything?"

Nate lifted a shoulder. "It wasn't my story to tell."

"We all make mistakes," Knox said, glossing over it. "And it seems like Jackson has learned from his. If Sloan is willing to trust him again, we should give him a fair chance."

Jasper leaned back in his chair, still unconvinced.

Graham opened his mouth, and I braced myself. "Sloan is worth significantly more than you are—financially speaking," he added, when Nate shot him a dirty look. "Are you willing to sign a prenup?"

"If that's what Sloan wants, of course."

Nate and Knox seemed satisfied.

"If you're asking if I'm interested in her money, the answer is no. I fell in love with Sloan without knowing who her family was or what she was set to inherit."

Graham leaned forward. "Even so, she's a powerful, independent, wealthy woman. Some men find that intimidating."

"I'm not one of them. If anything, I only admire her more for the woman she's become." I decided it was time to metaphorically lay all my cards on the table. I took a deep breath. "I understand that you all want the best for Sloan. As an older brother myself, I get it. I'm sure there are many things I could say to try to reassure you about me, but I've always believed that actions speak louder than words. All I ask is for you to give me a chance."

"Damn," Jasper said. "He really is perfect for her."

Nate and Knox nodded. Graham peered at me over his cards, and I detected a hint of praise in his eyes.

"Sloan doesn't need your permission," I said. "But I hope to have your blessing to marry her when the time comes."

Knox seemed to consider it, but it was Nate who spoke. "Yes. Absolutely."

I turned to him, touched by his enthusiastic vote of confidence. "Thank you."

Before anyone else could chime in, Graham's phone buzzed, and he scowled at it, muttering, "Fucking Lily."

Fucking Lily? Who's Lily?

"Hey." Jasper reached for Graham's phone. "No devices at the poker table."

Graham muttered a curse and shoved his phone into his pocket before looking at the cards in his hand.

"It's my turn to decide the prize," Knox said, turning to Nate. "Winner gets to borrow a piece from the vault."

The vault was a highly secured, hidden room in Nate's home where his mother's jewelry collection was stored and displayed. I'd been in there once. Dark walls and dramatic lighting made the gems sparkle. Tiaras. Necklaces. Rare gemstones. It was incredible.

"For how long?" Nate asked, turning more serious.

"One event."

With the terms settled, everyone returned their attention to the game. I leaned toward Knox and asked, "Who's Lily?"

Wife? Girlfriend? Sloan had never mentioned that Graham was dating anyone.

"Oh lord." Jasper rolled his eyes. "Please don't ask."

"The bane of my existence," Graham said, practically growling. Jasper pushed Graham's drink closer to his hand.

Okay. Interesting.

I made a mental note to ask Sloan about it later. Perhaps do some digging of my own.

"Actually," Nate said. "Since Jackson's now chief of security for the Huxley Grand, he should probably know about Lily."

"Why? Is she a stalker or something?" I watched the four of them for any tells. I knew Nate well enough to know his, but the others were a mystery to me.

Graham smoothed a hand down his tie. "She's annoying."

Knox leaned closer, keeping his voice low and his cards angled down. "She's a luxury travel blogger, and she posted a few less-than-positive reviews of some of the Huxley hotels."

"That's it?"

I'd expected something more nefarious. More threatening. A bad review wasn't great, but it also wasn't the end of the world. Nor was it a safety concern—at least, I didn't think so from what I'd been told so far. It sounded like more of a personal offense, and I was surprised to see Graham worked up so much over anything, let alone the opinion of one person.

"That's. *It?*" Graham sneered.

"Oh boy." Jasper sat back in his chair, shaking his head. "You've done it now."

Knox rolled his eyes, and Nate merely crossed his arms over his chest and grinned. Graham launched into a diatribe of Lily, the threat she posed to the brand, how inaccurate her review was, and so much more.

"That's not even the worst part." He practically growled the words. "She used to be my assistant."

Everyone's attention snapped to Graham, our questions overlapping.

"What?"

"Which one?"

"What about her NDA?"

Graham held up his hand, and everyone fell silent. "Lily was my assistant a few years ago. Her name is Liliana Fontaine. As to her NDA, it doesn't apply because her blog doesn't expose confidential or proprietary information."

"Liliana?" Jasper scrunched up his face. "Aw, man. I liked her."

"She was a pain in the ass," Graham grumbled. "Always butting her nose in where it didn't belong."

"Exactly." Jasper smirked. "She was good for you."

"Why did she leave Huxley Grand?" Knox asked.

"She gave some bullshit generic excuse about 'wanting to pursue other opportunities,'" Graham said.

"She certainly pursued other opportunities." Nate shook his head.

"Did you piss her off?" Knox asked. "Is that why she's decided to write a bad review?"

"Probably," Jasper muttered.

"I gave her a generous bonus while she was working for me." Graham clenched and unclenched his fist.

"Money doesn't solve everything," Knox said.

"Agreed," I said, though it certainly caused its fair share of problems.

"Do you have a plan?" Jasper asked.

Graham's posture was even more rigid than usual. "Not yet."

"Sloan mentioned a grand opening of a new location. Ixtapa, right?" I asked, an idea taking shape in my mind.

Jasper nodded. "Yeah. Why?"

"You could invite a bunch of travel bloggers, including Lily. Do a soft opening to show her what the Huxley Grand brand stands for," I said to Graham.

"That's a great idea," Jasper said. "You could confront her." He frowned, and I regretted opening my mouth. "Though, I might be more successful in obtaining information, considering—" he waved his hand through the air "—your history."

Graham narrowed his eyes at Jasper. "You are *not* seducing her for information. That will only make the situation worse."

"I meant that you could give her the VIC experience," I said, trying to get us back on track before this conversation completely derailed. "Fly her out in first class. Give her the best room. The most exclusive spa package. The works." I tried to think of everything that a very important client would expect.

Graham glowered. "I'm not going to reward her for her betrayal."

"No. I like this idea," Jasper said. "We already do this for high-spenders, the very important clients, as Jackson said. Why not extend it to someone with a lot of influence?"

"It's a good move," Knox said, and it was time to show our cards.

Nate folded. I had a strong hand, but Knox won the round. It didn't surprise me. He was a strategist. Patient. He feigned disinterest in the game, but it was all an act.

"Jackson," Nate said. "You're up."

"I get to name the prize?" I asked, unable to keep the incredulous tone from my voice.

Nate leaned back and spread his arms wide. "Anything you want."

I considered everything I knew about Sloan's family. Their fortune. Their fame. They owned luxury hotels, homes, cars, rare art, and gems, but I found myself asking for none of those things.

"Your company," I said.

Graham scoffed. "We're not handing over the Huxley brand or the Leatherbacks." He gestured to Knox, who owned LA's pro soccer team. "Or Rainshadow Productions." Nate's film studio.

"No." I ignored my cards, keeping them facedown on the table. "Winner gets to host an event where everyone has to attend."

"*That's* what you want?" Jasper asked, his tone incredulous. "I mean, of course, we're going to attend. We're a family. But why even ask for something that's a given, when you could have season tickets in a box at the Leatherbacks games, a night in our most decadent suite in the most expensive location of the Huxley Grand resorts. Or…"

"I think we get the point," Knox said with a bemused grin.

"Good," I said. "And I'm glad it's a given that you'd support your family. That's always been important to me."

Nate nodded, impressed. "Welcome to the family, Jackson."

"Let's not get ahead of ourselves," Jasper said. "They're not married."

"Yet," I added. "We aren't married yet. Now, deal. Because I'm going to win, and then you're all going to have to attend Sloan's and my wedding when the time comes." Assuming she said yes, but I had a feeling she would.

Jasper choked on his drink. Nate grinned from behind his glass, but it was Graham who responded, shocking us all. "Regardless of whether you win this hand, we're going to hold you to that."

"I would expect nothing less," I said as Knox dealt us in.

As I glanced around the table at these four men, I smiled to myself. My day had certainly turned out differently than I'd planned. And while I was eager to return to Sloan and finally finish what we'd started, I was happy with how things had gone. Despite her brothers' ribbing, I knew I had their support, and that was worth more than anything else I could've won.

CHAPTER TWENTY-NINE

Sloan

"Sloan!" Emerson hugged me as soon as I'd stepped through the front door. "I'm so glad you made it."

"Me too," I said, glancing around the house where the caterers and the event planner and her team were still setting up. "Sorry I'm a little early."

"Are you kidding? I've been looking forward to your visit."

"Same. Fortunately, traffic wasn't as bad as I'd expected. And since the guys kidnapped Jackson, I had more time to get ready."

She arched one brow. "Kidnapped?"

"You know how they are." I laughed. "I'm sure they're off trying to interrogate him about our relationship, but Jackson is a former Navy SEAL, so..." I shrugged. "Good luck to them."

Emerson leaned her hip against the back of the couch. "Nate mentioned that you were together. I'm happy for you."

"Thank you." I ducked my head. "Though I hope that isn't weird for you."

"Are you kidding?" She smiled, reaching out to squeeze

my hand. Her red diamond engagement ring sparkled brilliantly. "We all love Jackson. He's always felt like part of the family."

"Thanks. Let's just hope my brothers don't ruin it," I joked. After everything Jackson and I had been through, from high winds to blackmail to our own past mistakes and fears, I had faith that we could weather whatever trouble my brothers—or anyone else—might try to cause.

"I'm sure Jackson can handle himself," Emerson said. "If anything, I'd be more concerned about them all banding together to hatch up ways to protect you."

I blew out a breath. "Good point. I didn't even think about that. Though, honestly, my brothers try to protect me, but Jackson empowers me."

Emerson grinned. "Girl, you're lucky. Did I tell you about the time that Knox had Kendall's older car towed so he could give her a Range Rover?"

My eyes widened. "He did not."

"Oh yeah, he did," Kendall said, joining us. "And we weren't even together at that point. I was still just his house sitter."

I rolled my eyes. "Men."

"Crawford men," Emerson clarified. We all rolled our eyes at that.

"Congratulations." I hugged Kendall. "Let me see the ring."

"Thank you." She smiled and held out her hand. The large diamond ring was dazzling, and her accompanying smile even more so. "So glad you made it."

"I wouldn't miss it. It's nice to add more women to the family."

Especially women like Emerson and Kendall. They were both a lot younger than my brothers, sure. But it was clear how much they loved Nate and Knox, even if they'd both started as their employees. Emerson as Brooklyn's nanny, and Kendall as Knox's house sitter and his son's ex.

Nate was right. I shouldn't have been concerned. If everyone could get past all that, I had faith that they'd be just as welcoming and accepting of my relationship with Jackson.

Emerson wrapped her arm around Kendall's waist, and Kendall leaned her head against Emerson's shoulder. I smiled, thinking of Greer and wishing she were here. I'd spoken with her on the phone a few times since she'd left Puerto Rico, and we texted daily. It was a huge relief that our friendship hadn't changed since Jackson and I had told her about our relationship. If anything, we'd grown closer.

And Jackson's mom, Belinda... Oh my. I smiled. She had been over the moon when she'd found out we were together. Disappointed that Jackson wasn't moving to New York after all, but we'd promised to visit often or fly her to London on my private plane.

"Here." Emerson held out her hands. "Let me take that for you." I handed her the gift I'd brought and followed her inside.

I glanced over my shoulder and spied Shea standing near the door to the garage.

"How do you like your new bodyguard?" Emerson asked.

"Everyone from Hudson's been great, but I like that she's a woman. I feel like it helps her blend in more easily. And I think we could actually be friends."

"That's awesome," Emerson said. "Nicholas is great, but no one is Jackson."

I smiled and turned to Kendall. "It probably isn't my place to tell you," I said, but I felt like Kendall deserved to know. "But I feel like we girls have to stick together. Did you know that Knox hired a bodyguard for you and Jude?"

She dragged a hand through her hair. "Oh yeah. Since he's never bothered to tell me, I just pretend like I don't know. It's pretty amusing to see what kind of ridiculous situations I can put Knox in because of it."

"Oh my god." I laughed so hard tears came to my eyes. "That's diabolical. And totally genius."

"Thank you," Kendall said, looking pleased with herself. "If he's already this bad, can you even imagine how he'll be once I'm pregnant."

She'd made the offhand comment to her best friend, but my expression must have betrayed my shock. Kendall merely smiled. "You're surprised, aren't you?"

"I…" I smiled, thinking it was none of my business, but they'd brought it up. "I guess I am, yeah. Not that you'd want children, but that Knox does. Though he's always wanted a big family."

She nodded. "You know him well."

"He's always been there for me," I said. "Despite the fact that we had the biggest age gap of the five of us. It's funny to think that now we're going through similar things even though we're a decade apart."

"Meaning…" Emerson leaned in, her eyes darting from my bare ring finger to my stomach, giving each a pointed look.

"What?" I jerked my head back. "No. No. Jackson and I only recently reconnected. We're moving in together, that's it. No wedding. No children."

"For now." Kendall shared a smirk with Emerson. She didn't seem surprised, but nothing had ever stayed a secret long in my family.

Though their comment got me thinking about Jackson's and my future. About what we wanted and whether it would include marriage or children or both. We'd been so busy trying to figure out if we could even have a future together, we hadn't discussed what it might look like beyond where we'd live.

"Speaking of children," I said, needing a segue before this conversation derailed even more. "Where's Brooklyn?"

"Brooklyn," Emerson called. "Sloan's here."

"Auntie Sloan?" She came tearing down the stairs with a huge smile. For a minute, I could imagine doing this with my own kids. Jackson's and my kids. They'd have his eyes, and my gran's nose. Jackson would be a great dad—overprotective, of course, but also fun.

And then Brooklyn flung herself into my arms, tearing me out of that daydream. The force of her embrace nearly knocked the air from my lungs, and I knew I needed to talk to Jackson to see if we were on the same page about this. Because if we weren't… Well, I didn't know what I was going to do then. I wanted kids, had always wanted kids. But I was thirty-seven. I didn't have the luxury of waiting like Emerson or Kendall, who were both in their late twenties.

"I really missed you," she said, squeezing me tight.

"Hey, kiddo. I really missed you too. I brought you something." I reached into my bag. I pulled out a conch necklace I'd gotten her in the Bahamas. "This is for you. And Jackson picked this for you." I handed her a stuffed turtle.

"Thank you!" she squealed and hugged the turtle tight before asking me to help her put on the necklace.

"That looks so pretty with your dress," Emerson said, giving Brooklyn's shoulder a squeeze.

Brooklyn smiled up at her with a look of such adoration and love, it stole my breath. I was so happy for Brooklyn, for all of them. I knew how badly Brooklyn had always wanted a mom, and now she had an amazing one in Emerson.

"Before all the guests arrive, I have some exciting news. At least, I think it's exciting," I said, hoping it would be well received. I figured now—before the party had started and when it was just the three of us—was as good a time as any to tell Brooklyn about Jackson and me.

"What's that?" Brooklyn asked.

I took a deep breath and smiled. "Jackson and I are dating, and he's moving with me to London."

Brooklyn's eyes went wide. "You and Jackson, as in my Jackson?" She glanced to Emerson for confirmation. "Our bodyguard?"

Emerson grinned. "One and the same."

Brooklyn squealed. "Best. News. Ever!" Each word was spoken by Brooklyn with increasing volume and intensity.

I laughed. "Thanks."

After that, the guests started arriving. The party was small and intimate, and it was filled with so much love and support. A few of the wives and girlfriends of the LA Leatherbacks players even attended.

As much fun as I was having, I couldn't wait to return to Jackson. I'd texted him a few times, but they'd gone unanswered. So finally, I'd caved and messaged my brothers in the group chat.

> Me: I hope you're being nice to Jackson.

> Nate: When have we ever not been nice?

> Jasper: Right? Who does she think we are?

> Me: I think I'm justified in being nervous after how you treated pretty much every other guy I've dated.

> Graham: They were all dicks, especially Edward.

I didn't disagree. And his sister was certainly a piece of work. Though I no longer had to worry about her. Earlier today, Halle had texted me an article about the fall of the Burton Banking giant.

Edward and Amelia had both been arrested for fraud and

embezzlement and a number of other crimes. I secretly wondered if Graham was behind the "insider leak" that had led to their arrest, but I didn't ask. It was probably best that I didn't know.

> Knox: Most of the others were too.
>
> Nate: Seconded.

I rolled my eyes, tempted to ignore my phone at this point. I was getting nowhere with these jokers.

> Jasper: Thirded. Is that a word? Thirded. Regardless, Edward has been voted off the island.
>
> Me: That's not how this works. And Jackson better not get voted off the island because he's staying.
>
> Jasper: Ooh. Possessive. Defensive. She must really like him.

I considered responding but decided to focus on my goal. Rescuing Jackson from my brothers.

> Me: I'm heading back from the shower soon. Jackson better be at the hotel when I get there.
>
> Nate: Ooh. Scary.
>
> Jasper: Right?
>
> Jasper: I can imagine her wagging her finger.
>
> Me: Nate. Knox. You do remember that I'm in the same room with your fiancées, right? Do I need to tell them all your embarrassing stories?

Graham: If you need help, I can send pictures.

Knox: Not helping.

I laughed. Sure, my brothers could annoy the shit out of me. They could be overprotective and overbearing, but it was only because they cared. And I loved them for it.

Me: And that's why you're my favorite brother, Graham.

Graham might break laws with his hacking, but he lived by a code of ethics.

Jasper: What? I feel betrayed.

Knox: So do I.

Nate: Same.

I sighed. *Focus!* I mentally shouted at them through the phone.

Me: Thirty minutes, boys. The clock is ticking.

Jasper: But we're having so much fun. We were about to tell Jackson all your embarrassing stories.

Me: I doubt that. Besides, he's already heard most of them from Greer.

I was bluffing, but hopefully they wouldn't figure that out.

Graham: He'll be there.

I figured Graham was only complying because he was

done peopling. Jasper and I often joked that Graham could only handle so much social interaction in one day. And clearly, he'd met his quota.

> Me: Thank you, #1 Brother.

I closed out of the group message. I could only imagine the kind of trouble that had caused. At least it might give Jackson a break if they were grilling him.

I texted Shea, letting her know I was ready. And then I said my goodbyes to everyone. It had been so nice to spend time with Kendall, Emerson, and Brooklyn, but I wanted nothing more than to be alone with Jackson.

When I returned to the suite, he was sitting on the couch watching TV alone, much to my surprise.

"Hey." I set my purse on the counter.

He turned and glanced at me over the back of the sofa, his eyes darkening the moment he saw me. "Hey, *hayati*. Have a good time?"

I sank down on the couch next to him, and he immediately pulled my feet into his lap and slipped off my heels. "Yeah. It was nice. Did you?"

He started massaging my feet, and I relaxed into his touch. "Surprisingly, yes."

"What'd you guys do?"

"Played some poker. Drank some whiskey."

I jerked my head back. "That's it? Does that mean it went okay?"

"Yeah. It did. Why?" He chuckled. "What did you think we'd do?"

"Did they interrogate you?"

He lifted a shoulder, sliding his hand up to massage my calves. "It was nothing I couldn't handle."

"So, it really went okay?" I asked again, needing confirmation.

"Yeah. I like them, and they seemed supportive of our relationship. What about Kendall and Emerson?"

"So sweet," I said. "They were happy for us. Brooklyn too."

I thought back on my conversation with Kendall and Emerson about the future. About a wedding and kids. I thought about what I wanted.

"Something on your mind?" He continued working his magic on my muscles.

"Time is funny, isn't it? Sometimes things seem to take forever, and others happen too fast." And being held at gunpoint had a way of putting things into perspective.

"Are you talking about us?" He stilled his hands briefly before resuming his ministrations.

"Yes. Sort of. I just…" I sighed. How was I supposed to say this? How was I supposed to bring it up? I decided to just rip off the Band-Aid and blurted, "Do you want kids?"

Jackson froze, his eyes darting to my stomach.

"No. No. I'm not pregnant," I rushed to add, trying to get a read on his thoughts. "But would you…"

"Yes," he said before I could even finish my sentence. "Yes. Absolutely, I want to have children with you if we're lucky enough that it happens. Even if it doesn't, I love you. I want to be with you."

I smiled, a thrill going through me at his admission. Okay. That had gone better than I'd expected.

He cupped my cheek. "Hell, I'd marry you tomorrow if I thought you'd say yes."

I leaned into his touch. "I… Yes," I breathed out the word, surprising myself. It had always been a secret wish of my heart, but to think that it might come true…

He stilled. "Wait. What? I didn't think you'd actually agree."

"Jackson." I climbed onto his lap, straddling him. He rested his hands on my hips, his eyes searching mine "We've wasted enough time. I'm done waiting." I sensed that he wasn't taking me seriously. So I met his gaze. "I'm not kidding. I'd marry you right now."

"That wasn't an official proposal, though," he said. "I wanted to—"

I kissed him. "I don't need one. I just—" I kissed his neck, sliding from his lap to the floor "—need—" another lingering kiss to his chest, as I started to unbutton his shirt "—you." I peered up at him.

"Sloan, *hayati*." He grasped my chin. "I'm going to do this right."

"Who's to say what's right?" I yanked on his belt, pulling it free, before unbuttoning his pants. He stood and kicked them off, sitting back down on the couch. "Let's do what we want."

I smoothed my hands up his thighs, loving the way his cock jerked to attention.

"You're making it difficult to think straight." He gripped the cushions.

"Good." I smirked and placed a kiss to the tip of his already hard cock, closing my eyes briefly at the feel of his hands in my hair, his touch loving and possessive. I licked him from root to tip, gratified when his hips bucked.

"Mm," I hummed around his cock. I peered up at him, enthralled by the sight of this strong man coming undone. Losing control. Because of me.

"Fuck," he grunted when I licked his balls, pumping his shaft at the same time. "Yes. Fuck, yes."

My body was on fire for him, aching for his touch. He made me feel so needy, desperate even, but that no longer scared me like it used to. Because I trusted him—completely and absolutely.

345

He gathered my hair in a ponytail as I continued working him. "Show me how deep you can take me."

His encouragement spurred me on. And I loved the way his ab muscles contracted as he hissed. He was getting close, and I was so, *so* turned on by the sight of him. I mean...*damn.*

"Off," he rasped. "Dress. Off. Now."

I released him from my mouth with a pop. He roughly pulled my dress over my head, tossing it aside. It was dark now, the only light coming from the lamp.

He smacked my ass. "Lie down. Legs up over the back of the couch."

Huh?

He helped me get into position and then went to stand behind the couch. He pulled me closer to him, and the angle allowed both of us to see everything. When he put his head between my thighs and licked my clit, I nearly came undone at the sight of him looking at me. The entire time, his hands were on me—traveling over my stomach, my breasts, even playing with my mouth and pushing a finger between my lips.

He kept at it until my legs were shaking, and I was calling his name. Until my body was on fire, and I thought I might burn if he didn't let me come. If he didn't come with me.

"Please, Jackson." I was done waiting. I was ready.

He moved for the bedroom, presumably to retrieve a condom from the intimacy kit, but I sat up and placed my hand on his arm to stop him.

"Are you sure?" he asked. "I mean, I had my annual physical for Hudson recently and passed it with flying colors, but..."

"I have an IUD. And I've always used condoms in the past, but I don't want to anymore. Not with you. You're my forever."

He cupped my face and kissed me, his cock hard against my stomach. "I love you."

"I love you too," I said, feeling dazed from that kiss. Delirious from the need I felt for this incredible man.

He lined himself up with my entrance, and we both watched as he disappeared inside me. His eyes flitted to mine, and I held his gaze. I felt it to the depths of my core. His love. His devotion. His unspoken promise. He was mine, and I was his.

He interlaced our fingers, fusing our mouths together, sealing our connection in every way possible. I gasped when he hit a particularly sensitive spot.

"Oh god." My head dropped back, my eyes closed.

When I opened my eyes, his blue ones were the same as they'd always been. Warm. Loving. Endless like the ocean and full of the promise of forever.

We were still us. We would always be us. And making love was like coming home.

He wrapped his arm around my lower back, pulling me even closer. So close it was impossible to know where I ended and he began.

Jackson claimed my mouth, his movements rough and possessive in the way he knew I loved. His eyes burned molten, and I loved how attentive he was. Always checking in with me. It was hot.

"Harder," I said, needing more, though I wasn't sure what. I just...needed him.

I locked my legs around his hips, and his thrusts grew almost punishing in their intensity, my pleasure building and building like a gathering storm. I needed... I panted. Needed...

"Mine," he growled, nipping at my shoulder. "You're mine, Sloan."

"Yes," I sighed, both from his words and the sensations he

provoked in my body. He was feral, and I freaking loved seeing him lose control like this. "And you're mine."

"Always," he promised, and I was so close. "Always."

I sucked in a jagged breath, surrounded by his scent. His touch. His love. Our bodies moved in harmony, carrying us both toward release.

"Look at me," he said, slowing down, torturing me. "Look at us."

We glanced down to the point where our bodies were joined. He spread me wide with his fingers, adding another sensation to the mix. "Fuck. Look how well you take me."

He pulled out slowly then thrust in hard. He did it again, eliciting another gasp from me. And then he increased his pace, his eyes darting between our bodies and my face.

"Oh god, Jackson. That feels…" I panted. "So good. I'm so close. So…"

And then it crashed over me like a thirty-foot wave—powerful, inescapable, and unrelenting. All I could feel, all I could see, all I could hear was him. He was my entire universe, and I'd been a fool to ever think otherwise.

With a few more thrusts, Jackson spilled inside me, grunting, "Mine," again and again.

We lay there a minute, still intertwined, our bodies sticky and sated. I smiled, full of love for this incredible man. He kissed me then withdrew, and I felt empty without him.

"Fuck me." He rubbed a hand over his mouth, his eyes glued to my most intimate place. "The sight of my come dripping out of your pussy…" He growled and leaned forward to lick my clit, setting off a round of shudders. "Damn."

My legs were shaking, and I tried to push him away, laughing as I did so. "I can't take any more."

He chuckled and licked me once more before standing.

"Come on." He easily scooped me up, cradling me to him. "Let's get cleaned up."

I rested my head against his chest, content to listen to the cadence of his heart. When we reached the bathroom, Jackson set me down and turned on the water. As soon as it was warm, he climbed in the shower and held out his hand, waiting for me.

I slid my hand into his, filled with a sense of rightness. Of peace and contentedness. Jackson joined me beneath the water, wrapping his arms around me, holding me close.

We just stood there, my head against his chest, his body curled protectively around mine. It was...bliss. This was all I'd ever wanted.

CHAPTER THIRTY

Sloan

"Mm." I stretched, reaching out for Jackson, but when I opened my eyes, the bed was empty.

It was Saturday, and I couldn't believe we'd already been in LA a week. Jasper had gone back to London to oversee operations there until I was ready to return. I'd told him it wasn't necessary, but he'd said he was happy to go.

Jackson and I were supposed to go out on Knox's yacht with everyone this afternoon. I wished Jasper would be here for it, but I was looking forward to seeing Jude and his girlfriend Chrissy and spending more time with my family.

Between meeting with the board, catching up on what I'd missed while we'd been sailing the Caribbean, and getting Jackson up to speed as our new chief of security, my days had been busy but full. My nights had been spent in bed with Jackson. And I loved waking up with him every morning. Getting ready for work together and knowing I'd get to see him at the end of the day.

He seemed to get along well with my brothers, even Graham. And he was loving his new role. I knew Jackson would miss his coworkers from Hudson, but he didn't seem to regret his decision, which was a relief.

Part of me had worried how we'd adapt to living and working together. And while I knew there might still be an adjustment period when we actually went back to London next week, I wasn't concerned. If anything, I was excited to share all my favorite places with him. To get to show him one of my favorite cities—or stay home doing nothing at all.

Jackson entered the room a moment later with a breakfast tray and a smile. He was shirtless, and his gray sweatpants hung low on his waist. It was distracting, to say the least. I scanned his chest, my eyes lingering on the sextant tattoo where my initials were hidden.

He smirked, setting the tray on the bed. "Hungry?"

"Definitely." I sat up, letting the sheet fall to my waist.

His eyes darkened, and my nipples hardened beneath his eager gaze.

"Thanks for bringing me breakfast in bed. I feel so spoiled."

He leaned in, capturing my lips for a lingering kiss. "Good."

I lifted the silver dome to reveal the plate, but the only thing on it was a small box covered in royal blue suede. "This doesn't look like breakfast," I joked. But then it hit me. Wait. Was it… Was he…

He'd talked about proposing nearly a week ago. And with everything that had happened since, I'd pushed the idea from my mind.

"It's not breakfast," he said, seeming nervous for the first time. "But hopefully it's something better." He took my hand in his. "I love you, Sloan. You've always seen me and loved me for who I am. You are my home. My everything. And I can't wait to spend our lives together. Marry me."

"Yes," I said without hesitation, wiping away a tear. "Yes, Jackson." I smiled.

He opened the box, and I gasped. My grandmother's engagement ring was nestled inside—a vintage Tiffany setting that I'd always loved for its simplicity and sentimentality. My grandparents had been partners in every sense of the word. Their love had endured the loss of their children. The challenges of starting and growing an international business. The raising of their grandchildren. And so much more.

"Where did you get that?" I whispered. I hadn't seen her ring in years.

His expression was solemn when he met my gaze. "Graham gave it to me."

My eyes bulged. "Graham..."

Jackson caressed the back of my hand with his thumb. "He'd been saving it for you. For when you found the right man."

I swiped away tears. I couldn't believe it. Jackson slid the ring on my finger, and it was a perfect fit.

"I was going to buy you an engagement ring..." He smiled down at my hand. "But I knew this would mean more to you."

"You're right. And thank you." I pushed the tray aside and wrapped my arms around him. "I love you so much, Jackson. You are my protector and my home. And I cannot wait to be your wife."

"How about tomorrow?"

"How about what tomorrow?" I asked, still admiring the ring and the man who'd given it to me.

"Let's get married—tomorrow."

"What?"

"Tomorrow," he said again, a third time now. My brain still couldn't seem to comprehend the word in this context.

"You can't be serious? What about…a dress? And a venue? And our families? And…" There were so many details, it could make my head spin. It was inconceivable to think that we could make everything happen in a day.

"Do you trust me?" he asked.

"Of course," I said instantly. This was crazy, but also… kind of awesome. Could we actually pull it off? "Even if we wanted to get married tomorrow, what about a marriage license?"

"You can get married same-day in California. It happened a few years ago with one of Hudson's celebrity clients and caused quite the stir. And we have the perfect venue." He spread his arm wide to encompass the room and the Huxley Grand LA. "With catering and flowers. And multiple spaces available for a last-minute intimate wedding. Jasper offered to come back to help coordinate everything."

"Wait. Jasper knows?" I asked, and he nodded. First, the ring from Graham, and now, Jasper's assistance. "So my brothers not only know of your plan and are okay with it, but are actively helping?"

He grinned.

I stared at him in awe, and for the first time, I realized how serious he was. Jackson had not only figured out several of the biggest logistics to pulling off a quick wedding, but he'd gotten my family on board. Why was I even hesitating? I'd never wanted a big wedding, and the details didn't matter to me so long as my family would be there. But…

"What about Greer?" I couldn't get married without her by my side.

"I talked to Knox, and he offered to send the jet for her and Mom and the kids. All you have to do is say the word. Say yes."

My jaw dropped open. "What? When? When did you have time to do all this?"

"I may have made a few discreet inquiries the past few days."

"This is…" I blinked a few times, still in disbelief. "Crazy."
Wasn't it?

He lifted a shoulder. "I didn't think you'd want a big wedding."

"You're right. I don't. I can do without most of the traditions like the garter toss and a bridal party in matching outfits. But what do you want?" This wasn't just about me; this was about us. And while it was one day in our lives, it was an important one.

Jackson pinned me to the bed, and I was momentarily distracted by the feeling of his bare skin on mine. "I want you to be my wife. I don't care when or how it happens, so long as we're together."

Oh god, I loved the sound of that. *My wife.* It had a nice ring to it, especially when he practically purred with pleasure.

"That's exactly how I feel." I smiled up at him. "Okay. *Okay.* I guess we're going to do this. I need to find a dress—and a glam squad."

"Already taken care of, thanks to Nate." He kissed me then pushed off the bed. "His stylist will be here in thirty. And Emerson said she'd send over her glam squad."

I was speechless.

Nate's stylist, Jay Crow, was in high demand. He styled Nate and Emerson, Kendall and Knox. I'd worked with him a few times, and he was talented. I couldn't wait to see what he'd come up with for a wedding dress, especially on such short notice. But I knew if anyone could work their magic, it was him.

"Jay will be here soon, as well as Kendall, Emerson, and Brooklyn." He grinned, clearly pleased with himself.

"Emerson offered to FaceTime Greer and my mom so they could be part of choosing your dress if you wanted."

"You've really thought of everything, haven't you?" I asked, touched. Gah. This man was going to turn me into a puddle of goo if he kept it up.

"You know me." He kissed me deeply, thoroughly. "I have to think of all angles."

"Mm." I rocked my hips against him. "All angles, huh?"

He thrust against me, and I could feel how hard he was through his sweatpants. So when he moved to stand, I pouted. "Where are you going?"

"They'll be here in twenty-five minutes." He adjusted himself, and I tried to ignore the bulge in his pants.

"You were so sure I was going to say yes, huh?" I teased.

"Considering how enthusiastic you were when I mentioned marriage, I figured you'd say yes to marrying me. As to the quick wedding..." He lifted a shoulder.

I glanced at the clock on the nightstand. "Yikes!" I jumped up out of the bed. "I need to shower."

"I'll help." He flashed me a wicked grin.

"No." I pushed him toward the bedroom door instead. "I'll never be ready on time if you join me."

"Later, then?"

I shook my head. "It's the night before our wedding. You'll have to stay somewhere else."

He frowned. "Oh, so we're going to observe *that* tradition?"

"It's only one night. And...I don't know how you feel about it, but I'd like to give you a wedding ring."

"Of course I'm wearing a wedding ring." He looked offended.

"Okay, then." I bit back a smile, loving how serious he was about this. "Text me your ring size, and... Wait. What else do

I need to take care of?" I asked, my mind still trying to catch up with everything.

He glanced down at his phone. "Jasper wants to know if you have any color palettes you love or hate?" he asked, following me to the bathroom. I started the shower, knowing I was short on time. Jackson got dressed while we quickly brainstormed our wedding.

By the time I'd finished, we'd sorted out most of the details. He wrapped a towel around me, then kissed me. "See you tomorrow, fiancée."

I laughed. "That's probably the only time you'll get to call me that. This is the shortest engagement ever."

"Good." He paused, grinning. "Because I can't wait to call you my wife." He gave me a quick peck, and then he was gone.

I sat there in shock for a minute before leaping into action. I called Greer while I got dressed. I think she screamed for a minute straight because she was so excited that we were officially going to be family. I should've never doubted her.

I was just finishing breakfast when there was a knock at the door. I peered through the peephole and smiled at the sight of Emerson, Brooklyn, and Kendall.

"Congratulations!" they said in unison as I opened the door.

"Thank you. Thank you. Come on in. Room service will be up shortly with some snacks and drinks, or feel free to order anything off the menu."

It wasn't long before Jay and his team arrived. The rest of the day passed in a rush of fittings and wedding band shopping and pampering at the spa and just so much fun with some of my favorite people.

Brooklyn went home after lunch. She'd muttered something about needing time to prepare for something, and I wondered what that was about.

Greer arrived late afternoon, and the moment I flung open the door, she threw her arms around me. "You're going to be my sister for real."

We laughed and cried, and I was so happy. "Jackson thinks I'm marrying him, but we both know I'm actually doing this to legally be your sister."

"I knew it!" She wiped away a tear and then stood aside.

Belinda stepped forward, taking my hands in hers. "Oh, Sloan. I'm so very happy. I always suspected there was something between the two of you. Whenever you two are in a room, there's this...energy. Electricity."

I smiled and hugged her. "Thank you for coming."

"Are you kidding? We wouldn't miss it, especially not after Jackson told us we'd get to fly in the private jet," Belinda joked.

I laughed, giving her another hug before turning to Greer. "Where are the kids?"

"Hanging out with their new cousin at her Hollywood mansion. They're with Brooklyn and Nate."

"Nice," I said.

"And...we need to get ready," she said, after a quick glance at her phone.

"For what?"

She grinned, pushing me toward the bedroom. "We're going out for your last night as a single ladyyyy."

"Uh-oh. Should I be scared?" I was joking. Sort of.

"Nah." She grinned, but it was full of mischief.

The rest of the day was a whirlwind of champagne and presents and friends and so much fun. We went out on Knox's yacht for my combined bridal shower and bachelorette party. Kendall, Emerson, Greer, and Belinda had spoiled me, and I'd never felt more surrounded by love and support.

Kendall's present was a gorgeous navy silk robe with "Bride" embroidered on it in white. Emerson had given me some incredible lingerie, which had prompted a comment from Greer that she didn't want to think about the fact that her brother was the groom. Belinda's quip had been that maybe Greer's kids would finally get some cousins. Everyone laughed.

I loved the tote bag with "Honeymoon Vibes" on it from Greer. She'd filled it with fun snacks and all sorts of things. And I was touched by Belinda's gift. A silver plate that had belonged to Jackson's grandmother with "Shaw" engraved into it.

I didn't ask Greer about Logan; I was too afraid to. And she didn't mention him. But she seemed to be enjoying herself.

Before I realized it, it was time to go to bed. Belinda and the kids were staying at Nate's, and Greer was at the suite with me. I kept pausing when I'd catch sight of myself in the mirror. It wasn't just the engagement ring that was different. It was me. I was so happy. So full of joy.

My phone chimed with an incoming text.

> Jackson: Sweet dreams, fiancée. Can't wait to see you tomorrow.

> Me: Me either. I love you.

> Jackson: I love you, hayati.

I flopped back on the bed with a huge smile. I had no idea what to expect for the venue, the flowers, anything, but I didn't care. I was marrying Jackson, and I was practically giddy. Just the idea of walking down the aisle to him was a dream come true. The rest of it, the details, didn't matter. The only thing that mattered was him.

I knocked on Greer's door early the next morning. "I hope that's coffee," she called.

I laughed and flung open the door before running and diving onto her bed. "I'm getting married today!"

She rolled onto her back. "Not at all excited, are you?"

"Not at all," I deadpanned. And then we burst out laughing.

We ordered room service, and Greer checked in with her mom and the kids. I was looking forward to having the day alone with my best friend to get ready for my wedding.

Shortly after breakfast, there was a knock at the door. I hopped up and went to answer it, finding Knox.

"Hey." I smiled, leaning against the doorframe. "What are you doing here?"

"Came to deliver your dress." He held up a large garment bag. "May I come in?"

"Sure." I stepped aside for him to enter. "Thanks."

He greeted Greer before she went to shower. He hung the garment bag then leaned his hip against the kitchen counter. "So…how are you feeling?"

"I'm good. Actually, better than good. I didn't think this day would ever come, and now I'm marrying the love of my life." My cheeks ached from smiling. "Thanks for bringing the dress."

"You're welcome. It's my gift to you on your wedding day. Your dress, shoes, veil, everything. It's your 'something new.'"

I held a hand to my chest. "Knox, that's…" I fanned my

face to hold back my tears. "I'm going to cry. Thank you." I hugged him.

"I'm glad you and Jackson found your way back to each other. He's a good man."

I nodded. "The best."

"Also…I don't know what your plans were for the wedding night—"

"Ew. I'm not talking about that with you." And I didn't *ever* want to think about the fact that Graham had seen compromising photos of Jackson and me. I shuddered. I'd done what had to be done for Graham to find and destroy those photos.

"Yeah. We don't ever need to discuss that." He chuckled. "I meant, where you planned to stay, but I know how much you and Jackson love being on the water. So, I wanted to invite you both to enjoy my yacht for your honeymoon."

I placed my hand on his. "Knox, thank you. That's so perfect."

He opened his mouth as if to speak, but we were interrupted by someone else knocking on the door. "Must be the glam squad," I said.

It wasn't the glam squad. It was Graham, and he wasn't alone. "Graham. Jasper, hey." What was going on? And had my brothers planned this?

Jasper pulled something out from behind his back, and I gaped at the gorgeous bouquet of blue and white flowers. Roses and eucalyptus leaves, hydrangeas, thistles, and delphiniums. It was stunning.

"Jasper, that is…perfect." I accepted it from him, setting it on the kitchen counter. "I love it."

"Good. It's your something blue—both the flowers and the scarf wrapped around it, which was Mom's."

"Mm. I should've known." I ran my fingers over the material. I recognized the vintage Hermès pattern that was no longer available. "Thank you." I hugged him. "It's so thoughtful and beautiful."

He preened.

"And your engagement ring from me is your something old," Graham said.

I held up my hand to admire it. "Thank you. I had no idea you'd been saving it for me."

"Gran always meant for you to have it. And I think she and Pops would've approved of Jackson." He squeezed my arm. "I'm glad you found someone who will be a worthy partner."

I wiped away a tear. "Thank you, Graham." I hugged him.

"Where's Nate?" Jasper asked.

As if on cue, I heard another knock at the door. I laughed. This was getting ridiculous. "Right. That must be him."

I opened the door and welcomed Nate into the suite. "These are for you to *borrow* for your wedding, if you'd like to wear them with your dress. I had Emerson's help since she knew what your dress looked like."

He opened the velvet box to reveal the most gorgeous diamond necklace and matching earrings. "They are stunning." The diamonds just sparkled.

"Good choice," Graham said.

Jasper cleared his throat. "I came to give you the bouquet. But also to offer to walk you down the aisle."

"I'm her eldest brother," Graham said. "That's my job."

"I'm the eldest of the five of us," Knox protested. "She should choose me."

I tried not to laugh at them as they argued over who would get to walk me down the aisle. It was typical, but incredibly touching.

"But I'm her favorite." Nate grinned, winking at me. "So I should do it."

"She said I was her number one brother," Graham interrupted. "I have it in writing." He pulled out his phone. And I did laugh then.

"Okay. Okay," I said, ready to end this discussion before it got even more out of hand. "I appreciate the offer." I looked at each of them. "I do. And I'm so touched by all your gifts and support."

"But mine was the best, right?" Jasper asked. "I'm the one planning your wedding."

"You are. And I'm so very grateful, but…" I took a deep breath. Marrying Jackson was my decision, and I wanted to walk down the aisle alone. I wanted to give myself to him. Even so… "I couldn't possibly choose one, or even two, of you," I said, cutting off that line of conversation before it could start.

"Oh, that's a good idea," Jasper said. "Graham and I could walk you down the aisle."

"Why not Knox and me?" Nate asked, his brow furrowed.

I held up my hand. "Guys. I love that you're supportive, but this is something I'm going to do on my own."

"Wow. It's a party out here," Greer said, joining us.

"It sure is." I bulged my eyes out, silently begging her to save me.

She shook her head, and we shared a look as if to say, "Brothers."

Part of me still couldn't believe it was my wedding day. Not even after my brothers' show of love and support. Nor when the glam squad showed up and started doing Greer's and my hair and makeup. It still hadn't quite sunk in until my dress was on and the bouquet was in my hands. I stared at my reflection in the mirror, and I looked like a bride.

As we rode the elevator down to the floor where the wedding would take place, all I could think was, *Oh my god, this is really happening.*

I stood outside the doors to the room where our friends

and family were waiting, listening to the beautiful music being played by a string quartet. The song shifted and the doors swung open, and the only person I saw was Jackson. He was standing beneath a floral arch, his hands clasped before him. He looked so handsome in his dress whites, his back straight and proud.

The candles, the flowers, it was all so beautiful. I smiled at Jackson, filled with appreciation. I took a step toward him, proceeding down the aisle. He placed his hand over his heart, as overcome by the enormity of this moment as I was.

He looked so stoic, but I knew him well enough to know that he was trying to hold it all in. My heart felt as if it might burst. This was all I'd ever wanted. Jackson wiped away a tear, and I smiled, trying not to cry myself.

I couldn't believe Jackson was going to be my husband. That after all these years, after everything we'd been through, we'd made it here. Our journey hadn't always been smooth sailing, but a smooth sea never made a skilled sailor.[1]

I liked to think that our past—our heartbreak, our challenges—had made us stronger and more resilient. They'd help shape us into the individuals we were today. Strong enough to weather any storm together.

CHAPTER THIRTY-ONE

Jackson

I couldn't take my eyes off Sloan as she walked up the aisle toward me. Steady. Calm. Stunning. God, she was so beautiful. When the doors had opened to reveal her standing there, I'd gone weak in the knees.

She wore a strapless gown that was simple and elegant. The cream fabric draped across her chest before nipping in at the waist then flaring out again over her hips. It was sexy and classy, and I couldn't wait to take it off her.

When she joined me at the altar, I offered her my hand, eager to touch her, hold her. To confirm that she wasn't a figment of my imagination as I feared. But her hand was warm in mine, and her smile was watery and full of love as she gazed up at me.

"Hey," I said, keeping my voice low so that only she could hear.

She grinned, her green eyes dazzling in their intensity. "Hi."

Greer popped up from her seat in the front row, fluffing Sloan's train and veil before taking the bouquet from her hands. Sloan and I turned and faced each other fully, our eyes locked as the officiant welcomed everyone to the wedding.

He spoke of love and loyalty, but I couldn't concentrate on anything but Sloan. On her red lips that curved into the most beautiful smile. Her hair that was curled in loose waves like she'd worn when we first met. On how happy she looked.

When it was time to say our vows, I took a deep breath.

"Sloan." I drew in a shaky breath, trying my damnedest to hold it together. "You're my past, my future, my everything—forever. I love you, and I pledge to honor, love, and cherish you every day for the rest of my days." I smiled at her, wiping away a tear. "Today, I say 'I do,' but that means 'I will.'"

"*Acta non verba*," she mouthed, smiling through her tears.

I knew she'd understand perfectly. "I will hold your hand and stand by your side, no matter what challenges come our way."

I slid the infinity wedding band on her finger. I'd purchased it to go with Sloan's grandmother's engagement ring. Together, the two rings would symbolize both the past and our future.

"Jackson," she said, removing a ring from her pocket. *Damn.* "If it is our actions that matter, our deeds that define us, then know that I have never felt more loved than I do with you. You are my protector, my first mate—" She laughed at that, and our guests joined in. "And now, my husband. I promise to cherish you through all of life's adventures. To trust in you and our love. And to always honor our relationship."

She slid the ring on my finger, and the weight of it was both comforting and sacred. A symbol of our union and the power of love overcoming all obstacles.

I didn't hear much the officiant said after that until he spoke the words, "You may now kiss."

I stepped forward and placed my hands on Sloan's lower back, holding her to me. She slid her hands around my neck, and we smiled at each other. When I pressed my lips to hers, I was greeted with the smell of wild roses and sunshine, of home. I smiled against her mouth, kissing her until I realized the audience was whistling.

Sloan pulled away, her cheeks tinged with pink. She threaded her hand through my arm, and I placed my other hand on top of hers. Greer handed her the bouquet, wiping away tears with a tissue. Everyone was smiling and clapping, and even Graham gave me a nod of approval on our way out.

While everyone else filed out, I pulled Sloan into my arms and kissed her deeply. "Fuck, *hayati*. You look so damn beautiful."

"Mm." Her eyes were liquid heat as she surveyed me. "You clean up nice, sailor."

I twirled her around so I could admire her. She was stunning. She was mine.

"ARE YOU HAPPY?" I ASKED HER LATER, WHILE DINNER WAS being served. Everyone was seated at a single table, and I was so happy we'd decided to have an intimate wedding.

Everything from the candles to the flower arrangements were like something out of a magazine. It was luxurious, and I was pleased that everyone seemed so at ease. My mom was talking with Knox and Nate. Even Graham seemed to be enjoying himself. At least, as much as Graham seemed capable of enjoying anything.

Sloan smiled at me. "Incandescently."

"Indecently?" I teased, giving her thigh a squeeze through

the layers of her dress. For not the first time, I wondered what—if anything—she had on beneath her gown. I couldn't wait to find out.

"Perhaps that too." She placed her hand on my cheek and kissed me.

Someone tapped me on my shoulder, and I glanced over to see Brooklyn standing beside me. "What's up?"

"Now that you married Auntie Sloan, can I call you Uncle Jackson?"

I grinned. "You can call me whatever you want."

"How lucky am I?" she asked Sloan. "I got a mom and an uncle this year."

I laughed and pulled her in for a hug. "I'm going to teach you all the important things."

"Like what?" she asked. "Ooh." Her eyes widened. "Will you teach me how to punch someone?"

"Absolutely." I smiled. "But your aunt Sloan can you teach you that."

"Yes!" She fist-pumped the air, and Sloan and I laughed.

Someone tapped their glass, and I expected it to be one of Sloan's brothers, not Greer. Brooklyn returned to her seat, and I shot a worried glance at Sloan. "Uh-oh."

She patted my thigh. "It'll be fine."

Greer cleared her throat, glancing at her phone. "They say that a marriage doesn't just unite two people but two families. I guess you could say that I'm gaining a sister, but I've always considered Sloan my sister, so today merely cements that relationship." Everyone laughed.

She turned to us, meeting our eyes. "The two of you have been through a lot, and you deserve all the happiness in the world. I'm so glad you've found that in each other. And I wish you a lifetime of love, laughter, and adventure." She raised her glass. "To Jackson and Sloan."

Everyone echoed, "To Jackson and Sloan," and then drank.

Nate made a speech next, and I was touched by how accepting he'd been of my relationship with Sloan. My impulsive plan to marry so quickly.

After the speeches, Brooklyn surprised us by stepping up to the microphone. Her guitar was slung over her shoulder, and she smiled nervously at the guests.

"Did you know about this?" I asked Sloan.

She shook her head. "Not a clue."

Brooklyn started playing, and when she sang the lyrics, her voice was pure and beautiful. The song was about love and walking through fire for someone. About adoring them. It was incredible.

Everyone gave her a standing ovation when she'd finished. Her cheeks were pink, and her smile was proud.

After dinner, I stood and offered Sloan my hand. "Can I have this dance?"

She smiled and placed her hand in mine, allowing me to lead her to the dance floor. As we swayed to the music, surrounded by the people we loved, I knew that it had all been worth it. And the fact that we'd endured so much only made this moment that much sweeter.

Later, after the dinner and the dancing and the goodbyes, Sloan and I boarded Knox's yacht. I'd been on it a few times as Nate's bodyguard, never as a guest. I was still getting used to the fact that this was my life now. That I was married to a billionaire. It was...strange at times, but Sloan's money was the least interesting thing about her.

Sloan had removed her veil after the ceremony, but we'd stayed in our wedding attire. The crew welcomed us and opened a bottle of champagne before making themselves scarce. We were going to sail to Catalina Island, but I didn't care about our destination so long as Sloan and I were together.

I handed Sloan a glass of champagne. I lifted mine to hers. "To us."

She smiled. "To us."

We sank down on the outdoor sofa, and I wrapped my arm around Sloan. "This is gorgeous," I said, admiring the view. "Though I prefer the *Athena*."

"So do I." She grinned. "But it's nice to be pampered for our honeymoon."

I leaned in, grazing the shell of her ear with my teeth. "Oh, I'll pamper you on our honeymoon."

"Mm," she hummed. "And how do you intend to do that, Mr. Shaw?"

"Actually," I said, "It's Mr. Mackenzie-Shaw."

"Is it now?" She bit back a grin.

I lifted a shoulder. "Just an idea. I thought it might be nice to have the same last name, but I wanted it to be something that reflected both of us."

"I like that," she said, placing her hand on my thigh. My cock thickened. "Shaw-Mackenzie. It has a nice ring to it."

"It does. Plus, when we have kids, then we'll all have the same name."

"We just got married, and you're already talking about kids?" she joked.

"I'm not in any rush. But I have to admit, the idea of seeing you carrying my child brings me to my knees."

"Such a caveman," she teased.

She had no idea. Claiming her as my wife had definitely brought out my inner caveman. I could only imagine how a pregnancy would affect me. My cock twitched just thinking about it. But even if it didn't happen, I would still be happy. We were more than enough. We were a family.

I smiled down at her left hand and the ring that now sat on her finger. "Seeing my ring on your finger is hot."

"Oh, I get that." She lifted my left hand. "This ring, plus the uniform, is…" She swallowed. "*So* hot."

"Did you bring my favorite swimsuit?" I nipped her ear. "The white one."

She smirked. "I might have. Are you suggesting a swim?"

"Maybe tomorrow. Shall we go to bed, wife?"

Sloan nodded, and I stood and offered her my hand. I stepped back, once again admiring how beautiful she was. How *mine.*

"You're not going to tear this dress off me, are you?" she joked.

"Not until we're safely in our cabin."

"Another reason why the *Athena* is better," Sloan said, leaning into me as we proceeded to go inside. "No staff."

"I thought you wanted the staff to pamper us," I teased.

"And I thought you offered to pamper me." She elbowed my side.

I chuckled and opened the door to the stateroom. It was definitely a lot nicer than our accommodations on the *Athena.* Higher ceilings. Bigger bed. Hell, there was even a balcony.

Sloan laughed, and when I looked at her, she was watching me with her hands in her pockets. "This is fun."

"What's that?" I asked.

"Watching you get used to this life."

I shook my head. "I'm not sure I'll ever get used to it, nor that I'd want to. It's nice to have wealth, but it's worth nothing without you." I closed the distance between us. "You are priceless to me, Sloan. And all I need is you."

Her expression was full of love when she pressed up on her toes to kiss me. "All I need is you, Jackson. I love you."

"I love you." I smiled against her lips. "Now, turn around so I can undress you."

"Barely married a few hours and already you're trying to boss me around," she teased, even as she did what I'd asked.

"I thought you were supposed to love, honor, and *obey* me, wife."

"Husband," she said sweetly, "did you ever hear me promise to obey?"

I tugged on her zipper, only to realize there was still more fabric covering her, though it was sheer with boning. She pushed the material of the dress down her hips, and I stood there, unblinking. *Holy shit.*

She turned to face me, and she looked fucking beautiful. I smoothed my hand over her hip, unable to believe that she was mine. This beautiful goddess was my wife.

Her hair was tousled and grazed her collarbone. Her corset pushed her breasts up to the point they were nearly spilling over the cups then flared over her hips and generous curves. Her underwear was almost entirely sheer, and fuck me, I didn't know whether I wanted to take it off or leave it on, it was that sexy.

She didn't give me time to consider, placing her hand on my chest and pushing me in the direction of the bed. "Sit. Now."

When the mattress hit the backs of my knees, I sat.

"Do you know how many times I've fantasized about you in your uniform?" she asked.

"Oh yeah?" I smirked. "You like a man in uniform?"

"If the man is you, then yes," she said, her hungry gaze raking over me.

She stepped closer, still wearing her heels. I slid my hand up her leg, goose bumps forming in the wake of my touch.

"Good answer," I rasped against her throat, smoothing my

hand higher until I reached the apex of her thighs. I stroked her through the silky material of her underwear.

She closed her eyes in bliss and arched her back. "Jackson," she shuddered. "Oh god."

Fuck. She was sexy. Especially when I caught sight of us in the mirror, her hand on my uniformed shoulder. My ring on her finger. Her ass bare, apart from a thin strip of material.

I pulled her bottom lip between mine, swallowing her moans as I quickly brought her to release. Her pleasured sighs were music to my ears. Her body clenched then released. My cock strained against my zipper, needing to be inside her.

I yanked at the hooks of her corset, giving up after the first few since her breasts were free. She clawed at the buttons on my uniform, and we fell onto the bed in a state of partial undress. I didn't care. I just needed to be inside her.

"Lie back," I said.

"I'm ready. I don't want to wait any longer."

"Sloan," I sighed. "It's our wedding night. I want to make this good for you. Special."

"It's always good for me," she said. "You know that. Now, lie down. I want to be on top."

I chuckled, cupping the back of her neck and pulling her to me for a kiss. "So bossy."

"You love it." She smirked.

"I do." I stripped out of my clothes and lay on the bed with my arms behind my head. "Is this what you had in mind?"

"Yes," she practically purred, unhooking the rest of her corset and then stripping off her panties.

She crawled over me, and my cock strained toward her. She stopped to press a kiss to the tip, and the sight of her naked, mouth open, had me nearly coming on the spot.

"Tease," I said through gritted teeth.

I gripped the sheets in my hands, twisting them as she continued to torment me. I gathered her hair, holding it in a loose ponytail. Her eyes were locked on mine the entire time, and it was fucking hot.

"Sloan," I groaned. "Fuck me. Fuck." I squeezed my eyes shut, panting. This was happening way too fast. I was already on the verge of coming, but I was determined to make it last.

She stopped. And when I opened my eyes, she was smirking at me.

I grabbed her arm. "Get up here. Come on." I pulled her toward me. "Otherwise, I'm going to spill down your throat."

"Would that really be so bad?"

I groaned, throwing my arm over my face. "Sloan."

She straddled my hips, sinking down on me inch by inch. Once she was fully seated, she let out the most contented sigh. I sat up against the headboard, bringing her with me. I loved this position—it put her breasts right in my face and gave Sloan more control.

She gasped at the change in movement then held on to my shoulders, writhing her hips. I intertwined our hands, the metal of our wedding rings rubbing against our skin a new sensation. I smiled, content in the knowledge that she was my wife and this was now my life.

Sloan cried out, clenching around me. "Come with me, Jackson. Come now."

I tightened my grip on her hips, thrusting up into her until there was nothing but her and me and our love and pleasure.

I'd made so many mistakes in the past, but I'd come to realize that perhaps we'd needed the time apart—painful as it was. We'd both been so young; we hadn't yet grown into the people we would become. Into two strong individuals who were even better together. Who each knew their worth and the value of their partner.

Being together now, after spending so many years without Sloan, only made me appreciate what we had even more. And if it had brought me to this moment and this woman, then I had no regrets.

Later, after we'd cleaned up and were cuddling in bed, I said, "I wish my dad could've met you." I'd worn his medals on my chest today, bringing a part of him with me to the wedding.

"I wish my grandparents could've been there tonight, but I like to think they were all there in spirit. My parents too.

"Oh, before I forget—" She leaned over and removed something from the nightstand. "I have a wedding present for you."

"I didn't realize we were trading presents." I sat up a little more and unwrapped the gift. Inside the box was a leather-bound book. "What's this?"

I opened the cover, and the pages were filled with pictures from our sailing trip. Everything from me sitting on the deck drinking coffee to the two of us watching the solar eclipse. I paused when I came to an image of Sloan in the hot tub. It was one of the photos Amelia had used to try to blackmail us.

"I couldn't bear to get rid of them," Sloan said. "They were hot, and I wanted to reclaim them. They're ours. Our private moments. No one else's."

I couldn't have been prouder of her. She'd taken something so dark and sordid and turned it into a positive. "Thank you. I love it."

"You're welcome."

She rested her head against my shoulder, and I wrapped my arm around her. "Any regrets about the quickie wedding?"

"Absolutely none." I could hear the smile in her voice. "And I think everyone else really enjoyed themselves too."

"Me too," I said. "I was worried about Greer, but she seemed happy all weekend."

She nodded, caressing my chest. "I know. She didn't once mention Logan, and I didn't want to ask for fear of upsetting her. But she seemed so much better than when we were in Puerto Rico even just a few weeks ago."

"Maybe a divorce is what she needs," I said, though I knew it wouldn't be easy. But I didn't want to dwell on that. Not tonight. "And did you see how happy my mom was?"

"Everyone was." Sloan sighed happily. "I'm honestly still amazed by everything my brothers did for us."

So was I. They'd handled everything from the engagement ring to the honeymoon. It was incredible, and it reassured me that they were pleased with our match. "We couldn't have pulled off the wedding without their help."

"I know. Whatever you did to win them over..." She leaned back to peer up at me. "But for them to welcome you with open arms... It's crazy."

"Is it?" I knew it was a big deal, and I was grateful. But Sloan spoke of me as if I were a unicorn or some magical creature. I was just a man who loved a woman and wasn't afraid to show it.

"Yes. They were arguing over who would walk me down the aisle this morning. Did I tell you that?" She barked out a laugh. "All four of them. And they've never liked anyone I've dated."

I slid my hand into her hair. "Maybe—" I kissed her "—because they knew—" another kiss, this time longer, more intense "—all along that you were waiting for someone. Waiting for me."

She considered it a moment, and I half expected her to brush off my comment. But then she said, "You know, maybe you're right. I think I was going through the motions of dating, but I never really gave my heart to anyone. Probably because you had it all along."

I pulled her hand to my mouth, kissing her fingertips, her palm. "And you had mine."

THANK YOU FOR READING *REDEMPTION*. I HOPE YOU ENJOYED Sloan and Jackson's love story. If you did, please consider leaving a review.

Want more delicious, feel-good forbidden romance? Click here for **Inevitable**, a page-turning dad's best friend, age gap romance that will steam up your kindle.

When Sumner's dad asks her to intern for his best friend, Jonathan Wolfe, she knows she should say no. She hasn't seen Wolfe in years, but she's always had a secret crush on him. And from the moment she steps foot in the office, she wants him. He may be twenty-years older than her, he's still as hot as ever. And she's coming to realize that maybe, just maybe, Wolfe wants her too.

As hard as they try to fight their growing attracting, their relationship seems inevitable. There's just one problem: her dad.

Keep reading for a sneak peek...

Acknowledgements

"There was never anyone else but you."

God, I love it when Jackson admits that to Sloan.

Confession time: I always swore I'd never write a second chance romance.

Why?

Personally, I've never been a big fan of the trope. Maybe it was the ones I'd read in the past or maybe it was me, but I never really clicked with them. I typically felt like the reasons for the couple breaking up/staying apart were weak. I mean, if they really loved each other, shouldn't they find a way to be together?

But Sloan and Jackson showed me that sometimes, you have to spend some time apart to be able to come back together. Sometimes you need that time to grow and mature. To appreciate what you had and to be in a place where you can be the kind of partner your significant other deserves.

One of the things I loved most about writing Sloan and Jackson's story was the character growth. Between the present and the past, we see how much they've grown as individuals. And how right they are for each other despite all the obstacles in their path.

This was my first story with flashbacks, and I found that I LOVED writing them. It was so much fun to dip in and out of the past. To just show a snippet or a longer scene.

And gah...these characters. Jackson is an alpha--protective, possessive, former Navy SEAL. But he's also a golden retriever. He's confident in himself, and he wants nothing more than to support the woman he loves.

I think that's one of my favorite things about Jackson. Yes, it took him some time to get there. But when he does, he's not intimidated by Sloan's wealth or position. Nor does he try to coddle her. Even when it's his job to protect her, he wants to empower her. He's a true partner.

And Sloan...I loved how assertive yet vulnerable she was. I loved seeing her pain and her longing. I was so ready for her to stop doing what was right and do what was right for her. And Jackson was definitely right for her.

I mean...these two. They have so much freaking chemistry. I loved how they teased each other, how they complement each other.

Sigh.

I'm sad to leave them, but I'm also excited to see what's next for this family and this series. And don't worry...I'm sure there will be glimpses of Jackson and Sloan in future books. Just as we see glimpses of our favorite characters from *Temptation* and *Reputation* here. Heck, there were even a few mentions of characters from my Love in LA Series and the Alondra Valley Series. Did you catch those? ;)

Thank you for going on this journey with me. I've been blown away by the response to *Redemption* and the entire Tempt Series. And I am so so happy that so many of you love these characters as much as I do!

A HUGE thank you to all the readers who share your love for my stories. I could not do this without you.

Nor could I do this without my incredible team. Thank you to Angela for always being encouraging and supportive. For helping me with all the details, so I can focus on the big picture.

A huge thank you to my beta readers. Thank you for

making me a stronger writer, for offering your unique insight and advice. You each bring something different to the table, and I'm always amazed and impressed by your suggestions. I'm so incredibly honored to have you on my team!

Thank you, Jade. You make me a stronger writer, and you challenge me on pacing. You are so clever and always provide great insight. I'm so grateful for your friendship, and our long chats! This story wouldn't be the same without you. And I can't believe we're FINALLY going to meet IRL this year! Thank you for reading a million different versions of this story and always providing such valuable suggestions.

A huge thank you to Kristen for being such an amazing friend. I value your judgment and honesty, and I so appreciate your support. We've been through so much together, and I treasure your friendship and advice. Seriously, I cannot thank you enough for all that you do. You are my "hype girl." You always pump me up and make me feel fabulous.

Beth, thank you so much for jumping in at the last minute. Your encouragement and support mean so much to me. And I'm so delighted that we reconnected after all these years!

Thank you to Ellen, as always. Thank you for being so supportive and positive, for being a friend. And thank you for sharing your incredible eye for detail. Your comments are always priceless, and this book was no exception! I couldn't do it without you.

To my editor, Lisa with Silently Correcting Your Grammar. I so appreciate your attention to detail, and your patience with my questions. You always go above and beyond and this time was no exception. I value your insight and your friendship.

A huge shout out to all my fellow authors. Sometimes this

job can feel so solitary, but I know you're all out there. And we're all cheering each other on.

A big thank you to the Hartley's Hustlers and my Sweet-harts. You rock! I cannot possibly tell you how much your support means to me! I appreciate everything you do to promote my books and to encourage me throughout my writing journey.

Thank you to my husband for always encouraging me. For always supporting my dreams and believing in me. You are better than any book boyfriend I could ever imagine. You constantly build me up, and I couldn't ask for a better partner.

And to my daughter, for always putting a smile on my face. You are spirited and independent, and I wouldn't have it any other way. Dream big, my darling.

Thank you to my parents for always being so encouraging. For reading my books. For being my biggest fans!

Dear reader, if this list of people shows you anything, it's that dreams are often the effort of many. I'm grateful to have such an awesome team. And I'm honored that you've taken the time to read my words.

About the Author

Jenna Hartley is *USA Today* bestselling author who writes feel-good forbidden romance, much like her own real-life love story. She's known for writing strong women and swoon-worthy men, as well as blending panty-melting and heart-warming moments.

When she's not reading or writing romance, Jenna can be found tending to her growing indoor plant collection (pun intended), organizing, and hiking. She lives in Texas with her family and loves nothing more than a good book and good chocolate, except a dance party with her daughter.

www.authorjennahartley.com

Also by Jenna Hartley

Love in LA Series
Inevitable
Unexpected
Irresistible
Undeniable
Unpredictable
Irreplaceable

Alondra Valley Series
Feels Like Love
Love Like No Other
A Love Like That

Tempt Series
Temptation
Reputation
Redemption

For the most current list of Jenna's titles, please visit her website www.authorjennahartley.com.

Or scan the QR code on the following page to be taken to her author page on Amazon.com

NOTES

CHAPTER 30

1. "A smooth sea never made a skilled sailor." Franklin D. Roosevelt. Similarly, "Smooth seas do not make skilled sailors." African Proverb.

Made in the USA
Monee, IL
03 January 2025

75878881R00216